KT-151-414

Please return/renew this item by the last date shown on this label, or on your self-service receipt.

To renew this item, visit **www.librarieswest.org.uk** or contact your library

Your borrower number and PIN are required.

Libraries**West**

Also by Annie O'Neil

The Vet's Secret Son
Christmas Under the Northern Lights

Double Miracle at St Nicolino's Hospital collection

A Family Made in Rome
Reawakened by the Italian Surgeon by Scarlet Wilson

Available now

Also by Scarlet Wilson

Family for the Children's Doc
His Blind Date Bride

Double Miracle at St Nicolino's Hospital collection

A Family Made in Rome by Annie O'Neil
Reawakened by the Italian Surgeon

Available now

Discover more at millsandboon.co.uk.

A FAMILY
MADE IN ROME

ANNIE O'NEIL

REAWAKENED
BY THE
ITALIAN SURGEON

SCARLET WILSON

MILLS & BOON

First Published in Great Britain 2021
by Mills & Boon, an imprint of HarperCollins*Publishers*
1 London Bridge Street, London, SE1 9GF

A Family Made in Rome © 2021 by Annie O'Neil

Reawakened by the Italian Surgeon © 2021 by Scarlet Wilson

ISBN: 978-0-263-29760-7

MIX
Paper from
responsible sources
FSC® C007454

This book is produced from independently certified FSC™ paper
to ensure responsible forest management.
For more information visit www.harpercollins.co.uk/green.

Printed and bound in Spain
by CPI, Barcelona

A FAMILY
MADE IN ROME

ANNIE O'NEIL

MILLS & BOON

This is to the doctors who dedicate themselves
to the advancement of medicine,
helping women and children everywhere.
Thank you.

CHAPTER ONE

'HERE WE ARE.'

Leon's lips brushed against Lizzy's neck, his familiar touch and lightly accented voice sweeping through her nervous system like the New Year's Eve fireworks display they'd just slipped away from. Dangerous. Dazzling. Powerful enough to unearth a thousand memories she'd barely managed to stuff into a box over the years since they'd seen each other last.

She tried to sweep them away again, desperate to believe that the past didn't matter. That this chance meeting wasn't fate forcing her hand, demanding that Lizzy confess to Leon he was the only man she'd ever loved. An admission that would definitely send him running back to the seven hills of Rome.

It had been five years since their paths had last crossed. Hardly a surprise, considering she worked in Sydney and he worked in Rome, and their lives—professional and personal—had never intertwined as they had once before here in New York during their surgical internships.

Not one email. Not one phone call. No texts. Nothing.

But she still knew him well enough to know that telling him she loved him would put an immediate halt to whatever was about to happen behind this hotel room door.

And, God help her, she wanted to go into that room. She wanted him.

He ran his fingertips along her bare collarbone. It was all she could do to contain a low groan.

Of all the medical conferences, in all the world…he'd had to walk into hers.

He stroked her arm and a skittering of goosebumps added wattage to the flames already burning bright for him. When she realised the touch had been accidental—that his hand had been on the way to his pocket to check for his key—her body's automatic heated response offered a new perspective.

Perhaps the sentiment she'd been clinging to these last five years hadn't been love at all. Their shared passion for antenatal surgery, their mutual desire to be the best, the head-to-head competition their mentors had encouraged, pitting them one against the other to be the very best, and their obvious physical attraction… Perhaps all those things added up to nothing more than good old-fashioned lust.

It wasn't as if she wanted to sit and talk to him about feelings all night long. Or their pasts. Those types of moments had never defined what she—perhaps wrongly—had called their relationship.

What she'd felt for him then was remarkably similar to her response to him now. It was primal. Instinctive. An animal attraction. A shared hunger for the same goals in life colliding at the perfect time and place. The only difference being that last time they'd had two years together, while this time they had one solitary night…

Her body was responding to him as strongly as it had the first time they'd met. Crackling and sparking as if the seven years since that moment had never existed.

But they had. And ever since they'd both left New York there had been a part of Lizzy that believed their relationship might have been something more if only they'd given it the oxygen to breathe.

In fairness, she'd been as marriage-shy as he had. Not that she'd ever told him why. Who wanted to unload a mountain of childhood misery into a relationship that was fuelled by a shared belief that the world of antenatal surgery was theirs to conquer?

But now their individually built, hard-earned professional futures had led them here, to the most elite medical conference in their field. Where, once again, they were being drawn to one another like a moth to a flame.

But who was who in this scenario?

She definitely didn't want to be the moth. No way was she going to let a night with Leon consume the self-respect she'd built for herself after her move to Sydney. She'd beaten herself up for years for letting herself fall in love with him back then, despite a silent vow to keep things simple. No more moth behaviour for her.

No. Tonight she wanted to be the flame. Wanted this to be the night she finally understood that the energy they shared was purely physical. Was being with Leon tonight the best way to make those years of self-doubt disappear? Who knew? But she was tired of living on an emotional rollercoaster—being yanked this way and that, wondering if she had lost her one chance at happiness.

Maybe they were more similar than she thought. Two moths. Two flames. Neither of them willing to admit to feelings that were too frightening. Too raw. Or maybe they just fancied the pants off one another. And—wouldn't you know it?—there was a fancy hotel room waiting to help them out...

Her eyes drifted to the hotel room door, willing it to give her a nudge in the right direction.

Honeymoon Suite

Leon had seen her taking in the gold script on the door. Their eyes met and meshed with an intensity that blazed through her like wildfire. It had been a long time since she'd felt like this. Out of control. So she did the only thing she could think of to regain that control.

She snorted.

There were many things she believed were going to happen behind that closed door tonight, but consummating a marriage neither of them wanted wasn't one of them.

'Upgrade.'

Leon's shoulders hitched into one of those shrugs of his that spoke of countless similar upgrades. It wasn't vanity, or a limitless bank account, or his natural charisma that swept people under his spell. It was what Lizzy had used to playfully call 'The Cassanetti Effect'. She'd certainly not been immune. For two near-perfect years. Perfect right up until the end...when it wasn't.

Leon cupped her chin for a kiss she'd not yet let him take.

'Uh-uh.' She smiled and pushed him away from her.

Not too hard and definitely not too far. Arm's length. A safe enough distance for her to regain control. She was determined not to let him steal her heart for another five years. The next five hours, though... Could she allow herself one perfect night of passion and then walk away from whatever it was they shared once and for all?

She made an impatient noise, edging herself away from a tumultuous trip down memory lane.

C'mon, Lizzy. Get a grip. This is lust, pure and simple.

Sure, she'd been blindsided when she'd seen Leon surrounded by a crowd of admirers at the conference's celebration dinner. Her body had felt as though it had disappeared, leaving only untamed energy humming in the centre of the room where she'd stood. And a thousand emotions had collided into one vital sensation: desire.

Seeing the one man she'd thought she'd never see again had felt heady and frightening and thrilling all at once. An energy too powerful to dismiss.

But she'd tried to pull herself back into her body. Remind herself that tonight was about her career. That the only reason she was here was because she was the keynote speaker. Her focus and dedication to her career had paid dividends and, as such, feeling tingly because her ex-boyfriend was here was ridiculous.

He'd extricated himself from the group of people he'd been speaking to and crossed the room with the determination of a man who'd found the Holy Grail. He'd taken her hand in his and wordlessly lifted it to his lips.

His name, when she'd said it, had tasted like warm caramel on her tongue, without a trace of the bitterness she'd thought she might experience if she ever saw him again. And then, as if the years they'd spent apart had been swept away by an invisible hand, Lizzy and Leon had become inseparable, as if leaving one another's side wasn't a physical possibility.

They hadn't spent the time catching up, exactly. There hadn't been any need beyond her glimpse at his ring finger—which was still, unsurprisingly, bare. Just as her own was. She'd read about his work in medical journals and presumed he'd done the same about hers. Only a few people in the world dealt with the types of cases they did—which, she supposed, made it completely insane that she hadn't expected to see him here.

After half listening to their peers for a spell, their hands occasionally brushing, eyes catching, the energy between them had inched ever upwards towards the moment when, without speaking, they'd eased away from the crowd, his fingers weaving through hers as naturally as they had that first time they'd sneaked into an on-call room and confirmed what they'd both known for several months.

They wanted one another.

Tonight was no different. He wanted her as much as she wanted him. It was the perfect opportunity to tie a nice shiny bow on the end of five years of wondering *what if...?*

The answers lay just out of reach.

After one, possibly two orgasms, and a bit of a cuddle, she would have fulfilled her animal desire and then she could set herself free of Leon Cassanetti once and for all.

Another shiver of goosebumps swept across her midriff as his hand slipped along her hip, his fingers grazing the cut-out in the fabric that laid her skin bare just at that magic spot where waist began to swoop into hip. She couldn't stop a small sigh of satisfaction.

Again their eyes met, and a slightly more fevered quest for that missing room key got underway.

She took advantage of the moment to really look at him. *Leon Cassanetti.*

The man who broke the mould.

She allowed her heart one careless flip and then realigned her focus. This wasn't about spiralling back into an out-of-control, unrequited love dungeon. This was about closure.

Well...

Pleasure and closure.

The two could co-exist, right?

Maybe they cancelled one another out.

Of *course* they could co-exist, Lizzy assured herself slightly desperately. She wanted to feel that unbridled joy she'd felt when they were together just one more time. One night of hot hotel sex didn't have to mean reopening the scars of heartache. No matter what her father said, she was a modern woman. A modern woman, with modern needs, who'd felt like a modern-day Cinderella from the moment her eyes had met and cinched with Leon's a few hours ago.

But unlike Cinderella she wouldn't spend her days in the scullery, wondering if Prince Charming was going to show up at her door with that damned glass slipper. Just like last time, he'd get on a plane to Rome and she'd get on a plane to Sydney. Only this time she'd walk away first. Eyes wide open.

It was just after midnight now.

A symbolic moment to mark the beginning of a new era.

She glanced at the closed door again. Once they went in, there would be no turning back.

She caught him looking at her inquisitively. As if he'd seen the flicker of hesitation in her eyes and was leaving the final decision as to whether or not they went in up to her.

Was there still enough magic in the air to let this be the final chapter of their story? Give her the closure she so desperately needed? When she looked into his eyes she saw nothing but longing—a hunger that gripped him with the same intensity with which her love for him had held her to ransom all these years.

His desire was intoxicating. A stark reminder of why impressing other men hadn't mattered to her over the past few years. Because of this man there was a string of failed first dates and briskly wrapped up mini-relationships trailing behind her as long as a kite tail.

She'd never admit it to anyone, but that moment five years ago when he'd turned and gone had made her feel as if he'd ripped her heart out of her chest and taken it with him. It was her own fault, really. For letting herself believe emotions could be flicked on and off like a light switch. She'd had her reasons for wanting to keep her feelings for him under control, but the one thing she'd failed to do was tamp down that flicker of hope that he might ask her to join him in Rome. The hope that had flickered right up until he hadn't.

Now, here they were—five years later, a little older, a little wiser. As she'd planned, she had climbed the ranks and now had a great job as an antenatal surgeon in Sydney. She was a leader in her field, actually. That was what happened when all your unspent love and energy got poured into your work. And Leon had just taken the helm at the antenatal unit in Rome's most prestigious children's hospital, which suggested he'd possibly done the same. Worked to fill the void left by the relationship that had nourished them both.

She forced her gaze to turn clinical. Tricky, when she had the urge to tuck her finger into his belt buckle and tug him towards her as decisively as she'd pushed him away. He was more handsome than she remembered. Extraordinary, given the fact that merely thinking of him had the power to turn her insides molten.

His dark hair still fell in soft, gorgeous waves, lightly grazing his eyebrows and, more sexily, his shirt collar. It wasn't pitch-black, like many Romans' hair—a rare mention of his father had unearthed the fact that he was half-Scandinavian. His eyes, though, were pure Italian. As dark brown as the shots of espresso he'd always favoured when the alarm went off at an ungodly hour and they'd headed to the showers, pulled on fresh scrubs and begun another day at the hospital. His smile, often hard-won, might have been its own solar system.

At thirty-seven he was still young and vital, but there was a new, decisive aura of 'proper man' about him—as her father had used to call the men he'd admired. Those who took charge. Held the reins. Told women what they did and didn't want from them and stuck to it.

Leon brandished the key with a smile.

She masked her darker memories with her own smile, but she wasn't entirely sure it reached her eyes. Tonight wasn't about fulfilling her father's outdated beliefs that anything a woman did was fuelled by emotion, and that men were required to fulfil their duty and, as a result, could treat the women in their lives however they felt. Tonight was about closure. Full. Stop.

She felt her lips quirk as she gave the mental image of herself and Leon at a flower-laden altar a casual flick into an imaginary bin. She replaced it with a steamier image, her breath catching in her throat as it gained traction.

Leon took a half-step closer, his hands resting softly on her hips. He looked at her expectantly, his dark eyes scanning her features for any sort of tell.

'Lizzy? Are you sure? We don't have to do this.'

There were countless answers to the seemingly simple question. *Yes. No. Rip my clothes off, already.* But Lizzy didn't bother answering, choosing to let her gut do the deciding. Actions spoke louder than words, so she took the newly unearthed key card out of his hand and held it against the electronic lock before she could change her mind.

It flashed green and the door clicked open.

His full lips curved into a smile. He'd never disguised his pleasure when she took the lead, and this was a blatant show of her desire.

Yes. She wanted him. Had done for the five years they'd been apart. Well, the four years, eleven months and eighteen days. No need to get hysterical.

The small of her back grew warm and tingly at his touch as he held open the door and guided her into the suite.

The bright lights of Manhattan twinkled like stardust out beyond the twentieth-floor bedroom, giving the space an even more magical hue. As if they needed any external razzle-dazzle to increase the sparks that were flaring more and more with each passing moment.

Leon stood behind her as she feigned an interest in the view. She was actually staring at his reflection in the window. This was hello and goodbye to the ghost that had stayed with her for far too long.

She shivered as his fingers teased her shoulder-blade-length hair away from her neck, so that he could drop a few sensual butterfly kisses upon her skin. She felt his lips hover above her shoulder, where the thin strap of her dress held the lightest of purchase.

As if he'd rehearsed the move a thousand times, he slipped both straps off her shoulders so that the dress skimmed down over her goosebumps until it puddled onto the floor around her feet. Soon enough there was skin upon skin, heated breath matching heated breath, and kisses so deep and powerful the rest of the world faded away.

Yes. She'd made the right decision. For now the world was Leon. When morning came she'd get up, give his cheek a farewell kiss, and bid *addio* to this man who had held her heart captive for much longer than he deserved.

CHAPTER TWO

Three months later

'DOTTORE CASSANETTI?'

Leon blinked at the foetal echocardiogram he'd been staring at for quite some time. Prompted yet again, he looked across at the nurse who, judging by her slightly impatient expression, had clearly been trying to get his attention for a while.

He gave the high-tech screen a tap. 'Tough one, this, Constanza,' he said, meaning it.

Foetal surgery was never easy. In utero surgery on one half of a twenty-six-week foetal heart ratcheted the difficulty up to a level only a few antenatal cardiologists in the world could handle.

He was one of them. The only other one he'd trust was half a world away.

As if on cue, his eyes played the same trick they had been playing on him ever since he'd left New York... A cloud of straw-blonde hair briefly appeared just beyond Constanza's shoulder and along with it a soft hint of floral perfume. But every time he went to check if it was really her there was, of course, no one there.

He cleared his throat and forced himself to focus again. He'd earned his place among the elite in paediatric medi-

cine the old-fashioned way: by pouring every fibre of his
being into his work.

From a young age his mother had drilled the importance of self-reliance and the fallibility of love into his
psyche. Relationships didn't last. Professions did. She'd
led by example, dedicating every fibre of her own being
to her job at an art gallery when her relationship with his
father had fallen apart.

Thus cautioned, and unwilling to endure the years of
grief and bitterness that had become part of his mother's
cell structure, he'd planned his future with meticulous care.
University in England. Medical School at Harvard. Surgical internship at Columbia in New York City, gaining as
many contacts as possible before returning here to Rome,
his beloved home city, to practise at St Nicolino's—one
of the most prestigious paediatric hospitals in the world.

Its historic stone edifice belied what it was inside: a
high-tech epicentre of medical excellence that attracted
some of the most complicated cases from across the globe.
They were a fiercely passionate bunch here at St Nicolino's, united by a shared love of pre, ante and postnatal
healthcare.

The day he'd been made head of the antenatal unit had
been one of the proudest in his life. What could be better
than leading a massive team of medical specialists who
gave mothers and yet to be born babies a proper shot at
living a full and healthy life?

Having someone to share it with?

He shook the thought away. He wasn't built for relationships.

His conscience knocked him on the head.

Okay. Fine. Perhaps that wasn't entirely true. Seeing
Lizzy again had thrown a thousand barbed questions at

an ethos that had, up until now, always worked for him. *Work hard. Play at your own risk.*

Apart from during his internship in New York, when he'd come as close to having a proper relationship as he ever had, work had always been his lifeblood. It was the only way to avoid the type of pain his mother had endured when his father left them almost thirty years ago.

Leon had been unceremoniously sent to spend a summer with him once in Denmark, but his father had made it very clear that he wasn't regarded as family. The blunt reality was that he hadn't even acknowledged his presence. Not with one solitary smile.

He'd not returned to Denmark since, incising the pain of that visit with the same surgical precision he used on a daily basis. Neat. Clean. Permanent. As such, he had a reputation for going where other surgeons suggested caution. He performed procedures other specialists only read about. But since the New York trip he'd added a new and unwelcome string to his bow. He was now the only elite maternal and foetal specialist in the world who spent his spare time daydreaming about making love with a woman he'd likely never see again.

Lizzy Beckley.

Allowing her name precious headspace inadvertently gave it access to prowl through the rest of his body. Trying to push it back into the box he'd kept it in these past few years didn't work any more. It was as if chaining it up and then unleashing it for that one perfect night had only magnified its power.

Her name sounded silently again, reverberating from his head to his heart, warming his chest and then spiralling further down, producing darts of heat that expertly arrowed below the drawstring waistband of his scrubs.

She'd been on fire that night. They both had. It had been

as if everything that had ever transpired in the world had happened so that he and Lizzy could share those few rarefied hours of lovemaking. He'd never felt more connected to one person in his life.

When he'd awoken, she'd gone.

He'd felt the sting of her absence so sharply he'd struggled to draw a complete breath since.

Constanza's fingers drummed impatiently on her hips. There was also a foot-tap.

He gave the echocardiogram a final thorough examination to flush his system of inappropriate thoughts. A child's future was reliant on his unerring focus. He'd have to stop this. The daydreaming. It didn't do him any good, and nor would it change the fact that Lizzy had made it very clear she had moved on. He had to respect that. Even if it was driving him insane.

'If you could head down to the imaging lab…?' Constanza persisted, not unkindly.

She was clearly used to doctors being lost in their thoughts. Perhaps not the precise strain of thoughts Leon was having right now, but suffice it to say the woman was made of patience.

Leon followed her down the corridor towards a part of the ward he knew perfectly well. He'd spent countless hours in the imaging lab, poring over X-rays, echocardiograms and ultrasounds, ensuring his plans were in as perfect condition as possible before he began the complicated surgeries he regularly performed.

Constanza had fulfilled her name's meaning—constancy—during one of the hospital's most complicated times. In those Covid-19 days, when life and death had hung in a balance more precarious than any of them had ever experienced bar Constanza, who came from a wartorn African country. She said she'd looked a real enemy in the eye and lived. She wouldn't let an invisible one take her down either.

Seeing families separated at the most painful and vulnerable times imaginable because of fear of the virus had made him grateful he didn't have a family of his own to worry about...children's futures to fear for. He saved lives on a daily basis in tandem with his incredible team here at St Nicolino's, and when his work was done he went home to his clean, quiet sanctuary to recharge for another day of pushing the medical envelope.

He was, in short, a man who had fulfilled his mother's dreams for him. She'd ensured that her son relied on no one, because she believed it was easier that way. If you relied on someone, you'd only be let down. If you needed to indulge in a bit of male-female relations you must cut it down when you knew you could still walk away.

Unsurprisingly, it had been his mother who'd been the most bemused by his choice of medical specialty. Paediatrics. Why would he want to spend his life around something he'd never wanted? she'd asked. Children? Families?

He'd always laughed it off, but since she'd passed away a few months back going home to his empty flat after a day with pregnant mothers, anxious fathers and the newly delivered babies that magically turned a couple into a family had pushed him into an occasional uncomfortable moment of self-examination. One that went beyond what he'd been forced to see when his mother had died without a lover or a spouse by her side.

He'd felt only a hollowness since her death—not missing her, because she'd never given him enough access to her for him to truly feel a loss. The hollowness was more of an ache. A black hole that had opened up inside him, aching to be filled with light.

He knew exactly whose light he'd like to fill it.

Lizzy's.

How the hell he'd walked away from his most perfect relationship—his *only* relationship, really—was beyond him. Youth, he supposed. Naiveté. He hadn't really trusted that Lizzy would hold up her end of their unspoken agreement to walk away at the end of their internships, without remorse or tears, and yet she'd done it. Wished him well, boarded her plane, got on with her life...

If anything, he was the one who'd stumbled. Not back then. He'd been too blinkered back then. But seeing her again had made him wonder...

Holding her. Touching her. Feeling his body rejuvenated by her warm floral scent...

He'd thought he'd be able to walk away from that solitary night refreshed and charged for another intense, head-down assault on his surgical skills, but for the first time ever one night hadn't been enough. Not nearly enough. And he wasn't entirely sure what to do with that.

'Dr Lombardi is waiting,' said the nurse, in a way that suggested she was repeating herself. *Again*.

Giovanni Lombardi was one of the most respected surgeons he'd ever had the privilege of working with and he was lucky to call him a colleague. Widowed four years ago, he had a gorgeous little girl—Sofia—whom the entire hospital seemed to dote upon, and none more so than Giovanni himself, whose world largely revolved around her and his work.

Saying that, the man was never short of female attention. Whether or not any of it stuck Leon had no clue. He intentionally kept himself clear of post-op banter as it always ended up circling back to him and his own very distinct lack of a social life. It was a frailty in some of his colleagues' eyes. A strength in his own. Especially when the boss was waiting...

'*Si*. Of course. *Scusi*, Constanza. I—' He made a vague gesture with his hand for which he received an eye-roll.

He'd received a bounty of those over the past few weeks—as if a memo had been circulated around the hospital announcing that Dr Cassanetti was a few scalpels short of a surgical set so everyone should be on their guard. Which, of course, was unacceptable. He needed all his synapses firing. Particularly with this new case Giovanni Lombardi was waiting to share with him.

An hour later he was buzzing with adrenaline, his concentration crystal-clear. Giovanni had presented him with a once-in-a-lifetime opportunity: foetal surgery on conjoined twins. The list of complications was as long as his arm, but he'd have the freedom to build his own medical team to ensure things were done properly. More to the point, he was going to have the chance to help two little girls live normal, healthy and, with any luck, happy lives.

Giovanni ran through the case again, more quickly this time.

Conjoined identical twins with two near-perfect hearts. Early scans had suggested they were hugging. The twenty-week scans had shown otherwise. Now, at twenty-one weeks, having had much more detailed MRIs, advanced imagery had made it clear that the little girls shared one crucial aortic valve. Baby A, as she was presently called, also appeared to have hypoplastic left heart syndrome.

Long story short: if Baby A survived the pregnancy she'd endure a lifetime of hospital care unless there was a surgical intervention.

There were other complications. The girls shared a chest wall, the lining of the heart and a liver. These were largely surmountable problems for when the separation surgery happened—Giovanni's responsibility—but the mother's health, the babies' delivery and Baby A's left heart syndrome was Leon's focus.

As a maternal foetal medicine specialist he was best placed to oversee the mother and the babies' welfare until the children were born. He could, of course, do general foetal surgery if required, but he'd need a foetal cardiologist as part of his team. The mother and her babies would need monitoring throughout the duration of the pregnancy and, of course, during delivery, at which point Giovanni and his team would assume pole position in overseeing their health and, ultimately, the separation operation.

The mother, Gabrielle Bianchi, was twenty-eight years old and five months pregnant. Only married six months, this was her first pregnancy. She was scared, Giovanni cautioned, but having been referred by a trusted doctor in her native Switzerland, she and her husband were hopeful that their baby girls would live through their ordeal. Her husband would be staying in a nearby flat, owned by the hospital, whilst Gabrielle would stay here in St Nicolino's for monitoring.

Leon pored over the complex medical notes again. When he glanced up, Giovanni was looking him square in the eye.

'You sure you're up for this?'

'Never been more sure.'

'Only a couple of hospitals in the world have even attempted this.'

Leon grinned. 'What? And that's meant to intimidate me?'

'No.' Giovanni gave the back of his neck a scrub. 'I just—I'll want your complete focus on this. You know as well as I do it'll end up being much more complicated than those notes suggest.'

Leon nodded. 'I get that, but...' He tipped his head to

the side, his eyes still on Giovanni. 'You've never been worried about my concentration before.'

'I've never had to be before.'

That got his attention.

Leon pushed his chair back from the table, acutely aware of his temperature rising as his defences rushed to the fore. He pushed the paperwork to the centre of the table as if it were a prize only one of them could win.

'There's not been a solitary mistake made in my operating theatre.'

'I know, but you don't seem—' Giovanni stopped himself and sought a better word than the one he had clearly been about to use.

Whatever people said about Giovanni—that he was a charmer with the gift of the gab—he was a brilliant Chief of Surgery. He never played the 'Me Boss, You Underling' card. He fostered teamwork in a way that didn't always happen naturally in high-pressured, big-ego-filled hospitals like their own, where half the medicine practised was the stuff of science fiction novels.

This case would be no different. They'd pull in the 3D printers, the lasers, the robotics. Everything they had, they'd use. Not for show. But because the type of medicine they practised here at St Nicolino's was ground-breaking. Not by force, as Leon always explained to people who didn't know about their work. It was more organic. In the way a microscopic seed could grow into a beautiful plant or tree right in the middle of a city. The wildflowers that made a show every year at Rome's ancient Colosseum were testament to that.

He squared himself up to his boss. 'C'mon. Out with it.'

Giovanni wrote an invisible prescription on the table with his finger before answering. 'It's nothing you've done, per se, but ever since you've got back from New York I haven't been able to tap into that Cassanetti drive that assures me you and your team will be able to go where no paediatric hospital has gone before. It's not a slight. Your work has been flawless. But there's been *something*... something I can't put my finger on.'

Leon raised his eyebrows. 'Oh?'

Giovanni gave him a look. One that indicated he knew damn straight that Leon could tell him here and now what the problem was if he wanted to.

He was right.

The problem was about sixty-five inches of feminine wiles, with hair as soft as silk, skin to match, and a brain that put most mortal's to shame. Never mind off-the-charts surgical skills. But Leon wasn't really in the mood for opening up a Lonely Hearts Club Forum.

Giovanni rose and pushed the paperwork back across the table towards Leon. 'You know as well as I do that your work has been exemplary. I'm just saying if there's something going on in your private life that is sapping your focus...kill it, fix it, or put a plaster on it until this is over. For the next three months your life is all about the Bianchi twins. If you want it to be.'

'Oh, I want it to be.' Leon didn't need to think about that.

'Right answer.' Giovanni reached across the table and shook his hand. 'You're the one surgeon I know who will put together a team that will make these girls' lives a reality.'

Putting together a team...

A command to fix whatever it was that was distracting him...

An idea hit. It was mad, but...

Screw it. You only live once.

'I can bring in anyone?'

Giovanni nodded. 'It's going to be a high-profile case for us. We don't just want the parents fighting for their daughters' lives. We want them to know we've got the entire world crossing their fingers for them. And you know how I feel about crossed fingers.'

Leon laughed. 'Not necessary if you've got a St Nicolino's team on it.'

They shared a grin.

Leon hitched his fingers onto his hips and feigned a casual air he didn't quite feel. 'Have you heard of Dr Elizabeth Beckley?'

Giovanni looked out of the window to where the winter sun was setting in a late-afternoon fanfare of oranges and reds, lighting up the Vatican City on the far side of the river as if by celestial arrangement.

'Antenatal cardiologist, I'm guessing. British?'

'Australian,' Leon explained. 'One of the best. Antenatal cardiologist, though she's performed a wide variety of antenatal surgeries across a pretty impressive spectrum of specialties. I'd like to bring her in.'

'For the HLH surgery? Great.'

'No,' Leon corrected. 'For the rest of the pregnancy.'

There were valid reasons for having a cardiologist on hand throughout the pregnancy. One stent might not do the trick. The twins were joined at the chest and they shared that crucial aortic valve. There were any number of problems that might arise that would require a neonatal cardiologist beyond the HLHS. But having this particular cardiologist here for the duration would be expensive.

Giovanni's eyebrows shot up, but he said nothing. He was used to surgeons and their big asks, and this was definitely one of them.

'No one here would be suitable? We do have paediatric cardiologists who live a bit closer to home...'

Leon took the question on the chin. He could see that Giovanni was asking a bigger question here. Would Lizzy solve his little concentration problem or make it worse?

Professionally, of course there were a smattering of surgeons who could do the surgery. Any who could solve the other problem…? Not so much.

'She and I interned together in New York.'

That was as close as he was going to get to crying on Giovanni's shoulder and telling him that he'd once had a love life and what had happened was his own damn fault.

Giovanni gave him a slow nod of dawning understanding. 'Get me the paperwork and we'll make it happen.'

And just like that Leon felt the so-called Cassanetti Spark pour back into his system.

CHAPTER THREE

A SMILEY FACE.

Lizzy gave the stick a shake, almost willing it to turn into a frown. Nope. Still smiling. Why hadn't she gone for the one with lines instead? The smiley face felt so...personal. Lines were scientific. Anonymous. Not bright, shiny portents for a future that was suddenly a thousand times more complicated than hers had been three minutes ago.

She leant her head against the cool tiling of the hospital loo wall, willing it to calm the heated storm brewing in every corner of her body. The tiny tempests preparing to surge together to force her to accept what this little stick had already understood very clearly.

She was going to have a baby.

And not just any baby.

She was having Leon Cassanetti's child.

While the pragmatics of a surprise pregnancy didn't entirely elude her—women often experienced bleeding that seemed like a period, wrote off other symptoms as tummy trouble or working too hard, until—as had happened today—all the little dots began to connect together into a smiley face.

Her brain fuzzed and whirred and countless futures danced in front of her like film previews, each inviting her to dive in and explore. Not one of them involved a smiley face. None she would let herself believe in anyway.

Leon was… *Oh, man*. He was a thousand things and none of them all at once. Brilliant. Passionate. Driven. Devoted to his work in a way she'd never seen in any surgeon before or since those two remarkable years in New York. A commitment-phobe. Didn't want children. Didn't want a family. Didn't want her.

But…

Even with all those factors digging little knives into her heart, one thought persisted.

This is your chance.

She'd never let the thought crystallise until now, but somewhere buried deep inside her was a hunger to give a child the kind of carefree, deeply loving, innocent upbringing she'd never enjoyed. A future primed with possibility and hope and, yes, some cautionary notes, but not enough to make her—or him—as shy of relationships as she was.

It wasn't as if Leon was completely to blame for not falling head over heels for her, asking her to marry him and move to Rome, where the pair of them would live happily ever after, their lives full of surgical triumphs, lovemaking and, as they'd be in Rome, a lot of incredible gelato.

No. She'd fallen in love with the one man in the universe who was absolutely perfect for her apart from the fact he didn't love her. He'd had his chance. That ridiculous night when she'd told him she loved him.

To this day she still wasn't a hundred percent certain he'd even heard her. It had been in a busy bar in the middle of Manhattan at the end of their internships. The tequila had been flowing and everyone had been hugging and exchanging addresses and promising to stay in touch. Like a fool, she'd leant towards the man she'd spent the last two years with—either in the operating theatre or in a bed—and said, *'I love you.'* Nothing more. Nothing less. He'd said nothing, so she'd pretended she'd said nothing.

She'd tell him, of course. About the pregnancy. She had to. Morals. Ethics. Honesty. The triumvirate of principles she clung to in her professional life were stalwarts in her personal life too. Such as it was. Yes. She would tell him. But she'd also be very, very clear... Neither she nor this child would interfere in his life. The only thing she would ask was that his child be able to contact him. She'd like their child to hear it straight from the source why Daddy and Mummy were living separate lives.

Her hand flew, for the first time, to her belly. The protective gesture spoke volumes. She would do whatever it took to ensure Leon Cassanetti never hurt her child the way he'd hurt her—unwittingly or not.

A couple of hours and a lot of regrouping later, Lizzy was standing outside the NICU unit looking at all the tiny lives she'd helped bring into the world when a nurse ran up to her with one of the mobile phones they kept at Reception. Unusual... Normally they took messages.

'It's a call for you about a job.'

Her eyebrows went up. Good! 'A job' was always code for something difficult, and difficult meant she could temporarily keep her mind off the fact she'd be having a baby in six months' time.

'In Italy,' the nurse whispered, the way one might say *chocolate cake*.

Lizzy's hand was shaking as she took the phone.

'Lizzy?'

Her entire body hummed with nerves as she stood and listened to Leon as he told her about the conjoined twins, the shared aortic valve, the baby with HLHS, and said that he'd be honoured if she'd join him in Rome for the next three months.

'Sure,' she said.

She wasn't capable of saying anything more. Not on the phone. Not when so much was at stake. Not when she knew that the next three months would decide, once and for all, the kind of life her child would lead.

'Leon! Great to see you! Whoa! No need for two cheek-kisses— Oops… Oh, well…when in Rome…'

That was a little over the top, but in for a penny…

Arch an eyebrow. Pause. Wait for his response.

'What? Me? No, I look dreadful. Jet lag doesn't suit my complexion. Leon, listen…' Lizzy let her features re-arrange themselves into the expression she knew her patients saw when the news was serious. 'I've got something important to share right off the bat and I'm not going to beat around the bush. I'm pregnant. It's yours. Just under three months—*obviously*—so that does mean no flying after a while. Which leads me to logistics. I'm still very keen to play my role with the twins—*thank you*, by the way, for including me on the team. A real honour… Seriously… But as soon as we safely deliver them I'll be moving back to Australia.'

Pause. Nod. Furrow brow.

'Yes, permanently. I'm sure you'll agree it's for the best seeing as a girlfriend let alone children aren't really on your radar, so—'

She watched her mirrored expression falter and then crumple into the confused, strained mess it had been ever since she'd first stared at that positive pregnancy test.

The fact that Leon's call had come two hours later had shaken a thousand shards of 'not a coincidence' into her bloodstream. Her hands pressed one over the other on her stomach. Why did this have to be Leon Cassanetti's baby? The one man she'd tried and failed to wash out of her hair countless times? So much for her stupid one night of un-bridled passion wrapping up that chapter of her life. Now she was going to have to start writing an entirely new book. One with a baby in it.

She cleared her throat and tried to push a bit of confi-dence through her spine. The man was probably nothing more than a handful of metres away from her right now, so she had to get her act together.

Leon had been nothing less than professional on the call, so she knew her place on his team was solely about the conjoined twins, the boost to his hospital's profile and, with any luck, her own—although a boost in professional stature wasn't why she'd agreed to come. Obviously there was a part of her that had said yes out of professional curi-osity. But, more crucially, she was here to ensure her child knew where it stood with regard to its father.

Someone to keep at bay for ever? Or someone who wanted to play a role in his or her life? Doubtful, but—unlike Leon—she knew what it was like to have a father in her life, and even though her own father had definitely not set the bar very high she wasn't going to deny her child access, if that was what the two of them wanted.

She stared at herself, wondering how the hell she'd got herself into this predicament. The two people in the world least equipped to have a baby were having a baby.

If she ever had sex again, the man would have to wear three condoms. Four. Maybe she'd just never have sex again...

Outside the loo she'd locked herself in, she heard the tannoy. The voice was Italian, obviously, and as a result sounded sensual and impassioned with a splash of urgency thrown in. Italian, except when spoken during lovemaking, always sounded as if it were laced with urgency.

The soft, cadenced murmurs of appreciation Leon had

whispered into her ear as they had made love at the dawn of the New Year came back to her as viscerally as if he was there with her now, tracing his fingers along the downy soft skin on her cheek, her arms, her belly—

Right. Hashing over the past wasn't helping anything. Not that sleeping with her ex to get over him had been a particularly brilliant idea either, but what was done was done. The strawberry-sized baby in her belly wasn't going to be well served by hiding here in the ladies' room.

She jogged in place for a second, trying to loosen a reminder of why telling him in person had seemed such a good idea.

Because it's the right thing to do, Lizzy.

She tried to marry her conscience with her frazzled nerves, fixing her reflection with a bright, cheery smile only to watch it morph into a frown. No amount of rehearsing was going to make this any easier. It was rip-the-plaster-off time.

She gave her shoulders a little shake, pinched some colour into her cheeks and forced herself down the corridor.

A few moments later she stood in the doorframe of his office, her body buzzing as if she had one hand on an electric wire and the other on a jackhammer.

He was engrossed in something he was reading on the latest model tablet, looking every bit the Grade-A surgical specialist he'd set out to be in med school. His office was filled with high-tech screens, a pair of stylish yet comfortable-looking leather chairs, a sleek espresso machine—of course—and little else. No old-fashioned piles of paperwork in this hospital.

His hair was a bit longer than when she'd seen it last. His stubble more a 'nearly midnight' shadow than a five o'clock one. She must have got the highly groomed version of Leon on New Year's Eve. This one was a bit more…not free-range, exactly… Maybe feral?

There had always been an animal element about him she couldn't quite define. An attractive animal element. The poised, tightly controlled sensuality of a tiger on the prowl. How every woman in the world he met didn't swoon and leave her partner and beg him to be with her for ever was a bit beyond her, but—given what she was about to tell him—it would very possibly remain one of life's eternal mysteries.

She forced herself to knock on his door. 'Leon?'

He turned and saw her, his eyes flaring with something hotter than recognition.

'Lizzy. *Come stai?*'

He leapt up from his chair, his long legs diminishing the space between them in nanoseconds. His scent enveloped her as he lightly held her by the shoulders and doled out the obligatory Italian cheek-kisses, instantly rendering the pink she'd brought to them with a couple of pinches pointless. Vanilla and something spicy. Whatever it was, it smelt edible.

He held her out at arm's length. 'I was just about to send out a search party.'

Ha-ha.

'No need for that. Here I am.'

Me and your baby.

'Was the flight all right?'

He peered at her as if he truly cared. Her heart constricted in a way it wasn't meant to. *Did* he actually care? It was an angle she hadn't actively considered. Then again… he always looked as if he cared, no matter the secrets he was hiding.

'I'll always think of you with fondness…'

Okay, he was 'fond' of her—which was the kind of feeling you had for spinster aunties, which meant he genuinely was asking about her comfort on the flight.

She considered making a crack about the lack of peanuts taking it down a notch, but knew it would be petty and a delaying tactic not worth pursuing, considering a) the professional reason she was here, and b) the personal reason she was here.

So, instead of playing Let's Engage in Meaningless Chitchat, she skipped all the niceties and forced herself to voice the real reason she'd come.

'I'm pregnant.'

He shook his head in one short sharp move. As if she'd slapped him.

'Scusi?'

Remorse washed through her at the coarseness of her reveal. It wasn't the way she'd have liked to find out that an ex she'd had a one-night stand with was changing her life for ever. Was there even a good way? She didn't know. This was new to her, too. Even so, she heard herself pour apologies into the charged empty space between them.

'Sorry, I—I didn't mean it to be so blunt. I was going to soften the blow—'

His eyes eventually refocused, peering into hers, actively seeking answers to the logjam of questions she presumed were stuck in his throat.

'It's mine?' he asked eventually.

She nodded, her cheeks flaming an even deeper red—because if he'd known anything about her life these past few years he'd know the chances of her being pregnant by anyone else were pretty slim.

'But we—'

She nodded. Yes. They had used protection. His, in fact.

He went completely still. An intense motionlessness so powerful it felt as though an invisible, impenetrable energy field had surrounded him. It frightened her to the point that she actually dropped her eyes to his chest to ensure he was still breathing.

When she looked back up he still hadn't moved, but she could see his eyes darting back and forth, as if he was watching the denouement of a thriller. The moment when the true mastermind of a horrible plot to take over the world was revealed. In this case, she supposed it was her.

He was fact-checking her story, no doubt. She felt herself being swept into the journey he must be reliving. His face had softened. Was he remembering the moment when they'd been able to wait no longer? They'd been in bed, not a scrap of clothing between them. She'd already orgasmed, thanks to the luxurious amount of time he'd taken to reacquaint himself with her body's erogenous zones—as if their one-night surprise reunion was actually the beginning of a long journey they'd be taking together. With a groan of sheer longing, he'd grabbed his wallet, pulled out a little foil-wrapped packet...

He shook his head as if he was trying to let the facts settle into a new order. One in which he either did or did not make room for her.

'Come,' he said eventually, his closed-lipped smile warm but distracted. 'You must be exhausted. Why don't I introduce you to the team and then we can get you to your hotel for some rest? Then we start fresh tomorrow, *si*? The twins' parents are coming in at nine. We'll be keeping *mamma* in from there on out.'

He wasn't even going to acknowledge it?

Gosh.

Of all the responses she'd prepared herself for, this definitely wasn't one of them. Anger, joy, confusion... She'd had those bases covered. But full-on denial? Definitely not a reaction the Leon she'd thought she knew would have. He might not be the down-on-bended-knee-with-a-sparkling-ring-to-hand type, but he was a kind man. An honourable man. At least…that was what she'd thought.

She was forced to swallow the bitterest of pills. The Leon she'd thought she knew was a fiction. A man she'd let herself fall deeper and deeper in love with the longer they were apart. This moment was proof that she didn't know the real Leon at all.

Somewhere along the way she'd rewritten their New York internships into a fantasy of burgeoning love, when what it had actually been was two headstrong, horny, trainee surgeons having a brilliant time competing and bettering themselves at work and releasing their pent-up tensions in bed. And that had been that.

They'd both had provisional job offers in other countries well before their internships were over. Neither had ever offered to move to the other's country. Oh, she'd dropped a hint or two, but Leon had never picked them up. Deliberately ignored them, maybe. As he was ignoring the fact she'd just told him she was pregnant with their child.

She'd been a fool to think the chemistry they'd shared had been love. More of a fool to believe that one more night of lovemaking would lay it all to rest.

In a daze, she went through the motions. Smiling. Shaking hands. Laughing as the staff congratulated Lizzy on her halting Italian.

She wouldn't dare admit that she'd spent her first couple of years back in Sydney studying all the medical lingo she'd thought she might need when Leon rang her, admitted he'd made a mistake and invited her to move to Italy. The call had never come. And, not wanting to shame herself by begging for just a morsel of attention, as her mother had so often done, Lizzy had done her best to step away from her dreams of being reunited. She'd put them away in a cupboard, shuttered her mind to the fantasy of a bright, sexy, surgical future together, and let her Italian become dusty and lacking in fluidity with disuse.

Mercifully, despite the discord she could feel buzzing between her and Leon, the staff made her feel welcome, and she knew working here would be more pleasure than pain. If she didn't board a plane back to Sydney tonight...

When they'd finished the tour and found themselves alone again, Leon looked at her as he might any visiting doctor. Politely.

He held up his phone. 'I'll just let my team know I'll be out while I drop you.'

Wow. It looked as if they really weren't going to talk about it.

Wait.

He was going to drive her to her hotel?

Her brain reeled to make the necessary connections and came up short. The exhaustion she'd held at bay with nervous energy suddenly swept into place. Her limbs felt leaden and her clear, pre-prepared thoughts were fogged with fatigue. Sitting in a close space with Leon Cassanetti, her version of kryptonite, when she felt so vulnerable was definitely a bad idea. She didn't have the right kind of energy to do this. Not on her terms anyway.

'A taxi will be fine,' she spluttered. 'You don't have to—'

'Yes.' Leon cut her protest short. 'I do have to. You're a guest here. At my hospital. In my city. And,' he added, finally taking ownership of the child she had convinced herself he was preparing to deny, 'there is no chance I'm having the mother of my child wandering round Rome unescorted.'

A niggle of discomfort cinched round her heart. From one angle, his choice of words might be seen as protective. Kind and thoughtful—just as she remembered him. They were the words of a man who was going to step up. Accept the shared responsibilities of the child neither of them had expected. From another it was bordering on controlling. A childhood of living with someone who valued strength over compromise meant she didn't respond well to being controlled with alpha power. She wasn't sure she liked the way the conversation was going.

'C'mon, Lizzy.' He beckoned for her to follow him. 'Let's go.'

Instinct overrode the calm, controlled, adult way in which she'd hoped to handle this. Defensively, she hitched her tote up onto her shoulder. 'It's not the fifties, Leon. I think we can agree you've already done enough to "help", thank you very much.'

When she saw her words lance through his eyes, she regretted her sharp tone. She was floundering as much as he must be. She'd walloped him with a reality he had never wanted. She might not want to marry the man because... *bleurgh, feelings*...but she respected him professionally at least. And you didn't treat people you respected as if they were the enemy.

She tried again. 'Honestly, Leon. I'm fine. We can meet later, if you like, but I'm okay to find the hotel on my own.'

'Lizzy—' He caught hold of her hand, preventing her from leaving.

She tugged it free. *What the hell?* Her father had never hit her mother, but this was one of his standard moves. Holding her in place until he felt he'd been *heard*. She took back the respect thing. Respect had to be earned, and this sort of behaviour was not the way to start cashing in.

'Back off—all right?'

He held up his hands, but the energy emanating from him kept her caught in its snare.

'You have just told me you're pregnant with my child. *Our* child.'

He swept his fingers through his hair, and her body lived the sensation as if she'd done it herself.

'You've had time to digest this. Don't you think I deserve some time, too?' He took a steadying breath, then continued. 'My response might be clumsier than you'd like, but pushing me away isn't going to help either of us. Or the child.'

It was a fair point. Not that it stopped her heart from hammering against her ribcage or muted the fight-or-flight response her body was incapable of shaking off.

She forced herself to look at him—really look at this man who'd just been told he was going to father a child—and tried to see things from his perspective. What she saw made her heart stop and then do precisely what she'd willed it not to. Crack open far enough to allow the compassion she'd hoped to keep at bay pour in.

He looked every bit as scared and braced for battle and—yes—as strangely hopeful as *she'd* felt when she'd first taken the test.

Which, of course, added a ream of complications to what she'd hoped would be a black and white situation. She would tell him. He would say *Best of luck, mate*—or whatever the Italian equivalent of 'mate' was. Certainly not *patatina*, as he'd used to jokingly call her: his little potato. And then off she'd pop, back to Australia, to get on with the rest of her life, raising a child who would, one day, inevitably want to meet the man its mother had made love to as if her life depended upon it.

That was how intense it had been. Her need to get him in and out of her system during that one unexpected night.

As far as plans backfiring went, this was shaping up to be a doozy.

She forced herself to meet his gaze directly. 'Let's get a move on, shall we?'

CHAPTER FOUR

SIDE BY SIDE, Leon guided Lizzy through the busy hospital corridors, hoping she couldn't see his frown periodically quirking into a smile.

Same old Lizzy. Fiery. Fierce. As combative as ever when it came to good old-fashioned chivalry. As if an offer to open a door would lead to a life of indentured servitude.

The last thing in the world Leon wanted to do was trap Lizzy in 'a patriarchal system designed to subvert women for the sole purpose of big-upping male egos.' Her words. Not his. Something, he suspected, to do with her father—a leading cardiologist who, suffice it to say, wasn't known for his bedside manner.

They'd never really talked about their pasts, but he presumed if her relationship with her father had been warm, she definitely would have pulled him and his experience into conversation much more frequently than never.

He'd messed up big-time by grabbing her wrist, but he'd meant it when he'd said he would look after her. Her surprise announcement had tapped into the instinctive part of him that didn't just *want* to be protective—it *had* to be.

A child.

He, Leon Cassanetti—sworn bachelor and slave to his professional calling, a man who brought new life into the world for other people—already knew in his heart that he was going to cross that thick line he'd drawn in the sand between himself and the rest of the world. So much for the years he'd spent ensuring he was the kind of clear-eyed physician who kept his perspective purely scientific.

Emotions were things his patients dealt with. Men and women who, for reasons he'd thought he'd never understand, had decided to risk the foundations of their emotional stability by bringing a child into the world.

His arrival had signalled the beginning of the end for his own parents. What was it signalling for him and Lizzy?

To stop his thoughts reeling too far out of control, he forced himself to focus on the immediate pragmatics of their situation. He rang ahead to Reception, where she'd stored her luggage, to have it follow them in a taxi, and cleared his calendar for the rest of the day, all the while trying to push his mother's well-worn edict out of his mind: *Keep everyone at arm's length and all will be well.*

He glanced down at Lizzy as they made their way silently to the underground car park where he kept his scooter. There were light shadows under her eyes. She had just flown halfway around the world, but now that he looked at her—really looked—he saw that tell-tale glow about her. The one that assured him, without needing scientific proof, that she was carrying a child. There was an added lustre to her harvest-coloured hair, an extra wattage in the flares of connection they shared each time their eyes met.

He stopped abruptly, the memory of a colleague's experience bringing an unwelcome rush of adrenaline. 'I can't drive you there.'

She looked up at him, confused. The crinkle he'd used to run his thumb along to smooth away her worries formed between her brows. He shook off the instinct to do the same again.

'I brought my scooter,' he explained.

She shrugged in a way that suggested he was being ridiculous. 'Do you have an extra helmet?'

He did. And they had spares at the hospital's concierge desk. But—no.

'A car would be safer.'

'I'm not made of delicate crystal, Leon.'

'You are carrying our child.'

She crossed her arms and fixed him with a humourless smile. 'Interesting. Is this what you tell all your patients? That they should ride in crash-proof vehicles, wrapped in cotton wool, until they've delivered?'

She fixed him with a look suggesting that he had lost some brain cells between here and the antenatal unit. There was very possibly some truth to that. He was wading into something so unfamiliar to him he had no idea if he'd sink or swim.

She continued in her usual brisk, almost casually amused way. 'You know as well as I do that women have been getting on with their lives whilst pregnant for thousands of years. I'm guessing countless pregnant women right here in Rome have ridden scooters to and from their hotels with—'

She stopped herself, her upper teeth snagging her lower lip. Second thoughts, maybe? Or, more likely, feeling the enormity of what was happening now that they were together, absorbing the reality that in six months they would be having a child together.

As if on cue a young couple walked by, the woman carrying a newborn, cooing and whispering loving phrases of nonsense, the euphoria of having brought a life into the world blurring everything else.

Lizzy's eyes followed them, then clouded with a rush of emotion he couldn't put his finger on.

'Are you all right, *cara*?'

She didn't meet his eyes. 'Fine. C'mon. Let's go.'

They finished the walk to his scooter in silence.

Was this how the next few months would be? Each shared activity a small tug of war? One of them gaining a handhold here, the other the next, until at last their hands touched in the centre or, more likely, one fell down?

When he handed her his spare helmet, their fingers brushing as they made the exchange, he saw the tiniest hint of fragility fissure through the facade of the strongest woman he'd ever met. She caught him looking and once again looked away.

He frowned. This wasn't how he wanted things to go. He didn't want her to take his every suggestion as a power-play. He respected her. He cared for her. He might not have imagined a proper relationship or having a family with her, but that wasn't their reality any more. They'd have to figure it out. Together.

After he'd secured her helmet and climbed on, signalling Lizzy to climb on behind him, a suspicion rose. He knew exactly why she'd abruptly balked at the thought of a scooter ride. She was going to have to put her arms around him. Rest her hands on his hips at the very least.

When she climbed onto the seat behind him he felt the thrill of connection for a nanosecond. Then she pulled back, trying to keep a few centimetres of space between them. He revved the scooter and took off. Her hands instantly swooped round his waist.

He did his best not to respond to her touch...not to lean into those hot licks of response as her breasts brushed along his back. But it proved impossible as, with turn after turn, her fingers wove more tightly around his waist as if they'd done this a thousand times. To the point where he allowed himself a careless thought... *What if this was their reality?* Riding to and from work together…her hands round his waist…her breasts pressing into his back.

His hand instinctively slipped to her leg at some traffic lights, giving her thigh a light rub that spoke to all the feelings he felt for her but wasn't equipped to put a voice to. He hadn't been given the classic Italian gift for florid speech. The ability so many men had to call a woman *amore* or *cara*. Loved one. Dearest. Those words meant something pure and deep-seeded. Words that should only be spoken if the speaker had the emotional foundation to back them up. It was why he'd never called a woman *amore*, not even when he'd met Lizzy, opting instead for the more comical *patatina*.

'This doesn't look like a hotel.' Lizzy pointed up to the stone-and-marble-faced building he'd stopped in front of.

'No. It's my apartment building.'

Lizzy gave him the kind of double take he would've given himself if he'd been looking in a mirror. He was fiercely protective of his own space. Even in New York, where prices were insane and sharing a flat would've made so much sense—particularly for two people who spent the bulk of their spare time together—they'd each kept their own small studios, using the on-call rooms at the hospital more often than either of those.

He allowed himself a snapshot memory of their naked bodies tangled together, bedclothes heaven knew where, wishing fervently that dawn would never come.

'I thought I was staying at a hotel.' Her voice was guarded.

'This makes more sense.'

'To whom, exactly?'

'The both of us. *Per favore.* I have a guest room, so you'll have your own space. If it's too strange I'll take you to the hotel, but we have a lot to discuss.'

'That doesn't mean I have to stay with you to discuss it.'

No. But it did mean more hoops to jump through, and one thing neither of them had was excess time.

'Lizzy. Please. I want you to stay with me.'

For ever?

He didn't miss the sceptical narrowing of her eyes as, wordlessly, she climbed off the scooter.

'This isn't the largest of lifts, is it?' she crabbed as the two of them got into the small, wrought-iron-gated elevator built some seventy-odd years back. It moved so slowly he sometimes wondered if it was run by mice on a treadmill.

He looked down at the space between them, suddenly vividly aware that in six months' time it wouldn't be empty. It would be filled with the round, beautifully weighted orb of Lizzy's belly. Her hands might be resting on it to feel a kick or a squirm. Or his hands…

He stopped the daydream when his fingers twitched at the urge to massage oil into her back and belly to ease the strain her pregnancy might be taking on her. To hold their baby in his arms the moment it was born, then carry it to her so she, too, could embrace the tiny, beautiful child they'd created.

An unwelcome alternative arose. In six months' time Lizzy might be back in Sydney.

'How's your mother?' Lizzy asked, clearly uncomfortable in the silence. 'Is she still in Rome?'

'I'm afraid she passed away recently.'

All the fractiousness crackling between them disappeared. 'Oh, Leon. I'm so sorry. I didn't know or I would've—'

He waved away her apologies. 'Honestly. It's fine.'

It wasn't. It had knocked him for six. But in ways he hadn't expected. Ways that had given him mad ideas like inviting Lizzy Beckley to Rome. Into his *home*.

It was surprising to realise that what pained him was wondering what would've happened if he hadn't rung Lizzy. Would she have told him she was pregnant? The thought stuck like the poisoned tip of a blackthorn in his conscience. Of all the things he'd allowed Lizzy to know about him on a personal front, two things rose to the fore: he didn't want children and he didn't want a relationship.

Two long-held beliefs that had done a complete one-eighty in the space of an hour. Heaven knew what the next hour had in store—let alone the next six months.

'I always thought you became a maternal foetal medicine specialist because of her,' Lizzy said softly.

It was a leading question and they both knew it. Leon had never spoken about his mother to Lizzy. Talking about her was opening a can of worms and looking into a past that he would happily keep closed for ever.

He shook his head, but wondered if perhaps there was some truth to it. If a mother wasn't well, the child or children she was carrying would suffer. His mother has suffered enormous mental anguish. Relationship PTSD. The trauma and hurt had gone that deep. As such, Leon had not been immune either.

'Was she still living here in Rome?' Lizzy asked.

He gave a soft smile, grateful for the topic-change. 'Yes. I don't think anything could have pulled her away from here.'

'No?'

He shook his head and smiled. His mother might not have won any parenting prizes, but she had been a character. A very colourful character. And, more to the point, she had taught him not so much the power of love, but the fierceness of loyalty. When his father had left them, she'd stayed. Fed him, clothed him, drilled questionable survival skills into him when a piece of him had always known, but rarely acknowledged, that his mother would have liked to do exactly what his father had…walked away when the going got tough and pretended he didn't exist.

He cleared his throat and answered neutrally. 'She was a dedicated Roman. Occasionally, when the tourist population grew too much in the summertime, she could be tempted out to the Mediterranean… If the boyfriend was right.'

'She never remarried, then?'

'No,' he laughed. 'Pigs would've flown before my mother agreed to marry again.'

Lizzy's lips tweaked into a smile, but he could see her connecting these dots she'd not had access to before.

They'd had a very clear 'Don't Ask, Don't Tell' rule back in the day. His past was messy, emotional and unsettling. He knew very little of Lizzy's, but she had seemed equally happy not to air her childhood laundry. It was an unspoken policy that had worked for them right up until an hour ago. Now that they were going to have a child everything would have to change. And that included the way he looked at his own life.

Leon had never questioned his mother's embittered approach to love because he'd borne witness to its source. His father had never given her a reason for his abrupt departure. He'd simply risen from the supper table one night and walked away. Boarded a plane. Sent word through a secretary that he'd send a courier for his things and that had pretty much been that. No explanation. No hugs goodbye.

The experience had thrown Leon into the heart of the savage pain of loss. A loss so profound he refused to open himself up to that level of hurt and rejection again. Which had landed him here, in the world's slowest lift, with the woman who was carrying his child and, by all accounts, didn't want him involved in his child's life. A woman, in short, who didn't trust him as far as she could throw him.

He glanced again at Lizzy's flat belly and the space between them. Pictured the child that would one day come into the world and tried to imagine sitting down with him or her and teaching all the distrust and wariness his own mother had taught him.

What a selfish thing to do. An even more selfish way to love. The anguish his mother must have felt, to teach her child that his love would never be returned, must have been devastating.

He saw in a flash that what his mother had done was no better than his father's abrupt departure. He'd always thought he'd been protecting Lizzy and himself from an inevitable pain. But what he'd actually done was smash the foundations of what might have been an amazing relationship. If she'd wanted one.

Now that she was going to have his child would she want one? The chemistry was obviously still there. The professional respect. But the love...?

A tang of well-trained panic rose in his throat.

Lizzy looked up, a question in her eyes. 'Are you all right, Leon?'

'Marry me.'

She actually barked with laughter. 'Don't be mad.'

'I mean it, Lizzy.'

To his shock, he did. Mostly. Yes. Definitely. They could be a family. Here in Rome. At her place in Sydney. Wherever. He had no idea how it would work, but he did know he didn't want his son or daughter feeling the blunt heartache of rejection the way he had.

'Marry you?' Lizzy said dryly, and gave him an intense look as if scanning him for signs of insanity.

'I'm not the worst option.'

This elicited a trill of laughter too quickly. 'Nor are you the best.'

Her words pierced a place in his heart he hadn't even known existed. 'There's someone else?'

Indignation flared in her eyes, then reformed as a blaze of strength. 'I don't think my personal life is any of your business. Apart, of course, from the baby.'

Her hand instinctively went to her belly just as the lift churned the final few inches towards the top-floor flat.

'I'll be a father to this child,' he said, placing his hand over hers. 'Our child. And a husband to you. It's the right thing to do. It's my duty.'

CHAPTER FIVE

'No!' LIZZY LAUGHED as she spoke, but her heart was slamming against her ribcage so hard it physically hurt.

Marry him? It was the one question she had privately ached to hear five years before—but this way? Being brought to his flat without being asked. Being told he would parent their child without even considering the plans she'd already made for the baby? And she had plans, all right. Lots of plans. In Australia. Without him.

And marriage as a *duty*?

No. Freaking. Way.

It was exactly what her parents had done. Her mother had fallen pregnant during her first year out of uni. After a long talk between their fathers, Lizzy's parents had 'enjoyed' a shotgun wedding. And her father had never let her mother forget it. He stayed out of duty. Nothing more.

'No, what?' Leon persisted, as if there was any other question blinking in huge neon letters between them.

'No, I will not marry you,' she said more solidly. 'Not under these circumstances.'

Because he didn't really mean it. Right?

'Why not?' Leon asked, in the same way he might ask her why she thought a tricky surgery couldn't or, more to the point, shouldn't be performed.

It's not possible, came the small voice in her head.

A flare of light flashed through his eyes. She knew what it was. The acceptance of a challenge.

'Anything's possible, Lizzy.'

He'd used to say that all the time, back when they'd shared an operating theatre.

'You just have to find the right path.'

Lizzy ignored the tiniest waver fluttering through her heart and fixed him with her best *Be serious* look. Shutting him down was easier than pouring her heart out to him. Telling him she'd watched her mother fade from a beautiful, happy, smiling woman into a timorous, fearful shadow of a mouse, back-seating her own fledgling career as a social worker to support her husband and daughter.

How could Lizzy admit to someone so strong and solid that there was a part of her terrified of discovering that he would be like her father? A man who ruled with a *Because I said so* edict. And that, to keep the peace, she'd follow it. There was no way she could give up on everything she'd worked so hard for to enter into a marriage of emotional oppression and control.

When her mother had died three years back, never having received the love she'd so desperately deserved, something had changed in Lizzy. Hardened. She had vowed, then and there, never to let herself fall into the same trap. Never to live in a marriage hoping and praying for the day when her husband would finally realise he'd loved her all along.

Leon didn't budge, his expression expectant.

'You just have to find the right path.'

Seriously? Did he genuinely want her to consider this as an actual proposal?

Married. A family. With Leon.

It was exactly what Lizzy had dreamt of all their years

apart, so why did it feel more like a nightmare than a dream come true?

Because he had asked out of duty. Out of a need to control the situation. Not out of love.

Something must have changed in her expression, because after a moment of stillness his hand left hers and his eyes locked on the arrow inching its way to the seventh floor. From the brusque way he yanked open the lift door and crossed the marble-floored corridor to his flat, she wasn't holding out much hope that a declaration of undying love was forthcoming.

Missing Leon's touch upon her belly more than she cared to admit, she dazedly followed him into what was a surprisingly soulless apartment. A feat, considering how incredible it was. Floor-to-ceiling windows. Bifold doors that would open wide to the fresh spring afternoon. Richly coloured rugs took the echoey edge off the marble floors. Immaculate sofas formed an arc around a modern fireplace. Tactical displays of tulips dotted about the rest of the relatively monochrome furnishings provided bright, primary splashes of colour. Black and white photographs that might have been taken by anyone, anywhere, lined the walls.

It was more show home than comfort zone, unlike her own tiny house back in Sydney. It was her beachside cocoon away from the hospital where, every now and again, she had to rebuild herself after particularly tough cases. Her refrigerator was covered in crayon drawings. Her windowsills were filled with thank-you cards for her and her lodger, Byron, a scrub nurse who also worked at the children's hospital.

There were no signs of Leon's professional calling here. She had an entire wall made up of photos of proud parents holding the babies she'd helped bring into the world. The joy they elicited in her was as powerful as if they were family members. This place looked as if it had hardly been lived in—if at all. The building itself had an old-fashioned exterior that spoke of a deep human presence, but up here on the seventh floor…

She couldn't put her finger on it, exactly, but it felt lonely up here. Which, unexpectedly, made her heart ache for Leon.

The one place she warmed to as Leon gave her a swift tour of the two guest rooms she could choose between and the open-plan kitchen with its pristine marble breakfast bar, was the terrace that wrapped all the way around the building. It was wider than a balcony and canvas awnings were dotted about it, creating little protected seating areas, and just outside the kitchen there was a breakfast area where Leon said you could watch the sun rise.

'And…do you do that?' she asked, conscious that both of them were avoiding the 'Marry me' elephant in the room. 'Watch the sunrise?'

He shrugged. 'If I'm here and I see it, yes. If not, no.'

The response seemed so bereft of any engagement in his actual life that she had to ask. 'What do you do for fun?'

He looked at her, confused. 'Fun?'

'Yeah…' She warmed to the topic. 'You know—that thing we used to have back in the day, when we weren't in surgery?'

A midnight picnic they'd once shared in a sloshy bubble bath sprang to mind. Leon, however, still looked confused.

'I thought the *surgeries* were fun. The stuff in between was—'

He stopped himself, his eyes meeting hers, and she knew as they did that he'd been caught out. The 'stuff in between' had always been the two of them. Giggling over lattes and warm blueberry muffins as they rehashed the day's surgical rotation. Bashing out their frustrations if there'd been a run-in with a superior at a nearby batting cage, both of them ending up in hysterics over how bad they were as neither of them had grown up playing baseball. And, of course, the countless hours they'd spent in bed, not just making love but daydreaming of a time and a place when performing surgery would be second nature to them and the rest of their energies could be poured into enjoying life the way the rest of their peers who were already established surgeons did.

When she looked at it that way—clinically—she couldn't believe she hadn't seen it before. All their interactions in New York had been work-related. Well. Work and sex-related. What a fool to think he might have loved her as she'd loved him.

Channelling the woman who seemed capable of asking all the questions she'd kept to herself for the last five years, she plopped her tote onto one of the breakfast bar stools and challenged him. 'Go on. You were saying…?' She held her hands out. 'The stuff in between surgeries was what, exactly? A time-filler? Meaningless? Fond memories?'

The last words came out a bit more angrily than it should have if she actually wanted to know the answer.

He gave the back of his neck a scrub. 'It was great, Lizzy. You know that. It was time with you.' He pulled his hand up through his hair and rubbed his eyes. 'Look. You're tired, and I'm still digesting. I think it'd be a good idea if you had a rest. I'll go out and get us some food.'

She felt riled again. Would he *stop* telling her what to do?

He pulled open the refrigerator door and showed her the sparse pickings, as if to prove he wasn't making up an excuse to leave her on her own. A tiny bit of her fury drifted away. Okay. Fine. So maybe he was telling the truth about that part.

'When you get up, we'll eat and talk about this prop-erly—*all* of this. Tomorrow's going to be the first time the full team meets to discuss the twins' treatment, so I'm as aware as you are that we need to find some sort of happy place, *si*?'

Ha! Happy place? The man was mad.

She wanted to protest. Insist that now was the right time to talk. Sending her off to her room like a naughty child was just the sort of thing her father would have done if she'd dared to question his judgement. Saying that…there had been compassion in Leon's voice. Concern. Enough to throw her off her guard and, more pressingly, allow room for the jet-leg that adrenaline had been holding at bay to flood in.

She'd done the hardest part. She'd told him she was having their child. And rather than run away, which had been pretty much her number one choice of options for him, he'd stayed. Proposed, even. Offered her everything she'd ever wanted from him in the space of a lift journey. Everything apart from his undying love.

If there had been an eighth floor, would that declara-tion have revealed itself?

She considered insisting they talk it out now, but knew the chances that things would quickly degenerate because of her increasing fatigue were high. He was right. An-noyingly.

A huge yawn threatened to consume the remains of her brain cells, all but proving his point that she needed some rest. Reluctantly she acquiesced, and all but tumbled into one of the guest rooms, where a large wooden sleigh bed with a gorgeously inviting duvet beckoned her into a sound, dreamless slumber.

Several hours later she woke feelingly surprisingly refreshed. There were sounds of cutlery and plates clattering in the kitchen. Her phone, which had adjusted itself to the local time, said it was just gone seven p.m.

She walked barefoot into the kitchen in the airline T-shirt she'd managed to tug on before falling asleep. It was a hand-me-down from Byron, whose long-term boyfriend was a pilot.

Leon had also changed. In place of the navy scrubs he wore twill trousers which made the most of his long legs, and a white linen shirt that hung from his shoulders as if it were made to measure. His dark eyes met hers as she walked into the room, brightening in the first instance and then, as he took in her ensemble, emptying of light.

She tugged on the hem and threw him an apology. 'Sorry. I should've showered and dressed before coming out. I just heard you in here and wanted to make sure I had time before…you know…proceedings get underway.'

He didn't laugh at the sonorous voice she'd put on, instead giving one of those indeterminate head-shakes—*yes, no, whatever you wish*. He was being weird.

She looked down at the T-shirt. It was very clearly a man's. Did he think—?

'Like it? It's my housemate's. It's comfy to sleep in. Not exactly as stylish as I know you Italians are, but it does the trick.'

'You live with a man?'

Leon feigned an air of casual indifference to the point where it was actually kind of adorable. Leon Cassanetti… Jealous of a man he had no need to be jealous of. How long should she let this play out before she told him Byron was her very gay housemate, who would never in a million years like women?

Leon tipped some antipasti into a bowl and pretty much

missed the bowl. Definitely not a precision surgical move. Maybe she'd let this play out just a little bit.

She smiled, nabbing one of the amazing olives. Why was food so much better in Italy?

Leon bashed a glass against the tap, realised he'd cracked it, then threw it in the bin with a low curse.

Okay. Maybe she should explain...

'A few years back, when I bought my place, I thought it'd be wise to reduce the mortgage payments by having a housemate. Byron—one of the scrub nurses at the hospital—heard me talking about whether or not to let the room and volunteered himself. I thought... Why not?'

'Oh. Right...' Leon swept up a newly spilt pool of olive oil from the counter. 'So you two are colleagues, are you?'

'And friends.'

He began to chop some carrots with a pronounced *thunk* of the knife after each incision.

This was fun. And a little bit mean.

Her commitment to making Leon sweat was already wavering—which didn't really speak well to the whole getting custody of their child sorted, moving back to Australia and not worrying about seeing him ever again thing. Or maybe the fact that he'd proposed had given short shrift to that.

'So...you two socialise?' Leon asked.

'Byron is the only reason I *have* a social life,' she answered truthfully.

After her tenure in New York, and landing her job at Sydney's premier children's hospital, she'd fallen into a pattern that had been eighty percent hospital, fifteen percent sleep and the other five pretty much devoted to eating in front of the telly. Byron wouldn't have any of it, saying that life was for living, not box-setting. He'd said she was too pretty and too young to hang up her stilettos just yet. He'd even been the one to set up her profile on a rarely used dating app.

When she could see Leon trying and failing to find another question to ascertain if she and Byron were 'friends with benefits' she finally broke. She hadn't come here to be cruel. 'We occasionally go to the movies or a concert when he's not out with his boyfriend. Which is a lot.'

Leon's shoulders lowered about three inches, and his smile finally allowed a hint of the playfulness she'd once had full access to to surface.

'Could you maybe consider putting some more clothes on?' he asked.

His eyes dropped to her thighs and swept back up her body with such specificity that she felt her nipples grow taut against the soft cotton of the loose top. That was when it hit her. Leon still found her attractive. She didn't know why she had discounted that as an option. She gulped. He might have actually meant it when he'd asked her to marry him.

Heat sprang to her cheeks and, unable to sustain the eye contact he'd locked her in, she shot out of the room, took a quick, very cold shower, put on her most shapeless clothes and marched back into the kitchen, ready to deliver the little speech she'd rehearsed on the plane.

'I didn't come here to corner you into marrying me.'

Leon handed her a plate of antipasti, his lips parting in protest.

She held up a hand. 'Please. I'd like to get through this—mostly because I've been practising it for so long. I just need to get it out, okay?'

He nodded, poured her a glass of fizzy water, then joined her at the breakfast bar, giving her his full, undivided attention. Something her father definitely wouldn't have done.

'Okay. So… As you have probably guessed, my being pregnant is as much of a surprise to me as it is to you—but, as you say, I've had more time to digest. And, having given it a lot of thought, I definitely want to keep the baby.'

He nodded, his eyebrows burrowing together as if not keeping it hadn't even factored on his radar. It was another arrow into her heart. The warm, fuzzy kind that made saying the next part more difficult.

'My plan is to live in Australia. There will be no financial burden on you. Or emotional. Or anything else that you don't want. However, when the baby—my child—is old enough, I want to secure your permission for him or her to reach out to you… You know… To meet their biological father.'

'No.'

Lizzy physically recoiled at the bluntness of his response. 'What do you mean, no?'

CHAPTER SIX

LEON ALMOST REGRETTED not pouring himself a glass of wine, but he knew keeping a clear head was critical.

He took Lizzy's hand in his, trying not to react when she pulled it away, balled it into a fist and tucked it onto her lap under the counter. This wasn't just her child they were talking about. It was *theirs*. Their child. Their future. And that meant everything he'd believed before was now rendered null and void.

Did he know if he was capable of being a good husband? No. Would he be a good father? Perhaps better than his own, but that wasn't saying a lot. It would be a learning curve. A sharp one. But he'd never shied away from anything that scared him. Apart, of course, from relationships.

He started again. 'I meant our child won't have to seek me out because it is going to be a part of my life—*our* lives—from day one, so there will be no need for him or her to reach out, because I will already have been there every step of the way.'

His insides were echoing Lizzy's expression. One that very clearly asked, *Who stole the real Leon and replaced him with you?*

But rather than smile and relax with relief at the prospect of shared parenthood, her frown deepened.

It stung him to know that the deepest impression he'd

made on her was one of non-interest. It stung more to re-alise she hadn't been kidding when she'd said she didn't want him to be part of their child's life.

'Leon…' She teased at a loose string on her cuff. 'I live in Australia.'

He waved his hand between them. 'Logistics. You could live here. I could move there. We commute. Whatever it takes.'

'Bullshit.'

'Che cosa?'

'I said bullshit. You don't want to be married and have a family. I mean—' She gestured towards his flat. 'Look at this place. This isn't the type of home you'd buy if you wanted little ones and a wife around, is it?'

He took a look at the flat through her eyes. Chrome. Glass. Clean, clear lines. Nothing out of place except the jumper Lizzy had thrown on the back of a chair—which, he had to admit, he'd been itching to fold into an exact square and put back in her room.

La merda. She was right. Not a solitary thing in this flat spoke to a latent craving to be part of a family. And yet with Lizzy here, the place already felt nicer to come home to.

He gave himself a psychological thump on the back. She was right. He liked things as they were. But a child… A child changed everything.

'I could move. We could find somewhere together.'

'Oh!' She laughed. 'Sure! You could absolutely move. But not with me.' She said it with a smile, but her voice was fuelled by fierce protectiveness. 'I repeat: you don't want to be a father, Leon. You don't want to be married.'

'Nor do you,' he countered. 'At least you didn't back in New York.'

'I don't exactly remember you asking!' she snapped in a way that betrayed a vulnerability he'd never seen before.

Oh, hell. She'd wanted him to ask.

But they'd both talked so often about pursuing their careers—hers in Sydney, his in Rome—he'd just presumed it really was what they'd both wanted.

She flicked her hair over her shoulders and continued the speech she'd clearly rehearsed. 'You'd have to change your approach to work. And home-life, such as it is. There will be toys everywhere. And laundry. You'll be woken up in the middle of the night by the crying of a baby that you don't get paid to look after. And let's be honest, Leon. The only thing you want to be woken up by in the middle of the night is your beeper.'

'Lizzy,' he began, using his *now, let's be sensible* voice, 'if you can change, what makes you think I can't?'

She gave one solitary bark of laughter and shook her head in a vague way, her eyes not leaving his, as if answering the question would give him an opportunity to pounce and take control.

'I've *met* you, Leon.' Her features softened. 'Look. I'm not trying to be cruel. Honestly. I'm trying to be realistic. So…can we just take this whole "marry me" thing off the table?'

He scrubbed his hand over his face. He wanted to do the best by her. And now that he'd seen that glimpse of a part of her he'd never seen before—the part that had hoped for a long-term relationship…

No. She was right. He wasn't equipped for love, marriage or a baby carriage. How could he be? He'd been trained from an early age to think that love brought pain. Parenting equalled abandonment. But if Lizzy, a woman who had been very clear about not wanting children herself, could climb aboard the bandwagon, why couldn't he?

Because she didn't want him to be a part of it.

She was walking away years before his father had. Which, in some ways, was kinder than his father had been. But in other ways…?

His chest flooded with emotion, clouding his judgement as he tried to figure out the best way to proceed.

Lizzy, eagle-eyed, saw his indecision and slapped her hand on the marble countertop in frustration. 'We're not discussing real estate here, Leon. Or career moves. Or beepers. We're discussing a child. A baby. One I hadn't planned on having and one I know for sure you hadn't. Marrying you isn't going to put a nice pretty bow on everything and make it better.' She swept her hands along her cheeks and gave the back of her neck a rub. 'Look… How about this? Tomorrow, let's put our focus where it should be. On the twins. Then, after a few days, when we're both thinking a bit more clearly, let's do a scan together.'

'Have you seen it? The baby?'

She threw him a look as if he'd lost his marbles. 'I'm thirteen weeks pregnant, Leon.'

Yes. She'd seen it.

'Seen it and heard the heartbeat,' she confirmed.

His breath left his chest with such force it was as if he'd been kicked. In its place a memory shot to the fore.

A couple completely in love with each other who had been unable to physically be with their child during the Covid outbreak when it had developed pneumonia. He'd told himself at the time that heartache like theirs was exactly why he didn't want to be in a relationship. Now he saw how wrong he'd been. If he messed things up with Lizzy, he'd be the one on the outside looking in and he didn't like it. Not one damn bit.

He refilled Lizzy's water glass and took a sip of his own before speaking. 'I don't know how things were for you in

Sydney during the Covid outbreak, but at St Nicolino's we had people standing outside the hospital, hoping and praying their children would know they were there. Making video calls if they could…showing their child how close they were. One carer per family was eventually allowed in the hospital, but even then they often weren't allowed in the room. Siblings weren't allowed in at all. For far too many families the more relaxed visiting rules came too late. It was absolutely heartbreaking. As if the loss of a child wasn't enough, they weren't able to comfort one another as the situation worsened.'

'Yes…' she nodded, clearly having had a similar experience '…and your point is?'

'My mum. Her death.' He held up a hand to stop any flow of sympathies. He wasn't digging. He was explaining. 'When she died…the truth was, it was hard for me to feel anything.'

She furrowed her brow, clearly confused. 'What do you mean?'

He shook his head, still trying to figure it out himself. 'It was like my mother had created her own lockdown bubble around herself twenty-five years ago when my father left. I hadn't realised just how much she'd restricted access to herself until after she passed, when there was very little change in my life. In anyone's, really.'

Shockingly little. And although he'd only admitted it to himself as he'd shouldered the weight of her coffin along with five strangers he'd realised he'd barely known her. No wonder he approached life so scientifically. So clinically. It was the only emotional toolbox he'd been given access to.

Lizzy slid her arms into a tight cross over her chest. 'I thought you liked to keep yourself apart from all that messy emotional stuff.'

'I do. Emotional distance as a surgeon is essential. You know that. Emotion clouds judgement.'

She harrumphed.

'I believe that. *Professionally*,' he clarified. 'But as a son I was never given the chance to be emotional about my family.'

Not in public anyway. He'd felt the pain of abandonment when his father had left. The gradual cooling of affections as his mother had withdrawn her own.

He tapped his finger on the countertop, then looked up to meet Lizzy's eyes. 'It took my mother dying in the way she did—isolated, friendless—for me to realise that no matter how much you convince yourself keeping people you care about at a distance will help, it doesn't. It just means you'll be alone when you die.'

'And that's your big revelation from all this? You don't want to be alone when you die?' Lizzy couldn't keep the scepticism from her voice.

'No.' He shook his head, then looked her square in the eye. 'I don't want to be alone when I live.'

He watched his words land and take hold of her the same way the news he was going to be a father had gripped his heart and pressed the air out of his lungs in one swift blow.

She squeezed her eyes tight, then opened them, the aquamarine clarity of them piercing through to his chest. Somewhere deep within that kaleidoscope of blues and greens a *yes* was floating about, waiting to find purchase. A *yes* to the question he'd never imagined himself asking. *Will you marry me?*

Everything in him stilled as he waited for her to speak. If she said yes, he was going to have to throw himself at the relationship learning curve with the same blind focus he'd used when he'd poured himself into his career.

Lizzy shifted in her chair and ran her finger round the

rim of her glass. 'Maybe we should hold off deciding exactly what we're going to do. Like you said, I have jet lag and you have…' she scrubbed the air between them '…your "issues".'

It wasn't a no. It wasn't a *yes, let's all move in and play happy families* either, but they had time to figure out what to do without… *Ha!* Without letting all this emotion cloud their judgement. *As if.*

Just as he was about to suggest they move to the table out on the terrace and eat some of the antipasti he'd bought at the local *salumeria*, his mobile rang.

'Pronto?'

He locked eyes with Lizzy as he took in the details of the call. This was much more familiar terrain. An infant needing immediate surgery. The prematurely born boy had struggled with necrotising enterocolitis and the situation, which had been steadily monitored throughout his stay in the NICU, had reached critical. It was one of the most common problems for premature infants, but its likelihood made it no less lethal.

He rattled off a few instructions, ending the call with a promise to be there and gowned up within fifteen minutes.

'NEC?' Lizzy asked when he'd ended the call.

He nodded, then did a double-take. 'Your Italian's a lot better than you let on back at the hospital.'

She shrugged, as if it was completely natural that she should have added Italian to her list of skills over the years. 'I know enough to get by.'

No. She knew enough to move to Italy if she'd ever been asked.

He pocketed the information for later, pulled his jacket off the back of the chair he'd hung it on, scooped his keys from the ceramic bowl where he always deposited them at the end of a long day, when he propped himself up on one of the stools to eat yet another takeaway meal before crawling into bed and, a few hours later, waking up to start another day.

He looked up when Lizzy pointedly cleared her throat. Rather than looking annoyed that he was leaving, she looked expectant. As if awaiting an invitation. An invitation he knew she would accept.

'Want to come?' he asked. 'You don't have to. You can stay and sleep, eat—'

'No. I'd like to come.' She ran to her room and came back out tugging a sweater over her shoulders. 'Are we running or jumping on the scooter?'

'Scooter.'

Waiting for the lift seemed a waste of time, so by silent agreement they began to jog down the stairs, with Leon filling her in as they went.

'Luca Ricci was born fifteen weeks premature. He's been poorly for the duration of his stay in the NICU—infections in his bloodstream, problems with breathing—but lately he's been exhibiting intolerance to milk feeds. We've been trying to keep the intestinal inflammation to a minimum by introducing intravenous feeds, antibiotics and an abdominal drain, but it looks as though some of the bowel has become so damaged it's begun to necrotise.'

'What signs is he showing just now?'

'Swollen stomach. Dark external colouration indicating a further perforation. Bradycardia.'

Lizzy doubled her speed on the stairs. 'I've had a few of those back in Sydney.' She scrunched up her face. 'Do the parents know the risks?'

'Fifty-fifty chance of survival?' Leon put the cold hard truth into words. 'Yes. They know. But it's that fifty percent of children who make it that we're focused on, *si*?'

'*Si, Dottore.*' Lizzy gave him a small salute before accepting the helmet he was handing her.

None of the awkwardness of their first ride returned as, focused on the surgery ahead, the two of them climbed onto the scooter. Lizzy's hands slipped around his waist as if they'd done it for years and off they went.

Half an hour later the pair of them were in scrubs, standing on either side of an operating table with the small infant between them, all the earlier hostilities and tensions that had been vibrating between the pair of them evaporated.

It was just as it had been back in their surgical internships. Two focused, perfectionist surgeons working together with a harmony he'd let himself forget they shared. The Dream Team, the residents had called them. The Down Under Wonder and Da Vinci.

She'd come up with that one, Da Vinci, because he'd look at the same 'canvas' they all did and, where many of their peers only saw dead ends, see nothing but possibility.

'You just have to find the right path.' His mantra.

He looked across at her and she gave him an *Are you ready?* nod, hands up, ready for action. It was a silent signal to let him know that wherever he would go, she would follow.

For the first time the gesture spoke volumes.

She trusted him. Here at least. In the operating theatre.

Had there been a time when Lizzy had seen a completely different path? One that had included their careers and the two of them together. *Dio mio.* That must have been why she'd learned Italian. Because she'd believed that one day he would call. Admit he'd been wrong not to admit that he'd heard her whisper that she loved him and tell her that he felt the same way.

He threw the thought away, needing to focus on the surgery ahead of him. Besides, the very first thing that had attracted him to Lizzy was her single-minded focus on becoming the best. She would've spoken up if she'd thought he was being an idiot—just as she had today. Lizzy was nobody's fool—and certainly not his.

He channelled a fresh surge of energy and forced himself to see the infant's body afresh. What could they do to ensure this small, helpless child lived a healthy, happy life?

'How're the oxygen levels?' he asked.

Lizzy's eyes flicked up to the monitor. 'Okay for now. There are spare bloods to hand?'

'*Si.*'

Both of them looked back at the screen, where the images from the laparoscope showed the delicate workings inside the baby's abdomen.

'There doesn't seem to be any damage here, which is good. The drainage system seems to have kept the area clear of infection.'

'Risky for a little tyke under a thousand grams.'

He glanced up and met her eyes. Was that an accusation?

But her head was nodding in the way it did when she was bowled over by something—impressed.

'How much bowel do you think was compromised?' she asked after they'd removed the laparoscope and closed the microscopic incision.

It was a weighted question. Would Luca need ongoing healthcare? Would it last beyond his infancy or would this surgery set him up for a lifetime of never needing to know any of this had happened?

He watched her precise stitching and delicate tying of the surgical knot. The external scar, if there was one, would be no larger than a freckle.

Is she thinking of our own child when she makes each stitch? Ties each knot?

Leon was. Their own child's health. Its care. Its development. All the thoughts he should've slammed in a box were now charging each surgical move he made.

'You're opting for an external incision for the bowel removal?' Lizzy asked.

Again he looked up to see if it was a challenge.

But her eyes, when he met them, only held interest.

Not everything's a dare, Leon. Not everything's a move in a chess game.

Competition for that number one spot had fuelled them back in the day. Had she softened in that respect? Or, more likely, grown confident enough not to need to peacock her talents in an OR? The main objective was the welfare of the child. Exactly as it should be.

She was, in short, the exceptional professional he'd met and fallen for seven years ago when he thought he knew all there was to know about life.

He gave his head a small, sharp shake and realigned his focus. He began explaining step by step what he'd be doing, and what each of the surgical nurses, anaesthetists and other members of the surgical team would be doing to give the tiny child they had before them the best chance of survival.

Lizzy was her usual inquisitive self, but clearly she was refusing to showboat about the identical surgeries that he knew for a fact she'd done.

She was a picture-perfect surgical companion. She was always there to provide the second pair of hands when needed. Was waiting, needle poised, prepared to make an exact stitch wherever one was required without needing a prompt. It was a critical timesaver as, so often in surgery, timing was of the utmost importance.

Had their relationship been as easy? Had it even been a relationship? Neither of them had ever referred to the other as their partner.

An uncomfortable feeling that it might have been that simple teased at the back of his mind. He silenced it. Now wasn't the time to dwell on the past.

'Ooh!' Lizzy gave a quiet cheer when, twenty minutes later, he moved his hands back to let her take a look. 'Looks like the bowel is clear of all necrotic tissue and this little fella stands a good chance of a happy, normal life.'

They looked at one another, and he saw the crinkles by her eyes showing the smile her surgical mask was hiding. They'd deepened since their time together back in New York. As had the furrow between her brow.

'Bravo, Dottore,' she said.

'Brava, Dottore,' he echoed, trying not to betray the hint of sadness he felt that he hadn't been around to see the subtle, sweet changes in her face over the years.

Instead, he gave his usual brisk, efficient instructions about moving Luca back to the NICU and said that he'd be in shortly to have a look. Then he nodded towards the swinging doors that led to the private room where Luca's parents were no doubt biting their nails, waiting for news of their son.

As he walked alongside Lizzy it struck him afresh how fragile the lives of his tiny patients were. Obviously he knew it on a pragmatic level—saving those lives was at the very essence of his profession. But the woman who was carrying his child had just helped him perform surgery on a thirty-week-old baby, pushing aside the fact that what was happening to Luca, or to any of the other infants struggling for survival here in the NICU, might happen to theirs.

He was going to have to plumb the depths of the same strength if he wanted to make good on his promise to be there for their child. He was going to have to do a lot of things if he was going to give his child the best start in life.

CHAPTER SEVEN

'COFFEE?'

As Lizzy came out of her room Leon was already busy at his espresso machine, going through what was clearly a well-rehearsed morning ritual. His elegant surgeon's hands spooned coffee into a paper disc, then cinched the filter into place so that the hot steamed water could do its magic.

'No, thanks.' Lizzy dragged a comb through her shower-wet hair. 'I'm caffeine-free now, remember.'

Their eyes caught and her comb paused mid-journey. He held up a tin of decaffeinated coffee. Of course he'd remembered. The shadows under his eyes were proof that at least one of the two of them had been up half the night, remembering and making changes, preparing… Unlike Lizzy, who had slept like a baby.

'That was nice, last night.'

To an outsider, the comment might have appeared to be in reference to a night of passion.

'I can't believe I'd forgotten how precise your stitches were.' He raised his small espresso cup in a toast, then drank.

'Are,' she corrected playfully, pleased Leon's mind had gone exactly where hers had. The surgical ward.

Maybe this whole having a baby and working together for the next few months would work out. Somehow. Not the marriage part, obviously. Leon had clearly had a common-sense malfunction somewhere between his heart and his cerebral cortex. An information overload that had forced an old-fashioned response to a not so old-fashioned situation.

Although...

Her thoughts returned to that single, heartfelt admission: *'I don't want to be alone when I live.'*

The Leon she'd thought she knew would never have admitted as much. Maybe losing his mother really had changed him. Losing her own mum had certainly changed her. But in the opposite way. It had made her less willing to consider a relationship. Less willing to trust a man's intentions. Less willing to believe Leon Cassanetti had meant it when he'd proposed marriage.

As such, she'd not brought it up again after they'd returned from the hospital and they'd each—a bit awkwardly, a bit hastily—shut themselves behind the doors of their own very separate bedrooms.

Hopefully the next two or three months would follow a pattern. They'd go to work, do their jobs, find some sort of happy middle ground wherein he acknowledged that it was for the best that she raise her child—*their* child—on her own and then, when the little one was old enough, she would come over here and meet the other half of the gene pool.

Baby daddy? No. Gene pool made him easier to keep at arm's length emotionally. Gene pool it was.

She couldn't help but give him a quick scan. *Mmm...* It was a most excellent gene pool. Theirs was a lucky baby.

'Ten minutes enough before we set off?' Leon asked, his lightly accented voice sending too obvious a physical response through her body.

Gene pool. Gene pool. Gene pool!

'Scooter again?' She mimed putting on her helmet.

He shook his head. 'I thought we'd walk. I'll give you a mini-tour of Rome.'

Twenty minutes later it was taking all of Lizzy's self-discipline not to lace her fingers through Leon's. It wasn't just that their hands kept brushing as they moved in closer together on the pavement to let others pass, it was the sheer romance of the city.

Rome was everything she'd dreamt it might be. Like stepping into a postcard and having it smell and look exactly the way she'd thought it would. Fast and slow-paced all at the same time. Infused with a heavenly golden light. With scents of bitter coffee and sweet pastries wafting out on street corners as shopkeepers opened up for a day's business.

Taking a different route from the one they had on the scooter, Leon guided her through a glorious procession of high-end fashion boutiques nestled alongside centuries' old churches where women dressed all in black ducked in and out for their morning prayers as easily as they did the scrumptious-looking delicatessens and vegetable shops.

Produce you'd never find in a supermarket back home was presented in sumptuous piles: courgette flowers with baby vegetables attached, fresh, succulent artichokes, and a green vegetable she couldn't identify.

'What's that?' She pointed to the display of long, slender strands fashioned into a green wreath-like heart.

Leon smiled. '*Agretti*. It's… Do you know samphire? A sea vegetable? I think you call it saltwort.'

Lizzy laughed. 'I think I prefer *agretti* as a name.'

Leon signalled to the shop owner that they would take some. 'They also call it *barbe di frate*—friar's beard.' He stroked an invisible space below his own clean-shaven chin, grinning as the shopkeeper handed him a small brown bag full of the vegetable. 'We'll have it tonight with supper. Perhaps get some fresh seafood on the way home.' He held up the bag. 'The *agretti* are only in season a short time, so it is special that you're here for it.'

She bit down on the inside of her cheek to stop herself from saying it would be special to be here at any time of year because of her tour guide. She had no idea how, but because of him the city already felt familiar to her.

She'd obviously need a map if left to her own devices, but it was as if all the stories he'd told her about his home city had become a part of her. If she'd had a free hour to wander about, she wouldn't have felt anything but happy, knowing that familiar surprise after surprise waited around each corner. The Trevi Fountain and the Spanish Steps appeared as old friends sometimes did—unexpected but no less wonderful for it—and by the time they reached the hospital, fortified with two bags of pastries for a mid-morning snack which, of course, she had already sampled, she had to force her work hat back on.

Today and all the days that would follow were about ensuring the conjoined twins came into the world healthy and ready for the separation surgery that would follow. Then, when that had happened, she hoped she'd know exactly what was happening with her own baby. Or, more to the point, the role Leon would play in her baby's life.

After they'd changed into scrubs Leon took her on his morning rounds, with that same energy buzzing between them as when they'd practically raced to the surgery board each morning in New York, to see who was working on what and, more importantly, if they'd be doing it together.

They visited patient after patient, their energies concentrated on the all-important task of ensuring they gave each woman and the baby growing inside her the very best start in life possible.

Pre-eclampsia. Gestational diabetes. Hyperemis gravidarum—the intense morning sickness that had made headlines when Britain's future Queen had fallen victim to it. There were countless things that could go wrong with a pregnancy but, Lizzy reminded herself with a soft touch to her own belly, countless things that went right.

It was actually a genuine joy to watch Leon at work. He was like an energy bomb, infusing each mum-to-be with a confidence and comfort, telling her that her number one job was to relax. His job was to find solutions. And that was precisely what he would do.

They spoke with a woman who'd been admitted the previous day suffering from heavy blood-loss owing to placenta previa.

'You've had a blood transfusion and a steroid injection, *si*?' Leon asked her.

The woman, Valentina, gave a heavy nod. 'The nurse this morning said all I needed now was rest. So…' Her eyes pinged between Leon and Lizzy, as if she was unsure whose sympathies to play on the most. She ended with a small bat of her eyelashes in Leon's direction. 'I guess you could sign me out?'

Leon tipped his head from side to side—another familiar gesture that Lizzy had somehow let grow fuzzy as the years had passed. It said a thousand things at once. *You're right. There are other sides to that coin. I want you to have the best information I can give you so you can make a well-informed decision.*

'True,' he said. 'You do need rest. But because of the blood-loss and the Braxton Hicks you were experiencing yesterday, it'd be safer for you to stay with us here. Another blood-loss like that could cause immediate distress to the baby, and being able to respond quickly with all the right equipment and supplies is critical when it comes to such a fragile life. Your life could depend upon it as well.'

He rattled through a few statistics and gave her some solid historical examples of what might happen if she were to experience a similar bleed at her home—which was, according to her chart, a good hour outside of Rome.

'*Per favore,*' the woman pleaded with Leon. 'I can rest better at home. My husband needs me, and being here seems a waste when all I do is sit!'

Leon nodded, taking on board her concerns, and then gently explained—exactly as Lizzy would have—that her blood loss had been severe, and that at only thirty weeks they really would like to give the baby a bit more time to develop. In short, staying in hospital meant she was giving her child the best possible chance of a healthy start in life.

'But isn't it better for me and my baby to be relaxed? How can I relax here, with all this…this…mechanical stuff around me?' Valentina gestured at the monitors and screens flanking her bed. The cart filled with medical equipment prepped for emergencies.

'If you want your husband to bring some things in to make the room more personal, we're more than happy to ring him.'

'I don't want anyone to ring him! I want to go home!' Valentina cried with characteristic Italian passion.

Lizzy smiled. It was clear Valentina was in a happy, enriching marriage and that her safe place was with her husband. Her child's welfare, however, would be best attended to right here at St Nicolino's.

'You.' Valentina pointed at her. 'You're very quiet. You're a doctor and a woman. What would you do if you were in my shoes?'

Lizzy apologised for her stilted use of Italian, took the woman's hand and said truthfully, 'If there was anywhere

in the world I could be if I were you I'd be right here.'
Avoiding the possibility of more butterflies in her tummy,
she kept her gaze away from Leon as she continued. 'Dr
Cassanetti prefers patients to be at home if they can be.
He's well aware that there is added strain in being here,
away from your loved ones, but he's asking you to do it so
that you can return to them with your baby, both of you
healthy and well.'

Leon caught her eyes, gratitude capturing his features
in a way that seemed over the top for what had been her
genuine professional opinion. She respected Leon. On
a professional level and, begrudgingly, a personal level.
They'd never made promises to one another back in New
York. Had always been very clear that their number one
goals in life were to lead departments in their respective
countries. And now they did that. Job done.

So…was it possibly time for a new goal?

She forced herself to tune in again as he wrapped up
his talk with Valentina, promising to make her stay as
comfortable as possible. When they'd left the room he
said nothing, but shot Lizzy another look. One that felt
complicit…as if they now shared a secret mission. Her
spine tingled in response. A sensation, she realised, that
would only grow as they began to work with the conjoined twins.

Trying not to stare directly, she kept on throwing Leon
secret little glances as they made their way to the next
room. Was he experiencing it, too? This jolt of shared
connection that felt more like a muscle memory than
something new? Was it too dangerous to recapture? she
wondered? That feeling of togetherness? She'd felt invincible when they were a team. As if anything in the world
was possible so long as they were together.

Leon stopped outside a private room and tapped on

his tablet for a moment. When he looked up again, that hard-won smile of his was in place. 'You'll find this one interesting.'

'Oh?'

'Mmm...' He kept his voice low as he explained. 'Maria Paloma. Came in two days ago for a twenty-five-week scan and we discovered ABS.'

'Amniotic Band Syndrome?'

'*Si.*'

Lizzy instinctively swept her hands to the slight curve of her belly. So slight it might easily be mistaken for a large breakfast. She glanced into the room, only able to catch sight of the woman's swollen belly and her hands rubbing it over and over, as if for good luck. ABS was rare, but in this day and age, if it was caught early enough and treated by an excellent team of surgeons, it was something that didn't have to cause the profound trauma to an unborn child it once had.

'How bad?' She was, as Leon would know, asking after the fibrous, string-like pieces of tissue which had become detached from the amniotic sack and entangled the baby. This tissue, if attached to the growing child, would restrict blood flow and in some extreme cases cause stunted bone growth and even in utero amputation.

'Some of the bands are attached to the cheek.'

Lizzy's lips thinned to a wince. 'Risk of cleft palate?'

'High. I don't think it was caught early enough. We've informed our plastics team. They'll ensure any malformation is minimal. But at this stage it's always hard to say.'

There was regret in his features, as there always had been when he knew a child would have to go through a surgical trauma before its life outside the womb even began.

But that was life, she supposed. A struggle for survival from the very first day. Was it easier when you were part of a team? Knowing you had someone to lean on when the weight became too much? In other words, the total opposite of her parents' marriage where it had been fight or submit. Her father had always been more than happy to point out that there might be no 'I' in team…but there was an 'm' and an 'e' and as such that made him the boss.

'Lizzy?'

Leon was looking at her inquisitively. As if for just a second he'd caught a glimpse of something of her life she'd not let him have access to when they'd been together.

A part of her crumbled. There was no chance she could consider marrying someone she didn't know and who, more to the point, she hadn't trusted to know her. The *real* her.

Leon waved a hand in front of her face. 'Lizzy? *Buongiorno!* Are you feeling a bit of jet lag?'

She shook her head, unwilling to admit that she'd been raking over the past when she should have been focussing on the future.

Leon's forehead creased with concern. 'Maybe we should find you an on-call room before our meeting with Dr Lombardi and the Bianchis, so you can have a rest? I'm happy to finish the rounds on my own.'

She shook her head again, and gave what she hoped was a light-hearted laugh, feeling her topknot loosen into a very messy bun as she did. *Work.* Work was the one thing they could talk about without any sort of additional angst. That was what she would focus on for now.

'Any sign of the bands tightening on the umbilical cord?'

Leon's features sobered. 'No, thank goodness. Just the cheek, so the baby's getting all the nutrition it needs. I'll be in surgery this afternoon, if you'd like to join me?'

'Absolutely.' She gave him a play punch on the arm.

'You didn't think I flew all the way over here just to be a pretty face on the sidelines, did you?'

His expression clouded for a moment and then, as if he'd made a decision, cleared. For the first time since she'd arrived Leon looked exactly like the man she'd told herself she'd fallen in love with all those years ago. Intense, keenly passionate about his work, and *present* in a way few people could be. All his energies were trained on her, and with that came a heated rush of exhilaration. A spine-tingling energy that coursed through her as the world around her faded.

'Lizzy you are one of the most exacting, fearless antenatal surgeons in the world. That's why I wanted you to be part of my team. These conjoined twins deserve the very best, and as far as I'm concerned you are at the top of that list. Do not discredit yourself by even suggesting you're here to decorate the place.'

He waited until she gave him a nod to acknowledge the compliment. Not, she knew, because he wanted recognition for being so magnanimous, but because he wanted her to champion herself.

Even in the highly charged, ego-fuelled environment of surgical internships, where one surgery could make or break your career, Lizzy had never been comfortable tooting her own horn. Her father had drilled into her his belief that modesty was the only attribute a woman should fully embrace. That, and loyalty. In her mother's case, a loyalty fuelled by fear.

'If you want to join in any of my surgeries you are more than welcome,' Leon continued. He briefly broke his gaze, glancing over her shoulder as if, like her, he'd suddenly become aware of the people around them. He lowered his voice and said, 'I also appreciate you coming over for the personal reason. It was a brave thing to do.'

Lizzy's heart-rate accelerated yet again. Work talk she could do. But baby talk…? She'd thought they were going to shelve that for now. They had to. Until she knew exactly what was going on between the two of them and that would take time.

She hastily told the part of herself that knew the two were inextricably linked to be quiet. 'Maybe we can talk about that later?'

Leon fixed her with a solid look. 'Do you want to know why I asked you over here?'

She gave him a side-on look. 'You just said. The conjoined twins, right?'

'They were the excuse, but they weren't the reason.'

He reached out and tucked a tendril of loose hair behind her ear, his fingertips tracing down the length of her neck. It was a gesture that elicited far too many inappropriate memories. Memories she had vowed to consign to the past.

His fingers lingered just that infinitesimal bit longer than they should have. And when his eyes met hers she felt as though her body had finally, at long last, found the energy source it had been seeking for so long. Her heart bashed against her ribcage. Was this Leon's way of telling her he had actual genuine feelings for her? This was definitely not what she'd bargained on when she'd boarded the plane.

She must have stood there, blinking at him like an idiot, to the point when he felt she needed help. Because, with a hand on her elbow, he began to steer her towards an on-call room. 'Lizzy, there's something I think you need to know—'

'Ah! Leon. Just the man I was looking for!'

Leon's body language instantly shifted from doting father-to-be about to bare his soul to briskly efficient surgeon. Instead of relief, she felt a hit of loss that she might never know what Leon had been about to tell her.

'Giovanni. I'd like to introduce you to—'

'No need,' said the handsome doctor, tapping the side of his nose with a mischievous smile. 'I know all about Dr Beckley.'

CHAPTER EIGHT

LEON IGNORED LIZZY'S lightning-fast glare.

'It sounds like something other than my professional reputation precedes me,' Lizzy said, smiling and giving Giovanni's hand a shake.

'Nothing that wouldn't add to your accolades,' said Giovanni charmingly. 'How could one work in our business and *not* know about the world-famed Baby Heart Doctor Elizabeth Beckley?'

Lizzy gave Leon another look, this one saying, *What exactly have you told this man?*

She let go of Giovanni's hand. 'Sounds like you already know who I am. And you are...?'

'Giovanni Lombardi.'

Leon was about to jump in and apologise for his lack of manners, for not making a formal introduction and for his absence of brain power, but he was still trying to re-group from having been almost caught steering Lizzy into an on-call room, where he would have been dangerously close to repeating his foolhardy proposal.

The words were banging round his head. He *loved* her. It was a hell of an epiphany. He'd finally admitted to himself that he loved this woman and had done from back in those days in New York. He wasn't single these days by choice.

He was single because he loved the woman he'd arrogantly and ignorantly let slip through his fingers five years ago.

He didn't want to let it happen again. Perhaps his next proposal should be more thought-out. Now was his chance to change history. It would be messy. No doubt about that. He was a gifted bachelor, but he'd do everything in his power to make sure she knew he was going to change. Somehow.

What sort of evidence would she need? A diamond? A public declaration? Learning how to sing opera? No. She'd see right through those gestures for what they would be. Disingenuous. None of them were *him*, apart from the diamond, but his gut told him that with her colouring she was more of a sapphire girl.

Oh, Dio. That was a whole new rabbit hole he could disappear in. The whole point of Lizzy being here was to concentrate, not become a ring expert!

After a few more easily rejected ideas, he forced himself to tune in to a discussion that was in full flow.

'Amazing! Though I have to say with his track record I'm not surprised,' Lizzy was saying.

'Absolutely. A stroke of genius. Leon's ability to look beyond the obvious is exemplary.'

She threw him a quick, inquisitive look, clearly impressed by whatever it was she and Giovanni were talking about.

As he was completely clueless, and didn't want to betray the fact that he hadn't been listening, Leon put on what he hoped was a modest expression and gave them a benign smile. 'It was nothing, really.'

'It was innovative. Well,' Giovanni qualified, 'it was ancient. But it was an innovation we wouldn't have thought of if Leon hadn't put it forward.'

'Who would've thought it? Honey! I'm impressed.'

Lizzy gave Leon an admiring smile then turned back to Giovanni. 'Is it available elsewhere in the world?' Lizzy asked, looking truly interested.

He wished like hell he knew what they were talking about. And why was Lizzy calling him 'honey' in front of his boss? He'd thought they'd agreed to keep things professional here.

'Leon?' Giovanni prompted. 'It's available elsewhere, isn't it?'

Leon gave a cautious nod. 'In some areas…' He hoped that was true. Certain medical supplies or treatments would be difficult to offer in, say, Antarctica. Then again, he hadn't invented any medical supplies. His mind reeled, trying to catch up.

'Nonsense!' Giovanni cut in. 'You know as well as I do that it's available everywhere. It's just that not everyone sees medicine the way you do. A true Leonardo da Vinci, our Leon.'

'Hey!' Lizzy clapped. 'That's what I used to call him. Da Vinci. Ha! A visionary with a flow chart.'

Giovanni rocked back on his heels and roared with laughter. '*Oh, Dio!* That's him, all right. He likes to dot his "i"s and cross his "t"s—don't you Leon?'

Giovanni gave him a clap on the shoulder that felt strangely like a prompt to laud his own merits.

Lizzy laughed appreciatively. 'That's definitely the Leon I know.'

She started telling Giovanni about one of the first surgeries they performed together. Leon had made massive wall charts of the entire innovative surgery and posted them around the walls of the operating theatre, so that everyone had quite literally been on the same page as they'd changed a child's life for the better.

Giovanni laughed along with her, saying that sounded

just like the Leon he knew as well, and adding that his fastidiousness was one of the many reasons they had wanted him to head the antenatal unit at St Nicolino's. Did Lizzy know he headed the department? he asked.

She gave him a punch on the arm. 'You didn't tell me that.'

He forced a modest smile to come into play again. *What was going on here?*

Giovanni shook his head and said that he hoped while Lizzy was there she'd teach their cherished Dr Cassanetti a thing or two about sharing his genius in the world's medical journals, as she had done.

Lizzy's smile softened as her eyes lit on him. 'I'll do my best. He has a way of seeing the world that's...extraordinary.'

'Yes, he does,' said Giovanni, dropping a duplicitous wink in Leon's direction before drawing Lizzy's attention back to him. 'And I think you're just the woman to make sure he sees that for himself!'

Suddenly it occurred to him what was happening. Giovanni Lombardi was *flirting* on his behalf. Or—wait! His heart jammed in his throat. *Had Lizzy told Giovanni she was pregnant with his child?*

No. She wouldn't have done that. Not without checking with him.

Giovanni gave Lizzy a courtly bow. 'It's absolutely lovely to meet you, Dr Beckley. I can't tell you how grateful we are that you've joined us here at St Nicolino's. I look forward to spending more time with you.'

All right. No need to slather on the gratitude, Leon grumbled silently. Protectively. *Very* protectively.

Giovanni threw a discreet look over Lizzy's shoulder at Leon. A look that said very clearly, *Now I see why you've been so distracted.*

'Shall we…?' Giovanni gestured towards a small lecture theatre where they had agreed to meet the entire team and discuss the conjoined twins.

'Absolutely!' Leon said, a tad too enthusiastically.

As they entered the room Lizzy gave him a nudge in the ribs and blew out a low whistle of approval. 'Honey… Who would've thought it? Well, you did, obviously.'

What was she *talking* about? And, again, since when did Lizzy call him 'honey'?

And then he twigged. Giovanni had been talking about his idea to put medical grade honey around prematurely born infant's feeding tubes as an antidote to extravasation injuries—wounds that sometimes struggled to heal. *Let the honey do the healing*—that had been his tagline when he'd first tried out the ancient remedy, for its antimicrobial and wound-healing properties.

He forced his nervous system to cool its jets. Not everything was about him and Lizzy. Well… Yes, it was. Because as they entered the room a twenty-strong team of medical professionals rose and, as one, applauded their entrance as if they were royalty.

An hour later he was back on much stronger footing. Science. Medicine. One very specific goal.

'And that is how we see the procedure going from our end—pending, of course, any complications. We are a team, Dr Beckley and I. Think of us as one unit. Keeping Baby A well on a cardiovascular level is critical to both of the Bianchi babies' welfare—and, of course, their mother's. If you have any questions at any time about the Bianchis you come to either of us. We are one.'

He pressed his two fingers together so that the group could see that he really meant it. His eyes shot to Lizzy's. It was a speech he regularly gave whenever he worked with a visiting physician, but the language felt more potent when it was about Lizzy.

Lizzy cocked an eyebrow at him. *We?* it was saying. *One unit?*

The Lizzy he'd worked with five years ago had loved working with him as a unit. This Lizzy, for some reason, looked really annoyed.

'Dr Beckley and I will, of course, be keeping you updated in advance of the surgery. That's it for now. *Grazie mille*, everyone. Let's make this a sure-fire success so that Dr Lombardi and his team—as yet to be announced—will have two healthy babies when the time comes.'

Lizzy waited until the crowd of doctors who had swarmed around Leon to ask questions specific to their own roles had eased. Some of the team had, very kindly, taken the time to introduce themselves to her. She had never known there were so many Marias in the world!

She made a mental note to ask Leon for a cheat sheet later, so she could tell them all apart. Nothing made a surgical team work better than genuinely feeling like a team. Knowing everyone's name without having to look at their name tag was the easiest place to start. And another factor that made a team work was feeling included in the decision-making. Something she hadn't yet felt on this case. Sure, she'd only been here twenty-four hours, but...

She was used to being in charge of her own team— not following someone else's lead. Particularly when the 'leader' was a certain someone who was yanking her emotions hither and yon. *Marry me. Don't marry me. Let's be a family. Let's not be a family.*

Okay. Perhaps he hadn't said some of those things, but it felt as if he had, and that surely had to mean her gut was trying to tell her something, right?

But what, exactly?

Lizzy sighed. Maybe this up, down, all around stretchy emotional boundaries thing was what all the expectant mothers who burst into tears for no reason in the tinned vegetable aisle at the supermarket were talking about. She wasn't feeling weepy, though. She was feeling cross. *Very* cross. Which didn't make sense.

The logical part of her brain knew Leon was a fortnight ahead of her on the project, so of course he'd given the introductory lecture. But the part of her brain that had received a marriage proposal and that knew she was as good a surgeon as he was, shook with anxiety that this might be what life with Leon would be like. Taking a back seat to his opinion, no matter what she had to say. Just like her mother had done with her father.

She tried to shake some common sense back into her body.

It's his hospital, dummy! He's the MFMS. Of course he's taking the lead! He's also lauded you as critical to the twins' survival! The last thing he's doing is sidelining you. He's trying to include you, not exclude you.

Grr! Feelings. They were annoying when you didn't want them.

The part of her that wasn't a raging torrent of hormones knew for a fact that her time that day would've been better spent studying the case, not following him on his rounds like a lovesick puppy. She looked up at him, still standing on the small lecture hall stage, with staff gathered round him as if he were a superstar. Which he kind of was. Who wouldn't be with those looks and a brain like his? And the things that man could do with his hands…

She looked away, her body responding a little too viscerally to the mere suggestion of his touch. Maybe if she saw him every day the tingles would fade…or maybe she should have sex with Leon while she was here? Just to properly get him out of her system.

'Lizzy!' Leon appeared before her, his eyes bright with anticipation. 'So! What did you think?' He clapped his hands together and gave them a good rub, his eyes glinting brightly, the way they always had when a particularly complicated case presented itself.

'Nice presentation, Dr Cassanetti,' she said crankily, to disguise the fact that she had just been thinking of him naked and in an extremely compromising position.

'Thanks, I think...?'

'No, seriously.' Her clipped tone was making it entirely clear that she was annoyed. 'It was kind of you to make it look as though I actually know what's going on, but if you remember I haven't actually met the patients yet. A bit dangerous, wasn't it, to announce that I'm going to help make this operation "a sure-fire success"?'

Leon threw a look over his shoulder, as if he expected some sort of reason for her mood-change to appear before him. He looked back at her, more warily this time. 'What do you mean? You've done this kind of operation dozens of times before.'

'Not on a conjoined twin with a shared aortic valve.' She gave him a knowing look, indicating that it wasn't wise to make promises you weren't sure you could keep. Like, for example, proposing marriage when you didn't want to be married.

Or did he...?

Pregnancy hormones, Lizzy was beginning to realise, could quickly become exhausting.

'Hey. Where's this coming from? You're an excellent surgeon.'

Leon reached out to touch her arm, but she pulled it back before he could touch her. She could see what he was thinking. That it wasn't like her to be insecure. And he would be right. She wasn't. She was a strong, independent, very happy, not to mention incredibly well-adjusted woman, who didn't need the most gorgeous man in the universe, whose child she happened to be carrying, to make her feel better.

So she proved it by acting normal. She popped on a bright smile and said, 'I'd really like to meet the parents. See a scan. Earn the kudos you gave me, yeah?'

Leon held his arm out towards the doors to the ward. 'After you, m'lady.'

There, thought Lizzy, the smile on her face broadening as she swanned in front of him, *that's more like it!*

'Ooh, there they are!' Lizzy smiled in wonder as she ran the scanning wand over Gabrielle's stomach, all her wild emotions from just moments ago forgotten. This was what she loved. Seeing tiny little lives starting out in the world.

'It *does* look like they're hugging doesn't it?' Gabrielle asked, her eyes flitting between the screen and her husband.

Everyone agreed—it did look as if the girls were hugging. Lizzy guessed that warm thought added a level of comfort to what must be a terrifying experience for both Gabrielle and her husband Matteo. There were a lovely couple. She was from Switzerland and had, on a work secondment, met and married Matteo, who lived in Northern Italy. They'd both come to Rome on their doctor's advice, when they'd made the discovery about their babies.

A thick tumble of ebony curls cascaded over Gabrielle's shoulders, framing features softened by her advancing pregnancy. She was both frightened and brave. Stoic and nervous. Matteo, thankfully, was a picture-perfect doting husband. Holding her hand, checking she was warm enough, not too cold, not thirsty, or hungry, in need of a foot rub…

It made Lizzy smile. It also made her a little jealous, seeing the easy love they shared. They were a couple well and truly devoted to one another's happiness. What confidence that must take, she thought. To trust and believe in someone never to hurt you.

She glanced at Leon, then just as quickly looked away. History was powerful, and the reason it repeated itself was because people didn't learn from it. She didn't want to be one of those people.

She cleared her throat and focused on the screen. 'Shall we take a little look at…? Ooh…look there. Ten little toes on Baby A—'

'Oh, *scusi*!' Matteo interrupted her. 'We're not calling them Baby A and Baby B any more, if that's all right.'

Lizzy turned away from the screen, giving them both her full attention. 'Absolutely. What would you prefer?'

'Grace and Hope,' Gabrielle said, taking hold of her husband's hand.

'Beautiful names.' Lizzy smiled, her eyes catching Leon's as he concurred with a soft, *'Bellissima…'*

Collectively, they went back to the screen, taking the baby anatomy tour—or, as Lizzy liked to call it, head, shoulders, knees and toes. Lizzy loved this part of being an antenatal doctor. Showing a couple their child, the heartbeat…or in this case the one shared heartbeat. It sounded romantic, an ideal to strive for, but in this case it could prove lethal.

Had that been the problem with her parents' marriage? They hadn't been able to survive without the other? Divorce had never been discussed—and yet her father's powerful heartbeat had seemed to dominate her mother's more fragile, birdlike rhythm. The way he'd said things like

'That's the way we see things—isn't that right, Genny?' or 'We're not interested,' or any number of things her father had decided on behalf of both of them gave Lizzy a cold chill down her spine to this day.

She glanced again at Leon, who had moved to the far end of the bed, having turned things over to her once he'd made the initial introduction. Perhaps he'd read her mood. Realised she'd felt put on the back foot by having to meet the medical team without having so much as met the parents yet. Or perhaps, like her father—and this was a scary thought—she was a control freak.

She stuffed that thought into a box and squirted a whole load of mental superglue all over the lid.

The easy part of the 'tour' was done. Now it was time for trickier terrain. The conjoined chests and hearts.

Lizzy pointed towards the arrow on the sonogram. 'Dr Lombardi and his team will work out how best to approach the separation surgery, but if you look at the arrow, this little spot here is where Hope's and Grace's hearts are fused together.'

Gabrielle gave a little cry of despair.

Lizzy took her hand and gave it a gentle squeeze. 'You have got the very best medical team in the world at your disposal.'

'And you've done this surgery before? The HLHS?'

'Absolutely. Many times.'

'On conjoined twins?'

Lizzy shook her head. 'This is a first. But I know the surgery inside and out, and the aortic valve the twins share shouldn't change the standard procedure. If anything, it should enable their hearts to work better together up until the separation surgery.'

'There's a standard procedure for this sort of thing?' Matteo's eyes widened.

'Absolutely. I know having conjoined twins is a rarity, but one in four thousand babies is diagnosed with HLHS. There are specialised units around the world to help, and one of them is right here.'

'But you're not from here. Should we have gone to Sydney instead?' The couple shared an anxious look.

Lizzy could feel Leon's eyes on her, but he didn't jump in and make a case for his hospital. Interesting... He really was doing his best to show her he trusted her.

'This is the best place for the two of you. The *four* of you,' she corrected herself with a laugh. 'You're as close to home as you can be and, thanks to the hospital's facilities for parents, you don't have to be parted. Being together during your pregnancy is the very best thing you two can do to keep yourself happy. Those babies will feel your love. Your strength.'

She kept her eyes firmly on the Bianchis, vividly aware that she'd pretty much said the exact opposite to Leon.

What was it her father had used to say? *Do as I say, not as I do?*

The thought lurched uncomfortably close to the child in her own belly.

Tapping her pen officiously on her knee, she continued, 'Any specialist hospital will have a team of brilliant surgeons and physicians. This one is no exception. The fact that I'm here is—'

Foolishly, she looked at Leon. In the microsecond of eye contact they shared she finally believed him when he'd said he hadn't invited her here for the surgery. Well, obviously he had—but the real reason ran much deeper.

'I don't want to live my life alone!'

She tore her eyes away and put on her sensible doctor's voice. 'We've got around forty people dedicated to supporting you through this pregnancy, with Dr Cassanetti helming the ship as it were. And after the babies are born Dr Lombardi will literally have dozens of highly special-ised medical staff ready and waiting to help your two little girls to the best of their ability.'

Lizzy felt but did not see Leon pressing himself up to his full height as she talked the couple through the Hypo-plastic Left Heart Syndrome surgery. They nodded, asked questions, stopped and doubled back when they didn't un-derstand something.

Given the fact she'd just bitten his head off for making promises he couldn't keep, she knew she was standing on thin ice when she wrapped up the consultation by saying, 'We will do everything we can, Dr Cassanetti and I, to make sure Hope and Grace have the very best start in life.'

'But what if that start instantly comes with problems?' Gabrielle sniffed and, unsurprisingly, tears began to slip down her cheeks.

Lizzy startled herself by saying. 'That's life, isn't it? It's full of risks. Which ones do we take? Which ones do we leave for the more foolhardy? Or, more to the point, which ones do we regret not taking?' She smiled at the couple, who had to be so frightened. 'I know the surger-ies Dr Cassanetti and I perform come with a long list of potential problems, but we humans are a pretty resilient bunch. We're able to separate the bright side from the dark side and focus on the one that's going to bring the better outcome.'

It was a statement 'old Leon' would've billed as psycho-logical poppycock, but she caught him nodding out of the corner of her eye, murmuring 'Si...' and 'Absolutely...' as the Bianchis pulled them in for hugs of gratitude for their attention and care.

When it was Leon's turn to be caught in a fierce hug

from Gabrielle, he looked over her shoulder and caught Lizzy's gaze with his own.

'Some risks *are* worth taking, aren't they?' he said.

And she knew he was talking about their future when he continued.

'I believe this is one of them. Don't you, Dr Beckley?'

CHAPTER NINE

'*Buongiorno.*' Leon knocked on the doorframe of the hospital on-call room where, once again, Lizzy had spent the night on the premise of 'monitoring' Gabrielle's babies.

It was a job the overnight staff were well-equipped to do, and they were, of course, under strict instructions to ring either of them the moment they sensed trouble. It looked as if he wasn't the only ostrich who stuck its head in the sand—or, in this case, in the antenatal unit—when there were personal problems to confront...

'Oh, my God, you're an angel.' Lizzy grabbed the coffee, then flashed him a questioning smile. 'Decaf?'

'Obviously.'

'Pistachio?' she asked, already taking a bite of the flaky pastry he knew she favoured.

'*Si,*' he confirmed, enjoying watching her devour the pastry, and then another.

This had been how they'd done things since that first day of working together. She'd insist she needed to stay at the hospital to get a proper grasp of the overall medical situation with the Bianchis, and would send him home with a promise that she'd use the spare key he'd given her. The next day, her bed untouched, he'd find her, courtesy of a nurse, in an on-call room, either asleep or poring over case files. They would go over her thoughts, meet with Giovanni after they'd checked in on Gabrielle and the twins, and then he'd go on his rounds. Sometimes with her. Sometimes without her.

He knew better than to push, because he didn't like to be pushed either—and if he was the pot she was the kettle. In other words, it took a control freak to know one. Neither of them liked having matters taken out of their own hands, and that was precisely what having a child together did. Because life wasn't just about 'me, myself and I' any more. It was about 'us' and 'we' and 'it'. 'It', of course, being the baby, which would require changing and feeding and cuddling during bouts of late-night crying. Elements of life he'd never thought would be a part of his own.

Lizzy yawned and stretched, pressing her hands to her lower back, and then glared at the on-call bed. 'They could do with slightly comfier mattresses here.'

'You *can* sleep at the flat, you know,' Leon said, although an image of her tangled in his bedsheets inconveniently popped into his mind.

She barely glanced at him, but her thoughts had clearly gone in the same direction his had because her cheeks coloured. The only times that happened was when she was thinking saucy thoughts or when she was fuming—and she definitely wasn't fuming.

'I know,' she said. 'I just… I've got a funny feeling.'

Leon rocked back on his heels and nodded. Okay. The Lizzy he'd worked with before hadn't often spoken of feelings dictating her decision-making, but now, pregnancy hormones aside, he'd felt it himself. That kick in the gut that told him something wasn't quite right with a medical situation.

'Do you think we're wrong to wait to do the operation?'

She'd suggested holding back by only a few days, but

he knew as well as she did that sometimes life and death hung in the balance of a handful of seconds.

'No, but I...' She hesitated, scrubbing the sleep out of her eyes and then swooping her hair up into a messy and strangely adorable ponytail. 'Yes.' She gave him a solid look as she stood up and then added a foot-stamp. 'I was going over the scans a couple of hours ago—'

'You were up a *couple of hours* ago?'

She shrugged. 'Woke up full of beans, I guess. Then ran out of them. Anyway... Yes, I do think we're wrong to wait. These little girls are facing enough hard work in the womb as it is. Sharing a critical aortic valve means the left side of Hope's heart is having to work that much harder than it already is, and as such I think we should ease the burden. Then again...if it can gain strength on its own that's a plus. Also, the stent that would go in now would be minuscule—not that that's a problem—but...'

She gnawed on the inside of her cheek, hashing through the countless variables that factored into heart surgery for a twenty-three-week-old baby.

Leon leant against the doorframe, enjoying watching Lizzy whirl round the room, picking up her watch, her phone, trying to tie her hair up into a ponytail, again, even though she'd just done it. Even watching her scrub a tooth-brush against her teeth was fun. Was it possible to miss something you'd never properly had? A routine?

Sure, they'd spent a lot of time together in New York, but that had been different. They'd been a classic rom-com. Two ambitious surgeons battling it out to be the best whilst fighting—and ultimately succumbing to—a fierce mutual attraction.

Back then, they'd always known that whatever it was they'd shared was going to end. Now, with a baby in the picture, there was a real chance—if the pair of them could sort themselves out—that they would be in each other's lives for ever. Scrap that. They'd *have* to sort themselves out. Because their child wasn't going through life without a father. End of.

'Earth to Leon?' Lizzy spat out her toothpaste. 'I'm asking for your professional opinion here. C'mon. What do you think? Am I being paranoid?'

He straightened up. 'A lot of doctors would argue that it'd be better to wait until the babies are born. The fact that Hope has HLHS and a restrictive atrial septal defect could mean waiting until they're delivered—'

'No!' She made a strangled noise of frustration. 'You wouldn't have flown me halfway across the world if you believed that. You wanted this operation.' She turned the full blaze of her aquamarine eyes on him.

Unblinking he replied, 'And you agreed. You also decided that rather than race into an operation, we should wait until you had "the full picture".'

Why was she getting herself tied up in knots about this? She was Hope's doctor. If she thought they should do the operation, they should do it. As a maternal medicine specialist, he was technically Gabrielle's doctor. But as Gabrielle was carrying Hope and Grace he had to make the call, too. And right now he needed to force Lizzy's hand.

'I brought you in because I knew you would know when to operate. It's not my specialty. It's yours.'

Lizzy pursed her lips at him, then whirled round the room doing a very uncharacteristic final check for her belongings. This from a woman who had a photographic memory...

It made him wonder... What were they really talking about here? The Bianchi babies? Or their baby?

He decided to test the theory. 'Lizzy...there are many doctors who would caution waiting before making a decision.'

'Oh, really?' Lizzy turned indignant. 'Well, "many doctors" aren't me!' She poked herself in the chest and unexpectedly hiccoughed.

They stared at one another in silence for a minute and then, when the intensity of their eye contact began to morph into something else…something verging on a sexual frisson, Lizzy broke contact and began to laugh. 'Oh, goodness. Listen to me. I've lost the plot. I'm going to blame pregnancy hormones. Can I blame pregnancy hormones?'

Leon shrugged amiably. 'All you like—but please do bear in mind we have actual, real patients waiting for you to decide when you want to wheel them into the operating theatre.'

'I know.' She hung her head, that intense burst of energy now humming at a more manageable level. She looked up and met his gaze. 'I think we should do a scan.'

'Sure. I'll book them in. MRI? Echo?'

'No.' She shook her head. 'I'm not talking about the Bianchis. I'm talking about us. You. Me. Before we see the Bianchis.' She glanced at her watch. 'We have half an hour before they're expecting us, and I can't focus any more. Not with this vagueness hanging over everything. I need clarity, then I can proceed.'

It took all his power to bite his tongue. *She* was the only thing standing between vagueness and clarity. He had proposed to her. Offered to shoulder the load. Said he'd let her move in. Move somewhere else. Live in Sydney. Or had he taken it back? They'd definitely agreed to disagree on something.

Hell. She was right. It was a mess, and seeing the baby would definitely push them into making a decision.

Five minutes later, after Lizzy had downed a couple of glasses of water and he'd prepared the scan room, with the door firmly locked, Leon applied gel to the slight arc of Lizzy's belly, then picked up the wand.

'Ready?'

'If you are.' She smiled nervously.

He put the wand to her skin and... *'Oh, Dio. Amore...* look.'

He felt Lizzy's fingers wrap around his wrist as he moved the wand slowly over her belly, and then that magic moment he'd borne witness to for so many couples happened for him. He heard his child's heartbeat for the very first time.

'Hear that?' Lizzy asked.

'Si.' It was all he could manage.

He looked at her, and when their eyes met and meshed he felt that same perfect connection he'd felt when they'd first met. She was a kindred spirit. A woman who understood him perfectly because she was the same. Someone who wanted to be judged for what she was now—not who she'd been or where she'd come from, but for the future she hoped for.

Back then it had been all career, career, career.

Had those goals changed?

The pounding in his chest told him the answer.

Yes. Everything had changed.

Lizzy was the first to break eye contact, her eyes darting back to the sonography screen.

'Any guess as to the sex?'

'Too soon,' he answered as if by rote.

She knew as well as he did that physicians could make a rough guess from twelve weeks, but they also both knew it wasn't always an accurate one. When it wasn't necessary to know the sex, and it wasn't blatantly obvious, Leon liked keeping the big reveal until the twenty-week scan, enjoying the surprise along with the patients.

'We could—' she began.

He shook his head. 'No. No blood tests. Unless…?' He moved the wand towards their baby's neck, zooming in on the image so that they could see whether or not there was increased fluid at the base.

'I've already done the nuchal translucency screening. And the blood test,' she said quietly.

Leon cleared an unexpected knot of emotion from his throat. Of course she'd know what he was doing. Checking for Down's Syndrome. Lizzy was only thirty-five, but there was always a risk.

'We're good. The baby's healthy.'

Lizzy sounded as emotional as he felt.

'It's strange when it's happening to you, isn't it?' Leon voiced what he was sure they were both feeling. 'Completely different.'

She nodded, giving her eyes a quick swipe before returning her focus to the screen.

There was so much that wouldn't be a surprise about her pregnancy, given their professions. Without having to say anything, they both knew the baby would weigh about fifteen grams right now. Bones were beginning to form in the arms and legs. The vocal cords would be developing, as would its personality—whether it would suck its thumb, be a kicker or a nodder, when its tiny neck muscles would be strong enough to move the head from side to side.

'Let's keep it a surprise. Until I deliver.'

Her voice softened and her fingers began to stroke his wrist as he gently moved the wand back and forth across the soft, sweet belly he'd covered in passionate kisses just a few short months ago.

The power of what those kisses had culminated in hit him full force. He was going to be a father. It was up to him to decide what kind of father he wanted to be. A runner, like his own father, or a man who honoured the child he had helped create.

'Beautiful, isn't it?' Lizzy asked. 'All those little fingers and toes. And it's a thumb-sucker—look!'

They both smiled and laughed. Their child's hand could clearly be seen at its mouth, thumb in place between its miniature lips.

Leon could only nod, speech defying him. This was literally a picture-perfect baby. And, given their jobs, they knew how precious this news was.

'Should we call it something? You know…like, erm…' She tapped her chin, her eyes still glued to the screen. *'Pompelmo?'*

He laughed. 'What? Grapefruit? You want to call our child *grapefruit*?'

'Well…' She shrugged. 'It's about the right size.'

'So what are we going to call it next week? *Melone?* And the next? *Cantelupo?*'

Lizzy got the giggles. 'Okay, fine. We won't call it anything.'

Her expression suddenly sobered.

'What?'

'We're going to have to choose a name at some point.'

'We?'

'Well… I had thought of calling her Metrodora. Dora for short. Because Metrodora's a bit mean. I mean…if she's girl.'

Leon tipped his head back and forth. 'A Greek physician, eh? You know how us Italians feel about that.'

Lizzy pulled a face. He knew Metrodora wasn't just any old Greek physician. She was the first female physician to write a proper medical text.

'Don't you think it's time to move past of that Roman

versus Greek malarkey about who started civilisation?' she said.

'Sure. Happy to. So long as the answer is the Romans,' Leon said playfully. 'How about Trotula? She was the world's first gynaecologist. From right here in Italy. Or Dorotea Bucca. She was a physician *and* a professor. Nice, huh?'

He tried out a few variations of Dorotea. Dorothy. Téa. And, of course, Dora.

'Nope. Sorry. You don't get to choose,' Lizzy snipped, and the hum of shared delight disappeared as if it had been sucked into a black hole. 'Not since you won't be involved.'

Leon's hackles went up. Hormones or not, this wasn't her call. 'And when did we make that decision, exactly?'

'We made it on the day I arrived, remember? When you took back your proposal.'

'Hang on.' He put the wand on the desk beside the exam table and handed her a few paper towels to wipe the gel off her belly. The magic of the moment was completely gone. 'You made me take it back. And if I recall the conversation properly—which I do—I remember saying we'd put decision-making on hold. Not withdraw any offers made in good faith.'

'Ha! See? I *knew* you didn't mean it.' She shook her head and began muttering something to herself.

'I *did* mean it, Lizzy. It's the right thing to do.'

'Yes, but is it the thing you actually *want* to do, Leon? That's what matters here.'

'Hypothetically…' he said, before he could stop himself.

Lizzy's eyebrows shot up and she held him in a fierce glare as she slipped off the table and pulled her scrubs top down over her stomach.

'I think we should go and see the Bianchis now. They'll be expecting us.'

* * *

Lizzy was kicking herself over and over again. Why was she being such a pain with Leon?

It didn't take a brain surgeon to answer that one. Or an antenatal cardiologist for that matter.

She was scared. Scared right down to her very essence.

Of *course* she didn't want to do this on her own. She hadn't even known she wanted a baby until a fortnight ago, when she'd stared at that smiley face on the pregnancy test and then, of course, on the five back-up tests she'd done afterwards.

Of *course* she'd love to be all happy families with the one man in the world who set her on fire in so many ways—intellectually, professionally, sexually...

The 'sexually' part in particular had been driving her mad. She'd met plenty of pregnant women who said all they thought about was sex when they were carrying a baby, and lo and behold she seemed to be one of them. But having sex with Leon was out of the question. Especially as they hadn't decided on their long-term plan of action. Kissing, hugging, caressing and being totally naked with him would be sheer insanity.

That one night of mind-blowing sex they'd shared in January had changed her life for ever. If she were to have two to three more months of mind-blowing sex who knew what would happen? She might say yes to that ridiculously lovely cream-coloured dress she passed every single day when she sneaked out of the hospital for a secret gelato.

So, no way. There was zero chance she was going to go and stay in that flat of his, with him all naked and gorgeous and Italian, with his sexy voice, and super-sexy hands, and his sexy chin and his kiss-me-now lips and—everything. Especially if he smelt of burnt sugar and oranges as he had this morning. It had taken all the power she'd possessed not to rip her top off and beg him to have his wicked way with her when he'd come into the on-call room this morning. That was how big a game her hormones were playing.

Or maybe…her heart?

These questions and a thousand more plagued her as she sat through the morning meeting with Giovanni and his growing team and then went into the Bianchis' room, where they were now.

'Lizzy?' Leon was prompting. 'Gabrielle was just asking why you think another MRI is a good idea.'

He gave her a look that said a thousand things. *I know you're freaked out. I know you're hormonal. I know we have a lot to talk about.* And, more to the point, *I flew you across the world to help these people.*

'Is it really necessary?' Gabrielle's eyes darted between the doctors and her husband. 'I have to confess they're beginning to make me feel a bit claustrophobic.'

Lizzy retrained her attentions to where they should be. On her patient. 'We can get some music in there for you—or maybe an audiobook would help? Matteo, you're also welcome to stay. The way Gabrielle will be situated in the scanner means you could hold her ankle or maybe rub her feet?'

Gabrielle made a *Maybe that would work* face.

Matteo rubbed his hands together and feigned giving a foot-rub. 'Anything to help my good lady wife.'

Gabrielle bit down on her lip, indecision clearly gripping her.

'I don't know… It might be harder to stay still if he's doing something that feels good.'

Lizzy forced herself not to go in for a fist-bump. Gabrielle was preaching to the converted!

Concentrating on Gabrielle and her babies was exactly why she'd been sleeping on the hard-as-rock beds here at the hospital. Was there *no* hospital, no matter how fancy, that had comfy on-call rooms?

Lizzy sat down by Gabrielle's bed and took the young woman's hand in her own. 'You know more than anyone that the babies you're carrying are extra-special. As such, I want to know exactly what's going on before we take any surgical steps—yeah?'

Gabrielle's husband ran a hand through his already messy hair. 'I think we probably would've been happy doing something else extra-special, like…' he looked at his wife and grinned. '…like building the world's largest snowman or eating the most profiteroles in one sitting or swimming in the world's largest cheese fondue.'

'Food! That's what he is always thinking about!'

'How could I not?' he countered in mock horror. 'We're in Rome! Did you know this is the only month of the year you can get *puntarelle*? And *barbe di frate*! Monk's beard! I'd never even heard of it before.'

Lizzy felt Leon tickle her hand with his finger. She batted it away. She couldn't deal with butterfly swoops in her tummy and acting professional at the same time.

Matteo's wife gave him a loving swat, then tugged him down to her to receive a kiss. 'Enough about food. Can we talk about our children?'

He cupped her cheek in his hand, then bent to kiss her again. 'Of course, *amore mio*. I just don't want you to be stressed. And also… I know how much you love trying new food.'

His wife giggled. 'Don't! You'll make me hungry again and I only just ate.'

'Tell me what you want and I'll fetch it. Your wish is my command.'

The couple shared a warm look of such undiluted shared

purpose that a sharp blast of loneliness shot through Lizzy so powerfully she could hardly draw a breath.

She looked away and caught Leon's eye. Instantly that feeling of solitude switched to something powerful and charged. She could be with this man if she wanted. He'd asked her to marry him and there was a kernel of belief in her that he actually had meant it.

Granted, there were a whole load of 'ifs' attached. If she learnt to trust that he wasn't going to be like her father. If he didn't lay down his word as law. And if, the scariest of all, he didn't behave like 'old Leon' and disappear out of their lives when a bigger, better job prospect presented itself.

She didn't think she could bear the heartache. Trust was a much more precious commodity than she'd ever given it credit for.

'An MRI room can be made ready...' Leon's eyes dipped to his tablet '...now.'

Lizzy forced herself to regroup. 'Right. Good. Are you up for walking today, Gabrielle? Or are you happier in a wheelchair?'

Once they'd set Gabrielle up in the MRI scanner, and Matteo's foot-rub had been rejected in favour of a trip down to the local *piazza*, to see if he could find any healthy snacks, Leon and Lizzy went to the imaging room, overseeing the scan.

After a few minutes of silently staring at the images appearing on the screen, Lizzy turned to Leon. 'I'm sorry.'

'For what?'

'Behaving like a loon.' She pointed her index fingers at her stomach. 'It might be the cowardly option, but I'm holding someone else responsible for my behaviour.'

'Well, in that case, apology accepted.' Leon pressed a

hand to his chest and then, as if an idea had just struck him, held up a finger. 'On one condition.'

'What's that?' She grinned warily.

'Let me take you on a tour of Rome. Today.'

Oh! Well, that was loads better than baring all her deepest darkest fears. Even so...it was time away from the hospital—and, more dangerously, time *with Leon*.

'We've already seen the Trevi Fountain.'

He huffed out a supercilious laugh. *'Cara!'* He shook his head in mock sorrow. 'You think that's Rome?'

He reached out and tucked a wayward curl behind her ear, his fingers brushing the soft down of her cheek as he did so. *Goosebumps.*

'There is so much more to Rome than the Trevi Fountain.'

She looked at her patient, at the scans appearing on the screen of the babies she'd been tasked to deliver healthy and well. She was well known for her ability to pore over image after image for hours on end, but it would be a shame to fly all this way and not see even a few of the wonders of Rome. Beyond the gelato, of course.

Another image flashed onto the screen.

Her nerve-endings leapt to attention.

There. The left ventricle valve.

She squinted at the image, her brain whirring away, imagining herself placing a stent into the valve. It was going to be a tricky surgery, but achievable.

'Deal accepted. On one of *my* conditions.'

'Okay...?' Leon nodded for her to go ahead.

Her conciliatory expression morphed into the type of grin a child might wear when it was about to be presented with an ice cream sundae.

'Remember when you talked about the 3D lab?'

He nodded again.

'Can we print 3D versions of the babies now and at each week until thirty-two weeks? In utero. Obvs.'

'Assolutatmente.' His smile matched hers at the idea. 'We can get everyone in…do a few practice rounds of the surgery.' His eyes narrowed. 'On one more condition.'

She frowned and feigned a grumpy huff. 'What? An afternoon out and about in Rome isn't enough for you?'

'No,' he said. 'As a matter of fact, it isn't. I want you to come back and stay at my apartment from now on. Unless there is a genuine emergency.'

Her instinct was to protest. She stopped herself. It was becoming a bad habit, and one she would have to break if Leon really meant what he'd said about wanting to be involved in her and their baby's lives.

She closed her eyes and gave them a rub. From this moment on, she vowed, she would look at Leon through clear, unbiased, non-judgmental eyes. The past was the past and the future was a brand-new thing.

And God help her if he didn't look even more gorgeous when she opened them again.

CHAPTER TEN

L<small>IZZY</small> <small>REACHED OUT</small> and grabbed Leon's hand. 'I can't see!'

'You can.' He put his free hand to the small of her back and guided her to the centre of the glass flooring that was at the heart of the ancient, subterranean *palazzo*. 'Look— see the lights there?'

Lizzy drew in a quick breath. 'Are those...?'

'Public baths,' Leon said, his voice low to match the magical surroundings. 'Second century AD, they think. They would've been adjacent to what is now the *palazzo*.'

'And these other rooms, the tiles, the kitchen areas— those are all centuries old?'

'Around five hundred years,' he confirmed. 'The *palazzo* went through numerous renovations, of course, and as you can see...' he gestured to the walls soaring above them '...so has the rest of Rome.'

Lizzy shook her head in disbelief, leaning into Leon's hand, a movement that seemed so natural anyone around them would assume they were a couple. A movement that elicited a hundred questions for Leon, who knew they weren't.

'I can't believe we're *seven metres* below the rest of Rome!'

He laughed appreciatively. 'I couldn't either, when I first saw it. These elements of the *palazzo* were only discovered recently—and excavated this century—and the addition of the glass floors, so people can walk freely above the remains, is even more recent.'

'Palazzo Valentini...' Lizzy sighed. 'It sounds so romantic, doesn't it?'

Leon gave her hand a squeeze, and to his surprise received a small squeeze of acknowledgment in return. Tipping his head to give the top of her head a kiss, just as he would have five years ago, seemed the natural thing to do—so he did it. She leant into him again, then shot him a shy smile.

Perhaps it was being cloaked in the low lighting. Perhaps it was holding hands. Perhaps it was simply being with Lizzy. But standing amidst the remains of an ancient family's household, where lives had been lived and lost, filled him with a profound sense of longing.

What sort of history would the two of them leave behind? And, more to the point, what sort of future would they have?

He felt as if someone had taken the well-worn and very familiar carpet he'd been walking on his entire life, yanked it out from underneath him and—just like in this *palazzo*—uncovered metres and metres of memories and emotions to excavate.

Could he do that? Clear away the anger and the pain from his past to allow for a bright, loving future with Lizzy?

'And how was it you got us tickets?' Lizzy asked. 'The couple behind us in the queue said they'd had to book months ago.'

'A patient.'

She nodded. She'd clearly had a few of those as well. Patients who were so grateful they promised any favour at any time as thanks for bringing their child into the world.

They continued walking past the archaeological finds—ancient pots women had filled with water, tiled benches men would have relaxed on, no doubt professing to be 'thinking great thoughts', and of course bedrooms.

A thought struck him as they entered another pitch-black room, the glass floor their only support as they gazed on the archaeological finds a good three metres below them, lit by dim floodlights. Believing that love was enough to sustain a relationship was a bit like stepping onto one of these invisible floors.

Ahead of him he saw a young child drop to his knees and crawl along it, finding safety in proximity to the floor that supported him. Was that what he'd been doing? Clinging to a false support—to his belief that being alone meant less heartache—when in actual fact sometimes enduring the heartache made moments like this that much more rewarding.

His gut instinct when Lizzy had told him about their child had been to ask her to marry him. He had to trust that. Even if it did seem insane. Walking on the moon had seemed impossible at one juncture. As had painting the extraordinary arches and domes of the Sistine Chapel. But people who'd believed in the impossible had done it.

The magical atmosphere of the *palazzo* suddenly turned claustrophobic. Enough museums. Enough of the past. It was time to build his own future. One that included the gorgeous blonde by his side. One that made them a family.

He leant down and whispered into Lizzy's ear. 'Let's get some gelato.'

Lizzy looked up at him, her lips quirked into a smile, but her brows were furrowed together and she looked perplexed. 'Now?'

'Yes. Now.'

'We've not had supper yet.'

'Bah.' He waved away the feeble protest. 'It's only five o'clock. A perfect time for gelato and then…' An idea struck. He dropped her a wink. 'C'mon. Follow me. I know just the way to build up an appetite.'

Lizzy's heart pounded in her chest as she stumbled blindly alongside Leon as he led her through the darkened corridors of the subterranean *palazzo*.

Sex.

He was talking about sex, wasn't he?

What other way was there to build up an appetite for supper?

She raced back over the conversations they'd had which had led up to her agreeing to take this tour of Rome and wondered if there had been anything in her behaviour that had screamed, *Have your wicked way with me, you sexy Italian beast, you!*

Hmm…

There was nothing obvious…

But they were holding hands.

Was that a new signal that a lovemaking session was on the horizon?

Oh, God. She was so out of touch with how things worked. With her and Leon back in the day, things had been extraordinarily simple. Work. Sex. Sleep. Repeat. A spectacular combination of energies that had somehow morphed into her convincing herself she was madly in love with him. Something she was meant to have doused last New Year's Eve, when she'd left a sleeping Leon alone in his honeymoon suite.

Leon silently led her out of the *palazzo*, his hand holding hers, his thumb distractedly…or tactically…rubbing the back of her hand as thoughts of unbuttoning his shirt and whipping his belt out of the loops of his hip-hugging trousers stirred her nervous system into a frenzy.

By the time they'd bought the obligatory postcards, left the building and blinked and adjusted their eyes to the bright late-afternoon sunshine, Lizzy was so close to pouncing on Leon it was ridiculous. How could one solitary man smell like a pastry shop and the citrus aisle of a supermarket all at once?

So many questions to which there were no answers...

Which was why she adopted a casually uninterested air as she leant against a pile of rocks that had no doubt been part of a palace three thousand years ago, stared at Leon, and then huskily asked, 'So...what's this big plan of yours?'

'*Voilà!*'

Leon stepped to one side and threw out his arm, pointing towards an electric bicycle rental company.

Oh.

Her spirits deflated more than they should. She'd been quite keen on the idea of sanctioned sex.

'Yay!' She waved a pair of invisible pompoms. 'A bike-ride!'

'Electric bikes,' he corrected. 'I've always wanted to do this.'

'Really?' Weird... He lived here, and this was a very touristy thing to do.

'*Si!*' He gave one of those nonchalant shrugs of his. 'I grew up here, but I never really saw things fresh, you know? The Colosseum, the Parthenon, the *palazzo* we just went to. They were all just buildings I used as signposts rather than things I really looked at.'

She nodded, seeing his point. Sydney was the same for her. She'd only ever been to the Opera House on a school trip, and more recently on a blind date she'd had to abort before they'd even got to their seats because she'd been called to surgery. She'd never taken a harbour cruise, never seen an open-air film in the Botanical Gardens, never been up the Sydney Tower Eye…

Crikey. Was work the only thing she'd done since she'd returned from her internship? It was looking that way.

'This isn't some clever way to show off your glutes, is it?'

A girl could dream.

He snorted. 'I thought it'd be a nice way to build up an appetite. Unless you think it's too hot?'

Oh, she was hungry all right. But not for carbs.

She pursed her lips. 'You call this hot? Come to Australia, mate. I'll show you hot.'

The late spring air thickened between them. The sexual electricity she'd felt surging out of her was now zinging both ways.

Leon's dark eyes locked with hers. 'Would you like that? If I came to Australia?'

It wasn't a flippant question. It was a genuine one.

And it felt as intimate as if she were lying unclothed, waiting for his touch.

Did she want that? For him to see the little cocoon of work and home life she'd created for herself?

It was pretty embarrassing, actually. All her friends were from work. Since her mother had passed away she pretty much only saw her dad when she had to. Birthdays. Christmas. If she wasn't working. She didn't have any hobbies or social clubs to take Leon to. No surfing skills to show off nor masses of friends to introduce him to at a regularly scheduled champagne brunch.

In all honesty her life in Sydney wasn't that different from the little cocoon Leon had made for himself here. A bells-and-whistles workplace that demanded attention at all hours, most days of the week. A home literally a jog away from said hospital. The only difference in their life-styles was that her place was near the beach and had more Crayon drawings.

'Sure. One day. So...' She rubbed her hands together enthusiastically. 'Right, then! Let's get exploring.'

Two hours later they pulled their bicycles back into the hire station, smiles tugging their lips from ear to ear. Leon had been right. Seeing Rome through Lizzy's eyes had made his home town about a thousand times better.

She had a keen eye for finding small pieces of art tucked into doorframes and olive trees defying their cement sur-roundings and producing tiny little olives, just waiting for the summer sun to ripen them.

They'd stopped in the centre of Rome's oldest bridge, thought to have been built in 62BC, and marvelled at all the people and their outfits and the modes of transport it must have borne witness to.

They'd walked their cycles through the Jewish Quar-ter—one of the world's oldest ghettos.

They'd stood in silence, their hands brushing each oth-er's, in the centre of a two-thousand-year-old church so ripe with atmosphere in the form of incense and candlelight that they'd both, in tandem, turned to light candles, nei-ther one asking who they were lighting them for, but each knowing instinctively the solitary flames they lit were for someone close to them. Someone for whom they wished peace. Their mothers.

An unspoken peace had settled between the pair of them as they'd glided through the thinning crowds. Peo-ple rushing home or, as was the case with most tourists, couples wandering hand in hand, paying attention to anything and nothing, happy to be sharing this glorious city with someone they loved.

And Leon was one of them.

'That was great fun. Thank you.'

Lizzy went up on tiptoe to give Leon's cheek a kiss, but their helmets knocked together and she lurched backwards.

He grabbed hold of her waist and steadied her. Unbuckling her helmet, he slid it off her head, enjoying watching her hair as it tumbled out of the helmet and over her shoulders. He took his own off then, because nothing else seemed to be the right thing to do, and he kissed her properly.

It was the kind of kiss he'd been aching to give her since she'd arrived here in Rome but had been too afraid to lest it meant committing to something he wouldn't be able to make good on. Sure, he'd proposed. Lizzy had called him on it. But there had been a hell of a lot of water under the proverbial bridge in such a short time. They were sharing lives, a child, and the world they saw through separate lenses was being melded into one beautiful kaleidoscope of shared history...

It seemed like something he could do. And the only way to find out if they could be together was to be open and honest. And...like on those glass floors...he wouldn't know until he took the first step.

When they finally separated, Lizzy's cheeks were pink. 'You were right,' she said.

'About what?'

'I needed that before supper.'

He laughed, not asking for clarification as to whether she meant the cycle ride or the kiss.

'Want to eat Chez Cassanetti or out?'

She considered the options for a moment and then said, 'Out.'

He smiled. 'I know just the place.'

* * *

'This looks…erm…interesting…'

Leon's eyebrows performed a little *wait and see* jig.

After having walked past several dozen utterly gorgeous, flower bedecked, history-laden *ristorantes* and *trattorias, pescerias* and *tavolas* and, yes, even some rather alluring *pizzerias*, Lizzy had tried to summon a smile when they'd stopped in front of the plain-fronted, no-nonsense *osteria* Leon had chosen—the Italian equivalent of a gastropub, Leon explained, without the chalkboard menus and the aesthetically pleasing *olde-worlde* environment.

She was starving, so frankly a hotdog would do at this juncture, but she was trusting that some insider knowledge had made him pick this plain-tiled, sixties Brutalist streetfront eatery called, simply, Osteria Rosso.

She was also completely giddy. Her every nerve-ending was still crackling from that kiss. It had been the type of kiss that swept through her body over and over again in the best possible way. It had coincided with the golden hour—that perfect moment before sunset, when everything was bathed in a peachy-golden hue. So…weirdly… even Brutalist architecture didn't look half bad. Especially as she was holding hands with Leon—the same hand that had occasionally, almost absently, slipped to the small of her back to guide her this way or that as they navigated the ancient streets of central Rome, bringing yet another set of tingles for her body to enjoy.

What on earth any of it meant was another story. But for this moment she was happy to let her hormones enjoy the ride.

There was, surprisingly, a queue. Every now and again a large, rosy-cheeked woman appeared at the door and eyed up whoever was next in line, and then, seemingly randomly, admitted them or turned them away.

On her third such journey she caught Leon's eye. He gave a little wave. She beckoned him in.

After they'd been seated at what might easily be considered the best table—by the window, overlooking a leafy cobbled street—Lizzy asked, 'What favours have you done for her?'

'Grandbaby,' he answered.

Lizzy raised a *tell me more* eyebrow.

'Spina bifida,' he said simply.

'In utero?'

He nodded, his eyes dropping to the handwritten menu they'd been handed, along with a pair of soft drinks and a recommendation to try the fish special. It was, according to the owner, indescribably delicious.

Lizzy stared at Leon for a few moments as he read, absorbing what she'd always known about him but never acknowledged. That rare spinal surgery was a gamechanger. If left until birth, an unclosed spinal column could cause irreversible brain damage and severe trauma-based injuries to the nerves below a baby's waist. Surgery wasn't a cure-all, but it certainly gave the child a better shot at a normal life.

'You don't like to brag on yourself, do you?'

He looked across at her. *'Che?'*

'You don't make a big show of who you are and how unbelievable a surgeon you are.'

His shoulders did a tell-tale lift and drop. 'Why would I? It's about the outcome, isn't it? Not who created it?'

All at once she saw how generous and huge his heart was. He was like the very best chocolates at Christmas. A hard, crisp shell with an utterly gooey core. He didn't do any of his ground-breaking surgeries to raise his stature. He'd all but handed the baton to her when she'd arrived for the Bianchi case. Sure, he was the lead doctor, and he would also overseeing Grace's care while she focused on Hope's HLHS, but beyond that first day, when she'd been stupidly cross because he'd taken the lead at the group lecture, where—*duh!*—she had known about as much as everyone else bar him, he really wasn't a limelight kind of guy.

'Why do you do this?' she asked.

'What? Surgery?'

'Yeah, but…little tiny babies. Babies who don't have personalities yet. Babies who haven't yet breathed oxygen. When you claimed to never want babies for yourself.'

They both stared at each other a bit after that.

Then, 'Why do you do this?' she asked again.

He put down the menu and took a sip of his drink as he considered his answer. It was another trait she hadn't really etched into her portrait of him yet. He was a thinker. He liked to mull things over before committing. Which meant his marriage proposal genuinely had come from the heart. Which meant…*gulp*…that Leon had actually genuinely proposed to her.

'I don't want to be alone when I live!'

'I suppose… I suppose it's changed over the years,' he finally said.

'From what to what?' Lizzy asked straight away.

'From something that seemed impossible—something only extraordinary people could do—to something that is essential, regardless of the merit that comes with it.'

Hmm…that was too esoteric for her. 'Explain,' she demanded.

'I suppose I do it more for the mothers than anyone.'

'How so?' It was a laudable reason, but she really wanted to get underneath the reason *why*.

He traced his finger around the top of his water glass, then looked her in the eye. 'Have I ever told you about my childhood?'

* * *

Three times they waved away Concetta, the proprietress, until eventually she gave up and brought them what she thought they should eat.

A common practice in Italy, Leon assured her. For a place where restaurateurs did not believe the customer knew best. *They* did.

Half an hour and one plate of extraordinary *antipasti* later, Lizzy felt as shell-shocked as Leon looked. They were finally having the type of conversation most couples had in those first precious few weeks of courtship. The type of *Who are you, really?* conversation that demanded all the attention that neither Lizzy nor Leon had had the time or energy for, because of their insanely busy surgical schedules and because... Well, because that hadn't been what they *did*.

They'd worked. They'd competed. They'd sparked off one another. They'd made love. But they definitely hadn't talked. Not like this.

They both sat back in their chairs as their *secondis* were delivered. Pasta for Leon and—*oh, yum*—an amazing-looking risotto with fish for Lizzy.

When the waitress had left Lizzy asked, 'Why is this the first time you've told me about it? Your past?'

He twirled his fork through a tumble of *spaghettini* dappled with delicate little clams, glossy from a clear broth. 'Is your food all right?' he asked lightly, as if he hadn't just bared his soul. He poised his fork by his mouth, about to eat the expert swirl of pasta.

'Delicious.' It was—gorgeous grilled seabass with some beautiful tiny fresh peas in a lemony risotto—but she held up a finger. 'Can we go back to the whole thing of your father getting up in the middle of your supper and leaving for ever, please?'

He nodded, his eyes dropping to the bowl of pasta, his fork making half-hearted stabs at the clams swimming in the broth.

'What do you want to know?' he asked.

'Did you ever see him again?'

'Once.'

'So, he came back, then?'

'No. His wife in Scandinavia found out about me and invited me to spend the summer with them.'

'He'd remarried?'

'Si.' he confirmed tonelessly. 'Right away. Marriage, children, a holiday cabin on an island—the whole nine yards, as they say.'

He looked up, but appeared to be looking through her, as if reliving that summer afresh. His dark eyes took on a haunted hollowness that made Lizzy's heart ache. 'And…?'

He cleared his throat and gave her a tight smile. 'And it turned out he would've preferred it if she hadn't. He didn't like being reminded that he'd made mistakes.'

'He saw you as a mistake?' Lizzy put her fork down, unable to match the delicious meal with the awful story he was telling.

'He saw being with my mother as a mistake, and therefore anything that had been affiliated with her—like me—was also a mistake.'

And then it became crystal-clear to her. He was helping all those pregnant mothers have as perfect a baby as possible. He was preventing 'mistakes'.

Her voice caught in her throat as she reached out to him. 'I'm so sorry, Leon.'

'Don't be.' He accepted her touch but soon pulled away to take a drink of water. 'I'm not telling you for your pity.' His eyes flared, then steadied. 'I'm telling you because I want you to understand why I've behaved the way I have.

Why I held you at arm's length before we'd had a chance to see where things could go.'

She sat on this information for a minute. She'd been a willing participant in their *when the internships are done, we're done* thing, but if he'd heard her say she loved him… if he'd said he loved her too…would they be together now? Have children already? Be a family.

He toyed with his food for a minute, then abruptly his face tightened with unwelcome emotion. 'My father's wife had a stillborn baby when I was there. They sent me back straight away. She never said anything—she never would have—but my father did.'

'What on earth did he say?' Lizzy asked, though her churning gut was already telling her the awful answer to her question.

'He blamed me. Said my appearance had caused too much stress and strain and that I'd caused the baby's death.'

Lizzy's hands flew to her chest. 'I'm so, *so* sorry, Leon.'

She didn't bother telling him it wasn't true. He knew that. But knowing about the incident threw another swathe of light on Leon's complicated past. He didn't explain further, but he didn't have to. He had become an antenatal surgeon because he wanted to fix what he hadn't been able to fix as a child.

Her heart absolutely ached for him.

All the pieces of the *Why does Leon behave the way he does?* puzzle were in place now.

A boy who was abandoned by his father through no fault of his own.

A mother who withdrew her affections because of a broken heart that had swiftly turned bitter.

An adolescence spent being told to retreat from happiness because it only led to pain and, heartbreakingly, seeing the evidence to back it up.

No wonder he hadn't ever had faith in something as ethereal as love. His life had been mired in rejection and blame.

'Did you tell your mother?' Lizzy asked eventually. 'About what had happened?'

He shook his head. 'No point.'

'But she could have at least consoled you,' Lizzy shot back, knowing even as she spoke that the mother Leon had described would have defined love as a mirage designed to fool a person into giving their very best to another, only to be abandoned and left heartbroken and alone.

'Did you light your candle for her?' Lizzy asked, again already knowing the answer.

He nodded. 'And you?'

'My mum.' She left it at that, hoping they could leave putting the microscope to her own less than happy childhood for another day.

Leon tilted his head so that he could catch her eyes with his, those dark, beautifully familiar eyes of his searching hers for a cue as to whether or not she wanted to talk.

She dropped her gaze to his plate.

'Want some?' he asked.

She nodded, suddenly strangely ravenous.

He dipped his fork into the centre of the dish and created a gorgeous whorl of pasta and clams, then lifted the forkful, dripping, up to her mouth.

As she took a bite she looked up and met his eyes. What she saw made her heart skip a beat. She saw longing. The same longing she tried to hide from the world. A bone-deep ache to be part of a couple. So she would never have to worry about being loved. So she would never have to think about who she could turn to when she was happy, sad, tired, anxious or over the moon. Part of a couple with a partner in life who felt exactly the same way. Two people who were each other's homing beacons, providing a place of safety and security in a world where so many things were beyond their control. Two people who could raise a child together...

'Should we try it out?' she asked, after finishing the mouthful of succulent pasta.

'What?' He shook his head, not understanding.

'Us. Being a couple. While we're here.'

'What? You mean you're accepting my proposal?' His eyes went wide.

She wasn't going to go that far, but... 'How about we consider this a new beginning?'

He looked at her intently. He was listening. And looking damn hot. Which was distracting.

'Explain,' he said.

'We just...see how we go. Try being a couple.'

'In the same flat?' Leon asked, well aware that she hadn't exactly agreed to move back into his flat with him.

'Yes,' she said, her heart skipping a beat as she did so. 'In the same flat, in the same hospital, working on the same case. It's like an intensive cramming for a final exam.'

He laughed at that. 'What? You want to look at this as "cramming", to see if we'd be any good at marriage?'

She shook her head and gave him what she hoped was a cheeky grin. 'We're cramming so we can see if we'll be good together—warts and all. Because...babies mean warts.'

His expression sobered, the reality of their impending parenthood clearly taking a hold of him, and then that hard-won smile of his lit up his face as he took her hand in his and said simply, 'Our baby won't have warts.'

She laughed. 'You know I don't mean it literally. I just mean...this is scary. For both of us. Neither of us has any experience at being in a relationship—a proper one, that has peaks and troughs and mistakes and forgiveness.'

'You mean one that lasts a lifetime?'

His words landed in her heart with an explosion of heat. Yes. That was exactly what she meant. And it scared the living daylights out of her.

'I mean a happy, honest, *respectful* one,' she qualified, thinking of her parents' marriage, which had lasted her mother's lifetime, but certainly hadn't been a happy one. Nor respectful. 'We're heading into the wilderness here, you and I.'

'What do you mean?'

'Neither of us has really had the best of examples, have we?'

He shook his head, giving her the space to continue if she wanted to talk about her own childhood. But she didn't, and by then Concetta had cleared their dinner plates and brought two ridiculously beautiful servings of pannacotta, and it seemed a perfect time to let the intensity of their conversation have some room to breathe.

She lifted up the tiny glass of herbal digestif their hostess had slipped onto the table next to her dessert bowl. 'To seeing how we go?'

Leon lifted his own glass and shared a smile with her—one that actually looked as excited as she felt. 'To seeing how we go.'

CHAPTER ELEVEN

LEON HAD NEVER believed holding hands could deliver such promise. And yet here he was, walking through the streets of Rome, holding hands with the woman carrying his child, hoping he had the strength to make good on the commitment they'd just made to one another.

As commitments went it was fairly vague.

Let's see how it goes.

Not exactly *Till death us do part*, but it was a start. Not bad for two commitment-shy, work-obsessed control freaks like the two of them.

Abruptly he pulled her into a doorway, cupped her face with his hands and kissed her until they both lost their breath.

'What was that for?' she asked, her cheeks pinkened with, very possibly, a hint of shyness. This was, after all, the first time ever they had knowingly gone home together as a bona fide couple since New York. It felt like being a teenager. It felt like falling in love.

'Because,' he said, dropping a kiss on her nose.

Because he loved her, and he didn't know if his version of love was enough.

He pushed his fears to the side, reminding himself that they were taking this risk together. He wasn't alone. He had by his side the one woman he could trust to give him the room to make mistakes.

He slid his arm over her shoulders as they headed towards home. This felt nice. It felt good! It felt *right*...the *Let's see how it goes* approach.

When they reached his flat and got into the geriatric lift, the sexual tension that had been building between them on their walk home escalated.

Lizzy teasingly traced her finger from the base of his throat down to his belt buckle, and then suddenly, with a she-devil smile, tugged him in close.

Something deep and primal surged to the fore and spread like wildfire through his bloodstream. For the first time ever, he didn't care if it took a lifetime for the lift to inch its way up to the top floor. It gave him time to run the backs of his fingers along Lizzy's sides. To feel her arch into him as his fingertips lightly grazed the edges of her neck, her breasts, her waist...

His hands shifted to caress her thighs—which, to his satisfaction, elicited a soft moan. Without a second thought he lifted her up so that she was straddling his waist, kissing her as if his life depended upon it. And in this moment, it felt as if it did.

The moment the lift juddered into place on the seventh floor he yanked open the iron gate and, still carrying and kissing Lizzy, unlocked his door and took her, without any consultation, to his bedroom.

She didn't raise a solitary objection.

He sat down on the bed with Lizzy straddling him, her fingers already busy undoing his shirt buttons. In one swift, fluid move, he gathered the hem of her dress in his hands and pulled it up and over her head, relishing the sight of her body. Her breasts were fuller. Her curves softer. Everything about her was beautiful.

He shifted her gently to the bed, laying her down so that he could, for the first time, properly admire the soft curve of her belly. Their child was growing in there. Their beautiful, perfect child.

He dropped kiss after kiss upon her stomach as Lizzy ran her fingers through his hair—softly at first, and then, as the kisses descended, dropping her nails to his shoulders and scraping them against his skin as she groaned, 'I want you inside me.'

With each featherlight touch, kiss and caress, Lizzy felt as though her body was being lit from within—as if light was radiating like sunshine from a place she could only define as her very essence. It felt like being lit up by fireworks and enormous fistfuls of glitter.

They explored each other's body with a luxuriousness that didn't acknowledge time or space or the need for sleep or air. They were one another's oxygen. They were one another's life force. And Lizzy had never felt more alive in her life.

Leon lifted himself and then wholly, completely entered her, his eyes connecting with hers in an electricity she'd never known before—a shared energy that could only mean that for the first time neither of them was holding back.

She cried out in pleasure as he began to move with the rhythm of her hips. Arcing, pushing, savouring each moment as if it were a precious memory. There was a complexity to their lovemaking that was new. A feverish need to be as close together as humanly possible that went beyond those early lust-fuelled days in New York. What they needed now was different. Went deeper. Demanded more.

And that, Lizzy realised as she tipped her head back and Leon dropped kiss after heated kiss along her throat, was the key, wasn't it? Knowing one another's foibles. Knowing one another's pain. Hopes, dreams, desires, fears… All of it.

A sliver of her acknowledged that she'd not been nearly as open with Leon as he had with her, but she'd get there—now that they were taking on their fears…and hopes… together.

'Is this all right?' Leon asked as once again he eased his erection deeper into her, his hands pressing into the bed, his arm muscles growing taut as, with each movement, he turned her insides into liquid heat with stroke after stroke.

'More than,' she managed. And she meant it.

She'd thought the lovemaking they'd shared on New Year's Eve had been other-worldly, but she'd been wrong. That had been fuelled by…not revenge, exactly, but it certainly hadn't been by love.

This shared synchronicity they were experiencing now—the vulnerability of it—*this* was what making love actually was. Sharing the most intimate thing a couple could, knowing they might fail at being together and trying anyway.

Each time their stomachs touched, their thighs connected or, more urgently, she felt him withdraw completely and then tease at the junction of her thighs, she fought the urge to wrap her legs around him and tug him to her, so their bodies would reach that inevitable moment when they organically moved as one, urgently, uncontrollably, to reach the climax she was so desperately close to.

But she didn't. She forced herself to slow to the achingly luxurious cadence Leon had set, drawing out the pleasure as long as possible, trusting him, knowing that she could have faith in him to bring her to climax with him. Just as she had to have faith that he could change and that she too could change, she quietly acknowledged.

Life was complicated. Just like in the surgical ward, life was full of ups and downs, and, if there was anyone in the world she thought she could take that roller coaster ride with, it was Leon. The father of her child.

Their eyes caught and cinched.

She knew what they were communicating to one another.

Now.

By silent agreement, the intensity of Leon's movements gathered pace. Her hips met him thrust for thrust, her breath quickening, and soon enough her body was no longer having to obey her commands but merely following its natural rhythms, so that before her brain had a chance to catch up the two of them were pressed together so completely she felt as though Leon's body were directly communicating with her. His heartbeat matched hers. His racing blood ran in sync with hers. Their orgasms matched each other's with such force it doubled the pleasure and the intensity.

When, later, they were lying side by side, their breaths steadying, and as the long day began to take hold of them, she let herself focus on individual sensations. Leon's hand on her hip. His long, dark eyelashes. The hair on his leg brushing her smooth one. His scent, warm and citrusy, magnified into something like a warm summer afternoon in an orchard by his body's heat. Their eyes…his dark ones, her light ones…gazing sleepily into each other's.

She almost told him how she felt. That she loved him. But then a light fluttering in her stomach erased everything else from her mind. Her practical side told her it was far too soon to be feeling anything close to kicks or movements. That for a first-time mother such as herself, it was normal not to feel anything until twenty weeks. But…

'What? Did you feel it? Did you feel the baby?'

She grinned. Leon was clearly throwing his training to the winds, too.

'I don't think so—not really. But...' She moved his hand to her belly. 'Perhaps I sensed it? It's a bit of a learning curve, all this mother's intuition, isn't it?'

He shrugged. 'You're going to be the expert on that one. I suppose I'll be learning what it feels like to be an anxious father, unable to do anything apart from...' He pushed his full lips out as he thought of something a pregnant woman might want. 'I could peel some grapes for you?'

She laughed and rolled her eyes. 'No! I think, as we're in Rome, you being a gelato angel would probably do the trick. And salami. The peppery kind. With fennel.'

'A gelato angel, eh?' he said, his accent thickening as his voice lowered. 'Is that what you're going to make our child out of? Gelato and fennel salami?'

'Yes,' she quipped, feeling strangely happy that her baby was going to grow fuelled by the beautiful foods available in this equally beautiful city, occasionally fed to her, as today's perfect forkful of pasta had been, by the world's most beautiful man.

He gently eased her onto her back so he could spread his hand across her belly, dropping the odd kiss exactly where their baby was growing. One of the advantages, she thought, of having created a child with an antenatal surgeon. The disadvantages, of course, being that they both knew the countless things that could go wrong.

The moment was so perfect, though, that she pushed all that knowledge to the side and enjoyed feeling Leon's hand on her stomach, his lips whispering against her tummy as he... 'What are you doing?'

'I'm teaching our *piccolo pompelmo* Italian. It'll be an advantage in life. To enter the world bilingual, *si*?'

'You know it can't hear. A couple more weeks yet.'

He waved away the fact. 'Our baby is more advanced than other babies. Look at its parents!' He struck a Brainiac pose that, being done naked, made him look a lot like Michelangelo's *David*.

She giggled as his lips brushed against her tummy while he murmured words she was pretty certain were all food-based. 'Are you telling the baby what foods to ask for?'

'Maybe…' Leon threw her a cheeky grin. 'We don't want it being raised on sub-standard cuisine. Not when it has the best Rome has to offer, right?'

'Hang on a minute! My country has amazing food, too.' She shot him a mischievous look. 'If you don't watch it, I'm going to find an Aussie deli and feed it exclusively on Lamingtons and meat pies.'

Leon made a tsking noise and instantly began speaking to the tiny baby inside her in characteristically impassioned Italian. She fought the instinct to combatively counter with a list of the genuinely delicious foods Australia had to offer.

This wasn't a contest and Leon wasn't her father. He wasn't trying to dominate her, or box her into a way of living that suffocated the woman she really was. He was a proud father-to-be wanting his child to delight in the things he delighted in. To enjoy the things that brought him joy—or the things that, perhaps more realistically, he'd never been allowed to enjoy. Not with his family anyway.

This was his chance every bit as much as it was hers to give a child the life each of them had ached for. Happy, carefree, and full of love. She would have to learn to allow Leon the freedom to love their child in his way as much as she wanted to love the child in hers, the most important point being that they both wanted their child to feel loved.

Lizzy drew her fingers through Leon's silky hair, eventually dissolving into giggles as his lips brushed against her tummy with a never-ending menu. *Bucatini amatriciana, tonnarelli cacio e pepe, suppli, carciofi de fritte.* And the list went on and on.

She leant back against the pillow, little trills of excitement running through her each time Leon said *'mamma'* or *'papà'*.

The enormity of it hit her afresh. She was going to be a mother. Leon was going to be a father. The baby they would have was right here in her belly, growing, developing, just days away from being able to distinguish between its father's voice and its mother's laugh. She prayed those would be the sounds their child would hear throughout his or her life. Sounds of joy. Love. Happiness. She herself had no idea what it was like to grow up in a happy household.

'Let's find out,' she said abruptly.

'What?' Leon looked up, confused. 'You want to know what the special is at Osteria Russo tomorrow?'

'No,' she said, with an urgency she hadn't realised she'd been building up to. 'I want to know if it's a boy or girl. I want to call it something other than *pompelmo.*'

He looked at her, his eyes communicating all the things words simply didn't have the capacity to embrace, and nodded. 'As you wish.'

CHAPTER TWELVE

'READY?' LEON ASKED.

'As I'll ever be.' She gave him a nod. 'Go on. Do it.'

He laughed, considering the fact that she'd been saying she was ready for the past two weeks and then, just as he was about to put the sonography wand on her stomach, always changed her mind.

This sort of surprise, she'd told him as she batted away his hand, only came once. They didn't want to misread the scan, which might easily happen if they did it too early.

He'd nodded, bitten his cheek, and kept back all the things he could have said—like, *We do this for a living*, or *Who cares what sex it is so long as it's healthy?* or, more daringly, *We could always have another child after this one. Be a proper big, bustling family*. The type he'd always wanted to be a part of but never once admitted—not even to himself.

They'd reached a point where they were going to have to tell someone about the baby—Giovanni being the obvious candidate—but the more aware he was of the child growing inside Lizzy, the more her stomach arced and swelled, the more Leon wanted to stay inside the little private bubble the two of them had been living in since that magical night they'd made love.

There, had, of course, been other nights, other moments

of intimacy, but that night had marked a turning point. A sea change in his approach to the life he wanted to live and who he wanted to live it with.

They'd agreed to keep things professional at the hospital, not wanting to fuel the permanent hunger for gossip, but life had a way of forcing people's hands and they were no different. This morning, when Lizzy hadn't been able to fit into any of the clothes she'd packed, they had known that the truth, if not already out there, would have to become common knowledge. Which was why they'd decided to find out the sex of their baby today—before Lizzy's pregnancy was made public.

'Okay...' He held the wand above her belly. 'Are you ready to see the cucumber?'

She smirked at him. 'I thought we'd gone with *pompelmo*?'

He shrugged that easy shrug of his. 'You say *pompelmo*. I say *cetriolo*.' And then he put the wand on her belly.

They watched in silence as the screen flickered to life, their child's heartbeat almost instantly filling the room with that gorgeous *whoosh-whoosh* signifying life.

'He's got fingerprints now.'

'Or she,' Lizzy corrected softly, knowing from the way the baby was positioned that they couldn't yet know.

'Look at those little feet!'

Leon whispered something she couldn't quite catch in Italian, but it sounded like a prayer of gratitude. Then they watched as he moved the wand here and there, one of them occasionally saying a word like *ears* or *toes* or *perfect*.

'Do you see?'

Leon had finally hit the sweet spot in the scan.

Lizzy's face lit up. 'I do.'

'We're going to have a little girl.'

Her brows dived together. 'You're happy with that, right?'

'I'd be happy if you had a koala!'

She laughed, then made a dismissive noise. 'Don't be ridiculous. You look nothing like a koala.'

'Oh?' He put his head between her and the sonography screen. 'What *do* I look like, then?'

Her smile softened as her cheeks lightly pinkened. 'Like no one else in the world.'

'And that's a good thing?' he asked.

'That's the very best thing,' she replied, reaching out to press the kiss she'd put on her fingertips to his lips. 'The very best thing of all.'

It should have been a perfect moment. A moment when he told her, once and for all, that he loved her. A moment when he produced a diamond ring from his pocket. A moment when he got down on his knee and asked her to make him the happiest man on earth by agreeing to be part of a family with him and their daughter.

But something about the look in her eyes—the hope, the expectation she had, that things wouldn't come to a natural end as they had back in New York—shifted something inside him that unleashed a sharp, painful rush of age-old fears.

Would he be enough? Could he really stay the course? Was he the best man for Lizzy to raise a child with? And, more to the point, would loving Lizzy expose him to the heartache his mother had been subjected to when his father had decided he'd rather go leave and pretend none of his marriage had ever happened?

Mercifully, his beeper went off. He didn't want her to see this. To witness the uncertainty in his eyes when he knew what she needed more than anything was a confident, solid, committed man by her side.

Somehow, some way, he told himself as he strode through the hospital corridors towards the surgical ward,

where he would help another mother and her child sur-
mount their own difficulties, he hoped he would find a
way to hurdle his own.

Lizzy withdrew the laparoscope and discarded the instru-
ment on a tray with a clatter of frustration. The nurse who
was helping looked at her, startled. Lizzy wasn't normally
a clatterer. Or one to use blue language, for that matter.

'*Scusi,* I—'

Lizzy shook her head and tried to find the words to
explain how it was that she'd let emotions get the better
of her, but those same emotions seemed to have absorbed
her vocabulary. *Urgh.*

She tugged off the surgical cap she'd put on to try and
get herself in the zone, but even that hadn't worked. She
simply wasn't in the mood. And she'd just killed Hope.
And by proxy Grace. Pretend 3D-printed Hope and Grace,
but still… She'd killed them.

There was no chance she would be wheeling Gabrielle
into the operating theatre when she was feeling like this.
Emotional. Distracted. Wondering why the hell Leon had
abruptly left her in the middle of finding out they were
having a little girl.

Sure, he'd been paged, but she'd seen something happen. Something that had turned his eyes a dangerous shade
of dark that had absorbed the warm chocolatey depths
she loved.

A pretty dark-haired woman with a lovely Scottish burr
walked into the lab. Autumn Fraser. She was the surgeon
Giovanni had recruited to head Team Grace once the babies had been safely delivered.

If they got that far, Lizzy thought darkly, glaring at the
biocompatible model of the twins.

She grimaced, then forced on a smile. 'G'day. You all right?'

'Hi! Sorry. I was just hoping for a bit of…just trying to find somewhere—' Autumn stopped and started a couple more times until finally settling on, 'I didn't realise anyone else was in here.'

Lizzy instantly saw a kindred spirit. Someone hoping for a quiet space to mull over some extra-complicated thoughts. Her smile instantly grew warm with empathy. She'd had a nice impression of Autumn the smattering of times they'd crossed paths. Obviously they saw each other every day for the briefings, but somehow, apart from a short exchange in the locker room, when they'd promised to have a coffee together and talk about the joys of working with Italian surgeons, they hadn't yet got to know each other.

'Is it okay if I watch?' Autumn asked.

Lizzy stood back from the 'operating table' and held up her hands. 'Too late.'

'Oh?'

'I just killed your patient.'

'Ah…' Autumn stayed near the doorway, taking a quick read of the atmosphere in the room. Her concise nod and step back were an acknowledgement that she understood when a surgeon had had a bad day.

The nurse, whom Lizzy knew had live babies to look after, threw her a glance.

'Grazie mille,' she told her. 'Thank you for helping me work the mistakes out of my system.'

She threw in a laugh and a weird little victory punch, trying to prove she wasn't having an actual, proper meltdown in advance of the quickly approaching real-life surgery.

Autumn let the nurse pass, then hesitated, clearly unsure if she should go in or not.

'It's okay. Come on in, Autumn.'

Staying in a huff wasn't going to make this operation any easier. Also, if she was going to be performing surgery that would ultimately affect Grace's well-being, Autumn needed to be as up to speed as she was.

'Want to help me try again?'

'Delighted to.' Autumn's demeanour changed from wary to proactive. 'I want to get my head wrapped round as many angles of the twins' situation as possible.'

'Smart,' Lizzy said, moving the model she'd just used to one side and pulling another one into its place.

At least the technology was reliable here at St Nicolino's, she thought grumpily. Generous, even. Unlike the humans. The *men* in particular. Well… Not all men. Just the ones called Leon Cassanetti.

He'd been called away hours ago and hadn't bothered to come and find her again. Under normal circumstances she wouldn't have thought twice about it. She wasn't his keeper. But he'd been weird. Very weird…

Her mind raced back to the exam room for the nine hundredth time. What on earth had *happened* in there? They'd been so happy, sharing the joy of discovering they were going to have a daughter, and then, all of a sudden—*kablam!* His smile had disappeared as if someone had ripped his fuse out. Then off he'd gone with an excuse she'd used on at least a dozen dates she hadn't wanted to be on: surgery.

Sure, his excuse was legitimate, seeing as he was at work and a surreptitious walk-by of the surgical board did, in fact, have a list of surgeries Leon would be performing today, but a week ago he would've invited her to come along, or at least they would have had a private little kissing session in one of the on-call rooms in between. But this time….

Whatever. *Jerk.* The big chestnut-haired, espresso-eyed Italian so-and-so could take his 'marry me' to someone less gullible. She had known this would happen. Had known it from the start. The moment she'd agreed to fly over here, in fact.

Yes, she'd known in her heart of hearts that she'd be raising their child on her own—had embraced the fact, even. And then, just as he had back in New York, he'd spun her round that surgically perfect little finger of his and allowed her to believe things might turn out differently.

More fool her.

So it was back to Plan A. Because Plan B, which had always been half-formed at best, was quite clearly not destined for success.

Lizzy talked Autumn through the surgery—which, unsurprisingly, followed an exacting protocol. On the day, of course, there'd be a huge team of medical professionals. Perinatologists, cardiologists, radiologists, foetal surgeons, anaesthetists and, of course, Leon. Today, simply put, she needed to laparoscopically balloon dilate Hope's left heart valve in order to insert a small stent.

They began to work. Autumn asked the occasional question and Lizzy talked her through each move, occasionally lapsing into silence as she slipped first the laparoscope, then the tiny surgical tools, and finally the camera into place.

'And Leon will be monitoring Grace, throughout?'

Lizzy shot Autumn a sharp look. Why did she want to know about Leon? She sternly reminded herself that any normal surgeon working on a conjoined twins' case would want to know what was happening to 'her' baby during life-altering surgery to the other baby. It was a perfectly innocent and fairly essential question.

'Yes. He'll be there the whole time.'

Maybe Leon had wanted a boy. Could be as simple as that. He just needed time to rebuild the scenarios he'd built for himself and his son into new scenarios of him and his daughter.

Or... She paused mid-inflation of the balloon stent. Possibly...was he hurting?

She thought back to the childhood he'd had, with one parent walking out and the other keeping him at arm's length emotionally. There were studies proving that children raised without touch or affection could very easily veer towards sociopathic tendencies. Maybe that was why Leon was such a good surgeon. No actual feelings were running through him.

She remembered his caresses from the night before, his whispered terms of endearment, the sweet-as-honey kisses he'd given her before they'd left the flat that morning.

Nah.

She gave the balloon a microscopic inflation, then paused again.

'Everything okay?' Autumn asked.

'Just ensuring the left heart ventricle isn't increased at too rapid a rate of knots,' she lied, trying to figure out something—anything—that would explain why Leon had responded so poorly to the news that he was having a daughter.

Maybe he was experiencing hormones by proxy.

To be honest, if she loved him—if she really loved him as she thought she did—she'd have to learn to shake this kind of thing off. They were going to spend a lifetime together. Everybody needed alone-time, right? Everyone had occasional 'moments'. Especially when their life was going to change for ever in about four and a half months.

Then again...

'It isn't like he doesn't have options,' Lizzy said, with a frustrated harrumph.

'Sorry?' Autumn looked at her, confused.

'Leon!'

'Do you mean about Grace's heart? Were you planning on isolating the shared aortic valve during surgery?'

Lizzy stared at her for a minute, then withdrew her instruments from the model.

'I don't think I can do this.'

'What? Of course you can.'

The two of them stared at the model of the babies for a moment, and then Lizzy burst out laughing. 'No—sorry. I can do the surgery. I just don't think I can do it with, you know…' she pointed at her belly '…things up in the air the way they are.'

Autumn threw a look over her shoulder, as if hoping an escape route would present itself. The look said one of the two of them was acting a little bit irrationally, and it wasn't Autumn.

'I mean, why won't he just make up his mind?' Lizzy threw up her hands. 'One minute he's all "marry me" and the next he's all "I've got surgery…can't talk." What sort of father-to-be does that?'

Autumn, who obviously had absolutely no idea what Lizzy was talking about, said, 'Most of the fathers-to-be that I deal with are worse than the mums.'

Lizzy sat with that nugget for a minute. 'Yeah. I suppose you're right. Women have a much more present reality to cope with.' She pointed again at her swelling belly.

Autumn nodded. 'They're powerless, aren't they? The men? And men like to fix things. This is one thing they have absolutely no control over and it makes some of them a bit bonkers.'

'Especially surgeon men,' Lizzy said, with a *know what I mean* look.

Autumn gave an *oh, yes, I do* nod, shared a complicit smile and asked, 'Want to talk about it?' in a way that said she'd be a sounding board, but wouldn't be interfering.

'No!' Lizzy huffed. 'Yes…' She gave herself a little shake. 'Actually, it'd be nice to have a woman to talk to. But not just yet. I need to let all this maddening Italian man business marinate for a bit.' Her eyes shot to the door as a group of doctors raced past. 'Erm… Mind if we keep this little incident to ourselves?'

'What goes on in the lab, stays in the lab.' Autumn locked her lips with an invisible key and threw it away.

Lizzy gave her a grateful smile. She liked this woman. She hoped whoever she was avoiding wasn't half as frustrating as Leon.

A tiny exchange from that morning's briefing flared in her mind. One between Giovanni and Autumn. They'd been comparing notes and had begun speaking over one another, and then, just as quickly, deferring to each other to go first. It had ended in a weirdly awkward stalemate during which neither had spoken but they'd kept looking into one another's eyes.

Hmm… Lizzy's mind began to whirr. It wasn't often she was so caught up in her own personal dramas that she failed to notice a burgeoning romance. 'Coffee date some time?' she asked.

'Will there be cake?' Autumn laughed, then put on a nonchalant expression. 'Seeing as we're in Rome, and all.'

Lizzy's smile widened. 'Absolutely. Until then…enjoy the lab!'

'I consider it my new home away from home,' Autumn said, already settling in front of a fresh model of the twins.

Right, Lizzy vowed as she set off to find Leon. If they

were going to give this relationship a big dose of reality, maybe it was time they had their first proper fight.

Leon slid his key into the lock, hoping the occasional squeak his front door emitted wouldn't make a noise. It was late, and if Lizzy was asleep he didn't want to wake her.

'Hello, there.'

He knew in an instant that she'd caught his instinctive reaction—dismay—and also that he was in the doghouse.

'Don't worry. I'm making arrangements to stay at the hotel from tomorrow. Or,' she said, before he could protest, 'I can always go tonight. Don't worry about me.'

'I do worry about you, Lizzy. *Mea culpa.* I had surgeries.'

'Oh, I know. I'm not cross about that.'

He didn't have to ask her what she was actually cross about. It was written all over her face.

He'd shut her out.

It wouldn't have taken more than ten seconds to send a text saying he was held up. Telling himself it wasn't necessary, that she'd figure it out, was exactly the type of thing his mother would have done if she'd been out of sorts.

'*Scusi*, Lizzy. *Per favore.*'

He pressed his hands to his heart, on the brink of blaming it all on the day's surgical schedule getting away with him when he realised he owed her more than that. He owed her the truth.

'Don't move to the hotel. Stay. I had—how do you say it?—I had a blip.'

Lizzy screwed up her face, confusion taking over where there had previously been anger. 'What do you mean "a blip"?'

He sat down on the sofa beside her and took her hand in his. 'Seeing our daughter…knowing she was a she and not an it… I don't know… You think I'd be used to it. But because she's real…because she's *ours*… I suddenly felt inadequate.'

'What? What on earth would make you think that you, of all people, wouldn't be a great father?'

He shrugged. 'Conditioning, I guess.'

'You know your mother was wrong, right? She gave you bad advice about pretty much everything. No offence,' she hastily tacked on.

'Was she, though…?'

Leon wasn't defending her; he was genuinely trying to picture himself as a father. It was virtually impossible for him to picture it.

'You said so yourself, Lizzy.' He fanned his hand out across the immaculate flat. 'This place wasn't put together by someone who wanted a family.'

Lizzy gave him a hard stare, and after a moment said, 'I'm not going to try and talk you into having a baby you don't want, Leon. I told you that from the start. If you don't want me—'

He cut her off. 'That's not it at all. I do want you. Very, very much. And although I'm making a proper mess of it, I want our child, too, I just thought—'

'Oh, God.' Lizzy gave an exasperated sigh. 'You're not going to give me the "bad timing" talk, are you? Or— wait—is it the "it's not you it's me" talk?'

He gave her a sheepish smile. She was right on both counts.

Lizzy took her hand out of his and rearranged herself so she sat cross-legged on the sofa. She took a deep, shaky breath, then said, 'Did you ever know my father was emotionally abusive to my mother?'

Leon felt his heart slam against his chest. As if this dark

chapter of her past were a physical assault on the woman he loved and therefore, by extension, an assault on him. 'No.'

'She couldn't do anything right. Not in his eyes anyway. No matter what the situation, he always found a way to twist it so that she was to blame. But do you know the one thing she did do right, despite being totally screwed up and having no self-confidence and a huge closet full of unfulfilled dreams?'

Leon shook his head.

'She raised me to want something different. And up until I met you I thought I'd turned out mostly okay.'

Leon flinched. He knew he deserved that. 'Lizzy, you've turned out so much more than okay.'

She tipped her head back and forth, clearly unwilling to accept the compliment. Her eyes welled up as she continued. 'She loved me so fiercely. Protected me from whatever she could. Guided me as best she could. Did she do a perfect job? Probably not. I've got issues. I rarely speak to my father. I find it almost impossible to visit my mother's grave. I prefer to keep my past to myself—as evidenced by the fact that I'm only telling you this now. I fell in love with a man who finds it every bit as hard to fall in love as I do.' She threw up her hands, then unexpectedly smiled. 'I'm flawed. But who isn't? And do you know what else? Our child probably will be, too.'

'No. Lizzy. She's perfect.'

'*Now* she is,' Lizzy gently corrected him. 'But she's not lived yet. She's not had her pigtails pulled, or tripped on the street in front of laughing children, or been shouted at, or—'

Leon waved his hands for her to stop. He understood what she was saying. They needed to be this child's buffer against the world. And if he wasn't going to be there for Lizzy, there was no way he could be there for their daughter.

A hunger to prove to her that he was more than the sum of his past gripped him. He'd boxed himself into a world of work and recuperation that allowed for little else. Lizzy had been the one woman to let in all that amazing light the rest of the world had to offer. Their child would let in so much more. If he let her.

'Here.'

Lizzy sat up straighter, as if physically repositioning herself in order to dig deeper into the conversation than either of them would have done five years ago. And she was right to do it. They weren't singletons with nothing but their professions to worry about. They were going to be parents in a few months. He'd asked her to marry him, for heaven's sake. This was their future they were talking about.

'I'm going to give you a quiz,' Lizzy said brightly. Too brightly.

'What kind?' He shifted round on the sofa so that they were facing one another.

'A "How Prepared is Anyone for Parenthood?" Quiz.'

He laughed. Considering the hundreds of variations of parents he'd seen through the years this should be interesting...

She peppered him with questions about nappies and breast milk and E-numbers in baby food, and the sort of shoes he thought they should buy, and how important having a first birthday party was, considering the child wouldn't remember it. Then, abruptly, she shifted tack. 'How are clouds built? Out of marshmallows or cotton balls?'

'Neither,' Leon said, a bit surprised that she didn't know. 'Clouds are made up of water vapour—'

Lizzy cut him off with a buzzer sound. 'You're answering a three-year-old. At bedtime. A three-year-old who wants a story. Let's try again. "Papà?"' She put on a little girl's voice. "'How are clouds built?"'

Leon tapped his chin, then answered. 'They're built out of dreams, *cara*. That's why they come with silver linings.'

Lizzy nodded approvingly. 'Better.'

Leon ran his fingers along Lizzy's shoulder, then put his hand on her belly. 'Aren't you scared?'

'Terrified,' she answered, with a directness that, rather than frightening him, made him feel closer to her than he ever had. 'But I'll be less scared if I know I don't have to do it alone.'

'Right, then,' he said. 'Looks like I'm going to have to train myself to text when I'm going to be kept late at the hospital.'

'Old dog, new tricks?' Lizzy quipped.

'Something like that.' He laughed, giving her a soft kiss. And then, hand in hand, they went to bed.

CHAPTER THIRTEEN

LIZZY AND LEON were mid-chorus in the scrub room when Giovanni Lombardi walked in.

He looked between the pair of them: Leon mid-dance move at the scrub sink, Lizzy playing a rather exuberant air guitar.

'You two are full of the joys of life today,' Giovanni said, with a look that suggested he wasn't quite sure he trusted it.

They had told him about their pregnancy situation a few days earlier as a professional courtesy, after he'd found Lizzy asleep in the practice lab. He had appeared unsurprised, obviously having seen that Lizzy's floaty clothes wardrobe had pretty much become a clingy clothes wardrobe.

She must do that shop!

Giovanni, ever the gentleman, hadn't asked for details, merely an assurance that she was physically up to doing today's surgery—which, of course, he'd received. So, all in all, it had been a big week. Their first fight. Their first adult conflict resolution. Their first after-fight make-up session—extra-sexy. And now life-altering surgery on a little girl who still had all this glorious falling in love yo-yo ride yet to come.

'It's a big day.' Lizzy gave Giovanni a grin, taking a

surgical gown down from the supplies shelf and laying it out on the sterilised counter. She grabbed a packet of plastic gloves and dropped them onto the sterile gown without touching them. Protocol was everything on any day in the surgical ward, but today it felt even more important.

'Are you observing or scrubbing in?' Leon asked his boss, switching his scrub brush to his other hand.

'Observing,' Giovanni said. 'With Autumn.'

There had been, if Lizzy wasn't mistaken, the tiniest bit of weight added to Autumn's name when he'd said it. Hmm…perhaps she and Leon weren't the only ones holding a secret set of love cards close to their chests.

'Things are going well with her?' Leon asked, oblivious.

Giovanni made a noise that was hard to interpret, then muttered something about having to check on how Gabrielle was doing with the anaesthetist.

Lizzy joined Leon at the sink, opening the package that contained her sterile nail brush, scrub spine and nail pick, laying each one out on the back of the specialised sink while she worked a few drops of scrub solution into a thick lather.

'You look like you're preparing for a bubble bath,' Leon said.

'If that's a suggestion for a post-operation date, I'm all for it.' Lizzy gave him a light hip-bump.

She couldn't see his lovely mouth because, as protocol dictated, he was already wearing his mask, but she could tell he was smiling from the crinkles fanning out alongside those gorgeous eyes of his. She, too, put her mask on, then began the detailed process of scrubbing in.

This felt good. Really good. Standing next to her man. With surges of pre-surgical adrenaline adding an extra bounce to her step. She'd pretty much lived in the practice lab for the past few days and now she felt prepared for anything. Especially with things so good between her and Leon.

If she'd thought she loved him before their little contretemps last week, she loved him even more now they'd talked it out. Treated one another with respect. Given each other the room to be frightened and assured one another they were not in this alone.

She gave herself a smug little mental pat on the back. Theirs was shaping up to be an actual grown-up relationship. Something she'd never made room for in her life. She obviously hadn't been given a stunning example by her parents, so this was an incredibly steep learning curve, but, yes, they were happy. And about to make medical history.

All in all, a pretty good way to start a day. Especially when she factored in the pastries they'd bought on the way into the hospital. *Scrumptious.* She hadn't told Leon yet, but she was already actively considering staying here in Rome rather than asking Leon to move to Sydney...

She pushed away those thoughts. Logistics could come later. They still had months to figure those out.

'Here she comes.'

Leon tipped his head towards the operating theatre where Gabrielle and her ever-increasing tummy were being wheeled in. She was already anaesthetised via an epidural, and it was reassuring to see her features, increasingly tense these past couple of weeks, relaxed and at ease. She was awake, and would be throughout the procedure. A small grin appeared as she caught sight of Lizzy and Leon at the window. She lifted her hand, already fitted with a drip catheter, and wiggled her fingers.

Lizzy felt a gratifying squeeze in her heart. It was that expression that always gave her an extra fire to care for her patients and protect them from any harm that might come their way. They were so vulnerable. So trusting. And it wasn't just one life Gabrielle had entrusted them with today—it was three.

'Ready?' Lizzy stepped back from the sink, her arms crooking into the surgical gown the scrub nurse was holding for her.

'As I'll ever be,' Leon replied, his eyes flashing with that same flare of brilliance that had first drawn her to him during their very first surgery together all those years ago.

They entered the surgical theatre.

'How're you feeling?' Lizzy asked Gabrielle. 'I'd give your hand a squeeze, but—' She held up her gloved hands.

'No, you do exactly what you have to do for my little Hope,' Gabrielle said. 'We believe in you. And Dr Cassanetti, of course.'

Lizzy's eyes flicked to Leon's. He was shaking his head.

'It's all about Dr Beckley today, Gabrielle. I'm here as back-up. You've got one of the world's best surgeons here to help you, so your job is to lie back and relax.'

Gabrielle laughed. 'Relax? I'll try my best. At least I know I won't be moving. I can't feel a thing!'

'Sounds about right,' Leon said warmly. 'We've got you.'

He looked across at Lizzy, who somehow felt the words were meant for her as well. He had her back. He was there to be her support system. And knowing that meant the world.

'We'll all be putting our very best feet forward today, I promise you,' Lizzy assured her, before thanking the team for being there. Then she asked one of the surgical nurses to start the clock they used to time surgeries, gave Leon a nod to say that it was time for them to take their positions and, without any fanfare, the procedure began.

Time took on another quality as the first crucial keyhole incision was made. Though the entire procedure would take less than an hour, Lizzy knew that by the time they had finished it would feel as if the world had rotated on its axis. But the countless hours she, Leon and the team had spent in the practice lab were paying dividends. The dream team she and Leon had once been was well and truly back in action.

'How're Grace's stats?'

'Holding steady.'

'Mum? How are you doing?'

One of the obstetrics team in charge of Gabrielle gave a thumbs-up and Gabrielle herself, hidden behind a surgical drape, said she couldn't believe how lucky they were to have found St Nicolino's, and Leon and Lizzy, and Giovanni and Autumn. Then she began listing all her favourite nurses, and the puddings she had eaten that week, before rhapsodising about some deep-fried courgette flowers laced with truffled honey that her husband had brought her the other day from a street vendor.

Did they know she loved her husband? she asked. She loved him more than anyone or anything else in the world. That might change when the babies were born, of course, but who else would go out scouting for things she could eat? She hadn't been able to eat before today's operation and she was starving. Did stomachs rumble when there was an epidural?

Lizzy grinned at Leon. This was good. Having a relaxed, happy patient, a bit punch-drunk on the anaesthetic all factored into the feel-good environment critical to the kind of surgery that could so easily end in tragedy.

It was a precarious balance. Sharing the central aortic valve meant that each of the babies relied on the other's blood flow, and as Hope's blood flow was compromised by the underdevelopment of the left side of her heart, the strain would be felt by both girls.

Lizzy glanced up at the monitor, where she could now see a perfect image of Hope's heart. On the screen, of course, it was large, and showed all the details required to make the surgery a success. In reality, Hope's heart was the size of a large grape. And Lizzy was going to have to pierce through the thick wall of that heart with exacting precision, then guide the catheter through the chambers of the heart cavity into the left atrium—which was, at this point, about the size of a pea. She'd inflate the tiny balloon at the tip of the catheter before withdrawing the needle, touching absolutely nothing along the way.

No pressure, then...

She felt a scrub nurse reach up and pat her brow.

Yup. Things were getting serious.

Lizzy glanced around the room at all the concentrating medical professionals. They had the best team in the country here. Foetal cardiologists, obstetricians, imaging experts, maternal and foetal anaesthetists... The amount of brain power in this room could run a nation—but today they were saving a child's life. Without this surgical intervention Hope's chances of survival were limited. And as a result, so were Grace's.

'Are you ready?'

Lizzy looked into Leon's eyes, seeking that extra shot of confidence she needed to start the core elements of the procedure. She blinked once and saw trust. She blinked again and saw confidence. The third time she saw love. A rush of strength filled her with a tightly coiled burst of exacting energy. Precisely what she needed in this moment.

Apart from her voice, talking the team through her every move, the operating room was filled with little noise beyond the muted sounds of the equipment. Drips were in place. Extra pairs of hands were standing by if needed.

Surgical nurses had stepped into place to hold each of Gabrielle's hands.

Lizzy glanced up to the observation deck and saw Giovanni lean forward, elbows on knees, cupping his chin in his hands as she prepared to make her life-changing move. Autumn was there, biting her lower lip. This surgery was as important for them as it was for her.

Lizzy looked back at the monitor, took in a deep, steadying breath, then began to offer Hope a better chance of survival…

Everything in Leon stilled as he watched the high-tech ultrasound images appearing on the screen across the room from him. Though this surgery was precisely the reason he'd flown Lizzy halfway across the world, he watched in awe as she inserted the catheter with such unerring confidence it was as if she'd done it a thousand times.

She had done it once. On a single child. The risks with Hope and Grace were so much higher that he doubted more than a handful of surgeons in the world would have risked it. But if she didn't try—if they, as a team, didn't try—it would effectively be giving up on Hope and Grace. And giving up wasn't something they liked to do here at St Nicolino's.

He kept an eye on Grace's heart as Lizzy carefully inflated the tiny balloon that would open the stenotic aortic valve. The intervention would allow the left ventricle to grow properly, ensuring normal blood flow in the heart.

Lizzy carefully pulled out the needle, having inflated the balloon just enough, and after a few more minutes of removing surgical tools, said, 'And… Hope's got herself a happier heart. How're you doing, Mum?'

Gabrielle choked back a sob of relief. 'Is it done? Really?'

'All done.' Lizzy walked around the surgical drape so

she could look at Gabrielle, whose eyes were brimming with tears. 'We just need to close up the small incision and you can go back to your room to be with Matteo.'

The closing team stepped into place and began the small but essential procedure. Out of the corner of her eye Lizzy could see everyone in the gallery clapping, giving one another high-fives and fist-bumps.

'He won't believe this,' Gabrielle said, now openly crying. 'He simply won't believe it. Our little girls... They have a fighting chance now. Thank you. No other hospital would do this. We will owe you for ever.'

'No.' Lizzy shook her head. 'You owe your thanks to Dr Cassanetti. He's the one who rang me, so he's the one you should be thanking.'

Leon raised his hand in acknowledgement. Generous to a fault, Lizzy was. Talented, generous, fearless... They were all things he'd seen before in Lizzy, but never with the understanding that she had come from a home filled with fear. A home that had lacked paternal love and support—just as his had.

Medicine. An impassioned drive to help innocents have a better start in life. A fiercely guarded heart. Were those just a few of the invisible strings that had drawn them together?

Very likely. And doubtless there would be more.

They would also find things they completely disagreed on. Moral stances on world issues. Ethical decisions when it came to deciding which surgeries were and were not risks worth taking. Whether or not toast was actually edible if it was burnt.

But they'd stick by one another *because* of their differences, not despite them. And for the first time in his life the prospect of a complicated, messy life excited him.

'Catch up in twenty minutes?' Lizzy asked as she

passed Leon on the way out of the theatre, while the team prepared to take Gabrielle to her room.

'Sure. But...' He furrowed his brow, trying to figure out what she was doing.

'I'm just going to nip out and get some air before we talk the Bianchis through the next steps.'

When she didn't reappear as promised, instinct guided him to her.

He pushed open the door to the hospital's south wing rooftop terrace and looked across the broad expanse of the healing garden Giovanni had commissioned a few years back. It had a pair of shaded loggias, and trees heavy with blossom. There were water features and private little nooks where patients or anxious family members could sit and read, have their lunch—or, in Lizzy's case, have a quiet little weep.

Her back was to him, but he could see the tell-tale shake he'd become familiar with in his years as a surgeon. The shoulders of someone desperately trying to keep deep emotion at bay, but ultimately failing.

He walked through a waft of orange blossom scent as he made his way towards her. Above them, on the higher west wing roof, a helicopter came in. He heard the calls of the emergency staff, barely audible above the whirr of the helicopter blades. It was an acute reminder of the fragility of life. Two lives had been saved today. Others, most likely, would be lost.

He sat down beside her, not saying anything. She gave his knee an acknowledging pat. He handed her a clean handkerchief. He hoped they were tears of relief, not sorrow. A release after weeks of pent-up will I/won't I fears.

After her breathing had steadied, he said, 'You were brilliant today.'

She pursed her lips.

'Take the compliment, *cara*,' he urged gently. 'I don't hand them out that often.'

She parted her lips to protest, then stopped herself, a look of surprise taking over from where the disbelief had just been. 'You don't, do you?'

He shook his head. 'Not a big fan.'

She screwed up her face. 'Of compliments? Who doesn't like compliments?'

He hitched up a shoulder in response. Him. He didn't. Words never stood as proof to him that people felt a certain way. Actions did. And today Lizzy had made good on her promise to deliver a faultless surgery.

'You're just like my father.'

'What?' He shook his head. 'Sorry. I don't see the link.'

She lifted her phone from the bench. The face of it was freshly cracked, as if it had been hurled in anger.

'You rang your father?'

'Yup,' she said tightly.

'Why?'

She scrubbed her fingers through her hair, tugged out her ponytail and then did it up again, so tightly it looked almost painful. 'It was stupid. I rarely ring him—I mean, apart from birthdays and stuff—but I thought...' Her voice caught in her throat. She waited until the wave of emotion had passed before she spoke again. 'You know he's a cardiologist, right?'

Leon nodded. 'A well-respected cardiologist.'

Lizzy scrubbed her hands over her face, then through her fingers admitted, 'I thought what I did today—what *we* did today—might make him proud.'

Leon pulled her hands down, giving her knuckles a kiss. 'It should have. Any parent would be bursting at the seams to know their child had just changed another child's chances of survival.'

She put on a deep voice and a disdainful expression. '"What a waste of time and money. The child will most likely die anyway. The pair of them, probably. You think you've done something worthy today? Think again, Elizabeth. Think again."' She looked across at Leon, tears pouring down her face. 'I should have known this was what would happen. It's what always happens when I call home to brag.'

'It's not bragging, Lizzy—'

She shook her head. 'In my father's eyes, it is. There doesn't seem to be a single thing I can do to win his respect!' She wheeled on Leon with a ferocity he'd never seen from her. 'Did you know the only reason I accepted the job back in Sydney was for him? To prove to him—up close and personal—that I was worth loving?'

He wanted to cut in. To tell her that she had always been worth loving, and that if she'd let him he'd prove it. But she wasn't receiving information right now, and he had long ago sworn he wouldn't make promises he couldn't keep.

She carried on detailing her father's cruel tirade, and as she did so Leon felt as if she were plunging a knife deeper and deeper into his gut. So, this was how she'd been raised. With scorn. Contempt. No matter what Lizzy had done, her father had done something better. The actions of an insecure man taking out his unhappiness with the world on the only two people who had ever shown him true loyalty: Lizzy and her mother.

Lizzy's tears, he realised, as he felt his heart shredded into strips, weren't of relief. They were of sorrow. Bone-deep sorrow because no matter what she did it might never be enough to win her father's pure, uncomplicated love. It was something he didn't seem capable of.

And in that instant Leon knew that he couldn't ever,

ever subject his child to the sort of behaviour ingrained in Lizzy as normal.

Lizzy gave an angry *'Grr...'* Then, 'I just want to fly home and have it out with him, you know? March him through Sydney, past every child who's now in kindergarten, or grade school, or learning to ski, or doing their first somersault, and say, *See that child? That child would be dead if it weren't for me!'*

There was rage in her voice. But more than that there was anguish. And hopelessness. He got it. He'd tried to please a man who had walked out on him through no fault of his. A man he'd made himself intentionally lose track of so that he'd never have to go through what Lizzy was going through now.

The only difference between him and Lizzy, he supposed, was that Lizzy still actually spoke to her father. But the truth was, no matter how far away his own father was, how distant they were, he knew his father lived in his heart. Snagging and cutting and reopening those childhood wounds at unexpected moments like these, when he had to fight like hell not to cut and run. These were the moments his father hadn't wanted any part of. Moments his mother would have used as proof that she was right to keep her emotions closed.

'What do you want me to do?' he asked.

'Nothing!' she snapped. 'You can't do anything to help, so just back off—all right? It's what you're best at, isn't it? Walking away when things are good? Well, let this stand as proof that you should've handed me my walking papers after the surgery.'

Leon bridled, but didn't say anything. She was hurting and lashing out. Hitting him where she knew it would hurt.

He sat with her a moment longer, then pressed himself

up to stand. 'How about I let the Bianchis know you'll be down in a bit?'

She held up a hand, but didn't look at him. 'No. I'll speak with them. Give me five minutes and I'll be down.'

Leon didn't like walking away—not like this—but he knew she was right. In this instance there wasn't anything he could do.

A few splashes of cold water and a bit of freshly applied make-up later, Lizzy felt as though she'd reined in her feelings enough to face the Bianchis.

When she got to their room she discovered that Leon hadn't, as per her request, waited for her to speak to the couple. The three of them were laughing about something, and when they all looked across at her as one, instead of relaxing her, their camaraderie made her feel painfully isolated. Not so much Gabrielle and Matteo. They were innocents in this. It was Leon who was making her cross.

She'd asked him to wait.

Why was it that the men in her life steamrollered along without a care in the world about the feelings of the people who loved them? It wasn't as if she hadn't taken his feelings into consideration when she'd found out she was pregnant. She'd flown halfway around the world to tell Leon face to face that he was having a child. Sure, she hadn't done it with any particular grace or class, but she'd done it. She'd done what an honourable, decent person would do, regardless of the countless hoops she'd had to jump through.

She'd had to get a replacement—three, actually—to cover her long absence from the hospital. And that would have to be taken into account again, in a few months' time, when she actually had the baby. Not to mention that it was Leon's malfunctioning condom that had got them

into this mess in the first place! Sure, she might've insti-
gated things by looking completely and totally sizzling hot
at the conference supper—even if she did say so herself.
And she'd had just-in-case condoms, too. Reliable ones.
But, no! They'd had to use Leon's.

And now she was carrying the baby of the one man in
the world she'd ever loved. But today… Today she didn't
like him very much. Especially right now.

'Dr Beckley.' Leon's smile was tentative as his eyes
connected with hers. 'Good to see you. I was just telling
the Bianchis we have some recordings of the sonograms
if they want to send the audio and a few stills of their children's heartbeats to family back home. Apparently, their
phones haven't stopped ringing.'

Oh, terrific, she thought sourly, with a barely contained
eye-roll. Lucky Bianchis. *They* had families who *cared*.
Families who celebrated when it was appropriate. Families who celebrated when—

She stopped herself. She was being horrid. This wasn't
her. This wasn't the woman she wanted to be or the doctor she had trained herself to become. More to the point,
this type of reactive behaviour and self-sabotage wasn't
anywhere near the woman she wanted to be when she became a mother.

It wasn't anyone's fault—not even her own—that her
father was a jackass. But it could still make her mad.

She tried to shoot Leon a not entirely apologetic look
for being so awful to him up on the roof, but he wasn't
looking at her. He was doing what any good doctor offer-
ing antenatal care to a woman who had just gone through
exceedingly rare in utero surgery should. Focussing on
his patients.

Forcing herself to regroup, she managed to tag on to the
end of Matteo asking Leon what happened next.

She jumped in. 'The babies are in the best possible place right now. Gabrielle's beautiful natural incubator. There is a chance, of course, that Hope will need surgery shortly after she's born, depending on how long we can keep the babies where they are. She could outgrow the stent we put in today—which, big picture, is a good thing, because it would mean a longer gestational period, but as you know the risks are high.'

She rattled off a few things they'd been through before, including gestational diabetes and pre-eclampsia, then realised she had gone on for far too long and wrapped up quickly. 'But ultimately we're hoping it all goes like clockwork.'

She faltered as she saw their expressions shift from slightly confused to very confused, and then, more horrifyingly, to worried.

'Ah, *scusi*, Dr Beckley…?'

Leon was speaking in his 'polite' voice. The one that carried one very clear emotion—disappointment.

'We were talking about how to fry courgette flowers with ricotta.'

Lizzy gulped. 'You were…?'

'*Si.* Matteo's family are big foodies, and after these two enjoyed the *zucchini fritti* from Mercato Testaccio, they wanted to know if they were easy to make.'

'And are they?' she asked, at a complete loss as to how she'd got so caught up in her own problems she'd forgotten to focus on the people today was really about.

'Very. If you take your time and pay attention,' he added pointedly.

Even though his words hadn't entered her gut with the same cruel twist her father's words always did, Lizzy felt they were laced with the same disapproving venom. Her insecurities, having been contained as best she could these past few months, threatened to take over.

Leon thought she was careless. He thought she'd behaved poorly. He thought she wasn't worthy of the responsibilities he had given her. And, more devastatingly, he couldn't bear the idea that she was the woman who was going to be the mother of his child.

Completely flustered, she began explaining to the Bianchis about her brain being still caught up in the surgery, which she was so pleased about she'd not really been able to take anything else in. But she could feel an uncomfortable heat in Leon's gaze, and as quickly as she could she excused herself, assuring the Bianchis that she'd be back later in the afternoon to do another sonogram on the babies, so that they would have all sorts of recordings to send to family and friends.

'To anyone at all!'

She hot-rodded it to the changing rooms, almost knocking Autumn over in the process.

'Everything okay?' Autumn asked, her Scottish burr making the words sound utterly musical.

It was soothing. A foolish idea popped into her head. Wouldn't it be lovely to hear Autumn tell her a story? A fairy tale in which everything ended perfectly. Where the hero and heroine held one another close and promised each another a lifetime of joy, and the baddies melted away into little puddles of insignificance.

It would, of course, be completely ridiculous to ask. Even so, it would be so lovely to have someone outside her bubble of hysteria to speak with. Someone who had some perspective. Maybe she should ask her advice on what she thought a single, pregnant woman who had just snapped the head off her baby daddy and didn't really know if she was coming or going should do.

'Have you ever acted like a complete idiot in front of a patient?' she asked instead.

'Absolutely,' Autumn replied without a moment's hesitation. 'It's inevitable, given what we do.'

'What did you do about it after?'

The tiniest, most cowardly part of her was hoping that Autumn would say that she'd pretended it had never happened and life went on to be perfectly perfect.

'I marched right back in there, apologised, and set things straight.' Autumn pushed her hands into her scrubs pockets. 'If you deal with it straight away I find most patients are pretty forgiving. They want to believe we're extraordinary, but there's a part of them that takes comfort from the fact that we, too, are mortal. In other words you can make mistakes in your bedside manner, but you can't in Theatre.'

Lizzy hung her head. Yeah… That sounded about right. She looked back up at Autumn, whose green eyes were warm with compassion.

'Our patients come to us when they're vulnerable, scared, and have absolutely no control over what is happening in their own bodies. Being entrusted with their hope is an equally scary thing, but I'd rather be in my shoes than theirs. Wouldn't you?'

Lizzy nodded, grateful that Autumn's question was rhetorical and, mercifully, had been delivered without judgement.

They made another vague plan to 'do coffee' before Lizzy did an about-face and headed back to the Bianchis' room, where—thankfully—there was no sign of Leon. She apologised from the bottom of her heart. Even squeezed a few laughs out of them by re-enacting the time she'd dressed up as a unicorn one Halloween, only to get her horn stuck when the lift doors were closing, so the fire brigade had to free her.

Now for the harder part, she thought, as she forced herself to head to Leon's office. She owed him an apology for lashing out at him. For taking his appearance in the Bianchis' room personally. He was a doctor above anything—especially here at the hospital—and of course that meant his patients came first.

She heard him before she saw him. It sounded like a one-way conversation, so most likely he was on the phone. It couldn't be that private, because the door was open, so she hovered beside it, waiting for the call to end.

Thirty seconds later she wished she'd asked Autumn for that story instead.

'...and if my daughter's born here in Italy, her citizenship will be Italian, not Australian, right?' Leon was asking. He murmured a few 'I sees' and a couple of 'Interestings'.

Lizzy tried to tell herself the question was a perfectly natural one for him to ask. Even so...prickles of fear ran along her skin.

'So, no one can take her away, then?'

Lizzy's hands flew to her throat, where her heart had lodging too tightly for her to breathe. What was he doing? Was he trying to keep their little girl here? Trying to gain custody before she was even born?

Leon's voice had turned very serious now. 'And how quickly can I apply for parental responsibility? *Si?* Straight away. And the mother's parental responsibility is automatic? I see. *Va bene.*'

Blood was roaring so loudly in Lizzy's brain that she couldn't hear any more.

Leon was trying to take control of their child before she'd even given birth to her. It was precisely the sort of thing her father would have done. Precisely the kind of future she'd vowed her daughter would never, ever have.

So, she did the only thing she could think of.

She ran.

CHAPTER FOURTEEN

LEON WAS BESIDE HIMSELF. He couldn't find Lizzy anywhere. She wasn't answering his calls or his texts. She wasn't on the roof garden or in the flat. He'd careered around Rome on his scooter, revisiting the places they'd been together in the vain hope that he would find her. He'd even rung the airlines who had flights to Sydney that evening, only to be informed there was no chance he could get access to any flight manifest.

When he got back to the hospital he ran straight to the Bianchis' room, only to be told he had just missed her.

'Literally,' Gabrielle said, clearly clocking the frustration he didn't have the energy to disguise. 'Maybe five minutes ago?' She looked at her husband who nodded. It had been about that.

Leon's instinct was to page her on the hospital's PA system. Call Security and have them stop her. Or do more of what he'd been doing and run around with his eyes peeled for a glimpse of that singular swathe of straw-blonde hair. Surely he could catch up with a pregnant woman?

He turned to go but the Bianchis were feeling chatty. Wreathed in smiles, the couple told him how Lizzy had been so kind. She'd made both audio and video recordings from the surgery, and done a fresh sonogram just twenty minutes earlier, so that they had plenty of updates to share with their families back home.

'And what happened then?'

'And then she left,' Matteo said, hoicking himself up onto his wife's bed and pulling her into a cuddle. 'Said she'd check in tomorrow.' He grinned at his wife, then dropped a kiss onto her forehead.

The gesture doubled Leon's need to find Lizzy. He wanted what they had. The automatic instinct to protect each other. To care. To be there even in this kind of unbelievably frightening time and still find a way to line it with hope. The kind of hope he should have invested in a future with Lizzy a long time ago.

He'd got it all wrong on the roof.

He should've held her. Supported her. Told her that her father had absolutely no idea what he was talking about and that she was one of the most talented, amazing women he'd ever met. But most of all, he should've just been there for her.

She didn't need the situation to be fixed. No one was ever going to be able to change her father. But he could change himself. He could admit that he loved her. Admit that it scared him because love was like that first surgical cut. You didn't always know what you were getting, but you did it anyway because you had to. And that was where he was. At the do I/don't I crossroads.

'Did she say where she was going?'

They both shook their heads in the negative.

'And how did she seem?' he asked, trying and failing to ratchet down the intensity of his request. 'You know… in herself?'

Gabrielle and Matteo shared a look. One that indicated they had definitely talked about Lizzy and, very possibly, about him.

He gave up on being polite.

'Per favore...' He put his hands in the prayer position. 'Did she give any indication as to where she was going? I must find her.'

Gabrielle squealed and grinned triumphantly at Matteo. 'I *knew* it! I told you, didn't I? The baby may or may not be his, but he loves her!' Her eyes widened and she clapped her hand over her mouth.

Matteo shot him an apologetic smile. *'Scusi, Dottore.* My wife—she has far too much time on her hands, so she makes up little stories about everyone.'

Leon felt more exposed than he ever had in front of a patient—but, in another first, he found he didn't really care. Role reversal at its finest.

'No,' he admitted, priming himself for what he needed to say to Lizzy. 'You're right. I love her.'

'And the baby?' Gabrielle held her breath.

'Mine,' he confirmed, with a swell of pride gripping his chest so fiercely he knew what he had to do.

He ran to the nurses' desk, took the phone they used for the public address system and dialled in a code.

Lizzy cocked her head to one side.

Had that been—?

Her heart skipped a beat.

It was Leon on the PA system. He was calling a Code Aquamarine.

The colour he used to describe her eyes.

She was transported back to one particularly perfect bubble bath they'd taken together in her tiny New York studio. It had been early days for their internships and their relationship. She frowned. If you could even have called it that. They'd just led their very first in utero surgery as a team. Twin-to-twin transfusion syndrome. It had been a resounding success and they had left the hospital feeling on top of the world.

They'd walked to her place, grabbing some pizza and some ice cream on the way. Once there, they'd filled her tub with citrus-scented bubbles and sloshed around kissing, relaxing and reliving the surgery, revelling in how well they'd worked together. The dream team.

He had kissed her bubble-coated fingertips and told her that if he was ever floundering, if he ever needed to feel as positive as he did in that moment, he would commandeer the hospital's PA and call a Code Aquamarine.

She'd locked that moment in its own compartment inside her heart. It was, she believed, the closest he'd ever come to telling her that he loved her. She'd almost blurted out that she loved him, but knowing somewhere deep inside her that their time in New York was exactly that, she'd stayed silent.

So, like any career girl intent on climbing the ladder rather than walking down the aisle, she'd laughed and pointed out the flaws in his plan. She might not be in that hospital, for one.

He'd snorted and said, 'As if!'

And, of course, he'd been right. Because here she was, seven years later, feeling more torn that she'd ever felt in her life. And where had she sought refuge? The waiting room of the emergency department.

It was the best place to put things into perspective. Parents were bringing their children in, often in tears, as they sought help for a broken arm, or a fever that wouldn't go away, or a cut on the forehead from a run-in with a countertop. She felt their pain by proxy, itching to take it away, and almost physically felt their relief as one of her colleagues took the child in their arms and said, yes, they would help. Of course they would help.

The ones that really got to her, of course, were those terror-stricken parents racing in with a child in their arms, limp or screaming, clearly in need of immediate assistance. Those were the ones who got her back on her feet, adding herself to the 'pit crew' in the ED, proactively taking away both the physical and emotional pain the family were enduring and with it her own pain…whatever it had been.

But this time nothing had moved her from her seat.

She sat, her hands on her stomach, concentrating all her energies on her child—a baby who was little more than the odd flutter of butterfly wings in her belly—and praying for some sort of sign that would tell her what to do. Stay? Go? Endure the pain of loving someone who didn't love her as perfectly as a Prince Charming, knowing that without the lows there couldn't be the highs of making love, swapping ice cream cones, or sharing a secret smile in the operating theatre. The moments that made her world feel perfect.

Or, in Leon-speak, aquamarine.

Until this very moment the code had completely slipped her mind.

Because, she snippily reminded herself, *he'd never needed her before.* And the only reason he wanted her now was to make sure she didn't leave the country before he could take their baby away from her.

Or… The tiniest ember of hope sprang to life in her chest. Or maybe he'd realised he didn't feel whole without her…

Unable to put herself through any more emotional turmoil—picturing herself being handed over to police custody until she gave birth had a way of tying a girl in knots—she pulled out her phone and texted him. As Autumn had more or less said, it was better to face one's mistakes head-on, deal with the consequences, then move on.

* * *

Relief flooded Leon's chest the moment he saw her, tucked away in a corner of the ED waiting room. Why on earth was she there?

'*Amore mio.*' He dropped to his knees and took her hands in his. 'You scared me.'

'Why?'

There was wariness in her voice. That same self-protectiveness she'd worn like a shield when she'd told him she was pregnant.

'I couldn't find you. I wanted to talk.'

She stiffened. 'What about?'

He looked round the waiting room. It was relatively quiet, but it wasn't where he wanted to have *this* talk with *this* woman.

He glanced at his watch. 'Let's go out.'

She looked at him as if he were mad. 'I'm not going *anywhere* until you tell me whether or not my rights as a mother are protected.'

What the hell...? 'Your rights are precisely what I've been trying to figure out.'

She shook her head, not understanding.

'I've been researching what our child's legal rights are if she's born here—'

Lizzy abruptly stood up, her eyes blazing. 'Don't you think for one second you're getting sole custody of our daughter.'

For a second time the oxygen left his lungs. 'Lizzy, what are you planning?'

'I don't know yet,' she said, her chin jutting out, eyes blazing with defiance.

He caught the tiniest shake in her hands as she protectively knitted them together over the curve of her belly.

'But I know what you're trying to do. Get sole custody. I heard you on the phone.'

Compassion replenished his energy stores. She'd got it so wrong. His instinct was to pull her in close, hold her tight, but she was radiating anger and cuddling was definitely not on the cards. Yet.

'What exactly did you hear?'

'You were talking on the phone to someone—a lawyer, I presume—about whether or not you could have custody of the baby.' Her hands shifted protectively over her stomach.

He knew he shouldn't laugh at the misunderstanding. That was never a good way to react to an angry woman—especially an angry woman carrying your child. But huge blasts of relief and joy and, yes, love, were obliterating all the core-deep fear that had, mercifully, led him to her, each step opening his heart wide to their relationship and all its inevitable ups and downs.

He wanted it all. The laughter, the joy, the pain, the trust. But most of all he wanted the love he knew would only grow stronger. So, instead of laughing at her mistake, he crowded his myriad emotions into a soft smile and was met, unsurprisingly, with a defensive glare. She looked proud, brave, fiercely protective—everything he'd imagined she would be when their child was finally born. Everything he hoped she'd embody as a mother.

'Lizzy, I didn't want to do this here, but… I was talking to an immigration lawyer about you.'

He could almost see the flames stoking her fury.

'Why would you need to do that?'

'Because I don't want you to leave.'

Again, that defiant tilt to her chin presented itself. 'You don't get to tell me what to do.'

'I know. Which is why I am asking, right here, right

now, in the centre of the emergency department, if you would do me the honour of being my wife.'

'You've got to stop asking me that when you don't mean it!' she said automatically, and then she looked at him—really looked at him.

He watched her as what she saw caused her breath to hitch. He knew his eyes were alight with something she hadn't seen before. Commitment. Pure, unswayable, solid-as-a-rock commitment. He'd felt the transition happen somewhere between the roof, the Bianchis' room and the moment when her text had come through. The one that had said, I'm here.

He loved Lizzy. With every fibre of his being. He wanted her. He wanted to be a father to the baby girl she was carrying and, if they were blessed, all the other babies yet to come.

'I want you to stay. Here. As my wife. If you'd like that, too. That's why I was speaking to the lawyer. To see what we needed to do for you to stay here. Legally. Beyond the Bianchis' surgery. It's up to you, obviously, but if you don't want to go back to Sydney, it's possible. I've spoken with Giovanni. He's happy to offer you a job here. You can live with me. We can move flats, if you like. Move cities. Countries. Whatever it takes, Lizzy. I want to do whatever it takes to give you and our child a happy, loving life.'

She shook her head, clearly trying and failing to match up what she'd heard him say on the phone with what he was asking now. 'No. You were talking about the baby. How you wanted to keep her here.'

'*And* you!'

She shifted her feet, the tension in her shoulders giving a little. 'Really?' Her eyes narrowed, and her shoulders inched back up to her ears. 'Not just until the baby's born?'

Leon gave in to the urge to laugh. He clearly wasn't

going to get an answer to his proposal just yet. Not without a long talk.

'I wanted to find out how to get you an Italian passport.'

'Why would I need one of those?'

'It might be handy for when you travel with our daughter. It would also help if you want to work here. But if you'd rather be in Sydney, there are ways to make that happen, too.'

She frowned. 'So…you weren't finding out ways to keep me here against my will?'

Now he really did have to laugh. 'Lizzy, I love you. I want to do everything in my power to make you happy. To write our own history. One where you don't need your father's approval. Or mine, for that matter. One where you realise how amazing you are. How strong. How resilient. And how very much I love you.'

Her features softened enough to reveal the anxiety hidden in the creases of anger she'd been holding tight. 'And would that make you happy? Is that why you called the code?'

'Lizzy, you are the key to my happiness. You make my world a richer, better, much more interesting place to be. More than it could ever have been if I'd kept myself closed off the way I was taught.'

She put her hands to her belly and frowned. 'I'm hungry. I can't think until I've had something to eat.'

'Then let's go.' He held out a hand and pointed towards the exit.

She gave him a wary look. 'The canteen's just upstairs.'

'*Per favore,* Lizzy. My gorgeous, infuriating, deeply talented *pompelmo*… You're safe with me. We can leave a message at the nurses' desk, if you like. But let's go somewhere we can talk. Properly.'

She dithered, shifted her feet, looked anywhere but at

him, until finally she looked him straight in the eye. 'Okay, fine. But let's go to the flat via the deli. And that pastry shop—the one with the pistachio thingies. If I'm going to be subject to all these...' she scrubbed at the air over her swelling belly '..."emotions"... I'd rather do it away from the public eye.'

'As you wish, *amore*.'

He offered her his hand. She stared at it and then, to his surprise, took it.

'Shall we take the scenic route?' she surprised herself by asking.

Leon gave her a courtly half-bow. 'By all means.'

She realised as they walked that she wanted to look at Rome from a different angle. Not through a tourist's eyes, but from the perspective of someone who lived here.

Could she picture herself pushing a baby carriage through the higgledy-piggledy streets?

Yes.

Could she imagine Leon popping their little girl on his shoulders when her pudgy toddler legs were tired?

She threw him a secret sidelong glance, taking in his solid shoulders, his strong arms, and the way he walked so that none of the countless tourists bumped into her as they wove their way through the busy streets.

Yes. She could, actually.

She looked down at his left hand. Bare. Occasionally brushing hers. Making trills of response run through her body whether she wanted them or not.

Yes, she realised with a jolt. Finally, at long last, she could picture a wedding ring on his hand.

Which, of course, set off a ream of entirely different questions.

Should she keep her house?

Would it be lonely here?

She'd miss her housemate and her colleagues, of course, but her life pretty much revolved around her patients and that would be no different here. And Byron had his pilot, so...

Leon stopped at a street stall and bought two *arancini*. After they'd eaten, they continued to walk in a new but comfortable silence as they gathered their thoughts. She felt as if she needed to reach a decision before they got to his flat, because whatever it was she decided would be final.

The choice, she realised, was a simple one.

Did she want to risk giving her heart to Leon, knowing the baby that linked them for ever could grow up in the kind of happy family she'd never had? Or did she want to raise their child the way Leon's mother had? Alone. Too protective. So frightened of being hurt that her world would close in around her and, more to the point, around her daughter, excluding any possibility of love.

The answer was glaringly obvious.

Just then they turned a corner, and there was the Trevi Fountain, crowded as ever with families and couples throwing in coins, making wish after wish.

Leon gave her hand a squeeze and asked, 'Did you know it's still fed by aqueduct? For almost two thousand years Romans have gathered water from here.'

Lizzy shook her head in disbelief.

'Astonishing, isn't it?' Leon continued. 'To think something so beautiful—a frivolity at first glance—has endured as much history as it has. You know...' He held her away from him for a moment and looked at the fountain and then at her. 'I think the water's the same colour as your eyes.'

Lizzy shot him a look. Was he talking in metaphors? Saying *she* was a frivolity?

'War, famine, droughts, revolution—' Leon's list was long. 'It had to be shut down recently to be restored. It felt—' He laughed to himself. 'I know it sounds ridiculous, because it's so touristy, but it felt like the city wasn't completely alive without it. You know…?'

She nodded, still not entirely sure she was meant to be taking all this at face value. She pulled the analogy back to herself. The two years she'd spent with Leon had been the most vital, thrilling, dynamic years of her life. Since they'd been apart she'd never really ever felt the same. Like Rome with its fountain, she had felt as if something was missing. And that something was Leon.

Her heart doubled its cadence. This was her chance. An open door. A step away from her dark, unhappy past to make a fresh start.

Leon was studying the fountain with such intensity she was pretty sure he was mulling over the same questions. Hoping against hope that he was making the right call by asking her to share his life with him.

'Do you know the secret to the coins?' Leon asked, digging in his pocket and showing her a few.

Again, she shook her head.

'You can throw in one, two or three.'

'And that has different meanings?'

He nodded. 'One coin means you wish to return to Rome.'

'And two?'

His eyes flickered with heat. 'Two coins means you wish to fall in love with an attractive Italian.'

'And I suppose that means you?'

He gave one of those careless shrugs of his, but now she saw all the things she hadn't before. Things she'd been too busy protecting her own heart to notice. She saw his vulnerability. His strength of character. His moral compass.

And, most of all, she saw that he truly did love her. That he wanted this to work. For them to be a family.

'Are there any more options?' she asked, her voice barely audible above the noise of tourists laughing, telling one another their wishes and leaving it up to the fountain to decide whether or not they came true.

'Yes.' He took a step closer to her and held up a third coin. 'Three coins means you're wishing to come to Rome, find love and marry a handsome Italian.'

The space between them diminished. Lizzy's heart pounded against her ribcage. 'And are there statistics on any of these wishes being granted?'

He shook his head. 'Only for the lucky ones.'

'Do you think we're lucky?' she asked, her heart brimming with a level of hope she had never once let herself feel.

'Si, amore,' he said, ducking his head to hers, his lips brushing against her lips as he said, 'I think we're very lucky.'

And with that they turned their backs to the fountain, as tradition dictated, and she plucked three coins from his hand and threw them into the fountain.

CHAPTER FIFTEEN

'YOU LOOK BEAUTIFUL.'

Lizzy beamed at her reflection in the mirror, then back at Byron, who had 'hitched a ride' on his boyfriend's plane. 'D'you think?'

He rolled his eyes. 'Of course I think! You're going to have to trust your man of honour.'

'Trust you to what, exactly?' she giggled.

'Trust me to not let you loose on the streets of Rome looking like a ragamuffin!'

They laughed, and sighed, and caught one another's eyes in the full-length mirror Leon had bought expressly for this day. He had wanted her to have everything she wanted exactly where she wanted it, for this, their wedding day, and much to her surprise she had realised she wanted to get ready here, in the rooftop flat that had undergone quite a transformation over the past few weeks.

The waiting-room-style seats had been replaced by big sofas, good for a snooze or curling up and reading a book—also good for spills. The balcony had been baby-proofed. The second guest room had been turned into a nursery, its walls painted a soft natural green that made it feel as though you were walking into an enchanted sun-dappled woodland where the sole purpose was to protect and nurture the little girl growing inside her.

'I look fat!' She laughed.

'You look stunning,' Byron countered. 'You've got that pregnancy glow down pat.'

She gazed at herself. Her body was still vaguely unfamiliar to her, but she had to admit the lace and ultra-soft linen maxi-dress with a deep V cut down the back made her feel as beautiful as Leon did when he held her in his arms each night.

Her eyes dropped to her stomach, then to her engagement ring. The princess cut aquamarine jewel stood proud on the band of diamonds, looking as if it had been on her finger for ever. Today it would be united with a wedding band. A ring that would symbolise her lifelong commitment to Leon and their child.

Her hands swept over the taut, increasingly large ball that was their baby girl. Genevieve, they'd decided in the end. For her mother.

'I wish—' An unexpected rush of emotion balled in her chest as her heart lurched up into her throat.

'I know, honey,' Byron soothed. 'I wish your mum could see you, too.'

'Do you think I'm a bad person for not inviting my father?'

Byron shook his head. 'You said you and Leon had talked about it loads. Weddings are different things for different couples. Yours is about joy—not obligation. Yours is about choice.'

She nodded, blinking back tears, desperately trying not to mess up her carefully applied make-up. 'You're right. A real father doesn't do his utmost to make his child feel horrible about herself.' She drew in a shaky breath and managed to find a smile that made it all the way to her eyes. 'Today is about celebrating everything that's good about me and Leon and this little tyke.' She rubbed her hands on her belly, feeling the soft lace of her gown shift as she did. 'Oh! She just kicked.'

Byron's face lit up as she took his hand and pressed it to her stomach. 'Oh, wow. I'm definitely going to have to get to Rome more often. I don't want to miss this little one's life as she grows up.'

She gave him a grateful smile. 'Thanks for coming. And you know we'll come to Sydney every now and again?'

Byron laughed. 'I know you, missy. You'll come when there are some good surgeries on the board. And I'm guessing they're going to have to be pretty spectacular to get you away from that gorgeous fiancé of yours.'

Lizzy grinned. 'He is pretty cute, isn't he?'

'Cute?' Byron screeched. 'The man's a bloody catwalk model! And a world-class surgeon.' He gave her a hug. 'Well done, you. You deserve every gorgeous molecule of him.'

Lizzy's phone buzzed. 'Do you mind…?' she said.

Byron grabbed the phone from the bed and handed it to her. Lizzy frowned.

'Something wrong?' he asked.

'No, it's—it's the hospital number. I thought it might be Leon.'

'You said he was at the hospital, right?'

'Yes. He was going to pop in on the Bianchis before we went to the church.'

Five minutes later Lizzy was out of her dress and on the street, flagging down a taxi. *'Per favore*, St Nicolino's,' she said as Byron climbed in beside her. *'Pronto.'*

Byron elbowed her in the side. 'Check you out, Little Miss Italy.'

She grinned. 'That's Little Miss Almost *Mrs* Italy to you.' Her smile dropped from her face. 'Oh, gosh…'

'What?'

'This means I won't be getting married.'

'Seriously? You think it'll take that long?'

She gave him a solid stare and tried to shrug it off. 'Gabrielle has just had an eclampsic convulsion.'

Byron pulled a face. He knew what that meant. The involuntary contraction of muscles meant the babies needed to be delivered *now*.

'Gabrielle's health is on the line every bit as much as the health of the conjoined twins,' Lizzy said, even though she knew they both knew the score.

'Have they given her magnesium sulphate?'

Lizzy nodded, rerouting her mental energies into the operating theatre and away from the church.

Eclampsia was rare, but there was a small risk of permanent disability or brain damage from the convulsions and, if not treated immediately, it could mean both the mother's and the babies' lives were at severe risk.

'Can you ring the church, Byron? Let them know?'

'You've still got an hour. You might be able to make it.'

Lizzy gave him a look.

Byron promised to ring the church as soon as they got to the hospital.

In the end, they were both partly right.

The intensity of the scenario at the hospital demanded that Lizzy and Leon work in perfect synchronicity.

Gabrielle had had her seizure during Leon's morning visit. It happened sometimes, the total absence of signs that eclampsia was looming.

The babies were at thirty-one weeks. They'd been hoping for at least a couple more, but now Gabrielle's health was at risk as well there was no choice but to deliver the babies today.

Matteo was gowned up and holding his wife's hand as

Leon prepared to make the first crucial incision, and he apologised once again for the timing. 'We are so sorry to have interrupted your wedding.'

Lizzy shook her head, gloved hands held up, ready for whatever she might be needed to do. 'Honestly, this is more important. Besides,' she added, trying to add a bit of brightness to the tense atmosphere, 'bringing your girls into the world today is like an early wedding present.'

Leon agreed. 'It's these two little girls who helped bring us back together again, so it makes sense that they should want to be part of our big day.'

Lizzy looked across the surgical table, her eyes cinching with her future husband's, and smiled. She hadn't thought of it that way. How huge a role Hope and Grace had played in their lives. Without them— She shook her head and any other thoughts away. Here and now was where she both wanted and needed to be.

Up in the gallery Byron gave her a thumbs-up. Down here on the surgical floor both Giovanni and Autumn were gowned up and standing ready to help if anything went wrong. But, because Leon was doing what he did best, the C-section went like clockwork, and before any of them could fully grasp what had happened Matteo was holding his little girls in his arms, then handing them to his wife. Both of them were disbelieving that these tiny, practically perfect babies that they had seen so many times on imaging screens were finally out here in the real world.

'Looks like you've got about four kilos of baby,' Leon said, once each of the parents had had a chance to kiss and hold their children.

As they'd been born prematurely, they still had a long road ahead—and, of course, there was the complicated separation surgery Giovanni and Autumn would helm once the little ones had developed more.

There wasn't any need to put in a new stent straight away, Lizzy was relieved to see, but the girls would need to be under close scrutiny in the NICU as their lungs developed, their bodies gained a bit more weight and they were better able to regulate their own temperatures.

Mercifully, Gabrielle seemed to be all right, but she, too, would be under Leon's close care. The list of post-operative problems after eclampsia wasn't pretty. But Gabrielle had a core of strength. One that would only grow stronger now that she'd kissed and held the babies she'd been carrying all these months.

'Will we be able to hold them again soon?' Gabrielle asked, her mother's instincts already at full throttle.

'Of course,' Leon assured her. 'You'll be able to be with them every day, but for now let us look after *you*.'

'Are you going to be with them too?' she asked.

Lizzy nodded, her smile deepening as she felt Leon's hand slip round her waist as he joined her by the bedside.

'And Drs Lombardi and Fraser. In fact, Autumn and Giovanni are getting the twins settled into their incubator now.'

'So they're not alone?' Matteo asked.

'Absolutely not. They'll never be alone,' said Leon. 'Right now, your job is to rest, Gabrielle. If you or the babies need us, we're only a phone call away.'

Lizzy shot him a look. 'Why? Where are we going?'

He gave her a cheeky grin. 'You'll see.'

The moment Lizzy entered the church, Leon knew he was in the right place, at the right time, doing exactly the right thing.

The flowers they'd organised had been left in place along with another wedding party's flowers, so now, a few hours later than planned, as Lizzy walked towards him, it was as if she were Eve, walking through a Roman Garden of Eden.

He knew it was ridiculous, but he felt like the very first man ever to have got married. To have loved this deeply. To have been filled to the brim with the knowledge that his life was going to be so much richer for having his wife in it.

Would it all be smooth sailing from here on out? Probably not. They each bore the bumps and nicks and scars of lives that could have been kinder to them, but they'd both come out stronger in the end. Stronger and more resilient, now they knew they had someone they could turn to.

When she reached the altar in front of their friends, a smattering of hospital staff and, of course, Lizzy's best friend from home, Byron, who was at her side, Leon took her hands in his. They stood there beaming at one another as the celebrant said whatever it was he said—they weren't really paying attention, just staring into one another's eyes, seeing nothing but possibility, nothing but light, nothing but joy.

They both had to be prompted to repeat their vows, and when, at long last, they were given licence to mark the beginning of their married life with a kiss, they did so with relish.

'I love you, Dottore Signora Cassanetti,' said Leon, and nuzzled into her neck, dropping a kiss in that perfect nook between her chin and her ear.

'I love you too,' she said, happily walking back down the aisle to the applause of their colleagues and friends.

'Fancy a honeymoon in Rome?' Leon asked with a cheeky grin.

'I fancy a lifelong honeymoon in Rome,' Lizzy answered, then grinned and gave his hand a tug. 'But first… do you want to go to the NICU?'

Leon nodded. He had married the perfect woman for

him. And today had been the very best day to begin their lives together as husband and wife. He couldn't wait for the rest of their marriage to reveal itself, tantalising morsel by morsel. Just like the perfect Italian meal…

* * * * *

REAWAKENED
BY THE
ITALIAN SURGEON

SCARLET WILSON

MILLS & BOON

There's really only one person I could dedicate this book to, and that's my fellow author Annie O'Neil, who made brainstorming about hunky Italian doctors such fun!

CHAPTER ONE

IT HAPPENED IN the blink of an eye. Or maybe it was in a few seconds. But as Autumn watched her colleagues Sharon and Gavin turn to each other and laugh during the father of the bride speech she saw something.

It was like a giant neon sign pointing to the new bride and groom. The way that they looked at each other at that exact moment. The love. The connection. The promise. The life they hoped for together. All in that precise split-second.

Autumn Fraser swallowed, her mouth instantly dry as she smoothed her hands down the coral silk of her brides-maid dress. She automatically reached for the glass in front of her and gulped quickly, almost wincing at the slightly warm white wine.

It had been a fairly relaxed wedding, meaning that by the time the speeches had rolled around, she'd moved from the top table to sit next to Louis, the man she'd lived with for the last year.

Life was comfortable. Her job as a specialist paediatric surgeon meant she was frequently jetting off around the globe to assist in difficult surgeries. Louis was equally busy as a specialist neurosurgeon. Sometimes they were like ships passing in the night. They'd met a few years ago and had fallen into an easy relationship. She liked him.

She really did. But at this moment her heart was doing uncomfortable things inside her chest.

She glanced sideways and noticed that Louis, too, was watching the bride and groom closely.

'We don't look like that…' Her whisper was barely audible. She couldn't actually believe she was saying out loud the words that had been circling around in her head for months.

Louis's eyes didn't meet hers. 'No,' he said softly. 'We don't.'

It was an admission from them both. Part of her felt relief that he knew it too, but a little part of her felt empty.

Now her stomach was flipping over, joining the bedlam that was currently going on in her chest. It was the recognition. The agreement. Thank goodness she was sitting down, because she wasn't quite sure if her legs were up to the task of standing.

Silence hung between them. She blinked back tears. She wasn't sad. Truly, she wasn't. But Louis was a nice guy. An intelligent companion who made her laugh, who was thoughtful in lots of ways, and every bit as annoying in others.

The last thing she wanted to do was hurt him. The thought of doing that really pained her. But was it actually more painful to meander along in a relationship that wasn't right for either party?

They'd drifted along over the last year—their relationship was a convenience. She'd moved in with him, but left her own place unrented. Now she was wondering why she'd done that. Had she always known, deep down, that it would come to this?

Her parents had had a tight, restrictive marriage. It had rubbed off on her. She couldn't pretend that it hadn't. Control was everything to her. And falling in love—*really* in love—That wasn't control. She was a surgeon. Losing her heart and her head just wasn't on the agenda for her.

Which was why she felt so confused right now. Because that look that Sharon and Gavin had just exchanged was pure, unadulterated love. And she wanted *that*. No matter how much she pretended she didn't.

Maybe it was the fact that she'd had a glass and a half of wine that was allowing her to peek through the shutters she normally had firmly closed around her heart, but the realisation was startling. And upsetting.

Her parents had never directly shown love to her, her brother, or to each other. In fact, they'd been rapidly admonished for any outward show of emotion. Joy, love, pain had all been buttoned up and kept inside. Both of them had been so focused on their academic careers. There had been no room for emotion. They'd thought everyone should only strive to be the best, and put all other sensations aside. There was no room in life for emotions. It was energy best spent elsewhere.

That was what she'd always been taught. But something was making her do this. Something was making her hear the words that were circling in her head.

Autumn's heart ached a little as she turned to face Louis. It was almost as if the realisation had crumpled his face.

His voice was deep and cracked when he spoke. 'I want that, Autumn. I want what they have.' He was glancing back at Gavin and Sharon, who were holding hands and laughing again at another joke.

She let the surgeon side of her brain take over. The part that was decisive and direct. It was so much easier than the emotional side, which was threatening to tip her in a direction where she might end up a blubbering wreck.

She slid her hand over Louis's. 'I want that for you too,'

she said simply, working hard not to let her voice waver. 'It's time. We both know it's time. I'll go back to my own place.'

She didn't wait for a response. She just picked up her phone and walked out of the reception venue. She refused to let the tears that were brimming in her eyes slide down her cheeks. She wouldn't admit it out loud, but right now it felt as if a huge weight had just slid from her shoulders.

Giovanni Lombardi took a deep breath as his daughter Sofia climbed up into his lap. It was a hot, sticky evening in Rome. It didn't help that the air-conditioning he'd paid a fortune for a few years ago had decided to make some strange whirring noise and then clunk to a halt. He'd flung the villa's shutters wide, but there was no breeze outside— just more warm air.

Sofia was the equivalent of a hot water bottle, but Giovanni clutched her closer. She was his lifeline. The most important person in his universe. He would happily allow his body temperature to reach stratospheric heights in order to continue this moment.

His wife had died four years ago in a scooter accident on the roads of Rome. For a few months it had seemed as though the world was crumbling around Giovanni. Sofia had been his only reason for continuing.

'I like this one, Papà,' she said, pointing at a picture on the screen.

Giovanni was tired. He had one of the biggest cases of his career at St Nicolino's, the prestigious children's hospital in Rome where he was Chief of Surgery. His hospital—because that was how he thought of it—was renowned across Italy as a specialist hub for paediatric surgery and antenatal care, and five short weeks ago he'd been referred a case of conjoined twins, picked up at twenty weeks.

Most cases were picked up earlier than that, so he'd focused all his attention on making sure this family had the best antenatal care possible. His colleague, maternal foetal medical specialist Leon Cassanetti, had recruited Lizzy Beckley to partner with him in their birth. Now it was time for Giovanni to find a partner to work alongside him on the separation surgery.

He knew this case would have worldwide coverage. He didn't doubt he could persuade any surgeon, from any country, to be part of this surgery. Some surgeons he knew would probably fight over a surgery like this one. But picking the *right* surgeon was the priority here.

Whoever he picked would have to be happy to halt their life and come to Rome for at least the next four months. They would have to work alongside Giovanni and around fifty other members of the team to plan for this surgery. They would have to be happy to spend hours on research, hours on techniques specific to this case, with numerous practice surgeries. They would also need the ability to win the trust of the parents.

Giovanni already knew he would lead one team, and whoever he picked would lead the other. He had to trust them—he had to have faith that they could work alongside him, think the way he did, almost be in complete unison with him if they wanted both of these babies to survive. It was vital to pick the right person.

He had the details of hundreds of surgeons worldwide, and had spent the last two weeks filtering through them to find someone with the skill set and temperament that he needed. Volatile wouldn't work. Distracted wouldn't work. Passion and commitment were the absolute minimum of his expectations.

He leaned forward and inspected the photo that Sofia

was pointing to. 'Ah, yes,' he murmured to his daughter. 'Her name is Autumn. She comes from Scotland.'

He had eventually streamed his list down to ten potential surgeons. All brilliant. All capable of performing the surgery. But Autumn Fraser was actually neck-and-neck with another one at the top of his list.

'Scotland... They have castles,' said Sofia. She leaned into his neck. She was clearly getting tired. 'Do you think they have fairies in the castles in Scotland?'

He smiled and ran his fingers through her dark curls. 'I think they might have.'

'She's pretty,' Sofia replied.

Giovanni blinked. 'Is she? I hadn't noticed.'

He leaned forward to take a better look at the photo. The truth was he hadn't really looked closely at any of the photos of the candidates. He'd narrowed his potential field based purely on experience and skills. The faces hadn't even implanted in his head.

As he leaned forward he tilted his face naturally to the side. Autumn Fraser *was* pretty. Maybe even more than pretty. Her hair was similar to Sofia's. Dark and shiny with a hint of a curl. But he'd missed the searing green eyes completely, and her skin, with a hint of a tan and a few freckles scattered across her nose.

His gaze went back to those eyes. Sincere, compassionate, with a hint of fun. He blinked again and gave a shudder. He couldn't remember the last time he'd considered a woman so closely. It made him uncomfortable. He'd lived his life in a bubble these last few years, with no room for thoughts like this.

'What's wrong, Papà?' asked the sleepy voice on his shoulder.

'Nothing, honey.' He ran one hand down Sofia's back as he flicked back to the list of surgeries Autumn had performed. She was a specialist in abdominal and liver surgery on tiny babies. Her record was good. She'd published several papers on technique, and presented around the world on improving outcomes in these children.

People often assumed that the separation surgery was the most dangerous moment in separating conjoined twins. Those with more experience realised that, whilst separation was difficult, patching up two separate babies, often with completely different medical issues, and giving them a chance of the best possible life was much, much harder.

Giovanni sighed and flicked back to the details of the only other surgeon who could rival Autumn's stats. He'd only just started scanning them when something sparked in his brain. He flipped back to Autumn's page. Yes. There it was.

He'd skimmed the list of publications, assuming they were all surgery-focused. But, no. Here was another with Autumn's name on as lead researcher: *Psychological Trauma and its Effects on the Separation of Conjoined Twins. A Twenty-Year Study.*

He froze. He hadn't seen that before. A quick date-check showed it was listed on her bio, but due to be published in a renowned surgical journal in two months' time.

Giovanni smiled. Separation trauma had long since been in his thoughts for these children. So far he'd been involved in ten separation surgeries for conjoined twins, and this was entirely the area of research he'd wanted to pursue next.

It seemed that his potential colleague had beaten him to it.

He picked up Sofia and carried her to bed, tucking her in and placing a gentle kiss on her brow.

Once he was sure she was settled he moved back to his desk and picked up his phone.

It seemed he'd found his perfect fit.

Autumn's neighbour flung open his door and screwed up his face. It seemed to take him a few moments to place her. 'Autumn…?' He looked her up and down, his expression clearly saying that he thought he was in some kind of weird dream.

She still had the flowers in her hair. The long, slightly stained coral bridesmaid dress in place. The light rucksack in her hand only carried some make-up, her phone, her purse and credit cards, and her laptop—which she never left the house without—along with a sewing kit for wedding emergencies and some chocolate. What it didn't carry was the key to her flat. That was back at Louis's house.

'What are you doing here?'

'Sorry for the late call. I need access to my flat and forgot my keys. Do you still have the spare set for me?'

Barry didn't move. It was as if her words hadn't quite sunk in yet. He screwed his eyes up again and shook his head slowly. 'What have you done? Run away from some kind of wedding?' Then his eyes widened and his mouth moved into a perfect 'O'. 'Did you run away from your *own* wedding?'

Autumn shook her head and extended her hand, palm up. She hadn't seen Barry in over a year. But it was late. And she was tired. And she was kind of hoping that there might be a bottle of wine still in her flat. There was a good chance that any tinned or packet food would be out of date. Teabags and coffee would likely be the only things of use.

Barry was still looking at her. 'Actually, can I be a pest?' she asked.

'What…?'

'I'd really appreciate a couple of slices of bread and a tin of baked beans if you have them.' She shot him her best smile.

Barry blinked in stunned silence, then she saw him give himself a visible shake.

'Keys,' he muttered as he walked back into his kitchen.

She heard the opening of drawers and cupboards before he returned with her keys clutched in one hand, and a plate with two slices of bread, a can of baked beans and a couple of digestive biscuits in the other.

Autumn sighed in relief. 'Thanks, Barry—much appreciated.'

'Do you need milk?'

She shook her head. 'No, thanks. I'm fine.' Her phone vibrated in her bag.

'Does this mean you're moving back in?' asked Barry as she started to back away.

It did. Didn't it?

Autumn kept the smile pasted on her face, even though her muscles were starting to ache. 'Yes, I will be. Nice to see you again, Barry.'

He gave a gentle nod and then, with a final glance at her dress, closed his door.

Autumn stuck her key in the lock and walked into her flat. As she breathed a big sigh of relief, she tried to ignore the slightly stale air. It appeared that the automatic air freshener she had plugged into one of the sockets had run out of scent.

The air was still warm outside, so she flung the main window open wide and threw her bag on the sofa. After some moves that could have competed with a contortionist, she managed to let the coral dress drop to the floor at her feet.

Many of her clothes were now at Louis's. She still had

some supplies here—generally the kind of tired and boring clothes she hadn't worn for a while—but there was a pair of comfortable pyjamas that she slid into after standing under the shower for a few moments.

As she emerged back into the kitchen a thought sprang into her head. She hadn't actually said goodbye to Sharon and Gavin. *Oops.* But Sharon would likely not be too worried about the disappearance of one of her four bridesmaids. She would probably think Autumn had been called into work. It was fine. Autumn would send an apology tomorrow and tell them to enjoy their honeymoon.

Five minutes later she'd slumped on the sofa with her beans on toast and cup of tea when her bag made an odd noise. The phone. Of course.

She pulled it from her bag and frowned at the unfamiliar number. She'd missed three calls.

It was late. Autumn was drained. She'd been up since six this morning, helping Sharon get ready for her big day. She took a few bites of her food as she considered whether to call back.

It was as if someone was watching her. The phone started buzzing again. Autumn wasn't on call, but she often had calls regarding issues with newborns when she wasn't on duty. Her body reacted on automatic pilot and she answered, switching her mobile to speaker.

'Autumn Fraser.'

There was a pause. Had the caller actually not expected an answer at this point? Then there was a voice.

'Hello? Ah, good, Dr Fraser, I think I'm about to make you the offer of a lifetime.'

The voice was heavily accented, warm as treacle, and instantly had her attention. 'Excuse me?'

There was a gentle laugh at the end of the phone. 'Forgive me. This is Giovanni Lombardi, Chief of Surgery at St Nicolino's in Rome. I'm sure you've heard of us.'

This voice was assured and confident. Part of her wanted to cut off this stranger and tell him she'd never heard of his hospital and to contact her secretary on Monday if he wanted to chat. Who had handed over her personal mobile number?

But of course she wouldn't. She was far too curious already. The caller had addressed her as 'Dr'. She was a surgeon, and professional courtesy meant she should be addressed as Ms or Miss. But she knew that those in her own profession in other countries were sometimes addressed as 'Dr'.

She took a deep breath. 'What exactly do you want, Mr Lombardi?'

The soft laugh continued. 'Well, if you'd read the emails I've sent you over the last few hours, you would know exactly what I want.'

She bristled. Who *was* this guy? That sounded like a telling-off. Whoever he was, he clearly didn't know her at all.

'Guess what…' she paused as she tried to remember his first name '…Giovanni? This might come as a surprise, but I haven't sat around all day, waiting for random emails to fill my inbox. I've been off duty at the wedding of a friend. I didn't expect to answer my phone or read any emails today.'

Autumn was aware that the more tired and exasperated she was, the more clipped and thick her Scottish accent became. She made no apologies for it, but in her head she could almost picture this man's puzzled face as he tried to interpret.

She was already feeling out of sorts. Dumping a perfectly nice and safe man and moving back home to her flat without thinking things through properly had put her on edge. She knew that when she woke tomorrow morning she'd have to grab as much control of the situation as she could. That was if there was any left.

Annoyed with herself, she pulled her laptop from her bag and flipped it open. It only took a few seconds to come to life and she could see a stream of emails. She opened the first and leaned forward.

What?

Her eyes scanned that one and her finger automatically pressed for the next. This one contained details of scans. The next, measurements.

He must know exactly what she was doing, because a few moments later his smooth voice asked, 'Do I have your attention now, Dr Fraser?'

He was toying with her. And, whilst he might sound like some kind of dreamboat, she *so* wasn't in the mood to be played with.

Her heart-rate was quickening. And her breathing. So much detail. So much information. Two precious little girls, connected at the heart and the liver.

'How was this missed?' she asked as she kept on reading, her mind pushing everything else away and focusing on the case in front of her.

'The babies had their arms around each other in the scan at eleven weeks. It was a newly qualified sonographer who thought they were just hugging.'

There was so much she could say right now, but what would be the point? Time had already been lost. 'You have them with you now?'

'I have them,' he said reassuringly. He paused, and then continued. 'After delivery I'm leading the separation surgery. I'd like you to lead a second team,' he said.

Her heart leapt in her chest. She didn't care that it wasn't anatomically possible, she would swear in any court that she'd just felt it.

A smile crept across her face. 'Of course you would,' she said, trying to sound as confident as he had earlier. She needed to be a match for this man in every way. Surgeon's rules: *always believe you're a match for any other one*. 'No one else has the experience of liver surgery on neonates that I do.'

She was on her feet, flicking the phone to speaker, striding through to her room and dropping it on the bed as she pulled her suitcase from the top of the wardrobe.

Giovanni Lombardi gave an amused laugh. It seemed to be his signature. She was trying to picture this Italian man with the tantalising voice in her head. The last thing she needed in a case like this was any distractions—particularly when preparation time was at a minimum.

'There were a few others....' he said, as if trying to keep her in her place.

'Rubbish. You wanted the best. You've asked me. And, luckily, I've just made myself available.'

She rattled off a whole list of demands. None of them were outrageous and she knew it. This kind of surgery was history-making. She was almost sure this hospital in Rome wouldn't deny her anything. And for some strange reason—as crazy as this was—it made her feel as if she was grabbing a bit of control back from her day.

He replied quietly with an assured *'si'* to all her requests.

'I pick my own team,' she said as she threw random clothes into her bag. Her best work suits were at Louis's—as were most of her everyday items. She was left with half-full cans of deodorant, tubes of toothpaste and bottles of shampoo. Ordinarily she would have collected all her things herself, but it looked as if she might have to ask a delivery company instead.

'Of course you do. I have many staff you may feel are appropriate, but the assembly of any team is always down to the lead surgeon.'

'Great. What about flights?'

'I took the liberty of booking you a first-class flight tomorrow from Heathrow.'

She froze momentarily. He was presumptuous. But of course he was. No surgeon in their right mind would say no to this surgery. But she had her own tricks up her sleeve.

'Won't be necessary.' She grinned. 'I have my own transport available. I'll make arrangements right now. Expect me in Rome by early morning.'

Even though he couldn't see her, Autumn had a little fun by tossing her hair over her shoulder. Having a very famous billionaire brother was something she generally kept to herself. But she knew she could give Ryan a call and his company would file a flight plan and she'd be able to take off in a few hours. He was proud of her and her achievements, and he often helped her with travel arrangements when she needed to get to a place for work. He was one of the few people who understood her need to be in control.

Ryan had gone the opposite way. He'd left home, got away from their parents and lived a crazy life. No rules. No regulations. But then he'd made a discovery—one that had made him a billionaire. And instead of running from control he'd started to embrace it—in a good way. Along the way he'd met the perfect wife and had the perfect family. He'd even employed a few old friends he trusted to be part of his company. But all his money had kept his feet firmly on the ground, and he never forgot to check on his sister. He'd do anything for her.

'You will manage to get here by then?' asked Giovanni Lombardi.

'Absolutely,' she said with confidence. 'How about I meet you at the hospital at nine tomorrow morning?'

'Nine a.m.,' he agreed, although he certainly sounded a little bewildered.

She kind of liked the fact she'd thrown Mr Smooth off his game.

But it seemed he had a good recovery. 'You understand, of course, that before we formalise things I'll need to make sure that you're the right fit for the team.'

Heat rushed into her cheeks. That sounded completely personal. And it was. For a procedure like this, staff had to work in unison. It didn't matter that she and Giovanni would have teams of their own. They still had to fit together.

'I've never had a problem fitting in with a team, Giovanni.' She used supreme effort to try and mimic his smooth way of talking. 'Surely you can't be that difficult?'

The laugh she heard this time was deep and throaty. Every hair on her arms stood on end.

'Bravo,' he said. 'Or should it be *touché*?' There was a pause, and then he asked, 'Don't you need to clear this with your hospital?'

'No,' she answered quickly. 'I am literally a free agent. I have a sponsor. So, although I'm based in London, as long as I don't have surgical commitments and any current cases I am free to go to any case worldwide if it interests me and needs my skills.'

'That's a pretty unique arrangement,' he said quizzically.

'It is,' she agreed. 'But my sponsor gets credit in any research I publish, and in any publicity around the cases.'

She could almost see him nodding, contemplating her words. 'Understood,' he said after a few moments.

Autumn took a deep breath. The truth was, the timing of this couldn't be better. She'd be away for four, maybe five months. It would give her a chance to move on. Louis too. She hoped he'd find someone who'd look at him the way he wished for. Someone to give him the connection that they'd never shared. The kind of connection that she'd just witnessed between her friends, which had made her feel lonelier than ever.

Was there a chance that she could find that too? She gave a little shiver and pushed the thought from her head. She had long ago decided that lifestyle would never suit her. Too risky. Too much open to chance.

She was about to get the opportunity of a lifetime with this surgery. All her focus needed to be on *that*. She'd arrange for a delivery company to pick up her things from Louis and bring them back to her flat. With her in another country, the process would hopefully be painless for them both.

'Is there anything else you want to ask me? There's still much to discuss about the case,' said Giovanni.

Autumn shook her head, forgetting he couldn't see her. 'No, I'd prefer to do that in person tomorrow.'

'Then I'll be delighted to see you at…' he paused for a second '…nine o'clock tomorrow morning.' That laugh came again. 'I thought I might need to work harder to persuade you.' His voice softened a little. 'I'm glad you have no other pressing cases. Because this family really do need you. *We* need you.'

'And I'm happy to be invited,' she said. 'Until tomorrow.'

He closed the call and Autumn collapsed backwards onto her bed. Had that really just happened?

It was like a dream. A fascinating surgery. A chance to visit a beautiful country and work with other people. Time to build a relationship with the parents of these girls and for them to trust what she could do. The real possibility that she could improve the overall outcome for these babies.

And Giovanni Lombardi had thought he might need to persuade her…

Now it was her turn to laugh out loud. She stared out of her window at the stars in the dark sky. 'What can I say, Giovanni? You had me at hello.'

CHAPTER TWO

HE WAS PACING. He knew he was pacing, and it was ridiculous.

Giovanni always started the day early, and Sofia was a morning person too, which was easy to manage. He also had some family assistance. Sofia's aunt was happy to take her to and from nursery, and to look after her for a few hours at either side.

All of this meant that by eight a.m. Giovanni was pacing in his office. He'd already met with Leon and Lizzy to discuss the Bianchi twins. He'd also reviewed the variety of other patients he currently had in the wards, and answered a number of specialist queries from around the world.

Steam was rising in the air from the coffee on his desk as he spotted a black limousine pulling up outside the hospital entrance. Unusual...

He watched as a woman with dark brown hair just past her shoulders emerged, wearing low heels, a black suit and a bright pink shirt. She gave her hair a shake and walked around to shake hands with the driver and exchange a few words with him. Both of them laughed and she gave him a wave.

She only had a small bag across her body and a small pull-along case at her feet. Four months. That was how long Autumn Fraser was supposed to be here. Had she changed her mind already? He'd expected her to arrive with numerous bags. This wasn't looking good.

His brain raced. He had agreed to all the demands she'd made before she arrived. He was sure he could agree to anything else that she asked for.

A few moments later he heard his PA's voice, and the door to his office opened.

Autumn Fraser glided into his office. She didn't look like a woman who, less than twelve hours ago, had been at home in London. Nor did she look like a woman who'd spent frantic hours packing and travelling, negotiating the confusing airport at Rome, then picking her way through an unfamiliar city.

He held out his hand to her. 'You've made good time, Dr Fraser. I'm impressed.'

She shot him a beaming smile as she pulled her case behind her, taking a quick glance around the room. Giovanni's office was spacious, with wide windows that allowed him a view of both the car park beneath and the beauty of the city around him.

'Not everyone arrives in a limousine,' he said, and kept smiling as he shook her hand. Her grip was firm and steady.

'I have some connections,' she said easily. 'When I travel, I like to concentrate on the case I'll be working on—not the hassle of the journey.' She gestured with her head to the large table on the other side of the office. 'Shall we sit there?'

Before he had a chance to reply, she'd moved over to the table and opened her pull-along case. He'd expected it to be full of clothes, but instead she pulled out her laptop and a mountain of research papers. Even from here he could see that she'd highlighted certain parts of them. Had she been up all night? And how could she possibly have worked like that on a plane?

Giovanni pressed his lips together. It was clear she didn't want to sit across a desk from him. Was this a power move, to make sure he knew they were on an equal footing?

As if she'd read his mind, she looked up at him from the desk, her green eyes serious. 'Let's start the way we mean to continue,' she said as she spread her papers across the table. 'I'd like to review the babies and talk techniques.'

She clearly worked exactly the same way as Giovanni—she liked to get straight to business—but for the first time in his career he decided to buck the trend.

'Actually, Dr Fraser—or would you prefer I call you Ms? Or Autumn?'

'Autumn will be fine.' Her response was automatic.

'Autumn, then. I'd like to show you around the hospital, make a few introductions, and then discuss the case. Once we've done that, I'll take you to meet the Bianchis. But first, before all that, I'm going to take you to breakfast.'

She blinked, looking momentarily stunned. She'd obviously expected him to get straight to work with her. And normally he would have. But Autumn Fraser wasn't what he'd expected. She didn't appear to be tired. Or nervous in any way. He could already see the work she'd done in the last few hours.

Maybe this woman just had a smooth veneer, or some glossy outer armour. But she had to be tired. And she had to be excited about this case. He'd told her he'd have to check she was a good fit—for him and the team. Her confident demeanour surprised him. But that was fine.

The thing that wasn't fine was how right Sofia had been. Autumn Fraser *was* pretty. More than pretty. Unnervingly pretty—in a way that she clearly didn't realise. From those startling green eyes to the wavy loose curls and tall, slender figure. He didn't know a single man on the planet who wouldn't look twice. It irked him that he topped that list. He wasn't used to distractions at work.

'I don't normally eat breakfast,' she said, with a wave of her hand.

Those green eyes connected with his. *Wow.* His breath caught somewhere at the back of his throat.

He raised his eyebrows. 'Hasn't anyone told you it's the most important meal of the day?'

He liked her. She was sassy. In a good way. He'd had that feeling last night when they'd talked on the phone.

She rolled her eyes, but stood up when he gestured to the door.

'You're right,' he said. 'Let's start the way we mean to continue. Let me take you for a traditional Italian breakfast.'

This was all going so wrong. All the way over on her comfortable flight she'd thought about that smooth voice on the phone. She hadn't let herself do an internet search for Giovanni Lombardi because she was hoping her fears wouldn't be answered. But here he was in the flesh. Mr Italian Gorgeousness. *Ugh.*

His broad shoulders and tailored suit, along with those dark flashing brown eyes and his easy manner, made him a combination of every Italian dreamboat she'd ever seen on screen. Even down to the short moustache and beard that didn't really resemble a beard. More like four or five days of deliberate not shaving. Italian men knew how to wear facial hair in such a sexy way...

This was so not what she needed right now. This was a career-making case. The last thing she wanted was any distractions.

She gulped. This was verging on a disaster for her, and her brain didn't normally have such thoughts. Less than twenty-four hours ago she'd been sitting at her friend's wedding with Louis by her side. They might have parted ways amicably, but in her head she'd believed she wouldn't even contemplate looking at another guy for months—at least not deliberately.

This surgery was far too important to allow herself to be distracted by anything—least of all thoughts about men. Long-term relationships had never been on her agenda. The example of her parents had planted that seed in her head a long time ago. Her mother had been a brilliant physicist. Her father an esteemed professor of history. Neither of them had seemed interested in parenting.

She wasn't quite sure how she and her brother had actually got into this world. It was as if academia had told her parents they should have a couple of kids, and so they'd dutifully ticked that box. But with an entire childhood of being pushed towards perfection, control and study, she'd never really learned to play, let alone love. Whilst other friends had considered marriage and a family, Autumn had never contemplated that for herself. She hadn't allowed herself to.

Her career focus was all-consuming. The last thing she wanted was a husband and children. It had always been clear to her that her parents had never achieved a balance between career and family life. She didn't want to be the same. So a husband and children were off the table, and every single thing about Giovanni Lombardi was sending her into panic mode.

She hadn't been joking when she'd said he'd had her at hello. That voice just sent electricity dancing over her skin. How could she do this job without a) looking at him, or b) listening to him? Switching off her senses seemed to be the only way to go, because he just oozed magnetism in a way it would be hard to ignore.

She couldn't remember ever having a reaction to a man like this.

And that was entirely the problem.

She stood, following him as he gestured with his hand that they were to leave his office. Her brain tried to stay entirely focused on work. The hospital seemed impressive. On the outside, it looked like any grand old Italian building. But the inside was more akin to some kind of spaceship. The credentials she'd read on the website certainly showed that St Nicolino's had all the facilities she could need for this surgery and this case.

Giovanni tried to make small talk as they walked the long corridors. She was hoping he would take her to the impersonal hospital canteen—but, no, he ushered her out through the main door and into a large four-by-four. Her eyes noticed the child booster seat in the back.

Moments later the car stopped outside a small café on the outskirts of Rome. The traffic had been heavy, but Giovanni had woven the large vehicle down narrow streets that had made her hold her breath.

Before she had a chance to think, he was out of the car and opening up the door for her. 'Here,' he said. 'My favourite place for breakfast.'

Autumn was interested. It wasn't flash, or chic. It looked exactly what it was: a small business in amongst a hundred others.

He put his fingers to his lips. 'Best coffee and best *maritozzo* in Rome.'

He kissed his fingers and blew into the air and she laughed out loud. 'Best *what*?'

He guided her inside, towards a glass cabinet stocked

with food. 'Or, if you prefer, you can have a croissant, a *bombolone*, or *biscottate*.'

She was here for four months. She didn't doubt she'd try them all. 'I'll have what you're having,' she said. It seemed the simplest solution.

He nodded, and spoke in rapid Italian to the woman behind the counter. Listening to him talk his own language was magical. It took her a few moments to realise he was speaking to her again, asking her how she preferred her coffee.

A few minutes later they were sitting at a table outside. 'Your bags?' asked Giovanni. 'You have others?'

Autumn wrinkled her brow. 'I dropped them at my hotel on my way to the hospital.'

She could almost see his sigh of relief. He seemed to settle back into the slightly uncomfortable metal chair. She tried to hide her smile as she looked at the food on the table in front of her. Had he really thought she'd arrived with no luggage?

'You didn't want to catch a few hours' sleep or freshen up before coming to the hospital?' he asked, and then he seemed to realise how those words might sound and gave a slightly unnerved laugh. 'Sorry, I didn't mean it to sound like that.'

Autumn looked down at her old but still presentable clothes. They weren't rumpled. She gave him a direct stare. 'I showered on the plane and changed before I disembarked.'

There. Let him think that one over.

She could see the question form in his brain, but it never left his lips. *What kind of plane has a shower?*

'Actually,' she said as she took a sip of her coffee—*caffe macchiato*, coffee with a drop of milk, 'because you caught me at short notice, half my wardrobe was out of my reach.

I might need you to get someone to direct me to a few places in Rome where I can pick up some more clothes.'

Now he looked even more surprised. 'You don't need someone else. I can do that.' He waved his hand easily.

'You shop for women's clothes?' she asked.

Autumn was staring at the *maritozzo* on the plate in front of her. It had turned out to be an Italian sweet pastry stuffed with cream and likely a million calories. There was no way she could eat that without getting it all over her.

Giovanni handed her a large cloth napkin as he tucked one into his shirt collar. He gave a careless shrug. 'All Italian men know where to shop,' he said simply.

She wasn't quite sure what to make of that, and then she remembered the booster seat in the car. Her eyes went automatically to his left hand. No wedding ring was there.

But, like herself, Giovanni was a surgeon. There was a good chance he didn't wear a wedding ring. When scrubbing was a part of daily life, jewellery became a nuisance.

'I noticed the car seat,' she said, trying to say it as casually as possible. 'Do you have children?'

His eyes met hers and she would have sworn she saw them light up right before her.

He beamed. 'A daughter—Sofia. She's five and the light of my life.'

Everything about him changed in an instant. The tone of his voice, the relaxation of his shoulders. She'd thought he'd seemed quite easy around her already, but there was a visible difference now.

'Tell me about her.'

Autumn knew people. She'd been a doctor for years. This was a fellow surgeon she'd have to work alongside. It was essential that she knew what was important to him, and Sofia clearly was.

'She's fantastic. I may be biased, but I don't care. She's

smart, but she likes to pretend she's not. She's already told me that being a surgeon is too boring and she plans to be an astronaut. She's always trying to learn something new, but...' He paused for a second. 'I imagine she'll do something completely different.'

'Why?'

Autumn was curious. She didn't have much experience with kids. Babies, yes. But, as sad as it sounded, when babies were in the neonatal unit there was a certain element of control. They could be monitored carefully, their medication adjusted. Comfort given. Feeding regimes measured as much as possible.

Of course things did sometimes go wrong, but with babies in one place and under her guidance she generally felt she could do as much as possible for the tiny, gorgeous, helpless little people. Once they got a bit older, and could move, walk, run, eat anything they found, they generally became the biggest safety hazard around and a heart attack waiting to happen. No. The complete randomness and unpredictability of them terrified her. So, she was interested. Could a parent really predict what their child might do when it was only aged five?

'She's a people person. Like a moth to a flame. Sofia loves people. All kinds of people—everywhere. I've never gone to a place with Sofia where she hasn't found a person to talk to. And she talks to them because she's interested. She wants to know everything about them.'

He gave a shrug.

'She's too young to realise just how important that is.' A frown creased his brow for a second. 'She's intuitive too. Seconds after she meets someone, she'll tell me if she likes them or not. At first, I used to laugh it off. Because we all do that. We all form first impressions. But...' He breathed out slowly. 'There have been a couple of occasions when she's been right and I've been wrong.' His dark eyes met Autumn's. 'Let's just say I've learned to pay attention.'

A car's horn sounded right next to them and they both jumped. Autumn squeezed the pastry she'd just lifted, causing a large dollop of cream to land on the plate. A moped darted between two cars, narrowly missing a pedestrian.

The traffic here was crazy. Thank goodness she'd made the decision not to drive. But the hotel she was staying at was a little way from the hospital. She'd have to ask Giovanni about public transport.

She toyed with the idea of sweeping up the piece of cream with her finger, but decided it was too impolite. Even though she'd never eaten something like this for breakfast before, her stomach was starting to rumble in anticipation.

'It sounds like you have a great relationship with your daughter,' she said.

'Of course—it's just me and her.'

He said the words simply, and she realised he'd probably had to say them a hundred times before.

She didn't need to ask. His wife hadn't left him. She knew that instantly.

'I'm sorry to hear that, Giovanni. But I'm sure Sofia has everything she needs in her obviously doting dad.'

He gave a sigh and leaned back in the chair. He glanced at the roads around them, wincing as a few more scooters seemed to take risky chances.

He lowered his voice. 'My wife died just before Sofia's first birthday. She was travelling to the hospital for an emergency. She was on a scooter and she was hit by a speeding driver.'

Autumn shivered. She couldn't help it. There had already been several near misses in the time they'd sat here.

And the incident he'd just described... Things like that terrified her. Random, no reason, no control. She hated everything about those elements of the world outside her control.

As a medical student she'd taken some anti-anxiety medication for a time, and seen a counsellor to help her accept that there would always be things out of her control. It had taken four years, but she'd gradually accepted that. However, as soon as the counsellor had dug a little deeper about her feelings, repressed emotions and her upbringing, Autumn had stopped attending. She'd got what she needed to be able to function well enough in life.

But hearing stories like this always made her feel slightly panicky. One person's actions—a foot just a bit too heavy on the accelerator—had changed Giovanni and his daughter's life for ever. She'd always wondered how people coped after something like that.

'You must miss her.' It seemed the most obvious thing to say, and she didn't want him to see the tiny shake of her hands.

He gave a sad smile, his eyes looking a little darker than before. 'I'm sad that she's lost her part in Sofia's life. They were so alike. I think Anna would have got great joy from watching her grow every day. I also think they might have argued constantly...'

The smile grew warmer. He could obviously see them both in his head. But then he lifted his gaze again.

'But we can't live in the past. I have a duty to help Sofia live every day to the full. We talk about Anna, and I show her pictures, but I make sure her life is full of joy.'

Autumn could feel herself blinking back tears. *Wow.* This was the last thing she'd expected. But part of her was glad. She was glad she hadn't made a blunder and asked Giovanni about his wife. She was also glad that Giovanni was in a position where he felt as if he could share. He seemed sad, but not grief-stricken. A tiny, selfish part of her knew that meant he would be able to focus completely on their case.

As she watched Giovanni, he started to eat his pastry. He had the cloth napkin perfectly placed to catch any errant blobs of cream. It appeared he was an expert at *maritozzo*-eating. She took a few nervous bites herself, the burst of sweetness on her lips giving her an instant sugar rush.

She laughed. 'This can so *not* become a habit. Between the coffee and the sugar this morning, I will probably be jittery all day. Not to mention the pounds I could gain.'

He seemed back to his easy self, and the momentary shadows she'd seen flicker across his eyes had now vanished.

She glanced over at him, talking more before she thought. 'There's no way *you* do this every day!'

There wasn't a pick of fat on him. He was lean, but in a muscular kind of way. It was visible through his suit jacket, and the wicked smile he gave her in response made heat rush to her cheeks.

'Oh, sorry. That didn't quite come out how it should have.'

But now there was a cheeky glint in his eye, and she had to admit that she liked it.

'Maybe it came out exactly like it should have.' Giovanni glanced at his watch. 'Perhaps we should get back and I can give you the tour. Then we can get down to work.'

Autumn dabbed at the edge of her mouth with the napkin, praying she wasn't going back to her new place of work with cream on her face.

They jumped back in the car and Giovanni wove his way back to St Nicolino's.

Walking through the hospital with Giovanni was an enlightening experience. Everyone stopped to talk to him.

She smiled as she remembered what he'd said about his daughter. Did he really not realise where she got her 'people person' traits from?

Giovanni reminded her of a paediatrician she'd worked with when she was a student. Dr Blair had remembered the name of every patient he'd ever seen. He'd been a wonderful mentor, and she'd lost hours of her life waiting while random strangers stopped him in the street, thanking him for looking after a relative years before. He'd remembered every case.

Walking with Giovanni was like walking the streets of her home town back in Scotland with Dr Blair.

She'd heard a mixture of languages around her. She had been slightly worried, coming to Italy. Italian wasn't exactly a second language for her, although she could get by. But since setting foot in this hospital she had found most of the staff spoke English to her. It was a relief, but that didn't mean she wouldn't still make an effort to speak Italian.

St Nicolino's was a state-of-the-art hospital, and the sprawling tour wasn't for the faint-hearted. She saw the wards and ICU, and the operating theatre complex, where Giovanni reassured her that her surgical privileges had been put in place for her. Then they toured the X-ray department, and met the sonogram and radiology staff. He showed her the changing facilities, the offices, where he introduced her to the admin assistants, then the overnight rooms and canteen facilities.

Then he led her down a quieter corridor and threw open the door to a wide room. 'This is where we'll spend most of our time.'

She blinked for a moment, trying to take in the sight in front of her. It was clearly a training room—a room where doctors at all stages of their career could practise and hone their clinical skills. She'd been in many rooms like this over the course of her career. But none had been quite like this one.

This room was full of tiny 3D-printed mannequins. Perfectly made tiny babies, all anatomically correct, and all at various points in surgery.

She frowned as she turned to Giovanni. 'You practise every surgery?'

Cost. That was the first thing that flew into her head. She'd often asked for a specific 3D mannequin to be built, to allow her to practise a surgery that she hadn't performed before. She knew exactly how much each of them would cost. But right now, the fact that here she'd have the chance to practice surgeries again and again was making her smile from ear to ear.

She'd methodically ticked off all the people she'd met and the places she'd been today on a list in her head. There were still a few key staff and facilities she'd have to discover. But this room... There was a real danger this would distract her completely.

Giovanni nodded. 'We have our own design team and 3D printing capabilities. They have already made mannequins of the Bianchi twins that Lizzy and Leon can practise on. The truth is, we don't know exactly when we might have to operate on these babies. We have to be prepared at any point in time. And, as you'll know, size plays a huge factor in these surgeries. Of course,' he continued, 'I hope we have many more weeks to prepare. But our team are performing weekly sonograms, and every time they do another, our modellers make us 3D mannequins of the twins. Sometimes multiple mannequins. The surgery that you and I will perform will be very different from the surgery Leon and Lizzy will likely have to do.'

Autumn gave a solemn nod as she moved over to one of the pairs of mannequins. This one was sealed in the amniotic sac. One of the babies would likely need cardiac surgery before delivery. The delicacy and precision of the operation would be absolutely crucial. Performing in utero surgery was a real skill. She didn't envy Lizzy and Leon their task.

The lighting in this room was as bright as in any theatre, and a whole host of tiny instruments was laid out on the tables at one side. She walked over, her eyes scanning along the trays, instantly looking for the tools she might need for her surgeries.

She hadn't even heard Giovanni move, so the low voice behind her made her jump. 'Just give me a list of what you need. You'll have it in days.'

She could feel his warm breath at the back of her neck. He was very near, obviously looking at the trays too.

She should step to one side. They were too close for comfort. But she pressed her lips together for a second and closed her eyes, taking a deep breath.

It was too soon. Too soon to consider anything. She'd never felt a pull like this before. It unnerved her. She was always the calmest person in the room. So why didn't she feel like that today?

'Most of what I need is here already. There might be a few specialist instruments. I'll give you a list later.'

Now she did step to the side and turn to face him. 'Can we meet the parents now?'

He gave the briefest nod of his head. 'Of course.'

As he turned towards the door again she let out her breath. The air-conditioning in the room kept its temperature steady. She just wished her body would do the same.

She was just tired. That was what it must be. She'd been running on adrenaline since his call last night. Because what she really didn't want to do right now was acknowledge the way her skin prickled and her heart-rate picked up any time she was around this man.

They had to work closely for the next few months. All her focus had to be on these babies. And Giovanni Lombardi was a distraction she *definitely* didn't need.

CHAPTER THREE

GIOVANNI LED HER to a large, comfortable room on the far side of the maternity unit. It was close enough to all emergency facilities without being in the middle of an impersonal ward.

He beamed as he walked into the room. 'Gabrielle, Matteo—I want you to meet Autumn Fraser. She's a specialist surgeon from Scotland.'

He turned towards Autumn as he moved to a comfortable sofa.

'Autumn, this is Gabrielle and Matteo Bianchi. Gabrielle is from Geneva, where they live, but they are staying with us. Matteo is from here, and has rented a villa in Rome, and Gabrielle is being monitored on a daily basis.'

Autumn could see the worry lines on the faces of both parents. They'd likely had the shock of their lives when they'd learned about their babies. The nerves and the strain were apparent even at first glance.

Autumn walked over to them, holding out her hand to shake with each of them. 'It's a pleasure to meet you.' She knew how important it was to earn the trust of parents. And she was quite sure she would be every bit as anxious if she were in their shoes.

She sat next to Giovanni as he started talking again. 'I told you I was going to find a surgeon to lead the second team.' He put his hand on his chest. 'I'll be leading the team working with Hope, and Autumn will be leading the team working with Grace.'

Autumn's stomach gave a little flip. He'd mentioned this would be a trial agreement. But introducing Autumn as the surgeon leading the other team didn't seem like any kind of trial.

'The babies have names? That's fantastic,' she said. 'I love them.'

Gabrielle gave a nervous half-smile, her hands on her swollen stomach. She glanced at her husband. 'We did it a few weeks ago. We thought that if we gave them names now, it might bring us good luck.'

Autumn understood. Parents often had different opinions. She'd done other surgeries on conjoined twins where the teams had been called Twin A and Twin B. Some parents were terrified of naming babies who might not make it. They wanted to wait until they were actually born, then give them names.

Gabrielle and Matteo obviously wanted their daughters to be known by name from the beginning. Some people thought it might make their children more real. For them, as well as for others.

Giovanni gave a slow nod. Autumn knew he could have told her earlier, but it was clear he'd wanted to give the parents their place. She put her hand on her chest. 'So, I'll be in charge of Team Grace. I can promise you that we're going to plan for both your daughters carefully and do all we can to give them the best outcome possible.'

She could see Giovanni's sideways glance. It was always important in conversations like these that surgeons didn't promise they could save the babies. Autumn would have loved to do that. But these surgeries were filled with risks, as were the surgeries prior to separation. She could guarantee she would do everything she could for Team Grace, but anything else would be unethical.

Giovanni leaned forward. 'So, both myself and Autumn will talk you through all the aspects of the separation. But we don't want to overwhelm you. You know that Leon and Lizzy have to do their surgeries first? Once they have finished, we'll take over. But just know that we'll be working hard behind the scenes to get things ready for our surgeries after the Caesarean section.' He leaned forward and put his hand on Gabrielle's. 'One day at a time. Just know we're always here.'

Gabrielle blinked, unshed tears visible in her eyes. She gave a silent nod.

Giovanni stood up and Autumn joined him. 'Nice to meet you both,' she said. 'If you want to talk to me, just let one of the staff know and I'll be here.'

As they left the room Autumn could feel the weight of the meeting on her shoulders. Giovanni was walking alongside her, and his hand brushed against hers, drawing her attention. The buzz going up her arm was instant and undeniable.

'The first introduction is always the toughest. I'm trying to give them space to process everything without overwhelming them. Lizzy and Leon are their primary caregivers right now.'

She raised her eyebrows, sure that it must be driving him crazy, and he nodded.

'Yep, I find it difficult not to constantly check things. But I have a short meeting first thing every morning with Lizzy and Leon, then I drop in to see the parents at some point during the day.'

'You need them to have faith in Leon and Lizzy.'

'Absolutely. We'll take over when we need to.' He stopped for a moment and leaned on a railing to look out over the wide entrance and the floors beneath them. 'This is one of the most complicated cases we've ever had.'

Autumn joined him, leaning down and looking at the bustling hospital. She could see the sigh of absolute relief from everyone who walked through the front doors, out of the searing heat of Rome and into the air-conditioned space inside the hospital. She shivered, not sure if it was caused by the temperature around her, the man next to her, or the huge pressures of the surgery ahead.

'Do you have a gestation in mind that you think we'll need to work to?'

He nodded. 'I'm approximating around thirty-two weeks right now. Lizzy and Leon's surgery will be soon. From there, it just depends on how Gabrielle and the babies do after that. We could require immediate delivery, or we might manage a reasonable amount of time after that.'

Autumn nodded. Everyone knew that babies tended to do better the closer to normal gestation they were delivered. Most twins these days were delivered before forty weeks. These babies would never last to that point. But thirty-two weeks wasn't unreasonable. If things went well, both babies might be able to breathe with minimum assistance at that stage, and would also have the ability to suck, swallow and feed. Every baby was an individual, and they wouldn't really know until the twins were here, but thirty-two weeks was something to aim for.

She turned to face Giovanni. 'So, we're likely have a maximum of seven weeks to prepare for this surgery?'

Part of her body was going into panic mode. The intricacies of her liver surgery were going to be more than difficult. The separation between Hope and Grace would be tricky enough, and once that was done she would literally have to build Grace a liver, hoping she could also sort out an adequate blood supply.

'Are you okay?'

Giovanni moved quickly, his hand on her arm, and she caught the woody scent of his aftershave.

'Fine,' she said quickly. She wanted to start practising right this second. But she knew it was a bad idea.

Giovanni's fingertips on her arm pressed gently. 'How about an early dinner? I know a five-year-old who would love to meet you.'

She hesitated. She wanted to get back to her hotel room, lie down on the giant bed and just let it swallow her whole. Processing…there was so much processing her brain had to do right now.

'Sofia wants to meet me?' she asked.

One eyebrow flicked upwards. 'She picked you.'

'What?' His words came as a complete surprise and left her momentarily stunned.

He gave a serious nod as he steered her down the corridor again. 'Truthfully. She looked at all the faces I had on my computer screen and told me to pick you.'

Autumn's skin prickled in annoyance. 'I hope you're joking.'

Giovanni shrugged. 'Let's just say you were already joint top of the list anyway.'

Autumn stopped walking. *Joint?* She couldn't keep the indignation out of her voice. 'Who did you think matched me?'

He named another surgeon from the US, who specialised in paediatric liver surgery. She wasn't quite so offended, but still annoyed.

'I'm better than him…'

He opened the door to the office he'd shown her earlier, where her bag and jacket were stored. 'It was your studies into the psychological trauma of separation that swayed me.'

She'd just bent to pick up her bag and stopped dead. 'Really? You know about that?' That was another surprise. Most fellow surgeons just looked at her skill set and success rate. They didn't look into the other aspects of medicine she'd explored.

He nodded as he moved towards her. 'I've read your papers. I like your concepts. I don't have your depth of knowledge, but I've often wondered about the trauma of separation for conjoined twins. And I don't mean the physical trauma.'

Her mouth was dry. 'You believe there's a psychological side?'

She'd met other scholars who wouldn't be convinced about the principle of psychological trauma for neonates. It was almost a relief to find someone who believed in it and was interested to learn more. Too many other surgeons just wanted to talk about clinical procedures and techniques.

'Of course I believe it.' His husky voice revealed no doubt.

She could have sworn some magical creature had just run down the length of her spine.

Giovanni tilted his elbow towards her. 'Let's pick up Sofia and go for dinner. I'll drop you back at your hotel afterwards.'

'You don't mind eating early?' She knew Italians were known for their late dinners.

He shook his head. 'I have a five-year-old who I like to get to bed at a reasonable time. Believe me, Sofia needs no excuse to be up half the night.'

Autumn hesitated. She was tired, but she had to eat, and she still hadn't planned how to travel to and from the hospital. She gave a slow nod. 'Thanks,' she said, then added, 'I'd love to meet Sofia. Just to let her know that I'm truly the best candidate.'

She gave him a straight-eyed stare and he laughed.

As they walked out to the car park she wrinkled her nose. 'When you spoke to me yesterday, you said you had to make sure I was a good fit for the team. I'm assuming that as you've introduced me to the parents, you think that I am?'

He held the car door open for her for the second time today. There was a gleam in his eye. 'I might,' he said, 'but you still have to pass the final hurdle.'

'What's that?'

'Sofia,' he said, and grinned as he closed the door and walked around to the other side.

Giovanni could tell from the expression on her face that Autumn hadn't worked out yet that he was toying with her.

He went in to pick up Sofia and she dashed straight out to the car as soon as she knew who was in it. He hadn't even managed to collect her bag and jacket before she'd climbed into the car and started to fasten her seatbelt, the whole time talking constantly.

'You're Autumn? Do you know that's a season? I had to look it up. I'm Sofia. I'm five. How long will you work with my *papà*? Are you staying with us?' She started to bounce a little in her car seat, even though she was strapped in.

Giovanni slid into the car and gave Autumn a grin. 'Sofia, calm down. Wait until we're at the restaurant before you start asking questions.'

Autumn looked dumbstruck. 'Her English is amazing. Much better than my Italian.'

He nodded, the feeling of pride making his chest swell. 'Yes, her English is good. Obviously. As is her Italian. She can also speak a little Greek and a little Japanese. She attends an international school and she seems to pick up languages...' he wrinkled his nose for a second '...how do you say it? Like a sponge?'

Giovanni pulled away and moved into the traffic. It was busy. There was much horn-sounding, gesturing and shouting. It seemed that Giovanni wasn't shy about shouting either.

He let out a yell as someone cut in front of them and Sofia started laughing. Her laugh was light. But Autumn was gripping the sides of the seat. She'd heard about the traffic in Rome, but she'd never experienced it first-hand. She glanced sideways at Giovanni, wondering how it felt to drive in this every day, knowing that his wife had died in a traffic accident.

She literally felt as if an accident could happen around about them at any second. But Sofia didn't seem upset or worried. She was young... This was likely her everyday normal.

Around ten minutes later Giovanni pulled up in an older part of the city. As Autumn climbed out of the car, she pulled the damp hair from the back of her neck. The journey hadn't been quite what she'd expected. Stopping was a complete and utter relief.

Sofia jumped out and ran into the restaurant. Autumn turned and smiled wearily at Giovanni. 'Come here often?'

He let out a low laugh. 'Perhaps. Watch out or she'll order for you.'

As they walked inside, it was clear that this was a restaurant owned by his friends. Sofia had settled herself at a booth and was tapping the top of the table for them both to join her. 'Autumn, sit next to me,' she said.

Giovanni slid into the seat across from her. 'What am I? Old news?' he asked. But from the way he was grinning Autumn could tell he wasn't offended.

An older woman appeared, kissing Giovanni on both cheeks and putting some water and glasses on the table. She turned and said something in rapid Italian to Autumn, but Giovanni shook his head, clearly explaining that Autumn wouldn't understand.

He pointed to the water. 'Would you prefer some wine with dinner?' he asked.

She shook her head. She was already exhausted, and her head was so full. She felt as if even a sip of wine would knock her out. 'Water's great, thanks.'

The older woman switched easily to English, and spoke between two languages as she took their orders.

'Which is best?' Autumn asked Sofia, pointing at a few items on the menu, who then took great delight in deciding on her order.

Ten minutes later she had a delicious plate of rigatoni in front of her, in a creamy tomato sauce with bacon through it, along with a heap of garlic bread in a basket between them all. It was hitting all the right spots.

She'd also answered what seemed like a million questions from Sofia, who was currently tucking in to her dinner. Autumn smiled. Both Giovanni and Sofia had their cloth napkins tucked into their collars. Cute.

Giovanni glanced at Sofia. 'It's the only time she's quiet,' he said jokingly. 'Take advantage while you can.'

Autumn shook her head and looked at him steadily. 'She's a delight.'

She could see the pleasure in his eyes. He glanced back at his daughter and she could almost feel the strength of his love for her stretching across the table to grab her.

Sofia wasn't quite so terrifying as she'd feared a child might be. Drinks hadn't been spilled yet, nor dinner dropped on clothes—in fact, if anyone was going to do that, it was much more likely to be Autumn. She was struggling to keep her eyes open.

Her brain started drifting. Father and daughter seemed so easy around each other... She wondered if he ever got strict with her at home or if he was always like this.

It wasn't as if she knew anything about bringing up a child. Sure, Autumn had friends with children. She'd even offered to take a good friend's baby overnight, when her friend had started to look as if she might blow away in a puff of wind. She'd taken the baby back at lunchtime the next day and smiled sweetly, not admitting that she'd been up all night, terrified, watching the rise and fall of her friend's sweet son's chest.

She often stayed late in the ICU units at the hospitals she worked in in London. It was comforting, holding a baby against her chest, rubbing its back gently to settle it, all the while knowing she could be surrounded by ten people at a moment's notice.

It was easy being confident with tiny babies in a hospital. She didn't imagine for a single second it was easy being home alone in charge of a tiny person. And as Autumn watched Giovanni she couldn't pretend she didn't admire him right now. Sofia was a lovely kid—bright, fun and well-mannered.

'You okay?' he asked softly.

She gave a little start, embarrassed to have been caught staring.

'Just tired,' she said, pushing her plate away. 'The food here is delicious. I'll need to remember how to get here.'

A small hand landed on her arm. 'You can't come here without me.' Sofia's wide eyes were serious. 'I need to tell Mamma Pieroni what you want.'

Autumn put her hand over Sofia's. 'Well, I'll tell you

what—next time I want to come I'll let your dad know and he can see if you're free.'

For a second Sofia's brow creased, as if she were an adult contemplating something, and then her face lit up in a smile again. 'Okay, then.'

Giovanni had slid from his seat and moved away whilst she was talking to Sofia. He strolled back over. 'Sofia, it's time to go home. We need to drop Autumn back at her hotel. She's had a long day and she is very tired.'

Autumn realised distractedly that Giovanni must have settled the bill. 'Sorry,' she said quickly as she fumbled for her bag. 'Let me pay. I didn't expect you to buy me dinner.'

His reply was as quick as lightning and in a joking tone. 'But remember this wasn't dinner. This was a test.'

She sighed as she wriggled out of the booth. 'Then please tell me that I passed.'

As she slid into the car, she noticed what looked like a bus stop on the other side of the road. 'Oh, can you tell me the best way to get to the hospital from my hotel? Should I use the bus, the tram, or the metro?'

'None,' he said as he clicked his seatbelt into place. 'I'll pick you up.'

'You can't do that,' she said automatically. 'I don't want to put you to any trouble. Particularly when you have Sofia to think of.'

'It's no trouble.' His voice was smooth.

Autumn shook her head again. 'No, it would be a complete imposition. And I need to learn to find my way around the city by myself.'

The car eased into the traffic and Giovanni gave a nonchalant shake of his head. 'Maybe in a few days. But I'll pick you up for the next few mornings. Point out a few other places to you and give you some time to find your feet.'

He made himself sound like some kind of tour guide…
It wasn't that she didn't appreciate the offer—of course
she did. But Autumn had always been an independent
woman. She might not contemplate driving a car in the
complicated system around her, but she definitely wanted
to be mobile on her own.

'It's a kind thought,' she said firmly, 'but I like to find
my own way.'

There was a tiny crease in his brow. If she hadn't been
so tired, she might have been amused. She wasn't sure
if it was Italian chivalry or a colleague being protective,
but relying on Giovanni to get her to and from work was
a definite no-no.

They would be working closely enough already. It
hadn't even been a whole day and already she was trying
to pretend she didn't find this man attractive, compelling,
intelligent and incredibly sexy. She'd definitely need some
space to allow her senses a chance to recover.

Now, even though she could sense the tiniest hint of
annoyance, he gave a nod of his head. 'How about we just
settle on me collecting you tomorrow morning and I'll
show you where the transport links are on the way to the
hospital? There are a few places I'd warn you to avoid so
you can stay safe.'

'Tomorrow morning,' Autumn repeated, with a reluc-
tant nod of her head.

She was watching the fascinating attractions and the
streets of Rome stream past, and knew that she would want
a chance to explore this city herself.

She turned to him and kept her voice firm. 'And then
I'll be able to suit myself.'

There was an edge to her voice. She was drawing a line
in the sand. Sofia was singing quietly in the seat in the back
and Autumn didn't want to get into a fight with Giovanni.

There was a hint of a smile on his face. 'No problem,' he said, his accent thick.

He pulled his car up in front of her hotel and she let out a long, slow breath. She turned and smiled at Sofia. 'It was a pleasure to meet you, Sofia, and I hope we can meet again soon.'

Sofia stared at her with wide brown eyes. There were a few seconds of silence before the little girl gave a nod of her head. 'I think we're going to be friends,' she said solemnly.

Autumn smiled. 'I think so too.'

The door next to her clicked. She hadn't even realised Giovanni had slipped out of the car and opened her door for her. It seemed to be a habit of his.

She swung her legs out of the car, immediately swamped by the warm evening Rome air. As she stood up she stumbled a little, causing Giovanni to quickly slide an arm around her back.

'Okay?' he asked.

She turned her head—and froze. They were literally inches apart, and her body had decided to let her stop breathing. It was a close-up she hadn't imagined having.

His dark eyes seemed to pull her in. The remains of his aftershave drifted around her. His jacket was in her hands, and she was conscious of his warm fingers at her waist, their heat drifting through to her skin.

It was like being stopped in time. The noise of the city was there, but it seemed they were stuck in an imaginary bubble around them. Her eyes took in every part of his face. His dark hair, the short stubble of his beard and moustache, the tiny lines around the corners of his eyes…

'Did I pass the test?' she asked, in a voice so low she could barely hear herself.

His face creased into a smile. 'Always,' was his reply.

There was an instant of stillness between them, and then he dropped his arm and walked away.

Now she breathed. Sucking in the exhaust fumes of the others' cars around them. Numerous people were being dropped at the hotel. It wasn't as big as some of the others, but was obviously popular.

The noise around her seemed to amplify and she gave herself a shake. What *was* that? What had just happened?

'Seven o'clock tomorrow morning?'

Her head jerked up. Giovanni was at the other side of the car, ready to get back in.

She nodded her head. 'Absolutely—thank you.' She gave a wave to Sofia and headed to the hotel entrance.

A good night's sleep. That was all she needed. She'd been living on adrenaline since last night's telephone call. Today had been an overload. And she'd expected that... but not quite in the way it had occurred.

She walked through Reception and pressed the button for the lift. She would be fine. She would unpack the luggage she'd dropped earlier, shower, and drop straight into bed.

But even as she stepped into the lift her stomach gave a little twist. She already knew the face that would invade her dreams tonight...

CHAPTER FOUR

'WHAT'S WRONG, PAPÀ?'

Giovanni was staring out of the window, his head somewhere in the clouds. Sofia's voice jerked him back to attention and he finished buttoning the short-sleeved shirt he'd chosen to wear for work that morning.

'Nothing, darling,' he said quickly. 'I'll be ready in a moment.'

Sofia climbed up on to the chair next to him and gave him a hard stare. 'You keep doing that,' she said, a determined edge to her voice.

He tried not to smile. Sometimes Sofia acted like the adult in the household. Keeping Giovanni in line seemed to be her first priority.

He knelt down beside her. 'I keep doing what?'

'That thing.' She folded her arms across her chest.

'What thing?'

'The staring thing. Not paying attention.'

'To you?' The thought struck a pang through his heart.

'To everything.' She shrugged her shoulders, emphasising her folded arms.

Giovanni ran his hand through her hair. 'Sofia, you'll always be the centre of my attention. Sometimes Papà has to think about other things—work. But you always come first.'

'I know that,' she said in a small voice.

Giovanni held out his hand. 'Come on, then, let's get going.'

Sofia's hand slipped into his and he gave it a squeeze. He chatted easily until he dropped her off, then spent the rest of the way to the hospital swamped with guilt.

Called out by a five-year-old—and rightly so.

He'd been thinking about Autumn Fraser.

Ridiculous. One week. That was how long they'd been working together. His brain was constantly on overload, thinking about the intricate planning for the surgery. He couldn't spare any space—none at all—so he couldn't understand for a second why he continually found himself lost in thoughts about Autumn Fraser.

Of course, she was smart. Of course, she was unintentionally gorgeous. She definitely struggled with the language, but she was trying hard. He'd watched from the end of the corridor yesterday as she'd tried chatting to one of the domestic staff. Carla had been greatly amused with the new doctor trying out her Italian. But all of that was entirely superficial.

Giovanni knew that Autumn was here on a temporary basis. But from their first phone conversation he'd had a good feeling about her. This week she'd started to assess the staff around her as to their suitability for her team. She was pleasant to people, but had already revealed there were a few staff she was unsure of. He liked her honesty.

There had been no further breakfasts or dinners. She'd started taking the tram to work, and told him she was thoroughly enjoying the journey. But her office was right next to his. They spoke to each other every day. She'd started to accompany him on short visits to Matteo and Gabrielle.

'Giovanni?'

And there she was. Dressed in a pair of red scrubs.

He closed his laptop and moved over to join her, picking up his surgical cap as he headed to join her.

'Are you ready?'

He saw her hands were twisting together as they walked. He was dressed in his traditional navy scrubs and waved his hands down at his clothes. 'Do I look ready?'

'Oh, come on.' She nudged him as they headed to the clinical lab room, deliberately knocking him off his stride.

This was to be their first practice surgery. Of course, he was nervous.

Autumn kept talking. 'I'm worried about getting the positioning correct. I'm not sure I'll be able to reach the part of the liver I need to.'

She pulled her own surgical hat from her pocket as they opened the door to the lab. It was cream and covered in small red hearts. She tied up her hair and tucked the brown strands under her cap.

They'd both agreed to take this seriously. No one else was here for this first practice session. Autumn had seemed anxious to get started and had been impatient for their model to be ready. He wasn't quite sure if she was intimidated by this surgery—that would worry him—or just a control freak.

Giovanni mirrored her actions and tucked his hair under his own surgical cap. It had a little anchor at the front. It was like a ritual. He didn't know a single surgeon who didn't have their own cap.

Autumn stared at him for a few moments with those big green eyes. She gave a nod of her head. 'You tell me about yours; I'll tell you about mine.'

Her Scottish accent seemed a little thicker, making the words all run together. It took him a few seconds to work out what she'd said.

Then he laughed. 'My dad was in the navy. When I

told him about surgeons' hats, he produced this one a few days later.' He reached up and touched the cap again. 'He bought me a whole supply. Told me it was in case he wasn't around to see me wear them.'

Autumn tilted her head to one side. He could tell she understood without him having to say the words out loud. 'How long since you lost him?'

He gave a brief nod. 'Two years. He had cardiovascular disease. I'm just glad he got to meet Sofia. He was her biggest fan.' His fingers brushed his cap again, and visions of Sofia giggling on his father's lap played in his head.

He took a deep breath then, looked back at Autumn's cap. 'What about you with the love hearts?'

She shrugged. 'I lost a bet.'

'What?'

Autumn nodded. 'I don't need to tell you that surgery can be a pretty sexist area to work in. Most of the female surgeons I've worked under were power houses. One day me, and my fellow trainee surgeons, were talking about how most surgeons have a signature look, and contemplating what we'd choose if we made it through our programmes. One of the theatre assistants used to make caps for some of the staff. She had a ritual with trainees where she made what she thought suited them, laid out the caps and waited to see if they picked the right one.'

Giovanni was intrigued. He'd never heard anything like this before, but could imagine it taking place. 'So...?' he prompted.

'So, we came in one morning and there was a whole host of caps.' She counted off on her fingers. 'There were a few dark colours—some with motifs, like yours, or different patterns. There was one with bright yellow sunflowers, a green hat with a mountain range on it, another made of material that looked like the sea, one with rainbows, one with flames, and one with hearts.'

He wrinkled his nose. 'So how did you lose the bet?'

She waved her hand. 'Oh, we had to put our hand in a bag and pull out a number. I was last.'

'So you lost a lottery, not a bet?'

She smiled. 'You're being technical.'

Giovanni leaned against the surgical table he was next to. 'What would you have picked if you'd been first?'

She wrinkled her nose. 'I'm not sure. Probably leaves, because of my name.'

'But you got stuck with the hearts?'

She laughed and tucked another piece of hair under her cap. 'I did. And they've kind of stuck with me. Sometimes I imagine I want something crazy, like a unicorn or a space scene. But then I just revert back to my hearts.'

There was a gleam in Giovanni's eyes. 'Maybe you should switch to a liver.'

She gave him a gentle shove. 'Oh, very funny.' The last piece of hair disappeared and she stared at him. 'You know what turned out kind of nice? Avril—that's the theatre tech who made the caps— told me some time later that she'd meant the hearts for me anyhow.'

'She had?'

Autumn paused for a second, as if she was contemplating how she'd reply. Finally, she gave a nod of her head. 'Apparently I keep my heart close to my chest.'

Giovanni frowned and shook his head, not quite getting what she meant.

Autumn laughed. 'Sorry. It's a play on a figure of speech. You might have heard of keeping your cards close to your chest?'

'Ah, yes.'

'Well, she told me I keep my heart close to my chest.

I'm careful. And she was right. I do. I am. I've always been like that. She read me better than I expected her to.'

Every part of him was curious. Did Autumn have a reason to be guarded with her heart? It suddenly struck him that she hadn't even mentioned anyone back home. He'd made an assumption that she was single. But he didn't actually know that. For some reason, he knew he absolutely had to find out.

He chose his words carefully, but kept his tone light. 'So, do you still keep your heart close to your chest, or have you already lost it to someone?'

She gave him a curious stare, and he cringed at how forward his question seemed. She wavered. She didn't answer straight away. And all of a sudden the lurch of his stomach was so much more important than how cringeworthy his question had been.

She let out a long slow breath. 'I just...' she paused and chose her words carefully '...parted company with someone.' Autumn gave a hollow laugh. 'I didn't even have time to move out properly. I paid a company to go and pack up my things and drop them at my flat.'

Now Giovanni leaned back further on the trolley and folded his arms across his chest. He laughed too. 'Is it just me—or does that seem harsh?'

Her cheeks flooded with colour and she lifted her hands to them automatically. She let out a groan. 'It does, doesn't it?' She kept her eyes closed for a second. 'He's a nice guy. I like him—I do. I just had a moment when I realised he wasn't right for me.' She wrapped her arms around herself, as if she was trying to give herself some comfort, then opened her eyes and shook her head. 'No, that's not it. We *both* had a moment when we realised we didn't have that thing.'

Giovanni raised his eyebrows. 'That thing...?'

He couldn't believe how easily they were talking to each other. It seemed as though they'd tiptoed around each other for the last few days. Not awkward, exactly, just never really alone and talking. At least not like this.

She smiled and sighed. 'Don't start with me. You know that thing. The thing that quickens your heart and sets your skin on fire.'

She was staring straight at him. He unfolded his arms from across his chest and took a step towards her. The model they would be practising on was lying on a theatre trolley between them.

His voice dropped an octave lower. 'When your mouth goes dry and your brain won't focus?'

Recognition flashed across her eyes. He saw she was surprised. Her words had been easy, as if she'd been relaxed and with her guard down. But now she looked like a deer caught in the headlights.

As he watched she slowly licked her bottom lip. 'I guess…' It came out like a whisper. 'I'm not sure I've ever really experienced that. I'm not sure that I'll ever lose my heart to someone.' She gave a forced laugh. 'Anyway, we all know how important a heart is. It's too important an organ to lose.'

Giovanni took another step and laid his hands on his side of the trolley. She was trying to make light of those last words, but they hadn't gone unnoticed. He could ask more questions, but it probably wasn't the right time or the right place. So he took the easy way out. 'Then it sounds like you were right.'

Her head tilted slightly to the side. 'Right?'

'To walk away. Part as friends.'

She blinked. 'Of course. I'll always be his friend.'

Something lanced into Giovanni's heart. *Friends.* He hadn't told Autumn—or anyone—the truth about himself and Anna. Only a few short months after their daughter's arrival they'd been far from friends. The day she died she'd just launched a tirade at him before heading out on her scooter to go to work.

He'd told her she was still officially on leave. He'd been worried about her mental health after the birth of their daughter. A friend had been due to visit in a few days and assess her. Her behaviour had become, on occasion, increasingly erratic, with her flaring up out of nowhere. Other times she was calm and happy, but also a little restless.

Anna had always been like a butterfly, beating her wings against a window in a fight to get free. In the end, the last thing they'd been was friends, but he'd never shared that with anyone. Now, he was envious of the sad look in Autumn's eyes. She was sincere. She had genuinely parted from her ex as friends, and clearly wished him the best.

Her warm hand touched his arm. 'Giovanni? Are you okay?'

He jerked and looked up, putting a smile on his face. 'Oh, yes—sorry. Lost in my thoughts for a second.'

Her voice was soft. 'Thoughts about surgery, or thoughts about something else?'

Those green eyes were staring straight at him. She knew he hadn't been thinking about surgery and she was giving him an opening if he wanted it. But he couldn't. He couldn't share. Autumn was still almost a stranger, even though she didn't really feel like that.

He kept the smile on his face, knowing exactly how frozen it looked. Her gaze was steady. Almost as if she were peeling back his layers to see exactly what was there.

He looked downwards at the model of the babies beneath them. There was so much work to do. So little preparation time. He couldn't allow his thoughts to wander elsewhere. They both had a duty and a responsibility to Hope and Grace.

He cleared his throat loudly. 'I think we should get to work.'

If Autumn was offended by his change in tone and conversation she was professional enough not to let it show. 'Of course.'

She could feel the awkwardness in the air, but refused to acknowledge it or let it put her off her game. She was here to do a job.

They'd spent the last four hours talking technique as they worked. The surgical instruments they were using were understandably tiny. Steady hands were crucial. As was correct positioning. In an ideal world, they would be working on opposite sides. But surgery like this was never ideal.

'I need access to the renal vein,' she said in a low voice, as Giovanni worked on the side across from her. His dark eyes looked up. 'Come on over,' he said, clearly concentrating on what he was doing.

Autumn nodded and moved around. His large frame was bent over the models. His muscular arms held them in place. She dodged behind him, trying to find the best way to gain access.

'Problem?'

She hesitated. 'I may need to get a little closer.'

'Fine by me,' was the quick reply.

Her heart skipped a beat as she brushed up against his thin scrubs before ducking down and coming up between his arms. Her back was tight against his chest. One of her arms was intertwined with his, the other almost parallel. She shifted again, to allow her the optimum position to gain the access she would require.

She could feel the heat of his entire body, every bump, every ridge, against her spine.

Giovanni let out a low laugh. She felt his chest reverberate against her back.

'Sorry,' she whispered as she moved her hands delicately. 'But this is the only way to get access.'

His breath was at her neck and she knew he was watching her actions over her shoulder. 'It's a little up close and personal,' he whispered. 'But in the name of surgery I think we can sacrifice some personal space.'

There was laughter in his words and it made her tense muscles relax a little. With precision surgery there would always be an amount of tension. That was good. But too much tension could cause cramps and other problems. Truth was, this felt better than it should.

She didn't want to think about what she'd revealed earlier, and she hoped he hadn't picked up on it. The only person who'd caused her heart to race was this guy, the man she'd met just over a week ago.

She pushed back against him as she optimised her position in order to carry out the procedure she needed to.

He gave a little grunt and her stomach muscles clenched. Okay, this was maybe a bit *too* personal. She tilted her head, focusing, ignoring the rise and fall of the chest behind her. Another tiny clip and a positioning movement, to ensure the safety of the vein prior to separation… There—finally, she'd got it.

'Perfect.'

His voice was in her ear as she breathed a sigh of relief. Her muscles relaxed and she sagged back against him for a second.

'Wow,' she said.

But Giovanni didn't move. His hands remained entirely

steady, locked in place to enable him to carry out the next part of the procedure once she was finished.

It took Autumn a few moments to realise what she was doing. She was comfortable leaning into him, feeling the heat of him through their thin scrubs and the relief of the procedure being over.

Then her brain kicked into gear. She gave a nervous laugh. 'Guess I'd better move,' she whispered as she ducked down through his arms. Her head ran along the length of his thigh. He gave a cough and she flinched away, continuing to laugh nervously.

It felt strangely sad to move away from him. Which was ridiculous. She'd only known him for a week.

She watched without talking as Giovanni finished his part of the procedure, then straightened up, stretching his back and taking a deep breath.

As he pulled his head straight again, he gave her a wide grin, a hint of amusement in his eyes. 'I guess we'd better get used to that.'

'What?' she asked, praying her face wasn't as flushed as it felt.

'Getting up close and personal,' he quipped, his accent seeming a little thicker than normal. 'We might end up in all sorts of positions.' He paused for a moment, as her face definitely did a full flush, then added, 'In order to complete the surgery.'

One eyebrow gave the tiniest arch as he finished the last words. Deliberate. He'd done that deliberately. She didn't know whether to laugh out loud or throw something. So she pulled her cap from her head and shook out her hair, letting it cover her face momentarily.

It was hot in here. Too hot. Did the air-conditioning need turning up, or was it just her?

Through her hair she looked down at the model again,

trying her best to concentrate on the matter at hand. But it was hard. Her head was still swimming at the feel of Giovanni at her back, the sensation of his breath on the back of her neck, and the effect his voice had had on her.

She didn't do this. Not ever. She'd never experienced such an intense reaction to someone before and it all seemed so *wrong*. She was here to focus on two little girls.

'Let's do lunch,' said Giovanni, his words cutting through her thoughts.

Her mind went instantly to the nice dim restaurant he'd taken her to the time before. That was so *not* what she needed right now.

'I'm not sure that's a good idea.' The words came out before she had much time to think. She knew immediately they didn't sound quite right.

He stared at her, all humour lost. 'In the hospital canteen,' he said steadily, 'with a few of our potential colleagues for our teams. Let's brief them on how our first practice surgery went this morning, and how we would like to proceed.'

Embarrassment washed over her. He hadn't meant the two of *them*, specifically. Oh, no. His voice had a clipped edge, as if he were spelling things out to her exactly.

Giovanni had been welcoming and friendly when she'd arrived. Of course he had. Any surgeon would be. It was natural to pull out all the stops to entice another surgeon to stay if you wanted them to work alongside the team.

But she'd read too much into it.

She pulled her hair back. 'Of…of course. Of course. Give me ten minutes to freshen up. I'll meet you there.'

She was out through the door like a flash, her legs taking her rapidly down to the locker room. She flung open the door and leaned against the wall, her cap clutched in her hand. Within a few seconds she leaned over with her hands on her knees, groaning.

'Something up?' said an easy voice from the corner.

Darn it. She'd thought she was alone. Autumn snapped her head back up, ready to make some random excuses. But then her brain kicked in. The voice had spoken in English—not Italian. Lizzy Beckley was pulling on a pair of socks, sitting on a bench near the back of the room.

Autumn's shoulders sagged in relief. She tried to find words, but Lizzy gave her a knowing smile. 'That's the face of a woman who's been annoyed by an Italian man.'

Autumn took a few steps and sat down on the bench opposite her. 'You recognise it?'

They'd only met a few times, and had never had a chance to catch up properly, but she'd got a definite vibe of something weird between Lizzy and her Italian colleague Leon. What was more, it didn't seem to be on a professional basis…it seemed much more personal. From her rounded stomach, it looked as if Lizzy was pregnant, but Autumn didn't like to ask too many questions.

Lizzy nodded as she pushed her feet into her shoes. 'Oh, I know it well.'

She gave a little sigh as she picked up her bag and stood up. 'How about we talk some time? Is next week okay? I think us girls have to stick together.'

Autumn nodded. 'That would be perfect.'

She felt a wash of instant relief. They might not know each other well, but that recognition from another female who was likely in a similar position to herself was more than a bit welcome right now.

Lizzy put her hand on Autumn's shoulder as she walked past. 'We'll arrange a coffee next week. Hopefully away from this place.'

Autumn gave a grateful nod. Her eyes fell again to Lizzy's stomach as she watched her walk to the door, and Lizzy gave a little nod and rested her hands on her abdomen.

'How are you doing?' asked Autumn, keeping her words light and hoping they didn't sound intrusive.

'Eating for two.' Lizzy winked at her as she elbowed the door and walked out.

Interesting... The jungle drums were already talking about Leon and Lizzy. But Lizzy seemed remarkably cool about everything. How on earth was she feeling?

Autumn shook her head as she stood up again and pulled her scrubs from her body. She was slightly sticky, so she pulled her hair up on her head, grabbed new scrubs and headed to the staff showers. All the while wondering if Lizzy was as freaked out at the thought of having a child as Autumn knew *she* would be.

Giovanni wasn't entirely sure what he'd done wrong. Yes, they'd been up close and very personal. But, whilst it might not have been ideal, this type of surgery always carried that risk. Last time around, he and a male colleague had practically been breathing the same air in their attempt to position themselves appropriately for the sake of the separation surgery—and that one had been much less complicated than this.

Maybe it had been so long since he'd been that close to a woman that his senses were entirely off, but he could have sworn that when she'd finished her procedure Autumn had leant back into him, comfortably, for a few moments. She'd appeared relaxed, easy...but maybe she'd just been exhausted?

When he'd invited her for lunch it had been clear she'd

got the wrong message, and that had confused him again. She'd turned him down flat. And he might have been a little stung, and countered by being too direct with his clarification.

It wasn't as if the thought of lunch with Autumn hadn't entered his mind. Just not quite in the way she'd interpreted.

He wasn't sure what to do next to put any of this right.

Autumn was gorgeous. She was also from another country and would go right back there when her surgeries were complete.

He had a little girl to think of. No matter how attracted he might be to any woman, Sofia had to come first. Always.

The truth was he would take Autumn out in a heartbeat. It had been a long time since he'd had this kind of a reaction to a woman. Not even with his wife.

He had always played his cards close to his chest. His relationship with Anna had been rocky. They'd already decided to go their separate ways when Anna had announced she was pregnant. They'd reached an agreement to give their marriage another chance, and he'd marvelled as his wife's body had bloomed in pregnancy. He'd wondered if having a child would make Anna feel more settled. But it had become clear shortly after Sofia was born that she didn't.

It hadn't been any great surprise to Giovanni. His heart had already told him that was how she felt. Oh, Anna had loved their child. She'd doted on Sofia. But she'd struggled with being a mother. She'd wanted to return to work before her maternity leave was over. Not that Giovanni had minded.

He'd never told anyone they'd already had discussions about formally separating and sharing access to Sofia.

Anna had worked in the same hospital and Giovanni would never have spoken ill of his wife. Even though Sofia was too young to remember her, Giovanni had always made sure that every memory he repeated of Anna was good. Sofia even had a large photo on her chest of drawers, of Anna, beaming with happiness, holding baby Sofia in her arms.

He liked that photograph. It held happy memories. And those were the ones he preferred to keep, rather than memories of the exasperation that Anna had clearly felt when they'd fought. She'd told him she felt like a trapped bird. And he, in turn, had told her to spread her wings and fly. Their marriage had never been supposed to be a trap—for either of them—and if Anna hadn't been killed in the accident he was sure they would have managed to part in a fairly amicable way.

Instead he'd been left widowed, a single dad shrouded with doubts. Accidents were rife in Rome. But part of him had always wondered if Anna had been gripped by a moment of madness and thought of another escape.

It was ridiculous. And he knew it. She'd never expressed any suicidal tendencies. But late at night, when sleep was far from him, Giovanni's mind sometimes wandered into scary places. It might just be that he was avoiding the huge amount of guilt he felt about their parting words and their harsh argument. That had stayed with him—the fact that the last words between them had been in anger.

So, having a strong attraction to someone new was more than a little unexpected. Of course, he'd flirted, and occasionally dated over the last year or so. But no one had made his heart skip a few beats. Not even one. Until now.

He sighed and headed down to the hospital canteen, grabbing some food before joining a table with three other staff members. He could see the gleam in their eyes—all of them filled with hope that they would join one of the teams. They were hungry for it, and that made him glad. Hunger was what he looked for. Only the best would be allowed on his team. But first and foremost they had to really, really *want* it.

He didn't mind the reasons. To be part of precision surgery, for research, for the prestige of being part of a separation, or simply pure and utter passion for the project. Just as long as they had that passion.

He gave an easy smile and joined in their chat, only to be instantly distracted by the sight of Autumn walking through the doors. Her dark hair was slightly damp and piled above her head, and she was wearing a fresh pair of burgundy scrubs. She grabbed a sandwich and headed towards their table.

He could see the tiniest flash of hesitation in her face, and it made him sad, but Autumn sat down with ease, joining in the conversation at the table in a mixture of English and stumbling Italian. Her shoulders were tense and it took a little time for them to ease.

He kept on eating, nodding slowly and joining in. He was determined not to allow any of the others to pick up on any discord between them. Even he wasn't entirely sure if it was there or not. Maybe it was all just in his head and he was reading more into things than he should? Maybe parts of his brain were sparking back to life after slumbering for too long? But the truth was the other three were too busy trying to impress to pick up anything.

A few other people joined the table, one bringing coffee for both Autumn and Giovanni in a shameless ploy. Another brought a tray of donuts for the whole table. This doctor winked at the others and shrugged his shoulders at his colleague with the coffee. 'Hey, I didn't want to make it too obvious I'm trying to buy affection here. So I just bought for everyone.'

The rest of the people at the table laughed. All of them knew there was only one thing on their minds. The surgeries.

Giovanni watched Autumn. She was deep in conversation with the fellow surgeon sitting next to her. It was interesting to observe—particularly as he was a surgeon he'd planned to include in his own team, and Autumn had teased him about poaching.

As their conversation continued Giovanni shifted in his chair, wondering if it would be childish to interrupt. But before the thought could progress any further Autumn turned and gave him a stare that was a cross between haughty and challenging. His coffee slid down his throat the wrong way and he half coughed, half choked.

She pushed back her shoulders, lifted her eyebrows, and turned with her biggest grin back to the other surgeon.

Giovanni felt a wave of relief. Maybe he had overthought things. She certainly seemed to be relaxed enough now. That had seemed like a challenge. As if she were telling him, *I'm stealing your surgeon.*

He looked around the table and started talking. 'You'll all be well aware that Autumn and I still have to make selections for Team Hope and Team Grace. What you might not know is that this morning Autumn and I did our first practice surgery. There will be others—many others—and you will all have the chance to be involved. Our babies are at twenty-six weeks right now. We will need to have our teams in place, if possible, within the next few weeks. Whilst we hope our babies will remain in utero for as long as possible, we also know that we could be called at any moment.'

Everyone had stopped talking when Giovanni started,

but the silence that fell around the table now was heavy. It wasn't that his potential team didn't already know how serious this was, but he could see a few of them swallowing with difficulty.

The only person who didn't look fazed at all was Autumn. Her shoulders remained straight and her gaze steady. A little buzz shot through him. She would be ready at a moment's notice. Just as he would. That instilled him with confidence. For him and for the babies.

'My door is open for anyone who wants to talk to me about being on my team,' he said, knowing Autumn would see the glint in his eye.

'As is mine,' she added promptly.

She stood up and moved alongside him. She was making sure that everyone knew they were equals.

And they were.

Things seemed more relaxed now. What had happened earlier today must surely have been a blip.

He was still thinking when she turned to him. 'I have some work to do. I'll catch you later.'

Before he had a chance to reply, Autumn strode away across the canteen. He could see several staff members watching her leave, and he could almost write a list of who might approach her.

He tried not to smile. Healthy competition among staff was good. Everyone would be working at their optimum level to ensure a place on a team.

And that was entirely what he wanted—all staff at their absolute best to ensure the best possible outcomes for these babies.

CHAPTER FIVE

AUTUMN COULDN'T PRETEND she didn't feel a bit off. Whilst she'd had relationships with colleagues in the past, they'd never been with men she might potentially look at across the operating table.

The host of emotions that had swept over her while practising with Giovanni were simmering beneath her surface. It didn't matter how much she tried to ignore things, the air between them definitely sizzled.

Her brain told her it was too soon. She'd only just had a text to say that all her clothes had been packed up and delivered to her flat.

She pulled at her bright pink shirt. She hadn't asked for her clothes to be delivered to Italy. It would have been ridiculous and costly, and she'd rapidly realised the clothes she'd normally wear in the UK were just too warm for the current weather in Rome.

Her only choice was an immediate new wardrobe.

Via del Corso was one of the main streets in the historical centre of Rome, and several of the female staff at the hospital had pointed her in this direction to get some elegant dresses and suits for work.

Autumn couldn't believe quite how long and straight this street was, compared to the surrounding area that was littered with alleys and a variety of small *piazze*. What was also interesting was how narrow the street was by modern standards. It was busy, with only two lanes of traffic, and the pavements were packed with shoppers.

The buildings were a variety of colours—oranges, yellows, creams and a few red—with designer shop signs flickering in the light wind. The temperature was high today, and Autumn knew that as soon as she bought some new clothes, she would wear them straight from the boutique.

As she jostled with the crowds and listened to the chatter around her, she realised that there were just as many tourists as there were locals.

She strolled into the first designer boutique, pulled in by the elegant dresses displayed in the window. As she touched the first, the fabric light against her fingers, she knew it was perfect—just what she was looking for. The only trouble was the sharp intake of breath behind her.

She turned around. A woman in a beige suit was looking down her nose at her, speaking in rapid Italian. Autumn caught a few words and made a stammering attempt to reply in Italian. The woman wrinkled her nose, and Autumn felt embarrassed. She was surprised. These Italian boutiques must be filled with tourists on a regular basis.

She tried a few words in English. 'Excuse me, I'm looking for some dresses…' She lifted her hand again, wanting to check the size label on the dress, but the saleswoman stepped in front of her.

Autumn was immediately self-conscious, looking down at her clothes. She had on black trousers and a pink shirt. They were certainly a few years old, but perfectly serviceable. She had the most uncomfortable feeling that the woman didn't think she was good enough to shop in this boutique.

Maybe she was misunderstanding? Maybe it was just a

language barrier—and that flooded her with guilt. She was trying her best, but after less than two weeks she certainly hadn't mastered the language by any means.

The woman spoke to her again, rapidly and not entirely pleasantly. Autumn didn't need to understand the words to understand the tone.

She took a final glance at the emerald-green dress that would have been perfect, before giving a polite nod of her head and walking out of the door.

Her phone started ringing instantly, and she pulled it from her bag and answered it without even glancing to see who was calling.

'Hi.' Her voice was abrupt as frustration swept through her.

'Autumn? What's wrong?'

Giovanni's voice was like an instant balm. She wasn't thinking about earlier that week. Or about how she'd spent the last few nights barely sleeping, whilst he'd danced around in her thoughts.

'I've come shopping—' she sighed '—and I'm having some trouble.'

'What kind of trouble?' he sounded instantly concerned.

Now she felt a bit pathetic. 'I think it's just a language thing…'

'Where are you shopping?'

'Via del Corso. I wanted some lighter clothes for work. You know…smart, but something I can actually breathe in.'

He gave a soft laugh. 'Are you at one of the designer stores?'

She nodded, then realised he couldn't see her. 'Yes.'

'Give me a name?'

She turned and looked back at the pale-green-fronted store she'd just left and read the name out to Giovanni.

He gave a loud sigh. 'I told you to let me know when you needed to shop.'

'Don't be ridiculous. I don't expect you to come shopping with me.'

'Order a coffee at one of the nearby stands. I'll be there in ten minutes and I will take you to some places where they'll treat you the way they should.'

She didn't have a chance to say no before he hung up. She looked up at the door sign again. It was as if he actually knew something about the place.

She moved over to a coffee stand with a few tables and ordered coffee for both of them, sitting for a bit and watching the world go by. The heart of Rome was extraordinary. Partly filled with tourists, but also some of the most stylish people she'd ever seen.

A woman in a pale pink trouser suit with a bright silk scarf knotted at her throat strolled past as if she were wearing the most casual clothes in the world. Another woman moved along on the other side of the slim street, designer sunglasses on her face and wearing an elegant pure white dress that rippled around her model-slim frame. The crowd parted like the Red Sea around her, and Autumn held in a giggle.

She jumped as Giovanni sat down in the chair opposite her.

'There you are.' He beamed as if they were best friends.

'You didn't need to come,' Autumn said hastily. 'I'm sure I could have managed.'

He pointed down the street to the store she'd been in. 'Not in there. They're notorious. I'll show you where to shop.' His eyes ran down her body. 'There's some great places around here. Do you have a price range?'

Some might be offended by a question like that, but

Autumn wasn't at all. 'As long as we're not in the thousands, I'll be fine.'

He gave a nod, and she saw that he followed her gaze as she watched another woman in a dark green knee-length jersey dress stop to buy coffee from a nearby stand. 'I'd like that kind of thing,' she said. 'Smart enough for work, but still comfortable.'

'Dresses. No problem. Anything else?'

She thought for a moment. Whilst she might be a little embarrassed by Giovanni helping her shop, she might as well take advantage of the moment. 'Some tunic tops, a pair of shorts and some sandals…'

Giovanni laughed. 'You do realise I'll be in big trouble tonight, don't you?'

Autumn's brow furrowed. 'Why?'

'Sofia. She'll be annoyed that she's missed out on a shopping trip.'

'She likes shopping?' Autumn was surprised. Sofia hadn't struck as her a girl who would enjoy shopping trips.

'Are you kidding? My girl can shop like a pro. She *loves* shopping. When I tell her about this I'll be in so much trouble.' Giovanni let out a laugh as he shook his head. 'In fact, so will you.'

Something burned deep down inside her. He spoke about his daughter with so much pride—as he should. She could picture Sofia's face right now. 'I'm not too sure I want to get into an argument with your daughter,' she said with a smile as she stood up and put her bag strap over her head. 'I fear I might lose.'

He grinned as he stood up too. 'Oh, you definitely will. Come on, let's find some stores that are more fun.'

Autumn was amazed by how remarkably easy Giovanni was around the designer stores. He pointed at a few windows, unconcerned when she shook her head. Then they strolled down the street to look in some others.

When Autumn found a store with a large array of dresses in the window display that caught her eye, she was amazed when Giovanni greeted the sales assistant by name. Fifteen minutes later Autumn had found three dresses that she loved.

'The pink is great on you,' said the assistant, Marie, in easy English. 'And the floral print is so light. It will suit you in the hospital.'

'How did you know I worked in a hospital?' asked Autumn as she pulled the third dress, a comfortable green jersey, over her head.

Marie shrugged behind her. 'Giovanni told me you're work colleagues.'

'You're…friends?' Autumn asked as a button from the dress tangled in her hair.

Marie was a petite blonde, very attractive and equally nice. Was Autumn missing something here? And why did she feel a bit odd about that?

Marie leaned forward to unravel Autumn's hair. 'Yes, we're old friends. I know his sisters and I used to know his wife.' She shot Autumn a sorrowful smile.

'Thanks,' said Autumn as she shook out her freed hair.

She was glad of the distraction. Her stomach had clenched uncomfortably, but she was glad Marie hadn't tiptoed around about her. The staff at the hospital sometimes mentioned Anna. Almost in reverent tones. It was a little disconcerting at times, hearing how wonderful and beautiful Giovanni's dead wife had been.

Autumn gave Marie a little nod. 'Yes, Giovanni has told me about his wife. Obviously I'm new to the hospital, and didn't know her, but I've met Sofia. She's a delight.'

Marie's smile broadened. 'Well, if you've met Sofia,

you know who the boss is.' She glanced through the curtain towards the front of the store, where Giovanni was patiently waiting. 'It's such a shame he's on his own now.' She gave Autumn a sideways smile. 'We all keep hoping he might meet someone new.'

Heat rushed into Autumn's cheeks. Oh, no, it was like being a teenager back at school. In a few moments she'd gone from wondering if she might be a little jealous to wondering if Marie was trying to set her up. From one extreme to the other. And Marie's steady blue eyes were clearly sizing her up.

Marie tipped her head to one side. 'That's three dresses now. Do you need anything else?'

'S-sandals,' stuttered Autumn. Anything to distract the woman. 'And a few casual tops—maybe some capri pants.'

She didn't want to think about what all this might do to her credit card. It wasn't as if she couldn't afford to buy herself nice things—it was just she hadn't seen a single price tag on any of the items of clothing she'd tried so far. History told her that was never good a sign. It was just as well she loved everything that she'd tried.

Marie appeared again, as if by magic, with a pair of white capri pants and a short-sleeved fitted blouse that was white with pink flowers. She also had with her a second pair of capri pants, in navy, alongside a bright orange loose tunic top with a tie at one side, and a pair of flat cushioned sandals with some sparkle along the straps.

Autumn opened her mouth to talk, but promptly closed it again, taking the clutch of clothes hangers and closing the curtain on the dressing room.

Five minutes later she was glad she hadn't voiced any concerns. Marie's eye was good. She'd picked colours and styles that both suited and complemented Autumn's colouring. What was more, the clothes were actually comfortable. Almost unheard of unless it was a pair of pyjamas.

She kept on the sandals and the navy blue capris and orange top, and handed over the rest for bagging.

'Thank you,' she said to Marie appreciatively. 'You've made this so painless. I've got exactly what I need. How much do I owe you?'

Marie grinned and nodded over to Giovanni, who was sipping coffee in the corner of the store. 'Not a thing. Your bill has been covered.'

Autumn's credit card was already in her hand. 'What?'

Marie shrugged. 'Whether it's a friend or a sister, he always does this.'

There was something in the way she was looking at Autumn, with a hint of curiosity and humour.

Autumn spun around to Giovanni. 'You can't pay for my clothes! It's nice, but it's far too generous.' She was trying not to sound defensive and annoyed. Was this because he'd asked her what her price range was? Did he think she couldn't afford the clothes?

She heard the rustle of tissue paper behind her as Marie wrapped the dresses and other items, putting them in large bags. It was clear she was staying out of this fight.

Giovanni put down his coffee cup and stood up. He was wearing light trousers and a pale blue shirt, and with that darn dark stubble and the sunglasses on his head he might easily pass for some Italian model.

He gave her a nonchalant shrug. 'I like to keep the women in my life happy. You needed clothes.' He swept his arm out. 'We got you clothes.'

One of the women in his life. That was how he'd just referred to her. She was momentarily stunned. She couldn't even turn her head, because she was pretty sure that Marie's gaze would be searing into her.

Autumn took a deep breath and moved right in front of him. 'But, Giovanni, you can't pay for my clothes. It's not...' She struggled to find the right word.

'Not what?' He threw up his hands. 'Anyway, I might ask you for a little favour in return.'

Her skin prickled. 'What kind of favour?'

Giovanni threw back his head and laughed. 'You should see your face right now! Don't be silly. This will be fun.' He gave a thoughtful nod of his head. 'Better grab those bags.'

Autumn smiled quickly as she thanked Marie again, and left the shop clutching the large packages. Giovanni started to stroll back in the direction they'd started from. She was still a little uncomfortable. When was the last time a man had bought her clothes? She struggled to remember. It had obviously been a *long* time ago.

He named a popular movie from the nineteen-nineties. 'Ever seen it?'

She looked at him in confusion. 'Of course.'

His smile widened. 'Do you remember that scene where the women in a designer store are mean to the heroine and she returns later with lots of bags?'

Autumn looked down. She was carrying bags from the store that had been nice to her. She glanced up and saw the pale green store in the distance and started to laugh. 'Really? You want to do that?' She wrinkled her nose. 'Do people really do that kind of thing?'

The movie was playing in her head now, and she was seeing the similarities that she hadn't even considered. It might be fun...but it was also out of the ordinary.

She looked at Giovanni curiously. 'Is there something you're not telling me?'

If she hadn't been watching closely she might not have noticed the slight falter in his next footstep. He gave the briefest of nods. 'Maybe. Let's just say I have history with someone who works in that store. I can't believe they're still in business. They treat almost everyone the way they treated you today.'

Autumn's footsteps slowed. 'But why? Why not be like Marie? Why not be nice to people? I've never worked in retail, but surely that makes for better sales?'

Giovanni shook his head. 'I haven't worked in retail either, but courtesy goes a long way—no matter what field you work in.' He looked along the street. They were rapidly approaching the other store. 'Now, why not just have a little fun?'

Temptation was running through her veins. It felt like something a sixteen-year-old would do. But she couldn't pretend it wasn't a little amusing. Sad thing was, she probably would have bought a number of things in the other store if they'd been a little more friendly. Could she really pull this off?

He slowed as they approached the main door. Her bags were emblazoned with the name of the store Marie worked at. She guessed it must be a rival. Before she could overthink things, Autumn strode into the store. For a few seconds her wave of confidence evaporated, and then she lifted her head and started to stroll around, looking at the items on the rack.

Three saleswomen were standing gossiping at the back. As soon as they saw the amount of designer bags she was carrying, two of them were over in a few seconds. One of them was very familiar.

'Welcome, how can we help you?'

'Would you like some coffee? Some wine, perhaps?'

Autumn gave them a pleasant smile, but didn't attempt to speak. Didn't they even recognise her—remember that she'd been in their store only a few hours before? She started walking along the rails, looking at the clothes.

'What about this? It's one of our finest?'

One of the women had snatched a white jacket from the rail. It was as about as far removed from any item Autumn would ever wear as it was possible to be.

Autumn gave a brief shake of her head and kept moving.

The other woman moved seamlessly ahead of her, picking out a beige formal dress. 'Something in this shade?' Before Autumn had a chance to object it was pressed against her. 'This colour is perfect for you,' the woman cooed.

Autumn held up her bags and smiled. 'No, thank you. You weren't so helpful when I came in last time, so I shopped elsewhere.' She moved closer to the door and looked over her shoulder. 'Such a shame... You have lovely clothes, and I probably would have bought quite a lot.'

That was enough. That was more than enough.

She could remember the scene from the film exactly in her head, but she wasn't about to make any comments about commission.

Instead she finished with a steady gaze. 'Being nice is so important. We can have no idea of what kind of day another person has had, and I always try to remember that.'

She walked out through the door where Giovanni was waiting. 'You were nice to them,' he said in a surprised tone. 'You might even have taught them a lesson.'

'I doubt it,' she said, just as she heard a sharp voice behind her.

'Giovanni?'

She turned around in time to see one of the saleswomen, with an expression on her face that was a mixture of pinched and haughty. Her words came out in rapid Italian.

Giovanni crossed his arms across his chest. His voice

was low, deep, and from its tone Autumn could tell he had no intention of getting into a conversation with this woman.

The woman started throwing her arms about, her voice getting more staccato. Surely he hadn't said anything that bad? There hadn't been time.

Giovanni's voice remained low and steady. And as the woman kept ranting, he slid his arm into Autumn's and dropped into English. 'I think it's time for a change of scenery and I know just the place.'

He shot the woman a disdainful glance and started walking. They'd only gone a few steps when another woman approached him.

Autumn's head was spinning. What on earth was going on—all she'd wanted was a few dresses!

But this woman was entirely different. She was small, dressed in jeans and light shirt, with a broad smile across her face. Before Autumn had a chance to catch her breath the woman had flung her arms around Giovanni and stuck a kiss on his cheek. She was talking nineteen to the dozen, but clearly very pleased to see him.

Autumn was aware of the curious glance she got from her.

'Tua moglie?' the woman asked.

There was an awkward pause, then Giovanni shook his head and replied, *'Un college chirurgo.'*

'Ah!' The woman threw up her hands, grabbed Autumn around the neck and kissed both her cheeks.

Autumn's hands were still full of the shopping bags and she was frozen in bewilderment.

The woman then shook Giovanni's hand again, before hugging him for a second time and walking down the road with a final wave.

Autumn was shaking her head. 'Tell me what just happened!' she said, trying not to laugh out loud.

He put his arm around her back and they started walking again. 'That was the mother of a former patient. I saved her son and she's never forgotten.'

Autumn juggled her bags into one hand. 'And the woman from the store?'

His eyebrows were raised and there was a hint of mischief in his eyes. 'Oh, it's safe to say she hates me, but I never lose a moment's thought over it. It's personal.'

'Not now,' said Autumn quickly. 'You made me complicit, so you'd better tell me why.'

He nodded. 'Fair enough. I found out a few years ago that she was cheating customers—charging even more inflated prices than the designer brand had set for their clothes. One of Anna's friends suffered badly from postnatal depression. One of her ways of coping was buying designer clothes frequently and putting them at the back of the cupboard where they wouldn't be found. The family ended up in a large amount of debt.'

He'd mentioned his wife easily, and Autumn shifted a little on her feet. There was always chatter in the hospital. People mentioning how beautiful Anna had been, or what a great doctor she'd been to work with. But things seemed different when it was Giovanni talking about his ex-wife. She didn't like the way it made her feel. Why was that?

'What did you do?' she asked.

He sighed. 'When she asked Anna for help, we discovered the unworn clothes. They still had their tags and the original receipts in the bags. It didn't take long for us to notice that the prices of the items didn't match the prices on the handwritten receipts.'

Autumn's eyes widened. 'That woman did that?'

Giovanni nodded as they walked. 'Celeste—yes. When

I confronted her about clearly taking advantage of a vulnerable individual she was furious. But we had all the evidence. The store gave her the choice of paying back the difference to Anna's friend or facing criminal charges.'

'And did she pay the money back?'

Giovanni nodded. 'She did—and then the store sacked her.'

Autumn's footsteps faltered. She squinted her head back. 'So she hasn't always worked in the store I was just in?'

He shook his head. 'No, she's only worked there for the last year, but I heard she was up to her old tricks again.'

Autumn frowned. 'Darn it. Now I want to go back and make more of a scene.'

He rested his other hand on her arm and looked at her thoughtfully. 'Actually, I shouldn't have encouraged you. You were much nicer than I thought you might be. I wish I could say that might have taught her a lesson, but I seriously doubt it.'

They reached a taxi stand and he opened the door of the vehicle at the front. 'After you.'

The taxi driver rushed around and opened the boot, taking Autumn's many bags from her as she climbed in.

It was nice to get out of the heat for a bit and she settled back in the seat. 'Where are we going?' she asked.

Giovanni slid in beside her. 'How much of the city have you seen? Have you had time to do anything?'

She shook her head.

'So, it might be too hot to go tramping around the sights, but we can have a casual drink with your favourite place in view. Take your pick.'

She pressed her lips together, thinking hard. 'Either the Vatican or the Colosseum. But I'm not sure what the surrounding areas are like.'

He gave her an approving nod. 'Go with your heart. I'll find us somewhere good. I've lived here all my life.'

She closed her eyes for a second then gave a smile. 'The Colosseum, then.'

Giovanni gave some instructions to the driver, and half an hour later led her up some steps to a private rooftop bar, a few streets away from the Colosseum.

She sat down on a plush cream seat, with a large parasol shading them from the hot sun. There was only one other couple on the rooftop and the view of the Colosseum and surrounding bell towers was spectacular.

'Wow...' she breathed as she sat back and relaxed.

Giovanni was on the bench seat next to her, his leg close to hers, and he looked over the half-formed structure and smiled widely. 'It's magnificent, isn't it?'

A waiter appeared and handed them both menus, but Autumn's eyes were still on the Colosseum. She couldn't take her eyes off the sight.

Giovanni spoke to the waiter in rapid Italian and he disappeared. She wanted to pinch herself as she stole a glance at Giovanni. She'd noticed the looks he'd got on the street from women, who gave him more than a passing stare.

Whilst she'd been looking for clothes that morning she'd tried to push all thoughts of him from her mind, but then, like magic, he'd appeared, and her wardrobe worries had vanished. Now she was in the perfect place. She just wasn't sure if the man sitting next to her thought he was in the perfect place too.

The waiter brought two glasses of chilled white wine and put them on the shaded table. Giovanni watched as Autumn took a sip from her glass and visibly relaxed.

A smile danced across her face as she looked back at the imposing view. 'I can't quite believe I'm here,' she said quietly. She tipped her head to one side and held up one hand. 'This is right in front of me… Built more than two thousand years ago, a place packed with history where more than fifty thousand people would watch gladiators fight.' She closed her eyes. 'I can almost hear the roar if I try and concentrate.'

He loved that. He loved it that he'd shown her a tiny part of Rome and she was instantly trying to soak it up. He was also feeling a little guilty about what he'd asked her to do earlier.

He'd put most of his life with Anna behind him. But Celeste's manipulation of Anna's friend still made his blood boil.

When he'd heard Autumn's voice on the phone, he had instantly recognised the uncertainty and hurt in her tone. It had struck harder than he could ever have expected. Why? Did he feel protective of his fellow surgeon because he felt responsible for bringing her here and wanted to ensure she stayed for the surgery? That was the easiest explanation. But it didn't quite ring true.

As soon as Autumn had explained where she was, he had known exactly how she was being treated. Giovanni always tried to be logical. First solve the outstanding issue, then go back and deal with the original problem. That was what he always tried to do. But Autumn had handled things better than he had. Every time he found out more about her, it sparked something inside him.

'Bring many people up here?'

Her voice floated through his thoughts. He turned to her with a smile. 'Not many. But the view speaks for itself.'

She held out one hand. 'So does the shade, and…' she raised her glass '…the wine. This is a beautiful place to relax.'

He leaned forward a bit, a teasing edge to his tone.

'What? You don't want to stand in a long queue in the searing heat?'

She shuddered. 'Tell me that I can do a tour at night some time. That would be perfect.'

He could see her imagining it in her head.

'You know…standing inside as the night air cools and the sun is setting behind me. I can just imagine it.'

'Sounds romantic.' The words were out before he had a real chance to consider them.

Her gaze shifted from the building to him. She gave a thoughtful smile. 'Maybe I'm a hopeless romantic and you've just not discovered that yet.'

There was something about sitting under this cool shaded parasol while the world baked around them… From the moment he'd met her there had been an instant attraction—one he'd tried his best not to act on—but the glances, the smiles, the teasing tones and the full body contact were making it very hard for him to continue to fight something he wasn't entirely sure he wanted to fight.

Anna was long since gone, and the memories of their deteriorating relationship had left scars in his brain. Whilst there had been a few passing flings, there had never been anyone who had met Sofia. He'd deliberately never taken that step before. But Autumn had already crossed that bridge. And he wasn't sure how he felt about that.

All he could concentrate on right now was this woman with her soft brown hair and oh-so-green eyes, dressed in blue capri pants and an orange top, with her sunglasses pushed up on top of her head. She was so close he could see some tiny freckles across the bridge of her nose.

'What's the most romantic thing you've ever done?' he asked, his voice low.

She blinked, and he saw something flash across her eyes. The soft cushions on the bench seat seemed to push them closer together. The smile she gave him looked kind of sad.

'I've not really done anything romantic. Just the normal thing—a few nice dinners.' She gave a shrug. 'Nothing big. Nothing spectacular. I guess I've just not really been in that kind of relationship.'

Something pinged hard in his heart. In front of him was a gorgeous, intelligent woman. But she hadn't ever had those moments. Giovanni was struck by that. He could think of any number of romantic moments—silly things, gestures that had struck him at the time as a memory to keep and savour. Some before Anna, some with Anna, and a few after. But Autumn couldn't think of any?

'Didn't a boy ever make you a daisy chain when you were a girl?' he asked.

She looked surprised. 'What? No, never.' Then she frowned. 'Did you make someone a daisy chain?'

They were close. So close he could feel the heat from her skin… He grinned. 'I might have.' Then he pulled a face. 'I might even have made two at the same time.'

She let out a gasp of horror and her hand came down gently on his arm. 'The word I have for you doesn't really translate well from the Scottish,' she said, lifting her eyebrows, 'but in England they would call you a cad.'

'A cad? At five?'

'You were double-dating at *five*?' She shook her head and took a drink. 'I think I'm going to need more wine.'

He liked this. He liked this new, completely relaxed version of them. No hospital. No distractions. Just the chance for him to concentrate on the woman right next to him and finally let her set alight the parts of him that he'd been trying to temper.

As he signalled to the waiter for more wine, she gave

him a sideways glance. 'But you have sisters—how on earth did they let you away with that?'

He shifted on the cushions, which meant that his hip and leg were pressing next to hers. He'd turned to face her. There seemed to be little need to stay apart.

'They were actually in competition with each other. Both wanted to set me up with a friend.' His grin widened. 'You have a lot to learn about Italian families. You wouldn't have done the same in Scotland?'

She laughed. 'If anyone had given me a daisy chain between the ages of five and fifteen in Scotland, my brother would have likely beat them with a big stick.'

'Hmm...' Giovanni pretended to be thoughtful for a moment, then asked, 'So your brother...you haven't said much about him. Does he still live in Scotland?'

Autumn laughed again. Her hand was still on Giovanni's arm and she gave it a squeeze. 'The question you want to ask is, where *doesn't* he live?'

Giovanni wrinkled his brow. 'What do you mean?'

She made a flyaway movement with her hand. Giovanni immediately wanted her to put it back on his arm.

'You might have heard of him. My brother is Ryan Fraser.'

It only took a few seconds for the name to click in his brain. He shifted and looked at her in surprise. 'Your brother is Ryan Fraser the billionaire?' Tiny things started to make sense. 'He has his own jet, doesn't he?'

'Yep. That's how I got here. Ryan has places in Melbourne, London, LA, Washington, Spain and a castle in Scotland.'

Giovanni folded his arms across his chest and couldn't help but grin as he shook his head. 'Wow. Your parents must be delighted.' He gave her a nudge. 'A pair of overachievers—a billionaire, and a brilliant paediatric liver surgeon.'

Their wine glasses had been topped up and he took a sip. But Autumn tensed. It was as if every cell in her body had just contracted before his very eyes. 'They probably would have been.'

His skin prickled. 'Your parents are dead?'

She nodded. But he instantly knew it was more than that.

Her eyes dropped. 'My parents were very…controlling. With both me and Ryan. They were never bad to us. Just very strict. Much more so than any other parents I knew. They were academics. They probably should never have had children. They hated any element of life that was out of their control. They just wanted to focus on their work. So they tried to control us completely.' She gave a sad sigh. 'I guess it rubbed off a little. Ryan…he's a bit older than me…he managed to get out before I did.'

'You felt as if you had to "get out"?' asked Giovanni.

Her words and general demeanour were alarming. She'd gone from relaxed and composed to almost turning in on herself.

She gave a nervous laugh and shook herself. 'I'm being too dramatic. We just had a kind of odd experience growing up, with parents who made everything rules and demands.' Autumn paused for a moment and licked her lips. 'I guess it was my parents who made me think about childhood psychological trauma for separated conjoined twins.'

He was trying hard to follow the conversation here. She was saying that her parents hadn't been abusive, but Giovanni was wise enough to know that trauma for children came in many different forms. Part of him wanted to change the subject and get back to where they'd been before. But he wouldn't do that. Not when she was opening up to him.

'How so?'

She sipped her wine again. 'I guess that some of their controlling behaviour rubbed off on me. I didn't actually realise that for a long time—probably only when one of the girls I shared a flat with at medical school had a chat with me about my rules, my lists, and my own controlling behaviour.'

He nodded. 'But you're a surgeon. All of us have an element of control. We have to. When things happen in Theatre, control can be the most important element.' He met her gaze. 'It can save lives.'

She nodded and gave him a grateful smile. 'I know. I get that.'

'And your brother? Does he feel the same as you?'

She shook her head and her mouth curved upwards into a smile, her shoulders relaxing again. 'Oh, Ryan is entirely normal. Not like me at all. My parents' attitude gave him the remarkable determination to succeed at everything he does, but to do it in a completely different way.'

'That seems to have worked out well for him then,' Giovanni remarked. He gave her a sideways grin. 'Do you think he'd still hit me with a stick if I gave you a daisy chain?'

He was trying to read her. He was clocking up all the things she'd said. All the little reveals. But he didn't want to push too far. She'd already told him more than he'd expected her to. Autumn struck him as a bit like himself. She let the world see what she wanted it to see. Other parts of herself she kept locked inside.

After those few moments of tension she now seemed relaxed and comfortable around him, and happy to be close. He could feel the air sparking between them. But maybe it was just the surroundings and atmosphere. He'd hate to misread the situation.

She turned her head towards his, their noses only inches apart. 'Ryan has learned over the years to respect my choices.' She raised her eyebrows. 'Not that he always likes them—and it doesn't take him long to tell me when that happens.'

'What do you do when he does?'

His voice was barely a whisper. He could smell her shampoo, her perfume, her skin. They were *that* close. A tiny little flake of her mascara had smudged right in the corner of one eye. His fingers itched to reach out and touch it.

She moved again, a soft smile on her lips, her nose brushing against his. 'I tell him again,' she whispered, 'to respect my choices.'

Their lips brushed together, and without even looking Giovanni deposited his wine glass back on the table, freeing up one hand to cup her cheek and letting the other reach around her waist.

Her body shifted towards his and her breasts pressed against his chest. This was no crazy X-rated kiss. This was slow. Deliberate. Meaningful.

He doubted the other people on the rooftop would even notice. But Giovanni noticed. He noticed every second of it. The taste of her, the feel of her... The warm skin under his fingers as her top moved a little. The way her hair slid through his hand as he moved it from her soft cheek to the back of her head.

She didn't seem to mind the way his beard must be brushing against her cheek. In fact, her hand came around and she raked her nails through the short stubble. But after the longest moment she pulled back and pressed her forehead against his. 'Wow...' she breathed.

'Wow,' he agreed, staying exactly where he was.

They remained that way for the next few minutes, and then he felt a cold surface next to his arm. He gave the smallest flinch and looked down.

'Sorry…' Her laugh sounded nervous. Her wine glass had remained in her other hand.

Their heads parted and she sagged back against the cushions. The glass was at her lips a moment later and she took a drink, then let out a long slow breath.

Giovanni lifted his own glass, allowing the cool liquid to slide down his throat. What he really needed right now was an ice bucket over his head. Every sense in his body was currently on fire. The heat around them was nothing to the heat between them.

She still looked a little stunned.

'So…' he said gently.

Autumn licked her lips. 'So,' she said carefully, 'I usually don't mix business with pleasure.'

It was like a nail to the heart.

'You've never dated anyone you've worked with?' he asked.

She shook her head. 'Yes and no.' She glanced around, looking for the waiter. 'Do you think we could order some food? This wine is making me light-headed.'

He might have been offended. But she had a gleam in her eye. As if she knew how that had sounded.

He gestured to the waiter and rattled off the names of a variety of small dishes that he knew would arrive quickly, along with a bottle of sparkling water.

Autumn paused until the waiter had left and then continued. 'What I mean is, although I've dated colleagues, they've never actually been on my team—in my speciality.'

His hand reached up and he ran one finger down her soft cheek, finishing in her hair and winding a finger

around one of her locks. 'But I'm not in your team,' he
said hoarsely.

She took another deep breath and smiled again, her own
hand coming up and her fingertips running along his jaw-
line. 'No,' she breathed, 'you're not.'

And before he had time to say anything else her lips
connected with his again.

She honestly felt dizzy. Her brain was firing conflicting
messages at her.

He's your workmate.

He's the sexiest man you've ever met.

Go with your gut.

He has a child.

She was acting on instinct and not listening to the part
of her brain that was screaming *Proceed with caution.*
Waiting... She felt as if she had been waiting for this moment all her life. To have a guy who took her breath away
sitting next to her, to have a perfect setting, to be in the
perfect moment, and for said guy to be looking at her as if
she was the most desirable person on the planet.

She'd just ticked every box.

Moments like this didn't happen often. His words had
struck a chord with her and she'd opened up about a number of things she never normally would have. She wasn't
quite sure where those words had come from. In normal
circumstances she would never have revealed those things.
But Giovanni had made it easy. There had been no pressing, no judgement. Those words would always have been
awkward, but they hadn't felt uncomfortable.

There was just something about this man that made her
feel different. Different from the way she'd felt in every
other experience she'd had before.

From their earlier conversation, it seemed Giovanni had

had his life littered with moments like this, but Autumn couldn't remember a single one.

It must be the perfect time to start creating them.

She wasn't going to wait another second.

This wasn't a jump-on-each-other moment.

This was the perfect kiss, in the perfect place, with the perfect person.

She let out a little groan at the feel of his delicate touch on her skin. The taste of his lips against hers. The scent of his cologne on his skin. Her senses were on fire.

She reluctantly pulled her lips from his just as the waiter put plates of delicious-looking food down on their table, followed by some glasses and a bottle of water.

The sun was starting to dip in the sky, creating reds, oranges and purples. A few people came out onto the rooftop to appreciate the spectacular colours now framing the Colosseum.

Giovanni's arm moved around her shoulders as they leaned forward to grab cutlery.

'What do you think?' he whispered softly, glancing at the skyline in front of them.

She threaded her fingers through his. 'I like the view whichever way I'm looking,' she answered with a smile. 'And I think we should start the way we mean to continue,' she added, before they kissed again.

CHAPTER SIX

THE CLINICAL TEACHING room was packed. Multiple models had been made and every resident in the entire building was trying to find a space on either team.

Time was ticking. The in utero cardiac surgery on Hope had been completed successfully by Lizzy and Leon, and so far there had been no signs of early labour. But everyone was aware it could still happen at a moment's notice. It was essential that Autumn and Giovanni settled on their prospective teams.

Autumn was walking around all the potential candidates, checking their skills and competencies, taking notes the whole time. She knew how much pressure they were under, and occasionally she leaned forward and gave some advice.

'Try angling at around fifty degrees,' or, 'Our baby can't move. You'll have to move…get creative.'

She could hear Giovanni saying similar things at the other side of the room. Both of them were pacing, watching.

It was the oddest sensation. After their time on the rooftop last week, she'd called a cab and asked to be dropped at her hotel. If Giovanni had an alternative suggestion he hadn't made it—and she'd been glad.

Only a few weeks before she'd been living with someone else. She didn't want to jump from one man to another. And she wasn't entirely sure how wise it was to jump to a guy who a) lived in a different country from her and b) had a child.

She hated the way that thought felt in her head. Most people she knew around her age had past histories—many that involved children. It was just something else for her to consider. Sofia had to be Giovanni's priority and Autumn understood that. He might not have room in his life for a casual fling, and that was all she could offer him.

A child was a huge commitment. She would bet that Giovanni hadn't introduced Sofia to any potential girl-friends in the past. But she'd already met Sofia—albeit by default. And now that adorable little girl floated into her head yet again.

Something about the way Giovanni spoke about Anna bothered her. He didn't seem like a grieving and trauma-tised widower. But he did seem like a man who was a lit-tle sad and sorry. It would be nosey to ask why, and it was certainly none of her business. But Autumn couldn't help her natural curiosity.

She also struggled with the idea of responsibility, which for a specialist surgeon she knew was completely crazy. In her career she regularly had the lives of others literally in her hands.

But in her personal life she'd tended to shy away from responsibility. She'd spent the last few years telling herself it was due to the fact that she was trying to get a work/life balance. But the truth was Autumn knew that was garbage. Maybe she was a little terrified she would end up like her parents. Consumed by work, with no room for any fam-ily that came along?

She'd never had that burn, that desire to spend every minute of every day with another human being. Maybe if she'd experienced that, things would be different now. It might help her to take the next step. Learn to take a chance and accept the possibility that there could be hurt along the way and every element of her life might not be under her control.

Her life had been generally comfortable...pleasant. Just like her life with Louis. If at some moment he'd proposed, or mentioned children, she would likely have flown into a wild panic.

Because the truth was that 'look' she'd seen her friends exchange at their wedding had turned something on in her brain. *That* was what she was supposed to experience. *That* was what love was about. And it completely terrified her.

The thought of being that much in love with another person, giving your whole heart to someone, with no real guarantee it would be taken care of, made her anxiety levels soar. It was such a chance to take—letting go of an element of control and trusting another person with all your emotions.

She knew it started with an immediate heart-quickening, overwhelming rush of attraction.

And that was the sensation she'd experienced with Giovanni Lombardi.

Currently nicknamed in her brain as Mr Sex on Legs.

'Dr Fraser?'

The voice knocked her out of her thoughts. Probably just as well.

'Yes, Daniel?' He was a promising resident.

He gestured with his head. 'I was thinking about the formation of the hepatic artery and if there's a way to split it.'

She leaned forward, instantly interested. A major part of her surgery was based around reconstructing one of the major blood vessels to allow Grace's liver to function.

She'd already practised numerous ways—using the vessels already present, or trying to create a new one for Grace.

She moved alongside him and listened to his suggestions. All of them she'd already tried—but Daniel didn't know that, and she was glad he was taking the time to concentrate on thinking out of the box for her surgery. He was just the kind of resident she liked to train and develop.

As she bent down she looked over and Giovanni caught her eye. Neither of them was wearing a mask right now, in the clinical training room. There was a half-smile on his face. He raised one eyebrow and shook his head. *He's mine,* he mouthed.

No way, she mouthed back.

This had been their battle for the last few days. Both of them were picking their teams. It was, at times, like a stand-off, when they wanted a particular candidate. Autumn already had eleven on her team. A fellow surgeon, a trainee, an anaesthetist, five theatre nurses and three neonatal staff for the post-operative care of Grace.

But there were many slots on her team still to be filled. So it didn't help that while she was contemplating all these choices her head was full of snippets of Giovanni. A joke he'd made. A look they'd exchanged. She wasn't quite sure where their relationship was. That said, she wasn't quite sure they even actually *had* a relationship.

After he'd dropped her back at the hotel the other evening, she'd spent the remaining part of the night lying in her comfortable bed with the windows flung wide to the warm night air and sleep completely evading her.

What might have happened if she'd wanted to pursue things? What would he have said if she'd invited him up to her hotel room?

Thoughts like that made her pulse race, and her stomach roll. There was always a chance that Giovanni might have refused. And, to be truthful, she was glad she hadn't found out the answer to that potential scenario. Everything was still in her head as the perfect moment, and that was how she wanted it to stay.

But working alongside him every day was making her crazy.

Giovanni clapped his hands loudly, attracting the attention of all in the room. 'Ricardo, Erin, David—we all have a surgery in thirty minutes. It's time to prepare.' He waved his arms and gave the people in the room a broad grin, his eyes meeting hers. 'As for the rest of you—feel free to continue with your practice.'

Was there a secret message there? She didn't think so. But she couldn't pretend she didn't feel a little pull of something as Giovanni left the room.

There was an air about him…a magnetism that affected every cell in her body. She caught glances from some of the staff, and shouted some more instructions to them, walking slowly around the room and advising wherever she could. Trying to keep her mind on anything but Giovanni Lombardi.

When her pager sounded, her heart missed a dozen beats.

She wasn't on the regular staff here. She hadn't left messages anywhere in the hospital, and nor was she waiting for any tests results. Which meant her pager would only sound if there was an issue with Hope or Grace.

The number on the screen was unrecognisable. She moved to a phone outside the training room and dialled quickly.

The voice was initially Italian, but quickly switched to English. '*Scusi*, I'm looking for Dr Lombardi. He's not answering his pager.'

'Dr Lombardi is in Theatre right now.' Autumn pulled

her watch from the pocket of her scrubs and looked at it. 'He will be there for another few hours. Is there anything I can help you with?'

There was a brief pause. 'Dr Lombardi's sister is in the emergency department with his daughter, Sofia. They're asking for him.'

Her heart lurched. Of course she should go and get him. But Giovanni was performing a complicated follow-up surgery on a six-week-old baby with kidney problems.

Autumn took a deep breath. Instinct told her to assess the situation first. If she needed to get Giovanni, then she would.

'I'll deal with them,' she said into the receiver, before replacing the phone.

The ED was busy. It took her a few minutes to locate the unfamiliar woman with Sofia.

'Autumn!' said Sofia in delight as she walked around the curtain.

The woman with Sofia turned her head sharply. She was tall and slim, with dark brown hair and dark eyes. To put it bluntly, she was stunning, and her gaze was wary.

'Where is Giovanni?' she demanded.

Autumn stuck her hands in the pockets of her white coat. She wasn't normally intimidated, but it was strange to know that this was her first meeting with the sister of the man she'd kissed the week before.

She moved over to them, relieved that Sofia looked healthy. 'Giovanni is currently in surgery with a six-week-old baby,' she said softly, catching sight of a large white cotton patch on the top of Sofia's arm. 'Sofia, have you hurt yourself?'

Sofia nodded, looking almost proud of herself. 'I got in a fight,' she said.

Autumn washed her hands and sat down on a stool next

to Sofia, pulling on some gloves. She kept her voice steady and tried her best not to smile.

'The school phoned me,' said Giovanni's sister, who still hadn't introduced herself. 'Sofia injured her arm on the school fence. I thought it might need stitches.'

Autumn gave a nod. 'Sofia, can I have a look at this?'

Sofia nodded, and Autumn pulled up the edge of the soaked cotton swab. Underneath was an angry, jagged tear. Careful stitching would be required, and there was a possibility of some scarring.

A nurse wheeled in a trolley, as if she'd read her mind. She gave Autumn a curious stare, then glanced at her name badge. 'Ah, the paediatric surgeon. Welcome.'

'How do you know each other?' asked Giovanni's sister sharply, her head flicking between Sofia and Autumn.

'We went to dinner together,' said Sofia merrily, 'With Daddy.'

The hostility in the room seemed to move up a few notches.

'Can you call Giovanni, please?' his sister demanded.

Autumn took a deep breath and decided to start again. She took off her gloves and held out her hand to the woman. 'Hi, I'm Autumn Fraser. I'm a paediatric surgeon working with your brother. I've only been here a few weeks, and the first day I arrived your brother and Sofia took me out to dinner to help familiarise me with the area and, I think, to keep me awake after I'd had a very early start.'

The woman blinked. Then she held out her arm, shaking Autumn's hand. 'Eleonora. I'm Giovanni's sister.' Her other hand stroked Sofia's hair fondly. 'I help him out with Sofia.'

Autumn gave Eleonora a warm smile. 'It's lovely to meet you. I'm sorry it's under these circumstances. But let me assure you...' she nodded to Sofia's arm '... I will take good care of Sofia for you.' She paused, letting Eleonora consider her words. Then, 'The surgery that Giovanni is currently involved in is very delicate, and I'm not sure another surgeon could take his place right now.'

There was a flicker of annoyance on Eleonora's face. Or was it worry? Autumn didn't know her well enough to tell the difference.

She turned to Sofia. 'I'm going to clean up your arm, then put a couple of stitches in. Are you okay with me doing that?'

For the briefest moment Autumn thought she saw a little falter in Sofia's confidence, but then she tilted her chin up towards her.

'Can we have gelato after?'

Autumn was careful in her response. 'If your Aunt Eleonora says it's okay, then I'd be happy to get you a gelato.'

After another few seconds Eleonora gave a sigh. 'Okay, then. But you have to let Giovanni know as soon as his surgery is finished. He likes to be notified of anything about Sofia at once.'

'Of course.'

Autumn spoke to one of the nurses, first asking her to leave a message for Giovanni, and second to get some extra supplies, before washing her hands again. She cleaned the wound and used a numbing spray on the area before injecting a little local anaesthetic prior to doing the stitches.

Sofia only gave the slightest flinch, and it only took a few minutes to line up the ragged skin and place the careful stitches. Once she'd dressed the wound, she did a quick check to ensure Sofia's tetanus shot was up to date.

'How about that gelato?' she said as she snapped off her gloves.

Eleonora glanced at her watch. 'It's too late to return to school. I suppose gelato would be okay.' She picked up

Sofia in her arms, turning slightly away from Autumn. 'I'll take you.'

'No,' said Sofia quickly, a stubborn tone in her voice. 'Autumn said she would take me. She promised.'

Autumn suddenly felt like a pawn in a game of family politics.

'Sofia!' Giovanni rushed through the curtains, his face stricken.

'Papà!' Sofia yelled happily.

Autumn stood to the side as rapid Italian flew between the three family members. She was about to retreat discreetly when she felt a firm hand on her arm.

'Autumn, thank you so much for taking care of Sofia for me.'

'No problem. What about your surgery? I didn't expect you to be out for another few hours.'

He gave her a sorry look. 'Turns out we didn't even get started. There was a problem with the baby's clotting factor. We had to delay. Thank goodness we hadn't anaesthetised.'

Autumn pressed her lips together. From the dark furrows on Giovanni's brow she could see someone would clearly be in major trouble about this.

Eleonora started talking again and gave Autumn a sideways glance. But Giovanni waved one hand and started talking over her. Autumn shifted her feet uncomfortably. Why did she feel as if this was an argument about her?

Giovanni seemed to finish speaking abruptly. He walked over and kissed his sister on both cheeks, talking to her in a low voice. A moment later Eleonora kissed Sofia once more, before disappearing out through the curtains.

'Gelato?' asked Giovanni brightly.

Sofia was already clapping her hands, her injury forgotten.

Autumn hesitated for a second. But she wasn't on the

clock here. Unless something happened with the twins, no one would page her. Anyhow, she'd be with Giovanni, and they would page him too.

'Gelato sounds good.'

'Yay!' Sofia was still clapping. She tugged at the edge of Giovanni's scrubs. 'You can't wear this for gelato, Papà.'

'You're right. I can't. We'll head up to the locker room.'

Giovanni kept hold of his girl tightly. Autumn could see the relief in his face. She wasn't sure what his thoughts had been when he'd got the message about Sofia being in the emergency department, but from the way he'd burst through the curtains she assumed his heart had been in his mouth.

What was strange for her was the fact that her heart had been in her mouth too when she'd got the message about Sofia. There had been a distinct moment of panic. Autumn had been a doctor too long, and seen too many sights she couldn't un-see, for her head not to sometimes go to the worst-case scenario.

When she'd seen Sofia sitting awake and alert on the cubicle trolley, she'd breathed a huge sigh of relief. And her relief could only have been a fraction of Giovanni's.

They'd reached the locker rooms and Giovanni reluctantly set Sofia back down on the floor. The little girl automatically slid her hand into Autumn's. 'I'll come with you,' she told her. She wrinkled her nose at the sign on the men's locker room. 'That one is always stinky.'

Autumn burst out laughing. 'Okay, come with me to the non-stinky room while I get changed. Meet you in five, Giovanni,' she said over her shoulder as she pushed open the door.

Her locker held the white capri pants and the white shirt with pink flowers she'd bought with Giovanni the week before, and Autumn set them down on the bench as she pulled out her toiletries.

'This is pretty,' said Sofia as she held up the blouse.

'Thank you,' said Autumn as she took off her scrubs and held out her hand for the shirt. 'I bought it in a shop that your *papà* took me to.'

'Auntie Marie's?'

Autumn blinked. 'Marie is your auntie too?'

Sofia smiled. 'I call her that. Auntie Eleonora and Auntie Bella shop there too.'

Autumn gave herself a final spray of perfume and slicked on some lipstick. 'Okay, ready for gelato?'

She held out her hand to Sofia. It seemed like the natural thing to do, even though she wasn't really used to children this age. But Sofia reacted well, and as they walked out Giovanni was waiting, in a white open-necked shirt and light trousers.

He rubbed his hands. 'Our favourite place?' He smiled at Sofia.

'Yes!' she shouted.

He winked at Autumn. 'Let us take you to the best gelateria in Rome.'

All Giovanni could feel right now was relief. He was glad Sofia had only requested gelato, because he probably would have agreed to anything. When he'd been in Theatre and had got that message, his heart had pounded so much he'd thought he might die.

His staff were intelligent enough not to have passed on the message about his daughter when he was in the middle of surgery, but as soon as his surgery had been cancelled one of the theatre nurses had quickly come in and whispered in his ear.

He'd taken off like a rocket. And he'd never been so

glad to see Autumn in a cubicle. It had given him instant reassurance that Sofia was in good hands.

He took a breath for a moment. That was an unusual thought for him. Usually no one was good enough for his daughter. He remembered one night when her temperature had soared, and he'd thought the doctor in the emergency department too inexperienced and had demanded his superior.

He cringed now at how ridiculous that seemed. But thankfully his colleagues had forgiven him and Sofia had been fine.

It was odd, though. Because he frequently took referrals from other hospitals, with parents who demanded 'the best' to assess their child, often not accepting the opinion of their local surgeon who, most times, would make the same recommendation for their child. Being a parent had made Giovanni understand that behaviour, and he looked at Autumn curiously. How did she feel about those kind of referrals?

A taxi dropped them in front of Regallo's and they jumped out. Sofia dashed to her favourite seat at one of the white metal tables.

He pulled out a chair for Autumn and waited until she was seated. 'What's your favourite flavour?' he asked.

'Raspberry,' answered Autumn, with a broad smile on her face.

She was wearing the clothes he'd bought for her last week, and she looked fabulous. He nodded.

'What's yours?' she asked.

'Melon.'

'What?'

He shrugged. 'I can't explain it. It's always been my favourite since I was a child.' He nudged his daughter. 'And, Sofia, do you want to tell Autumn what your favourite is?'

'Chocolate and banana,' his daughter said without a moment of hesitation. 'With sauce.'

Autumn smiled. 'This gelato sounds like it might be fun.'

They ordered, and as soon as the gelato arrived Sofia was engrossed.

'Thank you,' said Giovanni.

Autumn looked up, spoon in hand. 'For what?'

'For looking after Sofia today.'

Autumn looked surprised. 'Of course. No problem at all.' Her mouth gave a tiny pull. 'She will likely have a tiny scar. But I hope it will fade with time. I never asked her about the fight where it happened, though.'

Giovanni gave Autumn a careful look, then aimed his eyes at his daughter. She caught on immediately.

'Sofia,' said Giovanni carefully. 'Do you want me to tell me why you were fighting at school today?'

Sofia's spoon paused midway to her mouth. She sighed and rested it at the edge of her dish. 'It was Enzo, Papà,' she said. 'He's mean to everyone.'

'Was he mean to you?'

She rolled her eyes. 'He tried to be. I wouldn't take it.' Sofia waved her hand, flicking chocolate sauce everywhere.

Autumn gave a little signal with her finger and Giovanni realised she wanted to take over the questioning. He watched as she leaned down so her head was level with Sofia's.

'So...tell me what he did?'

Sofia turned her full attention to Autumn. 'He stole my friend's *cioccolato*. I shouted at him and he pushed me into the fence.'

Giovanni bristled. And he saw that Autumn was automatically defensive.

'That's how you got hurt?' she asked.

Sofia nodded. 'But so did he.' She picked up her spoon again.

'What does that mean?' Autumn's tone was gentle, but curious.

Sofia grinned. 'I kicked him in the leg. Twice.'

Autumn pressed her lips together and glanced at Giovanni. The temptation to jump in was strong. This was his daughter. It was up to *him* to enforce what was right and what was wrong. But something made him stop.

Autumn put her hand on Sofia's. 'Do you think there might have been any other way to sort this out? One that meant you didn't end up with stitches and Enzo didn't have a sore leg?'

Sofia frowned instantly, her bottom lip pouting, but after a few moments she gave another sigh. 'I could have talked to the teacher...'

Autumn smiled. 'You could have. And that might have saved a visit to the emergency department.' She put her hand on her chest, where her heart was. 'I got a real fright when someone told me you were in the emergency department.' Her eyes met Giovanni's. 'I know your *papà* did too.' She lowered her voice. 'And I bet that Aunt Eleonora was upset about the call from school too.'

Sofia's shoulders slumped a little, as if her initial bravado was finally fading.

'Lots of people worry about you, honey. Everyone wants you to be safe.'

It only took a few moments for Sofia's doleful eyes to meet Giovanni's. He was completely and utterly biased, and he knew it, but his daughter could break his heart with one glance.

'Sorry, Papà,' she said quietly.

He did his best to stay silent for a moment. He was impressed by how Autumn had handled things. Was this a woman's touch with his daughter? He was much too fiery. His first reaction on hearing that a little boy had caused scarring to his daughter had been to want to yell at the world. Rage had raced through him. Then his rational brain had kicked into place within a few seconds, but he was conscious of his initial fierce protectiveness of his little girl—his whole world.

It had been a childhood spat. The kind that the school would handle on a regular basis. This one had just had unfortunate consequences. He was sure if he checked his phone there would be a call from one of the teachers. He would deal with that later.

'I'm glad you're safe,' he said throatily, trying to hide the emotion welling in his voice as he reached over and rubbed the top of her unaffected arm.

'Will you take my stitches out?' Sofia had turned to Autumn again.

This time Autumn looked a little nervous. It was clear she thought Giovanni would want to supervise that action himself, but he shook his head. 'We'll invite Autumn round next week and she can take them out for us at home.' He raised a questioning eyebrow. 'If that's okay with you?'

'Of course,' she agreed quickly, and then she tilted her head slightly and she gave him a quizzical look.

'I'm glad you were there today,' he admitted. 'I think my hands might have been—how do you put it?—all fingers and thumbs if I'd tried to stitch my own daughter.'

Autumn gave him a gracious nod. They both knew that a doctor wasn't really supposed to treat a member of their own family, but they also knew it happened all the time.

'I was glad I was there and able to help.' She touched the top of Sofia's covered arm gently. 'I think you'll have a little pink scar that will fade to white in time. You probably won't even notice it when you're older.'

She gave her a soft smile, and something shifted inside Giovanni. He'd been trying so hard to put their time together at the rooftop bar in a safe place. It had been an exception to his rule of not mixing his personal life with his professional life. When he'd dated colleagues before, it had never been someone in his team or involved in his surgeries. He also didn't introduce potential girlfriends to his daughter.

But it seemed he'd spent the last few weeks throwing all his rules out of the window. Today was an exception.

That was what he was currently trying to tell himself as he watched Sofia and Autumn together. They talked easily, but he could tell Autumn felt just a little awkward. Maybe she wasn't used to kids Sofia's age, and that was fine, but she was making an effort. And Sofia liked her. In fact, Autumn appeared to be his daughter's favourite topic of conversation.

He could only imagine the phone call later from his sister, Eleonora. He sensed she hadn't quite approved, but Giovanni had spent years doing battle with his feisty sisters, so that was nothing unusual.

Sofia put her hand up to Autumn's ear and whispered something to her conspiratorially, and they both looked at him and laughed.

'What?' he asked indignantly.

Sofia giggled and pointed her finger at his chest. There, on the pale blue shirt, was a stray drip of chocolate sauce. He groaned as he picked up a napkin, knowing it was stained for life.

'How did I get chocolate sauce on my shirt when I didn't even have any?'

Sofia's head bent next to Autumn's and the two of them started laughing again.

Giovanni's throat dried. It hit him in an instant. How much his daughter was missing by not having a mother. It wasn't that he'd never thought about it before—of course he had. But he'd convinced himself that his sisters filled that gap in Sofia's life, and up until this point had considered himself lucky.

He'd always done his best to be everything his daughter needed, but right now the simple moment of seeing the connection between her and Autumn made him feel like a failure.

It was like a punch to the gut.

He'd got this wrong. Sofia was bonding with Autumn—a woman he barely knew. He had no idea what she thought about kids—what she thought about him. He was allowing his daughter to see something that might not exist. This simple act of bringing Autumn with them for ice-cream might become a whole lot more in a five-year-old's head.

He should have known better.

That was his job.

To protect his daughter.

He stood up sharply and both Autumn and Sofia looked up in surprise. 'I'll just pay, then Sofia and I need to head home. I'll drop you back at your hotel, Autumn.'

He couldn't pretend that he didn't see the flash of hurt in her eyes. But he'd think about that later. Right now, he needed to get out of here. Process what had happened today and work out what on earth was currently going on in his life.

Because one thing was clear.

Giovanni didn't have a clue.

CHAPTER SEVEN

AUTUMN PULLED HER clothes out of the large carved wooden wardrobe. It was the kind of luxury item normally spotted in a country house, but here it was in the middle of her hotel room in Rome.

Four weeks. That was how long she'd been here. And even though she knew Rome had hills, she'd never expected it to be such a rollercoaster.

She'd thrown her windows open this morning and to her delight there had been a tiny smatter of rain. It had actually reminded her of Scotland, even though the noises and smells were completely different here.

Her hand ran across the soft green dress Giovanni had bought for her, and she almost rejected it from that memory alone.

She had no idea what was wrong with him. Maybe he was still upset about Sofia's little accident. But Sofia had appeared none the worse to Autumn. In fact, in two days' time she should be taking out the little girl's stitches.

But Giovanni had been distant with her. It could be anxiety. Gabrielle Bianchi had been feeling unwell yesterday—although there had been nothing wrong that anyone could find. Both of them were on edge in case the babies arrived early. But Lizzy and Leon had spent all day examining their patient, reassuring everyone that there was nothing of immediate concern, and Autumn trusted their judgement.

In fact, she was meeting Lizzy this morning, for their long-awaited coffee.

She shouldn't be nervous, but she was a little. Lizzy had amazing credentials as a neonatal cardiac specialist. The surgery that she and Leon had performed had been essential to the survival of the girls.

Autumn froze. When had she started calling Hope and Grace that? The girls?

She made a grab and pulled the soft green dress over her head. She liked it, it was comfortable and stylish, and whether or not Giovanni had paid for it was irrelevant.

She took another quick glance around the room, looking for her bag. With its giant four-poster bed, thick carpet and curtains, it was one of the most luxurious hotel rooms she'd ever stayed in. The thought of going back to her virtually empty flat didn't fill her with joy. She imagined her boxes, piled high in her sitting room, waiting to be unpacked.

Something twisted inside her. A sense of failure? Or a sense of loneliness?

Ever since she'd arrived in Rome and met Giovanni her head had been in turmoil. Her emotions were all over the place, and it didn't help that everyone in the hospital gave the impression that his dead wife, Anna, had been some kind of saint. How could she live up to that?

Growing up, she'd been used to feeling emotionally isolated. For her it was learned behaviour. Could she be capable of unlearning that?

Her brain kept going back, time and time again, to those romantic moments that everyone else on the planet seemed to have had except her. She never threw caution to the wind. Especially not with her heart. And not for the first time it struck her that she might end up on her own.

As an independent woman, that shouldn't worry her in the least—and on some points it didn't. But on others she wanted to hope that she could share her life with someone. Have a happy-ever-after like in the movies. But would that even be a remote possibility for her? She was starting to think that she might have sabotaged previous relationships by never really letting go. Never letting herself truly love someone and be truly loved in return.

Giovanni's face floated into her head again. That sexy smile, those deep dark eyes... She could swear her heart gave some kind of pang. She had never, ever felt like this about someone before.

That twist inside continued. She'd never wanted to let go. She'd always wanted to keep a piece of herself back. It helped with her feelings of being in control, being in charge.

But was life really all about always being in charge? Or could she trust herself to hand that piece of her heart into someone else's hands?

She shook her head and strolled across the room, grabbing her bag before heading out. She had to stop second-guessing every thought she had. Surgery—that was what she had to focus on right now.

Autumn had actually started to enjoy her commute to the hospital and around Rome. She liked the hustle and bustle of the people—even on the packed public transport. She picked up snatches of conversation. Her Italian was slowly but surely becoming a little better. Her attempts at conversation were still—in a word her brother would use—dodgy, but her understanding was improving every day.

She smiled now, as she heard two women a little younger than she was, discussing the merits of a particular group of men. She watched a young mother juggle a baby on her lap along with a few shopping bags. And she admired a conversation between two teenagers who were clearly at the first stages of flirting.

People were living life all around her, and Autumn was struck with a wave of sadness.

What did she have in life? Sure, she had a brilliant career, some good friends and her own place. She also had her health, and she'd met enough people in this lifetime to know that, for some, that was all they would ever want. So now she felt selfish. But that didn't stop the wave of emptiness that echoed inside her.

She'd never thought like this before. And she knew exactly why.

Giovanni.

There was something about the guy. And not just his electric kisses. The buzz in the air from that first look...

She'd never have dreamed that she'd be interested in a man with a child before. But Sofia was drawing her in. The inquisitive nature, the questions, the cheek, the heartbreaking smiles.

It wasn't even as if anything had really happened between her and Giovanni. Not really. Just a few kisses. But the urge to be around him was strong. Stronger than she'd ever experienced before. And the pull to be around Sofia was strong too. They were a partnership—a pair—and she couldn't think of them any other way. And that didn't terrify her quite the way it had before.

She pulled her diary from her bag and glanced at the dates. Depending on how things went with Grace and Hope, she could be here for another three weeks. If things stayed steady, maybe another five. No one could predict when the twins would need to be delivered. There was a good chance that the surgery Lizzy and Leon had performed could result in premature labour for Gabrielle.

Autumn pushed her diary deep back inside her bag, trying not to think about how that could turn out.

She reached the café and saw Lizzy sitting inside, out of the morning sun.

'Hey…' She smiled as she sat down beside her.

Lizzy had three drinks in front of her. Iced water, a pot of tea, and a diet soda. She gave Autumn a smile. 'Sorry, I couldn't decide, and as soon as I sat down I decided not to wait.'

Autumn grinned at Lizzy's protruding stomach. 'How many weeks are you now?' She looked up as the waiter approached and ordered a cappuccino and some toast.

Lizzy rubbed her belly. 'Only twenty weeks. But I feel much bigger than I actually am. I think it's just the heat in Rome right now. It's killing me.'

Autumn gave a nod and went for a careful question. 'So, how're things with you and Leon?'

Lizzy looked at her. 'I take it you know it's Leon's baby?'

Autumn nodded again. 'I had heard that.'

'Well, it's true.' There was a gleam in her eye and she leaned across the table to Autumn. 'I'll tell you how things are with me and Leon if you tell me what's going on with you and Giovanni.'

Autumn sagged back in her chair and let out a brief laugh. 'I wouldn't know where to start.'

Lizzy took a sip of one of her drinks, tucked a strand of blonde hair behind her ear and gave Autumn a thoughtful look. 'Okay, then, I'll start. I met Leon at med school in New York years ago. We were together then, and at the end I went back to Australia and he went back to Italy. We met again at a conference a few months ago and this…' she gestured down her stomach '…is the result.'

'Wow.' Autumn knew that her eyes had widened at this succinct sum-up.

'It's okay,' said Lizzy, waving her hand as the waitress arrived with Autumn's order. 'Go on—ask the million questions that just jumped into your head.' She bent forward and grabbed a piece of Autumn's toast from the plate. 'That's as long as you don't mind sharing with a pregnant woman.' She gave Autumn a wink. 'When it suits me, I'm eating for two.'

Autumn pushed the whipped butter towards her. 'Go ahead. I'm still in shock.'

'That's okay.' Lizzy smiled. 'I tend to have that effect on people these days. Give me a moment… I can probably shock you some more.'

'So, is Leon okay about the baby?'

Lizzy wrinkled her nose as she spread butter on the toast. 'Here's the thing: I've known him a long time. Leon never wanted kids. I knew that. And, to be honest, neither did I. This wasn't planned in any way, but…' She let her voice trail off for a second, as if she was deciding what to say next. 'For me, having our baby was the only option. Still, I struggled with how I felt about it all. Then I got the invitation to take part in the surgery. I knew I couldn't say no, and I knew it would give me a chance to be in the same room with Leon again and tell him we'd made a baby.'

Autumn shook her head in amazement. 'You make it all sound so simple.'

Lizzy let out a deep laugh. 'Oh, believe me, it's anything but simple. But if I say it out loud that way it keeps all my emotions in check.' She took a bite of her toast.

'Do you need to keep your emotions in check?' As

soon as the words were out of her mouth Autumn regretted them. The question was too personal.

But Lizzy answered in an instant. 'I did. But things have kind of turned around.'

She held out her hand. Autumn gave a gasp in surprise. A sparkling princess cut aquamarine with a diamond-encrusted band. It was stunning. She hadn't even noticed. 'You're engaged?'

Lizzy beamed at her. 'Told you I'd shock you again. Engaged and getting married at some point soon. It was a difficult road, but we got there. And I can't tell you how happy I am.' She took another bite of toast. 'Now, enough about me—let's give my pregnancy hormones a break. What about you? What's going on with you and Giovanni?'

Autumn gulped down some coffee, scalding the back of her throat and choking. She was still getting over the engagement bombshell. But Lizzy did look well and truly happy.

Lizzy laughed. 'That'll teach you to stall.'

Heat rushed into Autumn's cheeks. She liked this Australian woman, and it seemed that she'd got the kind of happy-ever-after that people liked to dream of. But she'd been honest. She'd said it hadn't been easy. And that made Autumn feel more comfortable around her. It wasn't as if there were many people to have a heart-to-heart with around here, and Lizzy was definitely her best bet. It was time to let out everything that was jumbling around in her brain.

'I kissed him…' she groaned.

Lizzy leaned forward again, snatching the second piece of toast. 'Really? When?'

'Two weeks ago. He took me shopping, then he took me to a rooftop bar that has views of the Colosseum. We kissed as the sun was setting.'

Lizzy gave a low whistle. 'Way to knock it out of the park with the romantic movie setting.'

Autumn shook her head. 'But since then nothing. I just don't know what's happening.'

'I could have matched you there for weeks!'

Autumn laughed. 'It's ridiculous. I'm only here for a short spell. Once the surgery is over, I'll head back to London. And he's got a kid, and I'm not sure I'm the kid type.' She put her hand over her mouth. 'Oops.'

It was too late. She stopped talking before she got herself into more trouble.

Lizzy didn't look hurt by the comment. She looked thoughtful. 'Kids aren't for everyone. I had to think long and hard about it.' She put her hand across the table and rested it on Autumn's. 'And it's fine for you to say that.'

'But I don't really know.' Autumn sighed as she lowered her head onto her other hand. 'And that's what's wrong. Does he even like me? Does he think of me that way? I've never really taken the time to consider kids in my life. And now I've met this dreamy guy, with eyes that just make me shudder, and a little girl who I think is great, and all I can see for myself is a whole lot of hurt.'

Lizzy pulled her hand back and folded her arms. 'Okay... Don't tell me you're one of those *I don't deserve nice things* kind of gals?'

Autumn gave a short laugh. 'No, not really. I'm just scared I'll do or say something wrong while I'm trying to work out things in my head. I think his sister already hates me.'

'Does Sofia like you?'

'Well, yes, I think so.'

Lizzy shrugged. 'Well, that's all that matters. She's Giovanni's world. And I can already tell that he likes you.

Maybe he's worried about some of the same kind of things that you are.'

Lizzy waved her arm and ordered more toast. And some cakes.

'I need to talk to him,' said Autumn softly.

'Yes, you do,' agreed Lizzy. 'And I had to do exactly the same thing.' She paused and wrinkled her nose. 'But why is it so hard?' She tilted her head to the side. 'I forgot to check—how was the kiss?'

Autumn groaned again and shook her head.

'That good? Darn it, I should have ordered even more food. We might be here for a while…'

CHAPTER EIGHT

THE GIRLS WERE at twenty-nine weeks. He'd started calling them that in his head, because Autumn was using the term more and more. It was like a term of affection. More personal than 'the twins'. Their heart surgery had been performed three weeks ago now, and there were no signs of imminent labour.

When they talked about the girls to their teams, they used the names chosen by Gabrielle and Matteo. It was Team Hope and Team Grace.

Giovanni and Autumn had finally chosen their teams after a little bit of cat-and-mouse games. It had been fun. They'd debated over a few members. Autumn had been fair. She had a wide team, with the skill-set she needed along with younger team members who would have a chance to learn and gain from the experience. It was a good mix.

Their longest debate had been over whether a certain team member was up to the job. Autumn had delicately raised a few issues about his suitability and Giovanni's first reaction had been to be instantly defensive of the person in question—he'd worked with him for years and liked him. It had taken him a few days to realise that Autumn was being far more objective than him. She'd seen things he'd been blind to and had excused. It wasn't that the person couldn't do his job, it was more that he shouldn't be doing *this* job.

It seemed Autumn Fraser kept surprising him time and time again.

The clinical training room was warm. It was as if the hospital's air-conditioning was objecting to having to work so hard. There were six different things happening at once—six teams all performing their own part of the procedure.

Tempers were fraying, and when he saw a scalpel hit a wall in frustration, Giovanni clapped his hands above his head.

'Enough. Everyone—time out. It's too warm. You've all been working extremely long hours. Unless you have immediate clinical duties, I want you to get out of here for the next few hours. We'll start fresh tomorrow morning. Seven a.m.'

Autumn pulled her hair from the nape of her neck and stretched out her back, giving him a silent nod.

There were a few stunned faces. Glances were exchanged. But eventually the room filled with the sound of surgical gloves being snapped off and the clink of instruments being put back on trays.

Slowly but surely the tired and various levels of sweaty staff all filed out of the room.

Autumn leaned on the wall and folded her arms. 'Should we be concerned?'

Giovanni moved across the room, pulling his surgical cap from his head. Every muscle in his body ached. 'Should we be concerned that our staff are so focused on these surgeries that they've forgotten how to take care of themselves or each other?'

She must be tired too—although he knew she would never admit it.

'There's one more job still to do today,' she said.

His brain started automatically filtering all his tasks for the patients he currently had. He never usually missed anything. 'What is it?' he asked, his brow creasing.

Autumn pulled her pale pink scrub top away from her chest, letting it flap for a few moments. 'The most important thing.' She had a smile in her eyes.

'Tell me.'

He was getting annoyed with himself now. What he really wanted to do was pull his own scrub top entirely over his head. Watching her flap her own to let the air circulate was giving him glimpses of pale skin that were more than a little distracting.

'Sofia. I need to take her stitches out today.'

She laughed at the expression he clearly had on his face right now. It had gone clean out of his head. His own daughter. He'd checked her dressing every day. Only cleaning and redressing when he felt it was necessary. The wound seemed to have healed well—due, of course, to the skill of the person who'd done the stitches.

Autumn's hand went into the pocket of her scrubs. 'She texted me. Didn't you know that?'

'What?' Sofia didn't have a phone. Which could only mean one thing...

He pulled his own phone from his pocket and scrolled down. His hand went to his head. *Oh, no.*

Autumn threw back her head and laughed. 'Your face! It's fine. I knew straight away it wasn't you. And—to be fair—she didn't pretend to be you.'

He read the messages quickly. His heart-rate started to slow from its panicked state. Then he got to the end and his eyebrows shot skyward.

He looked up and saw Autumn was nodding her head

and smiling at him. 'I see you've made me a promise. I expect you to see it through.'

It was clear from the text conversation that Sofia wanted them to spend more time together. She'd promised Autumn that Giovanni would take them both to a favourite place of hers.

Papà and me take you here.

'Where's "here"?' he asked.

She shrugged. 'I think the picture she meant to send got lost somewhere along the line. Where do you think it is?'

'I have no idea.' Then he stopped and put his hands on his hips. 'Wait—was Sofia wanting me to take you to a place she loves, or a place you want to see?'

Autumn shook her head. 'She's five, and her English is great, but honestly we didn't type that many words.'

Of course. Giovanni bowed his head, trying not to laugh out loud. He sometimes overestimated his daughter's abilities.

He gave a solemn nod. 'In that case I'm going to make a few presumptions. I think Sofia was saying we'd take you somewhere, and as the father of a five-year-old I'm assuming it's a place that she loves.' He met her green gaze. 'And I know exactly where that might be.'

The expression on her face told him that she was intrigued, and he decided not to give the secret away.

The more time he spent around this woman, the more time he *wanted* to spend around her. His sister Eleonora had asked a million questions about Autumn—some of which he hadn't been able to answer. And that annoyed him. He wanted to know more. He wanted to know everything about her. But that thought overwhelmed him.

Sofia had spent the last week talking about Autumn. He

shouldn't be surprised that his daughter had decided to use his phone. She was bright. He was just glad that Autumn had realised immediately that it was Sofia.

'How about we get changed and I'll take Sofia's stitches out this afternoon?'

He gave an immediate nod. 'Sure—thank you.' Then he paused a second. 'Let me check on a couple of patients and I'll meet you outside the locker rooms in half an hour.'

'No problem.'

Half an hour later Autumn was standing outside the locker room in the softly draped green dress that clung to her curves. That had been his immediate thought when he'd saw her try it on in the shop. But now, up close, he saw the best thing about this dress was the way it brought out the colour in her emerald eyes.

'Something wrong?' she asked.

He blinked and shook his head. 'No—sorry, lost in thought. Let's go.'

They headed outside to his car, and as he drove through the streets he realised this was the first time that Autumn would see his home.

His skin prickled, and he felt oddly nervous as he wondered if he'd left socks or shirts lying in places he shouldn't. Giovanni generally kept a relatively tidy house. But because his time was split between work and Sofia he didn't often have visitors, so didn't think much about how ready his house was for visitors.

As they pulled up outside the private gates of his villa on the outskirts of Rome, Autumn gave a light laugh as he pressed a button for them to open.

'Nice.' She glanced around the private neighbourhood. All the houses had similar gates and grounds. 'Do you talk to your neighbours around here?'

He moved the car up the paved driveway to the front

door and the gates closed behind them. 'I know some of them,' he said with a shrug. 'Others keep to themselves.'

'And you?'

He blinked, thinking about his answer. The truth was he pretty much kept to himself too. Some of the surrounding neighbours had known Anna. He didn't really want to have conversations with them about her or be reminded of how much other people had found her to be a shining light. Or see the sympathy in their eyes when they looked at him.

He didn't need pity. He and Sofia were doing fine. At least he'd always thought they were. But his connection and chemistry with Autumn was making him ask himself questions he wasn't sure he knew the answers to.

Autumn opened the car door and stepped out, clearly admiring the ochre and pale orange villa. 'Have you lived here long?'

'A few years. I had an apartment in Rome to begin with, but when Anna was expecting we moved here.'

He saw Autumn swallow, and realised he was taking another woman into the home he'd shared with his wife. She wasn't to know that all his memories weren't good ones. Maybe, because of their kiss, she was feeling intimidated. He hated the thought of that.

'Come,' he said quickly. 'I'll show you around. Sofia will be dropped here from school in a few minutes.'

He opened the door and led her into the wide cream hallway. Giving her a guided tour only took a few minutes. The villa had four bedrooms, a study, two bathrooms and a kitchen and living room with glass doors looking out over a spacious garden. The doors took up the complete back wall of the house.

Autumn gave a broad smile as she stepped into the room. He pressed a button for the doors to concertina back.

'Oh, wow. This is like something you see in those TV

shows. You know…the ones where people are trying to decide if they want to live in another country?' Then she gave a short laugh. 'And, of course, the presenters show them something they fall in love with that's *way* outside their budget.'

He laughed too. 'Of course.' Then he glanced around in surprise. He'd never thought of his home like that. 'These doors weren't here initially. I had them put in a few years ago.' He rolled his eyes. 'Sofia was a toddler at the time, and no matter how many times she was told to stay away from the building work…'

Autumn nodded, getting it immediately. 'You needed twenty sets of eyes in the back of your head?'

'Fifty.'

The doors were wide now, and a gentle breeze blew in, bringing in scents of evergreen, wisteria, azaleas and poppies.

'Coffee?' he asked, standing in front of his machine.

Autumn turned and walked over, running her hand along the countertop. 'You could fit my whole flat back in London into this big room. It's amazing.' She touched the silver machine, with its array of buttons and steam wand. 'You don't like to do things by halves, do you?'

He gave a pleased shrug as he lifted cups from the cupboard. Autumn made her selection of coffee and then walked outside to the garden. Humming to herself, she walked around touching a few bushes and flowers, then sat down at the table on the patio outside.

He carried out the cups. 'I have to admit I was a bit worried about what we might find when we got here.'

She laughed and shook her head. 'Well, I can assure you I don't have any right to comment. I can tell you exactly what you'll find back at my hotel room. Toothpaste on the sink and a pile of clothes on a chair that I should have sent to the laundry today.' She shook her head. 'No judgement here. In fact, I'm really impressed.'

'I'm relieved. Sofia can be a one-girl destruction module when she wants to be. I have a woman who comes in to help out a few times a week, but sometimes Sofia wreaks havoc just after she leaves.'

'Papà!'

Right on cue, Sofia came running through the main door and into the back room. Her eyes lit up like saucers once she realised Autumn was there too, and Giovanni's heart soared.

'You came! You got my message!'

Autumn grinned. 'Yes, I got your message. Of course I came.'

Sofia threw her bag onto the sofa and continued to barrel out, almost straight onto Autumn's lap.

He saw Autumn look back through the house and realised she was wondering who had dropped Sofia off. 'My sister,' he said, then clarified when he saw the widening of Autumn's eyes. 'Bella. She's working this evening, so she'll only come in if there's an issue. If my car is here, she knows I'm home and she can just drop Sofia and go.'

He could almost see her sigh of relief. 'Just how hard a time did Eleonora give you?'

Autumn shook her head. 'It's nothing…she was fine.' But she gave him a sideways glance. 'Just a little scary.'

He laughed and leaned forward. 'Does it help if I tell you she scares me too?'

Autumn took a sip of her coffee, and the smile she gave him reached up into her eyes. 'Absolutely.' She turned around to give Sofia her full attention. 'Well, Ms Lombardi, are you ready to get your stitches out?'

Sofia nodded and Giovanni stood automatically. 'Let

me collect what you'll need. Autumn, you know where the bathroom is so you can wash your hands.'

Five minutes later he'd opened a stitch removal pack on the carefully sterilised table. Autumn spoke gently to Sofia. 'I'm just going to remove this dressing. It might feel a little tuggy while I take it off. There. Good girl.'

The wound was tight, and a tiny bit red around the stitches, as if they could have been removed already. Her body was ready for them to be gone.

Autumn's face was right in front of Sofia's. 'I will have these out in a few moments. You just have to hold still. Do you want to stay standing—or do you want to sit on your *papà*'s lap?'

He could see the flicker on Sofia's face and resisted the temptation to automatically pull her into his arms. He had to let her choose for herself, and from the determined set of her jaw he knew exactly what she would say.

'I can stand here. I'm a brave girl.'

'Yes, you are.' Autumn nodded solemnly. 'Then give me a moment.'

She was good. She was very good. Autumn removed the stitches in literally the blink of an eye.

'You're finished?' asked Sofia in amazement.

'All done.' Autumn smiled, disposing of the tools and snapping off her gloves.

Giovanni leaned forward to look at the thin line on his daughter's upper arm. Autumn's prediction had been correct. The scar was neat and well-healed and it would fade with age. In a few years it would be barely noticeable at all.

'I don't think you need to cover it now,' said Autumn. 'Just try not to get into any more fights.'

Sofia dipped her head, looking sorry for all of two seconds before a grin lit up her face again and she clapped her hands. 'Now we can go to my favourite place!' She turned to Giovanni. 'Can't we, Papà? I promised we would.'

He raised his eyebrows. '*You* promised that we would on *my* phone.'

'You weren't using it,' she replied brightly. 'You were in the shower.'

Autumn gave him a knowing smile. 'No secrets here, right?'

He tried his best not to rise to the bait and turned his full attention back on his daughter. 'You know you're not supposed to use Papà's phone without permission?'

Sofia looked innocent. It seemed as though his daughter had mastered that art from birth. 'You were in the shower. I couldn't ask. And I didn't want Autumn to forget to take out my stitches.' She said it so matter-of-factly that he almost wondered what point he'd been trying to make.

He sighed and leaned back in his chair. 'Okay, tell me where you want us to take Autumn.'

'The pyramid!' she exclaimed.

Of course. Just as he had suspected.

'There's a pyramid in Rome?' Autumn looked amazed.

Giovanni nodded. 'The Pyramid of Cestius. It's Sofia's favourite place.'

Autumn's eyes were sparkling. 'Is that where we're going?'

'As long as you want to.'

'Of course! I can't wait. I had no idea there was a pyramid in Rome.'

Giovanni made a quick call, and then it took ten minutes to get Sofia changed and all of them into the car. They drove for another forty-five minutes to reach Via Raffaele Persichetti.

Autumn hadn't believed him when he'd said there was a pyramid until she actually saw the monument.

He parked the car and they walked up to it. Sofia raced ahead. The little girl could barely contain her excitement.

This afternoon had been illuminating. Autumn had seen around his home. He'd given her a whistle-stop tour of everything: the four bedrooms—Sofia's had a large bookcase crammed with books and the room that was clearly Giovanni's had rumpled navy bedding but was surprisingly tidy—the bathrooms, his study, and finally the kitchen and living space.

She'd felt a little nervous, but the house was breathtaking. It didn't have the feel of a pristine show house. It was warmer than that. Elements of Giovanni and Sofia were scattered around the house, but Autumn hadn't felt overwhelmed by the presence of another woman. There had been one photograph on a small corner table that she assumed was of Sofia and her mother, but it wasn't prominently displayed. Autumn had felt comfortable.

The glass doors and the garden had taken her breath away. It was amazing that leaving the busy heart of Rome behind could reveal such a green and tranquil space. Her heart had been struck by how impersonal her own home was back in London. Sure, she'd barely lived in it for the last twelve months, but even before then had it really felt like home?

She looked sideways at Giovanni. He had his hands in his trouser pockets as they climbed the hill, the warm breeze ruffling his dark hair. Her stomach gave a little flip. What was she more scared of? The possibility of a relationship with him and his daughter, or the possibility that he might not want that at all?

She had to find out.

She swallowed, ignoring how dry her throat felt, and

glanced at the monument they were approaching. 'Why on earth is there a pyramid in Rome?' she asked.

'Because I wanted one!' shouted Sofia, spinning around with her hands in the air.

Giovanni laughed, and when he spoke his voice was low. 'Despite what my daughter says, this pyramid has been here a lot longer than she has. Most people think pyramids are only in Egypt, Mexico or India. This is the only ancient pyramid in Europe.' He held his hand out towards it. 'This pyramid is over two thousand years old and was built as a tomb for Gaius Cestius, a Roman senator and general.'

'How high is it?' asked Autumn as she stared upwards. The sun was glinting off the white marble slabs on the outside of the pyramid.

'It's over thirty-five metres.'

'We can go inside.' Sofia had appeared, and she was looking around, making sure no one could hear her.

'We can?' Autumn was surprised.

Giovanni nodded. 'Yes, it's open to the public. Usually only a few Saturdays a month, but I gave a friend a call and he said it's fine for us to look inside today.'

They walked around to an entrance on the far side. Autumn shot him a curious look. 'Do you have friends everywhere?'

He gave her a sideways glance. 'I've looked after a lot of patients. And patients have families.'

She understood instantly. He wouldn't give her details. A doctor would never break patient confidentiality. And not every patient story had a good outcome—Autumn knew that. But whoever this family member was, and however they had met Giovanni, it was clear they were willing to do him a favour.

As they neared the entrance Giovanni pointed to two

spots on the ground. 'They did some excavations here in the sixteen-hundreds. They think the pyramid was originally in the countryside, but as Rome grew it became surrounded by other buildings. An enclosure, columns, other tombs... They found two marble bases with fragments of the bronze statues that once stood on them.'

Autumn stopped and took a deep breath, looking all around her. Rome stretched for miles. She shook her head. 'To think this was once the countryside,' she said in wonder. 'How on earth has it survived when so much else has been lost?' Then she laughed, 'Of course you have the Colosseum, and so much else in Rome. You seem especially good at looking after your famous artefacts.'

Giovanni held out his hands. 'It's not clear now, but this used to stand at the fork between two ancient roads. It was incorporated into part of the city's fortifications, which is probably why it's still here today.'

She loved this. She actually *loved* this. Exploring a part of the city she'd likely never have found for herself, with two guides who were enthusiastic and enjoyable to be around.

Sofia bounded up. 'Come inside,' she pleaded, tugging at Autumn's hand.

It was like a warm wrap of wool winding its way around her heart. The heat. The warmth. The look in Sofia's eyes. The way her heart expanded in her chest. It wasn't just Autumn's hand Sofia was tugging at...

Tears pricked in her eyes. The overwhelming surge was unexpected. She blinked the tears away. 'Of course. I'd love to.'

She stepped inside the quiet space. There wasn't much to see, but it wasn't a visual experience—it was a completely sensory one. Both Sofia and Giovanni seemed to know this, and they both stood quietly beside her, letting her breathe in the cool air around them.

The inside of the pyramid wasn't large—and it wasn't entirely what she'd expected. It was a barrel-vaulted cavity. The inside walls were light. It was apparent that at one point there had been frescoes, but only a few scant traces remained—just a couple of angels in the curve of the ceiling. There might not be much to see, but the room was filled with reverence. The city noise outside just appeared to fade away. The room was silent. But nothing about it was creepy.

Autumn rubbed her arms. Sofia was staring happily around, as if she enjoyed the quiet of the place too. Every step echoed. This had been the resting place for someone for years before it was plundered. She closed her eyes for a moment.

'You okay?' An arm slid around her waist and Giovanni's lips brushed against her ear as he whispered.

Her hand rested over his. 'Yes,' she said quietly. 'Just taking myself back in time and wondering what this might have looked like two thousand years ago.'

The heat from his body was comforting in this cool air. She was happy to stay resting next to him. But then a little voice interrupted them.

'I've got a drawing in my room. I can show you what it looked like.'

She smiled and looked down, Sofia's eyes were bright with excitement. She knelt down. 'I would love to see that. I bet it's perfect.'

Giovanni's hand squeezed her shoulder in support. He was letting this happen. He was letting her get close to his daughter. That filled her with a happiness she couldn't even have imagined.

Her brain jumped to a million possibilities and a billion

conversations they hadn't even touched on. She had to take her time. Think about this carefully. There was a little girl right in front of her who wore her heart on her sleeve, and Autumn was beginning to wonder if she did too.

She stood up and turned to face Giovanni, aware of how close they were. 'Thank you for bringing me here,' she said with a smile on her face. 'I really appreciate it.'

For a moment all she could see was his dark brown eyes, so deep they almost seemed to pull her straight in. She'd never been much of a romantic. She'd never really had the big romance dream. But something pinged in her head. For her, this look felt like the one she'd seen exchanged between her friends at their wedding. And while this flooded her with happiness, there was still a tiny element of panic in her veins.

She knew exactly how she felt right now. What she didn't know was how Giovanni felt.

She wanted to go with her gut and imagine that he was in exactly the same place as her. That would make her feel safe. Sure, it would open up a whole world of questions about her job, her life and her future plans. It would also challenge her to wonder if she could ever let go of her whole self and let someone else have her heart.

She so, so hoped he was in the same place as her.

But did she know that for sure?

Giovanni blinked and the edges of his lips turned upwards. Even though the air was cool, she just wanted to melt. This was it. This was what she'd been looking for.

'Giovanni—' she started, but a voice cut in behind them.

'We have to close now.'

She spun round, her heart sinking deep inside her. The man gave Giovanni a nod and he held out his hand to Sofia.

The moment was gone—wrenched away—and Autumn

struggled to catch her breath. Which was ridiculous, and she knew that.

'Will you come and see my pictures?' Sofia was skipping along as they exited the pyramid.

'Of course.' Her response was automatic.

Giovanni gave a nod. 'Shall we pick up something for dinner?'

She smiled, her head spinning. What she probably needed to do was go back to her hotel room and try to get her head straight. But her conversation with Lizzy was pushing her forward. She knew there was a chance here to have the talk with Giovanni that she needed to have. The chance to find out if he might want to take things a stage further.

The thought of being shot down in flames danced around her brain. She was pretty sure her adrenalin rates were currently topping out at their max. But she was an adult. She could do this. She could have this conversation and deal with the consequences.

Or not…

CHAPTER NINE

IT WAS LATE. Pizza had been eaten. Pictures had been shown. And Sofia had finally gone to bed.

The sun had disappeared in the sky and they were still sitting in his garden, drinking wine. The white fairy lights that Sofia had insisted they wind around the trees were twinkling in the dimming sky.

Autumn was looking like the most perfect woman in the world right now. But she lived in another country. She probably had career plans he didn't even know about. Could he really take the next step?

As he watched she lifted her wine glass to her pink lips and took another sip.

Every now and then her gaze met his, then flickered away. It was as if she wanted to say something but couldn't quite get up the nerve.

A feeling he recognised.

Giovanni wasn't sure where to start. Or if he should even start. All he knew was that if he was contemplating starting a new relationship that would involve his child, he wanted to be up-front right from the start. It seemed like the only way.

He reached for the wine bottle to top up her glass.

'You'd better stop doing that,' she said, in an oh-so-soft voice.

'Why?'

'Because I'm a lightweight. It only takes a couple of glasses for me to start to feel drunk.'

Giovanni picked up the remote on the table and flicked a button, turning music on around them.

Soft jazz sounds filled the air.

Autumn started laughing.

'You don't like my music?'

She shook her head. 'It's just the fact you have all this!' She flung her arms wide. 'This! This amazing house and even more amazing garden. Lights strung between the trees and speakers hidden in the bushes...' She raised her eyebrows. 'All these belonging to a man who masquerades as a master surgeon.'

He stood up and pulled her up next to him, wrapping his arms around her as he started swaying to the music. 'May I have this dance?' he asked, his voice low.

Her hands rested on his shoulders. 'If you must.'

Her head was against his chest, her gaze on the table. 'What are you looking at?'

Sofia had left her pictures on the table. She'd brought them from her room earlier, to show Autumn.

'Her pictures.' Her voice was quiet. 'The pyramid. The pyramid with a dinosaur. The dinosaur with a clown. And the space rocket with a hot air balloon.' She lifted her head and blinked heavy-lidded eyes at him. 'How do you manage to keep it all straight in your head?'

He frowned. 'Keep what straight?'

'The crazy kid stuff?'

'Sofia's not crazy.' He laughed softly.

She pulled back and looked up at him. 'Sofia is a delight,' she said flatly. 'But...' She leaned over and grabbed one of the pictures. It was another one of clowns. But they all had sad faces and glittery green shoes. 'How do you deal with this? How do you know if she's up or down? How do you know how to react?'

His chest tightened a little. 'Autumn, not every sad picture is a trauma reveal. Sometimes kids feel a bit sad. I let Sofia paint whatever she wants. That's what being a parent is. How on earth do I explain a clown and a stegosaurus holding hands when a stegosaurus doesn't even have hands? It doesn't always mean something. She enjoys painting, drawing, and generally getting glitter all over my house. Don't you remember tramping in dirt from outside? Drawing on the walls in your room? Climbing out of windows or up trees?'

When he caught the expression on her face he leaned back, moving his hands from her waist to her upper arms.

'Autumn, didn't you ever just play as a child? Do crazy things? Build a den where you weren't supposed to? Eat berries from a bush when you had no idea what they were?'

She looked so horrified that he knew the answer instantly.

'Why would you do things like that?' she asked in a small voice.

He reached up and stroked a strand of hair away from her face. 'Because that's what children do. It's normal play. And it's part of the heart failure of being a parent.'

She shuddered, and when she blinked he could see her eyes were wet. 'But doesn't every single second of that terrify you?' she whispered.

He could see the hairs on her arms standing on end. Now, he was really beginning to understand about her interest in trauma. She'd said her parents had never been bad to her—and he knew that she believed that. But didn't she know about the impact of constant controlling behaviour and its lasting effects? Because from where he was standing, she was living proof of that.

He took a deep breath and felt something fill his heart. He loved this woman. He wanted to take care of her, protect her. She was a good and true person. But could he take on someone with obvious lasting damage without worrying about her impact on Sofia?

'Autumn, you should know that when Sofia was a newborn I didn't sleep for weeks. I was a physical wreck. I used to hold a mirror in front of her face to make sure she was breathing. I actually thought I was losing it. Both Anna and I were the same.' He gave a sad smile. 'It wasn't until *much* later that I found out that lots of people do that. Most people are overwhelmed by their first kid and that whole new element of things being out of their control. Talking to others made me realise I was just a normal new parent. Not the person who was losing all reality and rational thought that I feared I was becoming.'

She took a few deep breaths, the expression on her face thoughtful. 'And once Sofia got older?'

He swung one hand towards the glass doors. 'I told you—when she was a toddler, I was in the middle of renovations and I was on my own. Sofia had an absolute gift of being where she shouldn't be. There wasn't a child gate in the world she couldn't get through.'

Autumn shook her head, the deepening sunset silhouetting her in shades of orange and red.

'But how on earth did you cope?'

'I took it one day at a time. That's all you can do. And I asked for help when I needed it.' He chose his next words carefully. 'Part of being a child is making mistakes and learning. It's my job to keep her safe to the best of my ability. But no matter how hard I wish for that to happen, there are always things I can't foresee.' He gave a shrug. 'Look at what happened at school the other day.'

'Yes...'

Her voice was quiet and he could tell she was still think-ing. 'Autumn, how much of a childhood did you have?'

She gave a little jerk and stared at him. 'What does that mean?'

Giovanni could sense her automatic defences slipping into place. He reached up and slid his hand into her hair. He kept his voice low. 'I mean that I have a woman in front of me I'm very attracted to. She's a brilliant surgeon, with a brilliant mind and a big heart.' He moved his hand and ran one finger lightly down her cheek. 'But sometimes she seems a little sad. As if she's never had the chance to live a crazy life and do things that seem stupid.'

Her gaze met his. 'But…do people *have* to do that?'

He ran his fingertip over her lips. 'Only if they want to. And I want you to know that if you ever feel like you want to be a bit crazy and lose control, I'm your man. I'll take your hand and show you how.'

A tear slid down her cheek and he resisted the urge to brush it away, wondering if Autumn had ever had a con-versation like this before. Inside, he knew that she hadn't.

She gave a small shake of her head. 'What if it feels like too much? What if I just want to take baby steps?'

Regret flooded through him. He was losing his heart to someone who might never be able to lose her heart to him. She was too closed-off. Too focused on control. Was he making a mistake?

'I'd say that baby steps are a start,' he whispered.

'Good.'

She slid her hands around his neck, standing on tiptoes and brushing her lips against his. Part of his brain was screaming at him. Telling him to be cautious. But his body had other ideas and he matched every move that she made.

Within a few moments he was frustrated by the con-fines of her dress, and he pulled back and held his hand out to hers. The message was clear. But he wanted her to be sure of their next move.

Her hand slid into his and they walked back into the house and into his bedroom.

Giovanni took a few seconds to go and check on Sofia. By the time he got back to his own room Autumn's dress was on the floor.

That was all he needed. He stopped thinking about everything else. He pushed it all away. Autumn was standing in her underwear, smiling at him. Her green eyes were still bright in the dim lights. She'd never looked more beautiful or more sure about anything.

She gave a smile and held out her hand. 'What are you waiting for? Let's try some baby steps.'

And he kicked his bedroom door closed behind him.

CHAPTER TEN

HE'D SLEPT WITH AUTUMN. And relived the experience a few times since. He'd brought another woman into his home, slept with her in that home, while his daughter was in the house.

If someone had asked him a few months ago about starting a new relationship he would have told them he had a whole set of rules. Those rules involved a certain length of time spent getting to know her, a judgement call over if she should meet Sofia, then the possibility of taking the relationship further—in the first instance far away from his family home.

But Autumn seemed to have thrown all that out of the window for him.

And he couldn't quite get his brain around it.

'You did *what*?'

He'd just confessed all to his sister, Bella. She was just as feisty as Eleanor, but easier to talk to.

'I know,' he muttered, pacing in front of the windows of his office.

'She must be something special.'

'She is.' Giovanni's shoulders sagged a little with the admission.

'So, what's wrong?'

'Who said something was wrong?'

'You did. As soon as you picked up the phone to me. You don't *do* this, Giovanni.' Bella knew him too well.

He leaned against the wall. 'I feel dishonest. She's let me know that she has issues with control. All related to how she was brought up.'

'Issues that mean your relationship won't work?'

He could hear the concern in Bella's tone. 'No, or maybe yes. I don't know.' He let out a giant sigh. 'She's terrified about things being out of her control. Even the whole child thing terrifies her. I don't think she realises just how good she is around Sofia. Or how good she is with the babies in ICU. The staff there love her.'

'Wait—I'm not really getting this.'

Giovanni rolled his eyes. 'Neither am I. I can't quite work things out.'

'Okay, tell me the problem from your side.'

Giovanni nodded and started walking again. 'Okay, I haven't really told her about Anna.'

There was a long silence. Then, 'She doesn't know you were married?' Bella sounded confused.

'No, no—she knows that. She just doesn't know that things weren't that great with Anna.'

'You told her about the accident?'

He stopped pacing again. 'Yes, she knows about that. But, like everyone else in the hospital, she thinks that Anna and I were...' His voice tailed off.

'Still completely in love?'

Giovanni's stomach clenched. 'Yes.'

'And why is that such a bad thing? Why do you need to tell her anything at all? Let her have the same impression as most people—that your beloved wife died and you've been a widower these last four years.'

Giovanni froze. 'But that's wrong,' he said deeply.

'Explain why.'

Giovanni ran his fingers through his hair. 'Because if I'm starting a new relationship I want to be honest from the start. I don't want to throw it in later. I want to sit down and tell Autumn that things weren't that great between Anna and me. That I think she probably wanted to leave anyway, long before the accident. And that I'm not even one hundred per cent sure it even was an accident.'

'Giovanni…?'

Bella's voice was full of concern. And he knew he had to say more. 'I don't know. I'm probably just overthinking things. I mean, I'm ninety per cent sure it was an accident, but we had a fight just before she left. She was still on maternity leave. She shouldn't even have been travelling into work. But she told me she'd do anything to get out of the house and away from me. Said I was trapping her.'

Bella didn't speak for a few moments. It was clear she was taking all this in. She'd known Anna better than most.

When she spoke, her voice was steady. 'Giovanni, how long have you felt like this? Why didn't you tell me?'

Giovanni swallowed. 'Because I didn't want to admit it might be a possibility.'

'And it's not. You can't be rational about this. She was your wife, but you'd fallen out of love with each other. I *can* be rational. I knew you both. Anna was ready to leave. But she loved Sofia. She would never have done something like that. It was an accident. That's all it was. Just a damn stupid accident. Park those thoughts, Giovanni. You are not responsible for this in any way, shape or form.'

She paused and Giovanni didn't fill the silence. He was mulling over what Bella was saying. It felt as if an enormous cloud had lifted from his shoulders.

'It also tells me something else,' she said.

'What?'

'Just how much you like this new woman. It's only

been—what? Five, six weeks? This is so unlike you. She's met Sofia, you've taken things further, and you want to tell her everything about you. Even your crazy fears that don't make sense. You know she has some issues herself and you're prepared to take them on board. Giovanni, you're making me think I should start to consider her as part of the family. She's special. You know she is.'

For the first time in the conversation the edges of Giovanni's lips moved upwards and his face broke into a smile. He nodded his head in agreement. 'You're right. She is.'

'Then whether you tell her you'd fallen out of love with your wife is entirely up to you. But focus on what you've got. This is the best news in the world for you and for Sofia. Take your chances, Giovanni. Grab them. If this is the woman you want in your life then work with her. Work together.'

The more Bella spoke, the lighter Giovanni felt. He should have spoken to her earlier. It would have helped him think things through.

'Thank you,' he said.

'Any time. I'm your sister. I love you. All I want for you and Sofia in this life is that you are both happy. And, Giovanni?'

'Yes?'

'Our whole family can love her just as much as you do.' Relief flooded through him.

The phone line clicked and Giovanni turned and stared out at Rome. Their time was ticking down. They would be performing surgery any day now, and what then? What if, a few weeks after Hope and Grace were separated, Autumn was called elsewhere, to another surgery? How would he feel then?

He knew the answer to that already. And he didn't like it.

* * *

'Can we talk?'

Autumn lifted her head and broke into a smile when she saw Giovanni standing in her doorway. 'Sure—come on in.'

Her head had been spinning, partly from how their relationship had rapidly developed, and partly because of how much it filled her heart with joy.

She'd seen both Giovanni and Sofia the last two nights and, whilst part of her still had fears about letting go, she knew they were both stealing pieces of her heart. Which was why the large crease in Giovanni's brow now made her stomach clench.

He sat down opposite her.

'What's up?' She watched as he shifted on the chair and put his elbows on the table, leaning towards her.

'I wondered how you might be feeling about things.'

It was the first time she'd ever really heard Giovanni sound a bit nervous. Now it was her turn to shift uncomfortably. 'Feeling about what things?'

It was an idiotic response. She knew exactly what 'things' he was referring to. But right now she was trying to buy herself some time to think of the appropriate response. Because *I think I'm falling head over heels in love with you and your daughter and it completely terrifies me* probably wasn't the best response to give.

He licked his lips. He knew she was stalling. And that was probably worse.

'Do you plan to go back to London after the surgery? Or do you have another surgery lined up here?'

Okay. That sounded a bit easier to answer. Except it felt as if he was asking her what her intentions might be. Towards him and his daughter.

'I haven't made any plans,' she said quickly. 'I haven't

been contacted about another surgery as yet. If things go well with Hope and Grace, I might go back to my place in London. I'm pretty much a free agent. I help out with general cases on a routine basis, but I can be called away at a moment's notice.'

Giovanni gave a slow, thoughtful nod, then his dark brown eyes met hers. 'Would you consider transferring your base to somewhere else?'

She knew she should say yes. Just about every pore in her body wanted to say yes. But the word stuck in her throat. Some people might call her crazy for considering upping sticks and moving her life and career to a new country, a new city, for a guy she'd only known for a few weeks.

Getting swept off her feet had never been Autumn Fraser's dream. In fact, she could almost feel the cells in her body panicking.

Giovanni's gaze was searing. The frown in his brow creased further and he leaned back in his chair. It wasn't hard for her to read what his concerns might be. He had Sofia to think of.

'I want to talk to you about something else,' he said gruffly. 'But maybe not.'

Before she had a chance to reply their pagers sounded simultaneously. Both them looked to their waists and then their gazes meshed.

'The girls,' they said in unison.

They both reached for the phone, but Giovanni got there first, dialling a number and asking a few questions in rapid Italian.

'Eclampsia. We need to deliver the girls immediately. Lizzy and Leon are scrubbing in now.'

She was on her feet in an instant. 'They're only at thirty-one weeks. We'd hoped to get a bit longer.'

'We're lucky we got this long. Let's go.'

There was no time for anything else. Both wanted to watch the Caesarean section and be ready to take over the twins' care once they were out of the womb. It might be that the separation surgery would be required soon afterwards.

There was no time for this.

There was no time for them.

She wished she hadn't hesitated. She wished she'd reached out and grabbed him. But she just couldn't be that person. No matter how hard she tried.

Maybe it was time for a rethink.

CHAPTER ELEVEN

AUTUMN STOOD OVER the warming crib that held Grace and
Hope. They were doing well. Although, to be honest, they
had so many wires and monitors attached to them that
it was virtually impossible to see any of their skin. But
though they both had tiny knitted caps, and were obviously
close together, Autumn could see their beautiful faces.

She pressed her lips together. The scan of the liver
hadn't been great. In fact, it was going to require even
more intense work than Autumn had planned for. The tiny
blood vessels were so friable... She was actually scared.

Her skill as a surgeon had never been questioned. But
now she was questioning it herself. Did she really have
what it took to give Grace the life she deserved?

Her mind drifted to how comfortable the girls seemed.
Neither of them had been upset or irritable since they'd
been born. Breastfeeding was out of the question because
of their positioning, and both currently had feeding tubes,
but Gabrielle was hopeful that once her girls were separated, she would be able to breastfeed them both.

How much trauma was she about to cause these babies?
It seemed alien to so many people, but was there a chance
that separating them would do more harm than good?

Giovanni appeared at her side. 'I know what you're
thinking.'

His voice was deep and low. She sighed, feeling his breath at the back of her neck. Things had been awkward this last week. There hadn't been time to sit down together and have the conversation that was badly needed. Both of them knew it wasn't the time.

There had been general agreement with all involved that they would allow Grace and Hope a few weeks of recovery time following the Caesarean section. Some time to establish their breathing, their feeding, and some time for Matteo and Gabrielle to get to know their daughters and to give the girls a chance to gain some strength for what lay ahead.

Autumn had spent hours here since they'd been born. Checking all the scan results, then rechecking them. She'd also spent hours in the clinical lab upstairs, practising surgeries.

'How do you know what I'm thinking?'

The tone of his voice held an edge of regret. 'Because I know you, Autumn. Better than you think. You're considering the surgery. You're thinking about childhood trauma.'

Her skin prickled and then she smiled. 'I am,' she said softly.

It felt good to know that someone could read her that well. She just wished she had the same confidence to know what Giovanni was thinking all the time.

She heard him suck in a deep breath.

'I think your work is excellent. I think it's really important,' he said. 'But have you ever asked yourself why it's an area of study you're interested in?'

She turned, automatically defensive. 'What do you mean?'

His fingers touched the bare skin on her arm. 'You know the lasting damage all types of childhood trauma can do. Physical, mental and emotional. It's the kind of trauma and behaviour that affects adults.'

'I know that.'

Her words were stiff. It was obvious he was trying to take her in a certain direction. But it was making her uncomfortable.

The look he gave her was full of sympathy and regret. 'Have you ever wondered why you find it so hard to give up control? To let go? To take a chance on giving a piece of your heart away—or even all of it?'

'You're saying I'm a victim of childhood trauma?' She could hear the indignant tone in her own voice. Tears pooled in her eyes.

He ran his fingers gently along her arm. 'You started this conversation with me some time ago. You told me your parents were never "bad" to you or your brother. But controlling behaviour can cause just as much damage as physical trauma. You must have thought about that sometimes, but I suspect you've just pushed it away.'

Autumn shook her head fiercely. 'This is ridiculous. Yes, they were controlling.' She put her hand to her chest. 'But me? I'm just me. Yes, I like to be in control of things. I don't like it when things happen that I can't plan for. That doesn't mean there's anything wrong with me. It's just who I am—and what's wrong with that?'

She stepped away from the warming crib and Grace and Hope. She was getting angry and irritated, and she didn't want anyone around to see two surgeons squabbling.

Giovanni ran his fingers through his hair. She could see the tiny lines around his eyes.

'I'm not saying there's anything wrong with you, Autumn. I just want you to understand how you got here.'

He put an arm around her waist and led her out of the unit and to one of the windows in the nearby corridor.

For the first time since she'd got here Rome was gloomy. The rain was lashing down on the streets outside and the clouds were low and grey.

'Have you ever gone outside and danced in the rain? Jumped in a fountain? Have you ever wanted to just turn up at the airport and pick the first flight that's available?'

She shook her head. None of those things were for her. The thought of turning up at an airport and getting a flight at random was ridiculous.

'Why would anyone do something like that? What if you've packed summer clothes and you end up on a flight to Iceland? Why wouldn't you want to plan your itinerary, get your currency in advance, know what you're going to do every day of your holiday? Time is too precious to waste.'

She saw his muscles tense. He closed his eyes for a second and she knew instantly that she'd disappointed him. This was why. This was why she'd tried to be so careful with her heart.

When he opened his eyes again, he gave a slow shake of his head. 'You are so right—time is too precious to waste. But what if, Autumn? What if my daughter hadn't looked at that screen of surgeons? What if she'd pointed to someone else? What if I'd called some other surgeon?'

Her skin chilled instantly.

'Some things are just random, Autumn. Some things— some meetings—are just happy mistakes. Or just darn good luck.'

She stared at him. Her head was flooding with thoughts. He could have picked someone else for this surgery. She'd still be back in London. In her flat. Alone. She'd never have met Giovanni. Or Sofia. Or Grace and Hope. Or Lizzy and Leon.

Her breath was hitching in her throat. This world, this

relationship…her brain wouldn't let her believe it was all down to chance. To the pointing of a finger by a five-year-old.

'I need to know,' said Giovanni quietly. 'I need to know that we can have a relationship together. I need to know that you can accept me and Sofia as a package deal. I'm not asking you to give up your life in any way. We can talk about all that.' He took a deep breath and looked at her again. 'But I need to know that you can give me your heart—your whole heart—just like Sofia and I will give you ours.'

He took another breath, and when he looked at her she thought her heart might melt in her chest.

'Because I love you, Autumn. *We* love you. And I want nothing more than to find a way to make this work between us.'

Something twisted deep down inside her. She hadn't expected this conversation. Not now. Not here. Her stomach was instantly in knots. These were words she'd wanted to hear but wasn't entirely sure how to respond to.

'Before you say anything else, I want to be honest with you about something,' said Giovanni.

He looked troubled. Autumn's chest was tightening. She wanted to tell him that of course she loved him. That she could give him her whole heart. But that part…it was sticking.

'Wh-what is it?' she stammered.

Giovanni fixed his eyes on the horizon. 'You've probably heard people in the hospital talking about Anna.'

'Yes?' It came out as a question.

He ran his fingers through his hair again. She'd realised that he only ever did that when he was either nervous or frustrated. Which was it here?

'Most people had a picture-perfect view of our marriage. Which, for a time, might have been true. We grew up here. Met at the hospital. Fell in love, got married and had Sofia.'

The pain sitting on Autumn's chest seemed to deepen. She didn't need to hear this. She didn't need to hear about Giovanni's perfect life. People around the hospital mentioned Anna all the time, with a sad and reminiscent look in their eyes. It was hard not to feel a little hostile about it. How could she ever compete with a perfect memory... a perfect ghost?

'But things weren't like that. Hadn't been for a while, at least.' He hesitated, then straightened his shoulders. 'We... grew apart. And after Sofia's birth Anna was frustrated. With me...with life.'

Autumn frowned. 'She didn't like being a mother?'

Giovanni shook his head. 'No, not that. She loved Sofia entirely. But she felt trapped.' He put his hand to his chest. 'By me. We'd been talking about splitting before she fell pregnant. We stayed together *because* she was pregnant. I thought—I hoped—that things might get better, but they didn't. She decided to return to work early and told me she still wanted to leave the marriage.'

He shook his head again and Autumn watched him swallow.

'We kept our fights away from our colleagues at the hospital. When Anna died... I found it hard. I had to pretend that my wife and I had still been perfectly happy and in love, when nothing could have been further from the truth.'

Autumn felt frozen. The wave of relief that flowed over her at knowing that Giovanni hadn't been in love with his wife was shameful. And now she was wondering about the authenticity of the man in front of her. This was the man she'd contemplated trusting with her heart. If he'd fallen out of love with his wife, would he fall out of love with Autumn too?

She'd spent days questioning herself. Wondering why this gorgeous, hot Italian man seemed to have picked her, out of the hundreds of adoring women who were around him. Then she'd wondered why she couldn't just jump into his arms and dance around the corridors with him?

Was this why? Because she'd recognised something in his eyes on the few occasions he'd spoken about his wife? Maybe her subconscious had known he was hiding something from her? It could be that her instincts to hold on to her heart had been entirely correct.

Her fingers wound around a strand of her hair.

'I wanted to be honest with you—' His voice was gravelly.

'But you weren't,' she interrupted.

'I'm trying to be,' he said. 'I want us to have the best chance of making this work. That's why I want you to know everything I think you should know, before we take the next step.'

Her brain was numb. 'You've lived a lie these past few years.'

He shifted uncomfortably. 'But I'm the only person to know that. I had Sofia to think of.' He held out his hands. 'What kind of a guy speaks ill of his dead wife?' He actually shuddered as he said those words. 'And what was there to gain from telling everyone we would likely have split up had she not been killed? I want Sofia to remember good things about her mother. Surely that's not too much to ask?'

Autumn's throat was dry. 'But I'm not "everyone". I'm the woman who met your daughter. Who shared your bed. If you weren't honest about this—what else have you lied to me about?'

She could feel the layers wrapping around her. Wrapping around her to keep herself safe. This was exactly what she'd feared about letting go and losing control of things—especially her heart. She would swear it was physically twisting in her chest right now.

It was about much more than honesty. But she couldn't quite articulate that right now. The words seemed the simplest to say. But he'd told her he'd fallen out of love with his wife. A woman who had given her heart to him.

Fear swept around Autumn, and again those feelings of a lack of control circled around and around. She couldn't control how he felt about her. She'd never be able to do that. He said he loved her now—but for how long?

She already knew how she felt about him. But she couldn't tell him. She couldn't tell him how much she loved and adored him. Couldn't return those words. Not right now.

In her head she could see pictures of being wrapped up in a family life with Giovanni and Sofia, only for him to change his mind a few years later and leave her on her own. Empty and useless.

The thoughts overwhelmed her.

'I haven't lied to you about anything, Autumn,' he said softly. 'I wouldn't do that. I didn't lie to you about this either. I wanted to take the time to get to know you. To know that I truly wanted to make this work between us. Because I think we can make a go of things. And I'm telling you now because I want to start this relationship with all my cards on the table.'

He was talking, saying words she wasn't really hearing. All she could think about was the myth that followed Giovanni around about him and his wife. It didn't matter that she'd found the whole thing intimidating anyway, and wondered how she could ever live up to the stories about his perfect wife. All that mattered was that it had all been an illusion. They hadn't been in love. Not when she'd died.

Did she really want to take a risk on something she had no control over? The future was so uncertain. Who was to say that in a few years' time he wouldn't want to walk away from her too? To take himself and Sofia back out of the life that she loved and leave her alone? She'd never risked her heart before—could she really do so now? It would be easier just to pull back, to insulate her heart the way she always had. To protect herself from any pain.

Flashes of her parents came into her head. Her brother had had the same upbringing as herself. He'd walked his own way, turned his life around and taken a million chances. He was happier now than she'd ever known him to be. But deep down Autumn knew that she didn't have faith in herself, or now in Giovanni, to do the same.

She shook her head and backed away.

'Autumn, don't do this.' His face looked stricken. As if he'd just realised what his words had done.

She kept on shaking her head. 'No. This won't work. I can't trust you.' She stared at him for a second. 'You fell out of love with your wife—how do I know you won't fall out of love with me? I can't do this.'

Every cell in her body was telling her to run. To get away. To keep herself safe and not open herself up to the level of hurt that was already tearing at her soul.

Giovanni squeezed his eyes closed for a minute and she could see his hands shaking.

'We need to talk about this more,' he said.

She held up her hand firmly in front of his face. 'No.' Her voice was firm and clear. 'We don't.'

His gaze met hers. It was as if shutters were falling down across his eyes. He looked as though she'd just stabbed him in the heart.

'We can't do this now…' There was a tremble in his voice.

'You're right. We can't.'

The girls. They were too important. The surgery was critical. Neither could walk away from this. They had a duty and a responsibility to perform the separation surgery and subsequent surgeries with no distractions.

This wasn't about them. This had never been about them.

She held up her head, not meeting his gaze. 'I came here with one purpose: to help save the lives of Grace and Hope. That's all that matters here.'

The words were breaking her heart, even though it was she who was saying them out loud. It was as if she trying to switch parts of herself off. If she said all this, it might convince her that she hadn't already let Giovanni and his daughter capture those parts of her heart she'd tried so hard to keep in her control.

Tears were forming in her eyes and she was determined not to shed them. But Giovanni's next words felt like a lance through her heart.

'You're absolutely right. This is about Hope and Grace. This has to be about Hope and Grace.'

She could hear the tinge of regret in his voice.

'I'm sure that you and I can conduct ourselves like the professionals we both are and do the very best for our patients.'

She hated him. In that second, she actually hated him. It didn't matter that she could see the pain in his eyes right now. She couldn't think about him and how he was feeling. She couldn't think about how he'd told her that he loved her and opened up to her completely. Her legs had turned to jelly. Her priority had to be to get out of here before she fell completely apart.

'Agreed.' That was all she could manage before she

turned and walked down the corridor, wishing she was anywhere else but in Rome.

Love wasn't for her. Happy-ever-after wasn't for her. She should have known better and continued to live her life the way she always had. The risks were just too great, and she didn't have the courage to take that final step into the unknown.

CHAPTER TWELVE

IT WAS AMAZING how easy it was to avoid someone in the hospital. He would enter a room and she would leave it. Both with smiles on their faces, and both giving no sense to those around them that there were any issues. That was what being a professional was. And, although every glance in his direction hurt, every time she heard the sound of his voice or, even worse, the echo of his laugh, she lifted her chin and kept going.

They communicated, of course. Emails back and forth about Hope, Grace and any logistics.

She'd left some test results on his desk with a query that he'd answered promptly. He, in turn, had left her a picture of a female doctor wearing a superhero cape that Sofia had drawn for her. There had been a note.

Sofia insisted I brought you this today. Would you mind sending her a text via my phone to let her know you've got it?

Tears had definitely been in her eyes at that point, as she'd admired the dark-haired, red-caped woman who looked as if she could move mountains.

She'd dashed off a text.

Sofia, thank you so much for my superhero picture. I absolutely love it! Xxx

She'd told herself she could do this. This wasn't about her and Giovanni. This was about the little girl whom she spent most days thinking about.

At night she sat in her hotel room with the doors wide, looking out at Rome. She'd stopped drinking alcohol, always aware that her pager might sound at any moment. Instead she would nibble on whatever food she'd found from a takeaway, and drink from a bottle of sparkling water, and contemplate what might come next.

No matter how hard she tried, all those thoughts focused around Giovanni and Sofia and the lives they had here.

Her brother called late one night, to check up on her. 'You haven't messaged me yet. When's the surgery? I keep checking every day.'

She sighed and ran her fingers through her damp hair as she walked through from the bathroom. 'Any day. Literally any moment. The girls are doing okay. There're a few things I'm worried about, but the longer we can give them, the bigger they'll get. They're breathing with only nasal oxygen support and seem to be tolerating their feeding tubes. If they could keep going for another two weeks that would be fantastic. But to be honest I think we'll need to do the surgery before then.'

'And how's Rome? What about the guy—the other surgeon? You sounded so happy last time we spoke. Should I buy a hat?'

Her stomach sank like a stone, and he picked up on her silence immediately. 'Has something happened?'

'He's just not who I thought he was,' she said finally.

Her brother took a few moments before he replied. 'He sounded pretty good last time we spoke...'

He let the words hang there.

Autumn couldn't think what to reply.

'Sis, there was something different this time. I've never heard you talk about someone like that ever—in all the years I've known you.'

'I must have,' she said dismissively.

'No, you haven't.' His response was firm.

'What are you trying to say?'

She was getting annoyed now. It had all been so easy for Ryan. He'd met the woman of his dreams at a summer camp in America when he'd been nineteen. They'd just 'clicked'. Miriam had been there when Ryan had made the discovery that had made him a billionaire, and they'd remained in their happy little bubble ever since.

Ryan breathed in deeply. 'I'm saying I'm sorry I left you with Mr and Mrs Perfect. I guess I didn't quite understand that me escaping left you as the focus for their whole attention.'

Her skin prickled uncomfortably. There was so much they didn't need to say to each other. 'They weren't so bad,' she said, with no confidence.

'Yes, they were. You proved just how clever you were and got out to become the brilliant surgeon that you are. But, Autumn, life isn't perfect. I sometimes worry that the guys you've met over the years are the easy ones. The pleasant, mediocre guys you think will give you an easy life, rather than the guys that would just blow you away in a heartbeat.'

She was stunned. Ryan didn't normally say things like that.

'I love you, Sis. But sometimes you need to take a chance on something. Go for it, whether it might work or not.'

'But that's crazy.'

'It can also be fun, and the best experience of a lifetime, whether it lasts or not.'

But those words left her chilled. She wanted guarantees. She didn't want to take chances.

'Not for me,' she said sadly.

She heard a noise in the background. 'Give me a minute!' she heard Ryan call, then, 'Okay, I need to run. But two words to think about.'

'What?'

'Learned behaviour. Think about it. And text me when you do the surgery. I want to hear all about it.'

The phone went dead and Autumn made a grab for her bottle of water, her throat instantly dry. *Learned behaviour.* He was talking about their parents and their controlling.

She stood up and started pacing, shaking out her still damp hair. No. She didn't want to think about that—to contemplate any of that. She flopped down onto the bed and picked up the room service menu.

Two minutes later she'd ordered one of everything from the dessert menu. Anything to distract her from actually examining the fact that she'd never got to shout, scream and play as a child, and that had turned her into the repressed adult she was now.

No one else had challenged her to have these sorts of feelings. No one else had pushed her to strive for a life and a love that had always been kept a comfortable distance away. Just a too-handsome Italian with electrifying stubble and deep, deep brown eyes.

As far as Autumn was concerned, those desserts couldn't come quickly enough.

CHAPTER THIRTEEN

THREE VERY AWKWARD days later, Autumn walked into Giovanni's office just as he was replacing the phone, to ask him to take a look at one of the latest scans. The blood supply to Hope and Grace's liver was looking more compromised by the day.

He'd just stood up when their pagers went off simultaneously. It was like Groundhog Day.

One glance at her waistband told her everything she needed to know.

Giovanni was quicker, but Autumn was on his heels.

The hospital staff appeared to have a sixth sense, and all slid back against walls to allow their sprint to the ICU.

Giovanni burst through the doors. 'What's wrong?'

Agatha, one of the nurses looked up. 'It's Hope. Her blood pressure is crashing.'

'Page Team Hope and Team Grace. Surgery is *now*.' The words were out of Autumn's mouth in an instant.

It was the oddest thing, but Autumn had experienced this in hospitals all over the world. In the most proficient units the worst-case scenario didn't send staff into a panic. It actually made them quiet, and they became the most organised people on the planet.

Agatha signalled to another nurse. 'We're going directly to Theatre. Come with me.'

A member of the admin team held her hand up at the desk. 'Paging everyone and dialling Theatre.'

One of the more junior doctors started unplugging equipment around the incubator to allow transportation.

Giovanni locked gazes again with Autumn. 'Do you want to go ahead and scrub?'

She shook her head. 'No. We'll *both* take our girls to Theatre.' She emphasised the word 'both'. It was a message. They were in this together.

Autumn licked her lips and closed her eyes, taking a few seconds for what lay ahead.

'Where are Gabrielle and Matteo?'

Agatha spoke clearly. 'I sent a member of staff to find them as soon as I'd paged you both.'

Autumn nodded. 'We start moving now. Your member of staff brings them to the theatre doors. Reassure them that they'll get to see their babies before we start.'

The next two minutes were frantic. As they moved into the elevator Giovanni started another infusion for Hope. By the time the doors opened at the corridor to theatre Izi, one of the anaesthetists, was waiting for them, slightly out of breath.

'Fill me in,' was all he said.

Neither Giovanni nor Autumn started to speak. They let Agatha give a report of the circumstances that had led her to page them.

'Something's bleeding, then,' said Izi, reaching the same conclusion as everyone else. 'We stabilise as best we can and start the surgery?'

Giovanni and Autumn nodded in unison.

Her heart was racing in her chest. This was it. This was the surgery she'd come here for. And this wasn't the set of circumstances she'd wanted. An hour ago the girls had been stable. But they'd always known this could happen.

The surgery had been scheduled for next week. They'd hoped for the girls to be a little stronger.

Some of their teams were already scrubbing as they reached the theatre.

Autumn noticed that the theatre next to theirs was still in session. 'How long?' she asked over her shoulder.

The theatre manager appeared behind her. 'Twenty minutes.'

Everyone knew that ultimately, they would need two theatres. Once the separation was completed, Hope and Grace would go into theatres of their own, where Giovanni would complete the necessary surgery on Hope, and Autumn would carry out the painstaking surgery on Grace. Part of her brain told her that this surgery could end up in the record books for its length and complexity, but these were things she couldn't think about right now.

There was a voice next to her. Asta—the theatre sister she'd appointed as her team leader for this surgery.

'Autumn, the parents are here. While you and Giovanni talk to them I'll do a check for all staff. Because it's short notice, some might not have got here yet. I'll get you a timeline for everyone.'

That was what she needed. Efficiency. And that was exactly why she'd picked Asta for her team.

She looked up from where she was scrubbing. Giovanni was in the same position as she was. Both had their gowns and caps in place; both were ready to put on their surgical gloves.

The lives of these little girls were at stake. But they had to make room for the parents too. Both she and Giovanni understood that this might be the last chance for Gabrielle and Matteo to see their babies alive.

She lifted her hands in front of her, careful to touch nothing. Giovanni did the same.

'I'll get the doors,' said one of the theatre orderlies.

They moved to the anaesthetic room, where Izi was with the girls and had allowed the parents in to see them as he monitored carefully. *One minute,* he mouthed to them both.

They understood.

'What's happened?' asked Matteo, his eyes bright with tears.

Autumn spoke softly. 'We think they're bleeding somewhere inside. We have to take them to Theatre to try and fix the problem.'

Gabrielle sniffed as she stroked both Hope and Grace's arms. 'You said this could happen.'

Giovanni started talking, defaulting into Italian. Autumn picked up most of what he was saying and was proud of herself.

He spoke plainly. 'Kiss your girls,' he told them. 'I promise you, we will do our absolute best.'

Tears brimmed in Autumn's eyes too. This situation was totally outside their control, and she couldn't imagine how terrified they were right now.

She nodded in agreement with Giovanni as Matteo and Gabrielle kissed their daughters and left the room, terrified.

'I have staff assigned to them for the whole time you're in Theatre,' said the neonatal manager from the door. 'Page me.'

She didn't need to say the words. They all knew what she meant.

Giovanni and Autumn went back through to the scrub room.

'Are you ready for this?' Giovanni asked, his eyes dark and serious.

'Are you?' she replied.

His reaction was automatic. He took a step towards her.

For the briefest moment their foreheads rested against each other, hands held outwards to avoid touching.

'We've got this,' she whispered, but she wasn't quite sure if she was saying it for him or for them both. She was downright terrified.

'We have,' he replied, sucking in a deep breath before lifting his head and stepping back.

As she headed to the theatre door his voice was deep behind her.

'And when all this is done we need to talk again. I'm not ready to let you go.'

She didn't react. She couldn't react. But it was as if he was reaching a hand out towards her.

His words soothed her soul and gave her hope. She was stepping into Theatre with a man she needed to trust implicitly. He knew that. And this was his olive branch.

'Autumn?'

Asta appeared at her elbow, a checklist of over twenty staff in her hand. She knew that Giovanni's team leader would be mirroring her actions.

'We have a problem.'

Words that Autumn didn't want to hear.

Her heart jumped. 'What's the problem?'

'Daniel.'

Giovanni lifted his head from the other side of the room, obviously in tune with their conversation.

'What's wrong with Daniel?' she asked, desperately not wanting to hear the answer.

Asta's face was grave. 'I've just spoken to him. He has gastroenteritis. Just in the last few hours. He can't come anywhere near the theatre.'

Her bright light. Her second in command. It was the worst news she could hear.

'You can have Akio.'

Akio was Daniel's equivalent on Giovanni's team. A superb surgeon. The temptation to say yes and grab him with both hands was strong.

'But he's done all that specialist training for your team,' she said. 'He should be used where his expertise is best.'

'He's adaptable,' said Giovanni.

She could hear the reluctance in his voice, and she completely understood why.

'There is another option,' said Asta softly.

'Who?'

'Ricardo. He hasn't done this exact surgery, but he's performed similar over the years.'

Autumn swallowed. Ricardo. The older surgeon she'd argued with Giovanni over, saying he wasn't quite good enough to be on any team. Giovanni had eventually reluctantly agreed with her.

Izi shouted from the theatre. 'Get in here, people, we need to start.'

Panic gripped her chest. Things were slipping out of her control. She'd picked her team carefully, ensuring there were no weak links. Part of her brain hated it that she considered Ricardo a weak link, but it was her job as lead surgeon to make that call.

Her brain scanned every other possible candidate. There were a few possibilities. But none had the previous surgical experience of Ricardo.

'Are there any models left?'

Asta frowned, but nodded.

'Okay, we'll be in here for a few hours. I'll need Ricardo for the second surgery. Can you call him and ask him to practise upstairs until we need him?'

Was that really cheeky? Maybe. But he hadn't been involved for the last few weeks. Grace's liver was basically going to be shredded. The model up in the clinical room showed the extent of the problem. It would also give him a good idea of the vein retrieval that was required.

She was swallowing her panic as best as she could. Her eyes met Giovanni's. He gave her a simple nod.

'Trust Ricardo,' he said quietly.

She couldn't see his mouth. Only his eyes.

She felt a flicker of panic starting to creep around her. She could do this. She could do this surgery with no assistance. But it would be long and arduous. Even she might get tired. The only person who expected her to be invincible was herself.

'Ask him,' she said to Asta. 'Then I need you back here with me.'

Asta gave the briefest of nods before disappearing.

Izi was positioned at the head of the table. Both girls were now anaesthetised. 'We're ready,' he said.

Autumn locked eyes with Giovanni. There was a gleam in his eye, a confidence in both himself, and in her.

She smiled underneath her mask. 'Let's do this.'

One surgery merged into the next. Every bone and muscle fibre in his body ached. He ignored the people watching the pioneering surgery from the gallery above them and focused only on Grace and Hope.

When they made the final incision to separate the girls, the whole room hushed.

Autumn leaned over and stroked both girls' faces and spoke in the sweetest voice he'd ever heard.

'Grace, Hope, we're going to keep you apart for a little while—just to make sure you both get better. But as soon as we can we'll have you next to each other again. I promise you that.'

Her bright green eyes locked with his and he could see the raft of emotions hidden behind the mask.

He spoke quietly too. 'Okay, Hope, you're going to stay with me, while Grace goes next door.' He touched the tiny dark hairs on Grace's head. 'See you soon, beautiful.'

And in the blink of an eye he was in Theatre with only his team.

Hope's surgery was quicker than Grace's. It was still painstaking and intricate work, but his team were well-practised and things went like clockwork. Six hours later he finished the neat row of stitches in Hope's abdomen and chest.

He took a moment, leaning back over her. 'All done, sweetheart. Now I'm going to see your sister while my colleagues look after you.'

He looked over his shoulder and through to the adjoining theatre. He could see Autumn, her strain evident in the set of her jaw and stiff shoulders.

'What's happening?' he asked, his focus shifting for the first time in hours.

The ICU sister was getting ready to transfer Hope. 'I think they had an issue with the vein retrieval,' she said. 'They had to change plans.'

His stomach clenched. Autumn had practised that part of the surgery over and over again. He tried to stay calm as he wondered how the lack of control was messing with her mind.

She was a professional. She had assistance. He should have faith in her. But he wanted to burst in and ask if she needed assistance. Every part of his body wanted to help the woman he loved.

'Giovanni?'

The ICU sister was looking at him expectantly.

'Matteo and Gabrielle? Are you coming to update them?'

Of course. That had to be his first priority.

He snapped off his gloves. 'Absolutely.'

He took one last glance over his shoulder and then followed his team out of the theatre.

She was calm. She was definitely calm. But she'd noticed the movement next door. 'Have they finished?'

'They have,' replied one of the theatre team who was standing against the wall.

'How did things go?'

'Just as expected. Hope's good and being transferred to ICU.'

Autumn took a few long, slow breaths. Hope was good. The surgery had been a success. She'd expected it, but was still surprised at the huge wave of relief rolling over her right now.

Ricardo's grey gaze caught her attention. He had his instruments poised carefully. There was a hint of hostility in the air between them that both were choosing to ignore. He clearly knew that she was the reason he hadn't been chosen for a team. But when he'd been called today, he'd come immediately. And he'd practised for a few hours in the lab upstairs.

She wondered if she would have been as forgiving.

Now he spoke in a low voice, showing parts of experience, resentment and knowledge. 'The radial artery is unsuitable. We'll need to use the saphenous vein.'

'Have you done this before?' asked Autumn.

In adult coronary artery bypass surgery, the artery in the arm, or the vein in the leg, were often the vessels used to replace damaged cardiac vessels. To give Grace's liver a blood supply she'd always known they would have to do a similar kind of surgery. But all her thoughts had been based on using the radial artery.

'Have you?' queried Ricardo.

Autumn swallowed. If they couldn't repurpose a suitable artery or vein, then Grace wouldn't survive this surgery. Her tiny lobe of liver wouldn't have a chance to heal and grow. But she wasn't going to let the panic that was trying to creep up and over her get a hold. Certain elements of this were outside her control, but she had to grasp the parts that she still had. Starting with Ricardo.

She heard a noise as the door opened. Giovanni. He moved as if it were the most normal thing in the world to come into another surgeon's theatre during a ground-breaking operation. He grabbed one of the wheeled stools and perched a leg on it, pushing back against the wall and folding his arms.

He was here for the long haul. She knew that. He wasn't going to interfere. He wasn't going to offer to help. But if she needed him to assist all she had to do was ask. It was like a warm comfort blanket being nestled on her shoulders.

She sucked in a breath and counted in her head, pushing the panic away from her. 'Ricardo,' she said steadily. 'Give me your professional opinion on whether the saphenous vein is the best option or whether we should consider something else.'

It was a question she would never normally ask in her theatre. She was the lead surgeon. This was her surgery. But she was willing to do whatever it took to make things work here today and give Grace the best possible outcome. If that meant she had to mend bridges with a surgeon she'd offended, then she would absolutely do that. Grace was what mattered.

There was silence for a minute. She tried to work out if Ricardo was being rude, or if he was genuinely taking the time to think. When his grey eyes met hers, he gave her the smallest of nods. He'd appreciated being asked for an opinion.

'Here's what I think we should do,' he said...

Nine hours later Autumn tugged the heart-covered cap from her sweaty head, the mask from her face, and walked around the table and kissed Ricardo on both cheeks. 'Fabulous!' she exclaimed.

There had been more than a few heart-stopping moments. Ricardo was much older than her, and at one point Giovanni had wheeled over his stool to let him sit for a few minutes' rest. The support had helped, and Ricardo had continued his part of the surgery with the stool adjusted to the height of the operating table, allowing him to lean over Grace's tiny body.

As Grace was whisked quickly away to ICU, Autumn stood in the theatre for a few moments with her hands on her hips.

The rest of the staff quickly disappeared until it was just her and Giovanni. His mask and cap were gone too.

'You have to speak to Gabrielle and Matteo,' he said slowly.

She nodded, knowing how important it was to let them know that the surgery had been a success. But that didn't help the way her heart was currently twisting inside her chest. Her part was over. She could stay for the recovery, and stall for however many weeks she wanted. But at the end of the day she would have to leave Rome.

And until this second she hadn't realised just how devastating that would be.

Slowly but surely her senses had started to awaken. She missed Sofia—the unpredictable five-year-old who also terrified parts of her. She missed her broad smile, her chatter, and the way she acted as though she'd been here before. She missed the way she could turn every book she read into a story about herself. And she missed the way Giovanni looked at his daughter when she did all those things.

Could she really face a life without seeing them both again?

Giovanni was looking at her. He'd said that after this they needed to talk. But talking was the last thing she wanted to do.

After years of living life by the rules. Of always being in control. Of never doing anything controversial or outlandish. Autumn knew entirely what she had to do next.

She held out her hand to Giovanni. 'Let's talk to the parents, and then I need you to come somewhere with me.'

He nodded, but glanced at her curiously as he stared at the clock on the wall. 'It's late—' he began.

She grabbed hold of his hand. 'I don't care what time it is. We'll speak to Gabrielle and Matteo, make sure everything is good with the girls, then we have to go.'

Giovanni was smiling, but his face was etched with amusement. 'Is this good or bad? Or shouldn't I ask?'

She grinned. 'Without a doubt, it's very, very bad.'

CHAPTER FOURTEEN

THEY HADN'T EVEN taken the time to change out of their scrubs. As soon as they'd spoken to the parents, and assured them everything was in place, Autumn had grabbed his hand and started pulling him down the corridor.

'Have you got your car keys?' she asked.

He nodded and pulled them from his pocket.

She dabbed something into her phone and then turned it around so he could see. 'Do you know where this is?'

'Of course.'

'Then that's where we're going.'

As they approached the main exit of the hospital it was clear that the weather was against them. Thunder sounded and lightning flashed across the sky. It wasn't just raining, it was pouring—a complete and utter deluge.

Giovanni stopped walking. 'I can't remember the last time it rained like this.'

He looked out in horror, but Autumn pulled him along. She smiled. 'It's like being home in Scotland. This is normal.' Then she paused and tilted her head, the smile spreading even further. 'Maybe it's a message for me,' she said quietly.

'What?'

'Let's go.'

She yanked him through the front doors and out into

the lashing rain. He started running across the car park towards his car, but she let go of his hand, holding her arms out and throwing her head back as she spun around a few times.

'Are you crazy?' he shouted, barely hearing his own voice above the thunder.

'Maybe!' She laughed as she joined him at the car.

They were already soaked as he started the engine and wove his way through the streets. 'Are you going to tell me what's going on?'

She shook her head. Speckles of water splattered from her hair. 'Just drive.'

He did as he was told, wondering what on earth was happening. It was late. As they glided up towards their destination the rain was still sheeting around them and the streets were empty of traffic.

'Here you are,' he said as he pulled the car over. 'Fontane del Tritone.'

Autumn pressed her face up against the window. 'It looks almost magical,' she whispered, her breath steaming the glass.

Giovanni killed the engine. The fountain was in the middle of a *piazza*—usually it was surrounded by traffic, but at this time of night, and in this weather, they seemed to be the only ones around. Lights on the fountain made the water gleam bright blue, and in the centre was the mighty Triton, his arms holding a conch to his lips, standing on four dolphin fins, with a rush of water spurting upwards from the conch.

In the dramatic black and purple background of the weather, the lit fountain did look magical.

'Let's go!' She grinned as she opened the door.

'And do what?' He still wasn't exactly sure what was going on.

But Autumn was already walking backwards towards the fountain. 'If I'm going to learn how to play and have fun, I might as well start somewhere good!'

She threw her arms apart again, spinning around before jogging towards the fountain. Her scrubs were instantly plastered to her skin, and he glanced quickly around to check for any traffic before sprinting after her. Before he had a chance to say anything she reached down and pulled her scrub top over her head.

'Autumn! What are you doing?'

'Living life!'

She swung her scrub top above her head. He ducked as he moved closer to her. Her dark hair was soaked, flattened against her head. Her pale skin glowed in the street lights. Her green eyes were gleaming as he put a hand at her waist.

Her breathing was fast. 'You asked me if I'd ever danced in the rain…jumped in a fountain? And my answer to everything was no. I'd never even considered any of those things. They were silly. They were ridiculous. But you've made me realise that if I want to love, if I want to have the life I long for, then I have to learn how to live first. I have to take risks…take chances. The things that have terrified me all my life. And I have to learn how to have fun.' She pressed her wet nose against his. 'Wanna have some fun with me?'

Before he had a chance to answer she threw her hands in the air and jumped into the fountain, kicking and splashing as she whooped out loud.

His head was spinning. He *had* said those things. Never realising just how literally she'd take them. But inside, his heart was exploding with joy. She was doing this for him. She was doing this for them.

There was nothing else for it. He jumped into the fountain with her, joining her in the splashing. She started singing. A kid's song. He joined in, laughing as she danced around the dolphins.

It only took one minute for a car to slow down as it drove past, with two people staring in complete confusion through the windows.

Giovanni grabbed her again around the waist and pulled her to him. 'Autumn, you don't have to do this for me.'

She shook her head as she laughed and put her hands on his shoulders. 'I'm doing it for me first and you second. I love you, Giovanni, and I love Sofia too. And that, and you, and Sofia—all of it—still...' she tilted her head back and shouted to the dark sky '...*terrifies* me!'

As she straightened her head he could see tears on her face as well as the sheeting rain.

'But this is it. This is my chance to let go of controlling everything in my life and take a chance. Take a chance on me, on you, on us and life.'

She ran her hands through his sodden hair and moved her lips next to his ear. 'You trusted me, Giovanni. You told me about your wife, your truth and your fears. You told me you'd fallen out of love with her. And I backed away. I backed away because I was scared. Scared that if I gave my heart to you the same thing might happen. That I might spend years loving both you and Sofia and then you might fall out of love with me and walk away.' She put her hand to her chest. 'I was already scared to take the risk, take the leap of loving you both. Don't you know I can't control that? I can't control how you both feel about me?'

'I love you, Autumn. I wanted us to start straight. The last thing I wanted to do was scare you off.' He put his hand to the side of her head. 'Why on earth would you ever think I might fall out of love with you?'

She put her hand on his chest. 'Because there's always that chance. That's what life is about. I've never met anyone like you. I've never felt anything like this before. I was scared that I might not be the person who could let herself love you the way you deserve to be loved.' Tears were pouring down her face, but she was smiling. 'My parents would be horrified by this behaviour. You told me to dance in the rain, jump in a fountain, and you were right. I have to let the world do what it needs to do around me. I can't control every little thing, and I have to take chances.' Her head dipped. 'I've missed out on so much because I was scared to take a chance on things.'

When he spoke his voice was deep, but shaking with emotion. 'Then I'm honoured that I'm the first guy you've danced with in the rain. That Sofia and I are the people you want to take a chance on.'

A car tooted on its way past. In a far part of the *piazza* a couple huddled under an umbrella...one of them looked as if he might be on his phone.

'There's one thing we still need to do.' He cupped her cheeks in both hands and kissed her nose. 'This adventure isn't over yet.'

Now it was Autumn's turn to look confused. 'What?'

'It's a secret.' He grabbed her hand. 'But let's go before we get arrested.'

They ran back to the car, where Autumn grabbed her top and pulled it over her head again before they dived back in, soaking the seats with their wet scrubs. Giovanni blasted the heaters as he manoeuvred around the Rome streets. He was still grinning at her. Autumn peeled the scrub top from her skin, holding it out to try and keep some of the water from pooling on the seat.

Her nose wrinkled as he stopped the car and she pressed her nose to the window again. 'Where are we?'

'Just where we need to be.'

The rain hadn't lessened as he led her across the grass in one of the parks in Rome.

She laughed out loud when he sat down on the grass. 'Which one of us is crazy?'

He patted the sodden earth next to him. 'You said you wanted to play. We are going to play.' He held out his hands and tipped his head back. 'A bit of wet weather isn't going to stop us.'

Autumn looked completely confused. But, 'Okay...' she said as she sat down beside him. 'Anything for the man I love.'

Giovanni didn't doubt for a second that he was doing entirely the right thing. He plucked a few simple flowers from the grass and used his short nail to split each of the stems, then threaded them together.

Autumn bent her head close to his, dripping even more water over his delicate operation. Her shoulders started to shake. When her gaze met his, her eyes were gleaming. 'You're making me a daisy chain?'

He shook his head. 'Oh, no. This is special. This is the first time I've ever done this. I'm making you...' he held it out '...a daisy ring.'

She stopped laughing, her eyes wide.

Giovanni took her trembling left hand. 'Autumn Fraser, will you do me the honour of making a life with me, and with my daughter—wherever that will be in the world—and filling our lives with love and joy for ever?'

She didn't hesitate for a second, throwing her arms around his neck. 'You have my complete heart,' she whispered in the rain. 'Take care of it. I can't afford for it to be broken. But somehow...' she pulled back and ran her finger down his cheek and beard '... I think I've picked the perfect keeper for my heart.'

She held out her hand and he delicately placed the now

slightly squashed daisy ring on her finger. 'You should know,' he said quietly, 'that not only did Sofia pick you, she also told me I had to give you a daisy ring when we got engaged.'

He couldn't wipe the smile from his face. The longest day of his life had turned into the best.

'The girl's got taste,' laughed Autumn. 'And now,' she said, and shook her head, 'would you do me a favour and take me home?'

'It will be my pleasure,' said Giovanni, and they walked slowly, covered in bits of grass and mud, back to the car and into their new life together.

EPILOGUE

HER BROTHER HAD insisted on paying for the wedding and flying all the guests to the venue—his castle in Scotland. Today Scotland had been blessed with good weather and the sun was high in the sky.

Sofia was beside herself. 'I'm a princess,' she kept saying as she twirled around in the cream satin dress with a peach waistband that she'd chosen herself. 'Are we ready now?' She was bouncing on her toes and glancing out at the people in the gardens beneath their room.

Autumn smiled down at her engagement ring. The central yellow diamond was surrounded by glistening white diamonds, and looked as near to a daisy as possible. Giovanni had presented her with the specially commissioned ring a few months after their daisy chain engagement.

'There's Lizzy and Leon and their baby!' said Sofia. A few moments later she turned with a deep frown. 'My aunties are fighting.' She laughed, 'Ooh, Eleonora and Bella have the same colour on!'

Autumn tried to stifle a grin as she finished fastening her rose gold earrings—a wedding gift from Giovanni. She stood up and smoothed down her own satin gown, straightening the peach tie that matched Sofia's around her waist.

She picked up her bouquet of peach roses and handed the smaller version to Sofia. 'We're ready to go now.'

Sofia ran back to the window. 'Daddy's there!'

Autumn's heart fluttered. She couldn't believe she'd actually reached this moment, when she would give herself wholeheartedly and completely without fear of losing control.

It hadn't come easily. Losing a lifetime of learned habits and behaviours had taken time. She'd had some counselling, and Giovanni and her brother had been with her every step of the way.

She bent down in front of Sofia. 'I can't wait to marry you and your *papà*,' she said sincerely, trying not to cry and ruin her make-up. 'It's going to make me the happiest person on the planet.'

Sofia was grinning and she flung her arms around Autumn's neck. 'You're my best friend,' she said with a few sniffs.

'And you're mine,' agreed Autumn. She straightened up and held out her hand to Sofia. 'Let's go.'

They walked down the aisle with Autumn's brother at her other side. Matteo and Gabrielle Bianchi were in the third row, Hope and Grace on their knees. Both girls were still small, but clearly thriving. Autumn blew them both a kiss as she walked past.

Sofia took things very seriously, timing her steps and waiting until she reached the front before she gave a big sigh of relief, hugged her *papà*, then sat on the red carpet under the floral arch.

Giovanni beamed at his bride. 'You made it,' he whispered.

'You thought I might get lost?' she asked, and smiled at her handsome groom in his tailored grey suit.

'I know you like to keep me guessing,' he said as he

leaned over and kissed her cheek, the short beard that she'd insisted he keep scratching her skin.

'Hey…' the celebrant laughed '…doesn't that come at the end?'

Giovanni put his hands on Autumn's satin-covered hips and pulled her close. 'Should we tell her?' he teased.

'I think so,' said Autumn as she put her hands on his shoulders.

They both turned at the same time. 'We'd like to start the way we mean to continue.'

Then they laughed, and kissed again, before the ceremony had even started.

* * * * *

MILLS & BOON

Coming next month

THE VET'S UNEXPECTED HERO
Traci Douglass

Lucy looked up at Jackson. "He's trained to be a therapy dog. He knows better than to jump up on people like that."

"Really. It's okay. I'm used to it. Like I said, some people find me irresistible." Jackson gave her a charmingly crooked, wry smile she felt all the way to her toes.

Oh boy. Not good. Not good at all.

Lucy needed something, anything, to distract herself from her unwanted awareness of this man. "Fine. Whatever. Good for you if people find you irresistible. I don't. I mean, there's nothing wrong with you, but—"

He crossed his arms, his smile widening as she babbled away like an idiot.

Her cheeks felt hotter than Hades now, and the more he teased her, the more frazzled she got.

Jackson studied her, his expression serious.

Flustered, Lucy forgot to be nervous and just laughed, easing some of her inner tension. She shrugged and stared down at her toes.

"Well, it was nice to meet you, Lucy Miller," he said, clasping his hands atop the table. Nice hands. Long, tapered fingers, well-kept nails. Strong hands. Capable hands. He was a paramedic, after all. He saved people. A small spark of warmth burst inside her. He'd certainly saved her just now, from dying from terminal embarrassment. "I wish I'd known earlier you were going to be here. I'd have brought a copy of the required binder with the emergency response team plan for you. I don't have a spare with me now, but if you give me your address, I'm happy to run one by your place on Big Pine Key tomorrow. It's my day off."

"Oh…uh…" Sitting beside him in the conference room was disturbing enough to her equilibrium. The thought of him at her compound had her quaking in her tennis shoes. "That's okay. Give it to Stacy and she can bring it to me. Or I can swing by the hospital and pick it up." She pulled a clean sheet of paper from her legal pad and picked up her red pen. "Just tell me what time would be best."

Jackson frowned. "It's really no problem, and it would be more convenient for me to drop it off. I'll be in your area anyway. Unless there's some reason you don't want me there?"

An awkward silence fell between them as they studied each other.

She couldn't help wondering what it might feel like to slide her fingers through his short black hair, learning its texture and temperament. The fluorescent overhead lights gleamed off his high cheekbones and there was a hint of dark stubble on his firm jaw. His lips were full and firm, with a slight tip to the outer corners that gave him a perpetual smirk, like everything amused him.

"Don't worry, I won't overstay my welcome. Promise. I'll Google your address," he said at last. Jackson stood and picked up his papers but didn't hold out his hand this time. The smile was there again though, still charming, too. "See you tomorrow, Lucy Miller."

Continue reading
THE VET'S UNEXPECTED HERO
Traci Douglass

Available next month
www.millsandboon.co.uk

COMING SOON!

We really hope you enjoyed reading this book.
If you're looking for more romance, be sure to
head to the shops when new books are
available on

Thursday 27th
May

To see which titles are coming soon, please visit

millsandboon.co.uk/nextmonth

LET'S TALK

Romance

For exclusive extracts, competitions
and special offers, find us online:

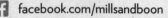

facebook.com/millsandboon

@MillsandBoon

@MillsandBoonUK

Get in touch on 01413 063232

For all the latest titles coming soon, visit
millsandboon.co.uk/nextmonth